PENGUIN BOOKS

THE KING'S GENERAL

Daphne du Maurier is the second daughter of the famous actor and theatre manager-producer, the late Sir Gerald du Maurier, and granddaughter of George du Maurier, the much-loved *Punch* artist and author of *Trilby* and *Peter Ibbetson*. After being educated at home with her sisters, and then in Paris, she began writing short stories and articles in 1928, and in 1931 her first novel, *The Loving Spirit*, was published. Two others followed. Her reputation was established with her frank biography of her father, *Gerald: A Portrait*, and her Cornish novel, *Jamaica Inn*. When *Rebecca* came out in 1938 she suddenly found herself, to her great surprise, one of the most popular authors of the day. The book went into thirty-nine English impressions in the next twenty years and has been translated into more than twenty languages. Sir Laurence Olivier starred in the film under Hitchcock's direction.

Since then, besides several best-selling novels, she has written plays, short stories, and a biography of Branwell Brontë. *The Du Mauriers*, her account of her relations in the last century, was published as a Penguin in 1949. Her latest novels are *The Glass-Blowers* (1963), *The Flight of the Falcon* (1965), *The House on the Strand* (1969), and *Not After Midnight* (1971), a collection of short stories.

Her three most popular novels were all inspired by her Cornish home, Menabilly, where she and her family lived for over twenty years. Daphne du Maurier is the widow of the late Lieut-General Sir Frederick Browning, wartime commander of Airborne Forces, Chief-of-Staff to Mountbatten, and, until 1958, Treasurer to the Duke of Edinburgh. She has two daughters and a son.

D1331666

Daphne du Maurier

THE KING'S GENERAL

PENGUIN BOOKS

Penguin Books Ltd, Harmondsworth, Middlesex, England
Penguin Books Australia Ltd, Ringwood, Victoria, Australia

—

First published by Victor Gollancz 1946
Published in Penguin Books 1962
Reprinted 1965, 1966, 1969, 1970, 1972

—

Copyright © Daphne du Maurier, 1946

—

Made and printed in Great Britain
by Hazell Watson & Viney Ltd
Aylesbury, Bucks
Set in Linotype Times

TO MY HUSBAND
ALSO A GENERAL, BUT, I TRUST,
A MORE DISCREET ONE

Acknowledgements

I WISH to tender my grateful thanks to John Cosmo Stuart Rashleigh of Throwleigh, and to William Stuart Rashleigh of Stoketon, for giving me permission to print this blend of fact and fiction. I trust that they, and especially Oenonie Johnson, whose labour in copying family papers proved so helpful, will enjoy this glimpse of their forebears at Menabilly in days long vanished and forgotten.

I am grateful also to Miss Mary Coate, Mr A. L. Rouse, and Mr Tregonning Hooper for their great kindness in lending books and manuscripts.

D. DU M.

Chapter 1

SEPTEMBER, 1653. The last of summer. The first chill winds of autumn. The sun no longer strikes my eastern window as I wake, but, turning laggard, does not top the hill before eight o'clock. A white mist hides the bay sometimes until noon, and hangs about the marshes too, leaving, when it lifts, a breath of cold air behind it. Because of this, the tall grass in the meadow never dries, but long past midday shimmers and glistens in the sun, the great drops of moisture hanging motionless upon the stems. I notice the tides more than I did once. They seem to make a pattern to the day. When the water drains from the marshes, and little by little the yellow sands appear, rippling and hard and firm, it seems to my foolish fancy, as I lie here, that I too go seaward with the tide, and all my old hidden dreams that I thought buried for all time are bare and naked to the day, just as the shells and the stones are on the sands.

It is a strange, joyous feeling, this streak back to the past. Nothing is regretted, and I am happy and proud. The mist and cloud have gone, and the sun, high now and full of warmth, holds revel with my ebb-tide. How blue and hard is the sea as it curls westward from the bay, and the Blackhead, darkly purple, leans to the deep water like a sloping shoulder. Once again – and this I know is fancy – it seems to me that the tide ebbs always in the middle of the day, when hope is highest and my mood is still. Then, half-consciously, I become aware of a shadow, of a sudden droop of the spirit. The first clouds of evening are gathering beyond the Dodman. They cast long fingers on the sea. And the surge of the sea, once far-off and faint, comes louder now, creeping towards the sands. The tide has turned. Gone are the white stones and the cowrie shells. The sands are covered. My dreams are buried. And as darkness falls the flood-tide sweeps over the marshes and the land is covered. Then Matty will come in to light the candles, and to stir the fire, making a bustle with her presence, and if I am short with her, or do not answer, she looks at me with a shake of her head, and reminds me that the fall of the year was always my bad time. My autumn melancholy. Even in the distant days, when I was young, the menace of it became an institution, and Matty, like a fierce clucking hen, would chase away the casual visitor. 'Miss Honor can see nobody today.' My family soon learnt to understand, and left me in peace. Though peace is an ill word to describe the moods of black despair that used to grip me. Ah, well ... they're over now. Those moods at least. Rebellion of the spirit against the chafing flesh, and the moments of real pain when I could not rest. Those were the battles of youth. And I am a rebel no longer. The middle years have me in thrall, and there is much to be said for them. Resignation brings its own reward. The trouble is that I cannot read now as I used to do. At twenty-five, at thirty, books were my great consolation. Like a true scholar, I worked away at my Latin and Greek, so that learning was part of my existence. Now it seems profitless. A cynic when I was young, I am in danger of becoming a worse one now I am old. So Robin says. Poor Robin. God knows I must often make a poor companion. The years have not spared him either. He has aged much this year. Possibly his anxiety over me. I know they discuss the future, he and Matty, when they think I sleep. I can hear their voices droning in the parlour. But when he is with me he feigns his little air of cheerfulness, and my heart bleeds for him. My brother. Looking at him as he sits beside me, coldly critical as I always am towards the people I love, I note the pouches beneath his eyes, and the way his hands tremble when he lights his pipe. Can it be that he was ever light of heart and passionate of mind? Did he really ride into battle with a hawk on his wrist, and was it only ten years ago that he led his men to Braddock Down, side by side with Bevil Grenvile, flaunting that scarlet standard with the three gold rests in the eyes of the enemy? Was this the man I saw once, in the moonlight, fighting his rival for a faithless woman?

Looking at him now, it seems a mockery. My poor Robin, with his greying locks shaggy on his shoulders. Yes, the agony of the war has left its mark on both of us. The war – and the Grenviles. Maybe Robin is bound to Gartred still, even as I am to Richard. We never speak of these things. Ours is the dull drab life of day by day. Looking back, there can be very few amongst our friends who have not suffered. So many gone, so many penniless. I do not forget that Robin and I both live on charity. If Jonathan Rashleigh had not given us this house we should have had no home, with Lanrest gone, and Radford occupied. Jonathan looks very old and tired. It was that last grim year of imprisonment in St Mawes that broke him, that and John's death. Mary looks much the same. It would take more than a civil war to break her quiet composure and her faith in God. Alice is still with them, and her children, but the feckless Peter never visits her. I think of the time when we were all assembled in the long gallery, and Alice and Peter sang, and John and Joan held hands before the fire – they were all so young, such children. Even Gartred with her calculated male-volence could not have charged the atmosphere that evening. Then Richard, my Richard, broke the spell deliberately with one of his devastating cruel remarks, smiling as he did so, and the gaiety went, and the careless joy vanished from the even-ing. I hated him for doing it, yet understood the mood that prompted him.

Oh, God confound and damn these Grenviles, I thought afterwards, for harming everything they touch, for twisting happiness into pain with a mere inflexion of the voice. Why were they made thus, he and Gartred, so that cruelty for its own sake was almost a vice to be indulged in, affording a sen-suous delight? What evil genius presided at their cradle? Bevil had been so different. The flower of the flock, with his grave courtesy, his thoughtfulness, his rigid code of morality, his tenderness to his own and to other people's children. And his boys take after him. There is no vice in Jack or Bunny that I have ever seen. But Gartred. Those serpent's eyes beneath the red-gold hair, that hard, voluptuous mouth. How incredible it seemed to me, even in the early days when she was married to my brother Kit, that anyone could be deceived by her. Her power to charm was overwhelming. My father and my mother were jelly in her hands, and as for poor Kit, he was lost from the beginning, like Robin later. But I was never won, not for a moment. Well, her beauty is marred now, and I suppose for ever. She will carry that scar to the grave. A thin scarlet line from eye to mouth where the blade slashed her. Rumour has it that she can still find lovers, and her latest conquest is one of the Careys, who has come to live near her at Bideford. I can well believe it. No neighbour would be safe from her if he had a charm of manner, and the Careys were always presentable. I can even find it in my heart to forgive her, now that everything is over. The idea of her dallying with George Carey – she must be at least twenty years the elder – brings a flash of colour into a grey world. And what a world! Long faces and worsted garments, bad harvests and sinking trade, everywhere men poorer than they were before, and the people miserable. The happy aftermath of war. Spies of the Lord Protector (God, what an ironic designation!) in every town and village, and if a breath of protest against the State is heard the murmurer is borne straightway to gaol. The Presbyterians hold the reins in their grasping hands, and the only men to benefit are upstarts like Frank Buller and Robert Bennett and our old enemy, John Robartes, all of them out for what they can get and damn the common man. Manners are rough, courtesy a forgotten quality. We are each one of us suspicious of our neighbour. Oh, brave new world! The docile English may endure it for a while, but not we Cornish. They cannot take our independence from us, and in a year or so, when we have licked our wounds, we'll have another rising, and there'll be more blood spilt and more hearts broken. But we shall still lack our leader. Ah, Richard – my Richard – what evil spirit in you urged you to quarrel with all men, so that even the King is your enemy now. My heart aches for you in this last disgrace. I picture you sitting lonely and bitter at your window, gazing out across the dull flat lands of Holland, and putting the final words to the Defence that you are writing, and of which Bunny brought me a rough draft when he came to see me last.

'Oh, put not your trust in Princes, nor in any child of man, for there is no help in them.' Bitter, hopeless words, that will do no good, and only breed further mischief. 'Sir Richard Grenvile for his presuming loyalty, must be by a public declaration defamed as a Banditto and his very loyalty understood a crime. However, seeing it must be so, let God be prayed to bless the King with faithful councillors, and that none may be prevalent to be any way hurtful to him or to any of his relations. As for

Sir Richard Grenvile, let him go with the reward of an old soldier of the King's. There is no present use for him. When there shall be the Council will think on it, if not too late. *Vale.*'

Resentful, proud, and bitter to the end. For this is the end. I know it, and you know it too. There will be no recovery for you now; you have destroyed yourself for ever. Feared and hated by friend and foe. The King's General in the West. The man I love. It was after the Scillies fell to the Parliament, and both Jack and Bunny were home for a while, having visited Holland and France, that they rode over from Stowe to see the Rashleighs at Menabilly, and came down to Tywardreath to pay their respects to me. We talked of Richard, and almost immediately Jack said, 'My uncle is greatly altered – you would hardly know him. He sits for hours in silence, looking out of the window of his dismal lodging watching the eternal rain – God, how it rains in Holland – and he has no wish for company. You remember how he used to quip and jest with us, and with all youngsters? Now if he does speak it is to find fault, like a testy old man, and crab his visitor.'

'The King will never make use of him again, and he knows it,' said Bunny. 'The quarrel with the Court has turned him sour. It was madness to fan the flame of his old enmity with Hyde.'

Then Jack, with more perception, seeing my eyes, said quickly: 'Uncle was always his own worst enemy. Honor knows that. He is damnably lonely, that's the truth of it. And the years ahead are blank.'

We were all silent for a moment. My heart was aching for Richard, and the boys perceived it. Presently Bunny said in a low tone: 'My uncle never speaks of Dick. I suppose we shall never know now what wretched misfortune overtook him.'

I felt myself grow cold, and the old sick horror grip me. I turned my head so that the boys should not see my eyes.

'No,' I said slowly. 'No, we shall never know.'

Bunny drummed with his fingers on the table, and Jack played idly with the pages of a book. I was watching the calm waters of the bay and the little fishing-boats creeping round the Blackhead from Gorran Haven. Their sails were amber in the setting sun.

'If', pursued Bunny, as though arguing with himself, 'he had fallen into the hands of the enemy, why was the fact concealed? That is what always puzzles me. The son of Richard Grenvile was a prize indeed.' I did not answer. I felt Jack move restlessly beside me. Perhaps marriage had given him perception – he was a bridegroom of a few months' standing at that time – or maybe he was always more intuitive than Bunny, but I knew he was aware of my distress. 'There is little use', he said, 'in going over the past. We are making Honor tired.' Soon after they kissed my hands and left, promising to come and see me again before they returned to France. I watched them gallop away, young and free, and untouched by the years that had gone. The future was theirs to seize. One day the King would come back to his waiting country, and Jack and Bunny, who had fought so valiantly for him, would be rewarded. I could picture them at Stowe, and up in London at Whitehall, growing sleek and prosperous, with a whole new age of splendour opening before them.

The civil war would be forgotten, and forgotten too the generation that had preceded them, that had fallen in the cause, or had failed. My generation, which would enter into no inheritance.

I lay there in my chair, watching the deepening shadows, and presently Robin came in and sat beside me, inquiring in his gruff, tender way if I was tired, regretting that he had missed the Grenvile brothers, and going on to tell me of some small pother in the court-house at Tywardreath. I made a pretence of listening, aware with a queer sense of pity how the trifling everyday events were now his one concern. I thought how once he and his companions had won immortality for their gallant and so useless defence of Pendennis Castle in those tragic summer months in '46 – how proud we were of them, how full our hearts – and here he was rambling on about five fowls that had been stolen from a widow in St Blazey. Perhaps I was no cynic after all, but rotten with sentiment. It was then that the idea came first to me, that, by writing down the events of those few years, I would rid myself of a burden. The war, and how it changed our lives; how we were all caught up in it, and broken by it, and our lives hopelessly intermingled one with another.

Gartred and Robin, Richard and I, the whole Rashleigh family, pent up together in that house of secrets – small wonder that we came to be defeated. Even today Robin goes every Sunday to dine at Menabilly, but not I. My health pleads its own excuse. Knowing what I know, I could not return. Menabilly, where the drama of our lives was played, is vivid enough to me three miles distant here in Tywardreath. The house stands as bare and desolate as it did when I saw it last in '48. Jonathan has neither the heart nor the money to restore it to its former condition. He and Mary and the grandchildren live in one wing only. I pray God they will always remain in ignorance of that final tragedy. Two people will carry the secret to the grave. Richard and I. He sits in Holland, many hundred miles away, and I lie upon my couch in Tywardreath, and the shadow of the buttress is upon us both. When Robin rides each Sunday to Menabilly I go with him, in imagination, across the park, and come to the high walls surrounding the house. The courtyard lies open, the west front stares down at me. The last rays of the sun shine into my old room above the gate-house, for the lattice is open, but the windows of the room beside it are closed. Ivy tendrils creep across it. The smooth stone of the buttress outside the window is encrusted with lichen. The sun vanishes, and the west front takes once more to the shadows. The Rashleighs eat and sleep within, and go by candlelight to bed, and to dream; but I, down here three miles away in Tywardreath, wake in the night to the sound of a boy's voice calling my name in terror, to a boy's hand beating against the walls, and there in the pitch-black night before me, vivid, terrible, and accusing, is the ghost of Richard's son. I sit up in bed, sweating with horror, and faithful Matty, hearing me stir, comes to me and lights the candle.

She brews me a warm drink, rubs my aching back, and puts a shawl about my shoulders. Robin, in the room adjoining, sleeps on undisturbed. I try to read a while, but my thoughts are too violent to allow repose. Matty brings me paper and pen, and I begin to write. There is so much to say, and so little time in which to say it. For I do not fool myself about the future. My own instinct, quite apart from Robin's face, warns me that this autumn will be the last. So while my Richard's Defence is discussed by the world and placed on record for all time amongst the archives of this seventeenth century, my apologia will go with me to the grave, and by rotting there with me, unread, will serve its purpose.

I will say for Richard what he never said for himself, and I will show how, despite his bitter faults and failings, it was possible for a woman to love him with all her heart, and mind, and body and I that woman. I write at midnight, then, by candlelight, while the church clock at Tywardreath chimes the small hours, and the only sound I hear is the sigh of the wind beneath my window and the murmur of the sea as the tide comes sweeping across the sands to the marshes below St Blazey bridge.

Chapter 2

THE first time I saw Gartred was when my eldest brother Kit brought her home to Lanrest as his bride. She was twenty-two, and I, the baby of the family except for Percy, a child of ten. We were a happy, sprawling family, very intimate and free, and my father, John Harris, cared nothing for the affairs of the world, but lived for his horses, his dogs, and the peaceful concerns of his small estate. Lanrest was not a large property, but it lay high amidst a sheltering ring of trees, looking down upon the Looe Valley, and was one of those placid, kindly houses that seem to slumber through the years, and we loved it well. Even now, thirty years after, I have only to close my eyes and think of home, and there comes to my nostrils the well-remembered scent of hay, hot with the sun, blown by a lazy wind; and I see the great wheel thrashing the water down at the mills at Lametton, and I smell the fusty, dusty golden grain. The sky was always white with pigeons. They circled and flew above our heads, and were so tame that they would take grain from our hands. Strutting and cooing, puffed and proud, they created an atmosphere of comfort. Their gentle chattering amongst themselves through a long summer's afternoon brought much peace to me in the later years, when the others would go hawking, and ride away laughing and talking, and I could no longer follow them. But that is another chapter. I was talking of Gartred as I saw her first. The wedding had taken place at Stowe, her home, and Percy and I, because of some childish ailment or other, had not been present at it. This, very foolishly, created a resentment in me from the first. I was undoubtedly spoilt, being so much younger than my brothers and sisters, who made a great pet of me, as did my parents too, but I had it firmly in my mind that my brother's bride did not wish to be bothered with children at her wedding, and that she feared we might have some infection.

I can remember sitting upright in bed, my eyes bright with fever, remonstrating with my mother. 'When Cecilia was married, Percy and I carried the train,' I said (Cecilia was my eldest sister), 'and we all of us went to Mothercombe, and the Pollexefens welcomed us, although Percy and I both made ourselves sick with over-eating.' All my mother could say in reply was that this time it was different, and Stowe was quite another place to Mothercombe, and the Grenviles were not the Pollexefens – which seemed to me the most feeble of arguments – and she would never forgive herself if we took the fever to Gartred. Everything was Gartred. Nobody else mattered. There was a great fuss and commotion too about preparing the spare chamber for when the bride and bridegroom should come to stay. New hangings were brought, and rugs, and tapestries, and it was all because Gartred must not be made to feel Lanrest was shabby or in poor repair. The servants were made to sweep and dust, the place was put into a bustle, and everyone made uncomfortable in the process.

If it had been because of Kit, my dear easy-going brother, I should never have grudged it for a moment. But Kit himself might not have existed. It was for Gartred. And like all children I listened to the gossip of the servants. 'It's on account of his being heir to Sir Christopher at Radford that she's marrying our young master', was the sentence I heard, amidst the clatter in the kitchens. I seized upon this piece of information and brooded on it, together with the reply from my father's steward: 'It's not like a Grenvile to match with a plain Harris of Lanrest.'

The words angered me, and confused me too. The word

'plain' seemed a reflection on my brother's looks, whom I considered handsome, and why should a Harris of Lanrest be a poor bargain for a Grenvile? It was true that Kit was heir to our Uncle Christopher at Radford – a great barracks of a place the other side of Plymouth – but I had never thought much of the fact until now. For the first time I realized, with something of a shock, that marriage was not the romantic fairy legend I had imagined it to be, but a great institution, a bargain between important families, with the tying-up of property. When Cecilia married John Pollexefen, whom she had known since childhood, it had not struck me in this way, but now, with my father riding over to Stowe continually and holding long conferences with lawyers, and wearing a worried frown between his brows, Kit's marriage was becoming like some frightening affair of State, which, if worded wrong, would throw the country into chaos.

Eavesdropping again, I heard the lawyer say: 'It is not Sir Bernard Grenvile who is holding out about the settlement. But the daughter herself. She has her father wound round her finger.'

I pondered over this awhile, and then repeated it to my sister Mary. 'Is it usual', I asked, with no doubt irritating precocity, 'for a bride to argue thus about her portion?'

Mary did not answer for a moment. Although she was twenty, life had barely brushed her as yet, and I doubt if she knew more than I did. But I could see that she was shocked. 'Gartred is the only daughter,' she said, after a moment. 'It is perhaps necessary for her to discuss the settlements.'

'I wonder if Kit knows of it,' I said. 'I somehow do not think he would like it.'

Mary then bade me hold my tongue, and warned me that I was fast becoming a shrew, and no one would admire me for it. I was not to be discouraged, though, and while I refrained from mentioning the marriage settlement to my brothers, I went to plague Robin – my favourite even in those days – to tell me something of the Grenviles. He had just ridden in from hawking, and stood in the stable-yard, his dear handsome face flushed and happy, the falcon on his wrist, and I remember drawing back, scared always by the bird's deep, venomous eyes and the blood on her beak. She would permit no one to touch her but Robin, and he was stroking her feathers. There was a clatter in the stable-yard, with the men rubbing down the horses, and in one corner by the well the dogs were feeding.

'I am pleased it is Kit and not you that has gone away to find a bride for himself,' I said, while the bird watched me from beneath great hooded lids, and Robin smiled, and reached out his other hand to touch my curls, while the falcon ruffled in anger.

'If I had been the eldest son,' said Robin gently, 'I would have been the bridegroom at this wedding.' I stole a glance at him, and saw that his smile had gone, and in its place a look of sadness. 'Why, did she like you best?' I asked. He turned away then, and placing the hood over his bird, gave her to the keeper. When he picked me up in his arms he was smiling again. 'Come and pick cherries,' he said, 'and never mind my brother's bride.'

'But the Grenviles?' I persisted as he bore me on his shoulders to the orchard. 'Why must we be so mighty proud about them?'

'Bevil Grenvile is the best fellow in the world,' said Robin. 'Kit, and Jo, and I were at Oxford with him. And his sister is very beautiful.' More than that I could not drag from him. But my brother Jo, to whose rather sarcastic, penetrating mind I put the same question later in the day, expressed surprise at my ignorance. 'Have you reached the ripe age of ten, Honor,' he inquired, 'without knowing that in Cornwall there are only two families who count for anything – the Grenviles and the Arundells? Naturally, we humble Harris brood are over-whelmed that our dear brother Kit has been honoured by the august hand of the so ravishing Gartred.' Then he buried his nose in a book and there was an end of the matter. The next week they were all gone to Stowe for the wedding. I had to hug my soul in patience until their return, and then, as I feared, my mother pleaded fatigue, as did the rest of them, and everyone seemed a little jaded and out of sorts with so much feasting and rejoicing, and only my third sister Bridget unbent to me at all. She was in raptures over the magnificence of Stowe and the

19

hospitality of the Grenviles. 'This place is like a steward's lodge compared to Stowe,' she told me. 'You could put Lanrest in one pocket of the grounds there, and it would not be noticed. Two servants waited behind my chair at supper, and all the while musicians played to us from the gallery.'

'But Gartred, what of Gartred?' I said with impatience.

'Wait while I tell you,' she said. 'There were more than two hundred people staying there, and Mary and I slept together in a chamber bigger far than any we possess here. There was a woman to tend us, and dress our hair. And the bedding was changed every day, and perfumed.'

'What else, then?' I asked, consumed with jealousy.

'I think Father was a little lost,' she whispered. 'I saw him from time to time with the other people, endeavouring to talk, but he looked stifled, as though he could not breathe. And all the men were so richly attired, somehow he seemed drab beside them. Sir Bernard is a very fine-looking man. He wore a blue velvet doublet slashed with silver, the day of the wedding, and Father was in his green that fits him a little too well. He over-tops him too – Sir Bernard, I mean – and they looked odd standing together.'

'Never mind my father,' I said. 'I want to hear of Gartred.'

My sister Bridget smiled, superior with her knowledge.

'I liked Bevil the best,' she said; 'and so does everyone. He was in the midst of it all, seeing that no one lacked for anything. I thought Lady Grenville a little stiff, but Bevil was the soul of courtesy, gracious in all he did.' She paused a moment. 'They are all auburn-haired, you know,' she said with some inconsequence. 'If we saw anyone with auburn hair it was sure to be a Grenvile. I did not care for the one they called Richard,' she added with a frown.

'Why not? Was he so ugly?' I asked.

'No,' she answered, puzzled. 'He was more handsome than Bevil. But he looked at us all in a mocking, contemptuous way, and when he trod on my gown in the crush he made no apology. "You are to blame", he had the impudence to tell me, "for letting it trail thus in the dust." They told me at Stowe he was a soldier.'

'But there is still Gartred,' I said. 'You have not described

20

her.' And then, to my mortification, Bridget yawned, and rose to her feet. 'Oh, I am too weary to tell you any more,' she said. 'Wait until the morning. But Mary, and Cecilia, and I are all agreed upon one thing, that we would sooner resemble Gartred than any other woman.' So in the end I had to form my own judgement with my own eyes. We were all gathered in the hall to receive them – they had gone first from Stowe to my uncle's estate at Radford – and the dogs ran out into the courtyard as they heard the horses.

We were a large party, because the Pollexefens were with us too, Cecilia had her baby Joan in her arms, my first godchild – and I was proud of the honour – and we were all happy and laughing and talking because we were one family and knew one another so well. Kit swung himself down from the saddle – he looked very debonair and gay – and I saw Gartred. She murmured something to Kit, who laughed and coloured, and held his arms to help her dismount, and in a flash of intuition I knew she had said something to him which was part of their life together, and had nought to do with us, his family. Kit was not ours any more, but belonged to her.

I hung back, reluctant to be introduced, and suddenly she was beside me, her cool hand under my chin. 'So you are Honor?' she said. The inflexion in her voice suggested that I was small for my age, or ill-looking, or disappointing in some special way, and she passed on through to the big parlour, taking precedence of my mother with a confident smile, while the remainder of the family followed like fascinated moths. Percy, being a boy and goggle-eyed at beauty, went to her at once, and she put a sweetmeat in his mouth. She has them ready, I thought, to bribe us children, as one bribes strange dogs. 'Would Honor like one too?' she said, and there was a note of mockery in her voice, as though she knew instinctively that this treating of me as a baby was what I hated most. I could not take my eyes from her face. She reminded me of something, and suddenly I knew. I was a tiny child again at Radford, my uncle's home, and he was walking me through the glass-houses in the gardens. There was one flower, an orchid, that grew alone; it was the colour of pale ivory, with one little vein of crimson running through the petals. The scent filled the

21

house, honeyed, and sickly sweet. It was the loveliest flower I had ever seen. I stretched out my hand to stroke the soft velvet sheen, and swiftly my uncle pulled me by the shoulder. 'Don't touch it, child. The stem is poisonous.'

I drew back, frightened. Sure enough, I could see the myriad hairs bristling, sharp and sticky, like a thousand swords.

Gartred was like that orchid. When she offered me the sweetmeat I turned away, shaking my head, and my father, who had never spoken to me harshly in his life, said sharply, 'Honor, where are your manners?' Gartred laughed and shrugged her shoulder. Everyone present turned reproving eyes upon me, and even Robin frowned. My mother bade me go upstairs to my room. That was how Gartred came to Lanrest.

The marriage lasted for three years, and it is not my purpose now to write about it. So much has happened since to make the later life of Gartred the more vivid, and in the battles we have waged the early years loom dim now and unimportant. There was always war between us, that much is certain. She young, and confident, and proud, and I a sullen child, peering at her from behind doors and screens, and both of us aware of a mutual hostility. They were more often at Radford and Stowe than at Lanrest, but when she came home I swear she cast a blight upon the place. I was still a child, and I could not reason, but a child, like an animal, has an instinct that does not lie. There were no children of the marriage. That was the first blow, and I know this was a disappointment to my parents, because I heard them talk of it. My sister Cecilia came to us regularly for her lying-in, but there was never a rumour of Gartred. She rode and went hawking as we did, she did not keep her room or complain of fatigue, which we had come to expect from Cecilia. Once my mother had the hardihood to say, 'When I first wed, Gartred, I neither rode nor hunted, for fear I should miscarry,' and Gartred, trimming her nails with a tiny pair of scissors made of mother-of-pearl, looked up at her, and said, 'I have nothing within me to lose, madam, and for that you had better blame your son.' Her voice was low and full of venom, and my mother stared at her for a moment, bewildered, then rose and left the room in distress. It was the first time the poison had touched her. I did not understand the talk between them, but I sensed that Gartred was bitter against my brother, for soon afterwards Kit came in and, going to Gartred, said to her in a tone loaded with reproach, 'Have you accused me to my mother?' They both looked at me, and I knew I had to leave the room. I went out into the garden, and fed the pigeons, but the peace was gone from the place. From that moment everything went ill with them, and with us all. Kit's nature seemed to change. He wore a harassed air, wretchedly unlike himself, and a coolness grew up between him and my father, who had hitherto agreed so well.

Kit showed himself suddenly aggressive to my father, and to us all, finding fault with the working of Lanrest and comparing it to Radford, and in contrast to this was his abject humility before Gartred, a humility that had nothing fine about it but made him despicable to my intolerant eyes. The next year he stood for West Looe in Parliament, and they went often to London, so we did not see them much, but when they came to Lanrest there seemed to be this continual strain about their presence, and once there was a heated quarrel between Kit and Robin one night when my parents were from home. It was midsummer, stifling and warm, and I played truant from my nursery and crept down to the garden in my nightgown. The household were abed. I remember flitting like a little ghost before the windows. The casement of the guest chamber was open wide, and I heard Kit's voice, louder than usual, lifted in argument. Some devil interest in me made me listen. 'It is always the same,' he said, 'wherever we go. You make a fool of me before all men, and now tonight before my very brother. I tell you I cannot endure it any longer.'

I heard Gartred laugh, and I saw Kit's shadow reflected on the ceiling by the quivering candlelight. Their voices were low for a moment, and then Kit spoke again for me to hear.

'You think I remark nothing,' he said. 'You think I have sunk so low that to keep you near me, and to be allowed to touch you sometimes, I will shut my eyes to everyone. Do you think it was pleasant for me at Stowe to see how you looked upon Antony Denys that night when I returned so suddenly from London? A man with grown children, and his wife scarce cold in her grave? Are you entirely without mercy for me?'

That terrible pleading note I so detested had crept back into his voice again, and I heard Gartred laugh once more.

'And this evening,' he said, 'I saw you, smiling across the table at him, my own brother.' I felt sick, and rather frightened, but curiously excited, and my heart thumped within me as I heard a step beside me on the paving, and looking over my shoulder I saw Robin stand beside me in the darkness. 'Go away,' he whispered to me. 'Go away at once.' I pointed to the open window. 'It is Kit and Gartred,' I said. 'He is angry with her for smiling at you.'

I heard Robin catch at his breath, and he turned, as if to go, when suddenly Kit's voice cried out loud and horrible, as though he, a grown man, was sobbing like a child. 'If that happens I shall kill you. I swear to God I shall kill you.' Then Robin, swift as an arrow, stooped to a stone, and, taking it in his hand, he flung it against the casement, shivering the glass to fragments.

'God damn you for a coward then,' he shouted. 'Come and kill me instead.' I looked up and saw Kit's face, white and tortured, and behind him Gartred with her hair loose on her shoulders. It was a picture to be imprinted always on my mind, those two at the window, and Robin suddenly different from the brother I had always known and loved, breathing defiance and contempt. I felt ashamed for him, for Kit, for myself, but mostly I was filled with hatred for Gartred, who had brought the storm to pass and remained untouched by it.

I turned and ran, with my fingers in my ears, and crept up to bed with never a word to anyone, and drew the covers well over my head, fearing that by morning they would all three of them be discovered slain there in the grass. But what passed between them further, I never knew. Day broke, and all was as before except that Robin rode away soon after breakfast and did not return until after Kit and Gartred took their departure to Radford, some five days later. Whether anyone else in the family knew of the incident I never discovered. I was too scared to ask, and since Gartred had come amongst us we had all lost our old manner of sharing troubles, and had each one of us grown more polite and secretive.

Next year, in '23, the smallpox swept through Cornwall like

a scourge, and few families were spared. In Liskeard the people closed their doors, and the shopkeepers put up their shutters and would do no trade, for fear of the infection.

In June my father was stricken, dying within a few days, and we had scarcely recovered from the blow before messages came to us from my uncle at Radford to say that Kit had been seized with the same dread disease, and there was no hope of his recovery.

Father and son thus died within a few weeks of one another, and Jo, the scholar, became the head of the family. We were all too unhappy with our double loss to think of Gartred, who had fled to Stowe at the first sign of infection and so escaped a similar fate, but when the two wills came to be read, both Kit's and my father's, we learnt that although Lanrest, with Radford later, passed to Jo, the rich pasture lands of Lametton and the Mill were to remain in Gartred's keeping for her lifetime.

She came down with her brother Bevil for the reading, and even Cecilia, the gentlest of my sisters, remarked afterwards with shocked surprise upon her composure, her icy confidence, and the niggardly manner with which she saw to the measuring of every acre down at Lametton. Bevil, married himself now and a near neighbour to us at Killigarth, did his utmost to smooth away the ill-feeling that he sensed amongst us, and although I was still little more than a child I remember feeling unhappy and embarrassed that he was put to so much awkwardness on our account. It was small wonder that he was loved by everyone, and I wondered, to myself, what opinion he held in his secret heart about his sister, or whether her beauty mazed him as it did every man.

When affairs were settled, and they went away, I think we all of us breathed relief that no actual breach had come to pass, causing a feud between the families, and the fact that Lanrest belonged to Jo was a weight off my mother's mind, though she said nothing.

Robin remained from home during the whole period of the visit, and maybe no one but myself could guess the reason.

The morning before she left, some impulse prompted me to hesitate before her chamber, the door of which was open, and look at her within. She had claimed that the contents of the room belonged to Kit, and so to her, and the servants had been employed the day before in taking down the hangings, and removing the pieces of furniture she most desired. At this last moment she was alone, turning out a little secretaire that stood in one corner. She did not observe that I was watching her, and I saw the mask off her lovely face at last. The eyes were narrow, the lip protruding, and she wrenched at a little drawer with such force that the part came to pieces in her hands. There were some trinkets at the back of the drawer, none I think of great value, but she had remembered them. Suddenly she saw my face reflected in the mirror.

'If you leave to us the bare walls, we shall be well content,' I said as her eyes met mine. My father would have whipped me for it had he been alive, and my brothers too, but we were alone.

'You always played the spy, from the first,' she said softly, but because I was not a man she did not smile.

'I was born with eyes in my head,' I said to her.

Slowly she put the jewels in a little pouch she wore hanging from her waist. 'Take comfort and be thankful you are quit of me now,' she said. 'We are not likely to see one another again.'

'I hope not,' I told her. Suddenly she laughed. 'It were a pity', she said, 'that your brother did not have a little of your spirit.'

'Which brother?' I asked.

She paused a moment, uncertain what I knew, and then, smiling, she tapped my cheek with her long slim finger. 'All of them,' she said, and then she turned her back on me, and called to her servant from the adjoining room. Slowly I went downstairs, my mind on fire with questions, and coming into the hallway I saw Jo fingering the great map hanging on the wall. I did not talk to him, but walked out past him into the garden.

She left Lanrest at noon in a litter, with a great train of horses and servants from Stowe to carry her belongings. I watched them, from a hiding-place in the trees, pass away up the road to Liskeard in a cloud of dust.

'That's over,' I said to myself. 'That's the last of them. We have done with the Grenviles.'

But Fate willed otherwise.

Chapter 3

My eighteenth birthday. A bright December day. My spirits soaring like a bird as, looking out across the dazzling sea from Radford, I watched His Majesty's Fleet sail into Plymouth Sound.

It concerned me not that the expedition now returning had been a failure, and that far away in France La Rochelle remained unconquered; these were matters for older people to discuss.

Here in Devon there was laughing and rejoicing and the young folk held high holiday. What a sight they were – some eighty ships or more, crowding together between Drake's Island and the Mount, the white sails bellying in the west wind, the coloured pennants streaming from the golden spars. As each vessel drew opposite the fort at Mount Batten, she would be greeted with a salvo from the great guns, and, dipping her colours in a return salute, let fly her anchor, and bring up opposite the entrance to the Cattwater. The people gathered on the cliffs waved and shouted, and from the vessels themselves came a mighty cheer, while the drums beat and the bugles sounded, and the sides of the ships were seen to be thronged with soldiers, pressing against the high bulwarks, clinging to the stout rigging. The sun shone upon their breast-plates and their swords, which they waved to the crowds in greeting, and gathered on the poop would be the officers – flashes of crimson, blue, and Lincoln green, as they moved amongst the men.

Each ship carried on her mainmast the standard of the officer in command, and as the crowd recognized the colours and the arms of a Devon leader, or a Cornishman, another great shout would fill the air, and be echoed back to us from the cheering fellows in the vessel. There was the two-headed eagle of the Godolphins, the running stag of the Trevannions from Caer-hayes, the six swallows of the numerous Arundell clan, and – perhaps loveliest of all – the crest of the Devon Champer-nownes, a sitting swan holding in her beak a horseshoe of gold.

27

The little ships, too, threaded their way amongst their larger sisters, a vivid flash of colour with their narrow decks black with troopers, and I recognized vessels I had last seen lying in Looe Harbour or in Fowey, now weather-stained and battered, but bearing triumphantly aloft the standards of the men who had built them and manned them and commissioned them for war – among them the wolf's head of our neighbour Trelawney, and the Cornish chough of the Menabilly Rashleighs.

The leading ship, a great three-masted vessel, carried the commander of the expedition, the Duke of Buckingham, and when she was saluted from Mount Batten she replied with an answering salvo from her own six guns, and we could see the Duke's pennant fluttering from the mast-head. She dropped anchor, swinging to the wind, and the fleet followed her, and the rattle of nearly a hundred cables through a hundred hawsers must have filled the air from where we stood on the cliffs below Radford, away beyond the Sound to Saltash, at the entrance of the Tamar River. Slowly their bows swung round, pointing to Cawsand and the Cornish Coast, and their sterns came into line, the sun flashing in their windows and gleaming upon the ornamental carving, the writhing serpents, and the lions' paws.

And still the bugles echoed across the water and the drums thundered. Suddenly there was silence, the clamour and the cheering died away, and on the flagship commanded by the Duke of Buckingham someone snapped forth an order in a high, clear voice. The soldiers who had crowded the bulwarks were there no longer, they moved as one man, forming into line amidships, there was no jostling, no thrusting into position. There came another order, and the single tattoo of a drum, and in one movement it seemed the boats were manned and lowered into the water, the coloured blades poised as though to strike, and the men who waited on the thwarts sat rigid as automatons.

The manoeuvre had taken perhaps three minutes from the first order; and the timing of it, the precision, the perfect discipline of the whole proceeding drew from the crowd about us the biggest cheer yet from the day, while for no reason I felt the idiotic tears course down my cheeks.

'I thought as much,' said a fellow below me. 'There's only one man in the west who could turn an unruly rabble into soldiers fit for His Majesty's Bodyguard. There go the Grenvile coat-of-arms – do you see them, hoisted beneath the Duke of Buckingham's standard?' Even as he spoke I saw the scarlet pennant run up to the mast-head, and as it streamed into the wind and flattened the sun shone upon the three gold rests.

The boats drew away from the ship's side, the officers seated in the stern sheets, and suddenly it was high holiday again, with crowded Plymouth boats putting out from the Cattwater to greet the Fleet – the whole Sound dotted at once with little craft – and the people watching upon the cliffs began to run towards Mount Batten, calling and shouting, pushing against one another to be the first to greet the landing boats. The spell was broken, and we returned to Radford.

'A fine finish to your birthday,' said my brother with a smile. 'We are all bidden to a banquet at the Castle, at the command of the Duke of Buckingham.' He stood on the steps of the house to greet us, having ridden back from the fortress at Mount Batten. Jo had succeeded to the estates at Radford, my Uncle Christopher having died a few years back, and much of our time now was spent between Plymouth and Lanrest. Jo had become, indeed, a person of some importance, in Devon especially, and besides being Under-Sheriff for the county he had married an heiress into the bargain, Elizabeth Champernowne, whose pleasant manner and equable disposition made up for her lack of looks. My sister Bridget, too, had followed Cecilia's example and married into a Devon family, and Mary and I were the only daughters left unwed.

'There will be ten thousand fellows roaming the streets of Plymouth tonight,' jested Robin. 'I warrant if we turned the girls loose amongst them they'd soon find husbands.

'Best clip Honor's tongue then,' replied Jo, 'for they'll soon forget her blue eyes and her curls once she begins to flay them.'

'Let me alone – I can look after myself,' I told them.

For I was still the spoilt darling, the *enfant terrible*, possessing boundless health and vigour, and a tongue that ran away with me. I was, moreover (and how long ago it seems), the beauty of the family, though my features, such as they were, were more impudent than classical, and I still had to stand on tiptoe to reach Robin's shoulder. I remember, that night, how we embarked below the fortress and took boat across the Cattwater to the Castle. All Plymouth seemed to be upon the water, or on the battlements, while away to westward gleamed the soft lights of the Fleet at anchor, the stern windows shining, and the glow from the poop lanterns casting a dull beam upon the water. When we landed, we found the townsfolk pressing about the Castle entrance, and everywhere were the soldiers, laughing and talking, encircled with girls, who had decked them with flowers and ribbons for festivity. There were casks of ale standing on the cobbles beside the braziers, and barrow-loads of pies, and cakes, and cheeses, and I remember thinking that the maids who roystered there with their soldier lovers would maybe have more value from their evening than we who must behave with dignity within the precincts of the Castle.

In a moment we were out of hearing of the joyful noises of the town, and the air was close and heavy with rich scent, and velvet, and silk, and spicy food, and we were in the great banqueting-hall with voices sounding hollow and strange beneath the vaulted roof. Now and again would ring out the clear voice of a gentleman-at-arms. 'Way for the Duke of Buckingham,' and a passage would be cleared for the commander as he passed to and fro amongst the guests, holding court even as His Majesty himself might do.

The scene was colourful and exciting, and I – more accustomed to the lazy quietude of Lanrest – felt my heart beat and my cheek flush, and to my youthful fancy it seemed to me that all this glittering display was somehow a tribute to my eighteenth birthday. 'How lovely it is! Are you not glad we came?' I said to Mary, and she, always reserved among strangers, touched my arm and murmured, 'Speak more softly, Honor. You draw attention to us,' and was for drawing back against the wall. I pressed forward, greedy for colour, devouring everything with my eyes, smiling even at strangers and caring not at all that I seemed bold, when suddenly the crowd parted, a way was cleared, and here was the Duke's retinue upon us, with the Duke himself not half a yard away. Mary was gone, and I was left alone to bar his path. I remember standing an instant in dismay, and then, losing my composure, I curtseyed low, as though to King Charles himself, while a little ripple of laughter floated above my head. Raising my eyes, I saw my brother Jo, his face a strange mixture of amusement and dismay, come forward from amongst those who thronged the Duke, and bending over me he helped me to my feet, for I had curtseyed so low that I was hard upon my heels and could not rise. 'May I present my sister Honor, your Grace?' I heard him say. 'This is, in point of fact, her eighteenth birthday, and her first venture into society.'

The Duke of Buckingham bowed gravely, and, lifting my hand to his lips, wished me good fortune. 'It may be your sister's first venture, my dear Harris,' he said graciously, 'but with beauty such as she possesses you must see to it that it is not the last.' He passed on in a wave of perfume and velvet, with my brother hemmed in beside him, frowning at me over his shoulder, and as I swore under my breath (or possibly not under my breath, but indiscreetly, and a stable oath learnt from Robin at that) I heard someone say behind me, 'If you care to come out on to the battlements, I will show you how to do that as it should be done.' I whipped round, scarlet and indignant, and, looking down upon me from six foot or more, with a sardonic smile upon his face, was an officer still clad in his breastplate of silver, worn over a blue tunic, with a blue and silver sash about his waist. His eyes were golden brown, his hair dark auburn, and I saw that his ears were pierced with small gold rings, for all the world like a Turkish bandit.

'Do you mean you would show me how to curtsy or how to swear?' I said to him in fury.

'Why both, if you wish it,' he answered. 'Your performance at the first was lamentable, and at the second merely amateur.'

His rudeness rendered me speechless, and I could hardly believe my ears. I glanced about me for Mary, or for Elizabeth, Jo's serene and comfortable wife, but they had withdrawn in the crush, and I was hemmed about with strangers. The most fitting thing, then, was to withdraw with dignity. I turned on my heel, and pushed my way through the crowd, making for the entrance, and then I heard the mocking voice behind me once again. 'Way for Mistress Honor Harris of Lanrest,' proclaimed in high clear tones, while people looked at me astonished, falling back in spite of themselves, and so a passageway

31

was cleared. I walked on with flaming cheeks, scarce knowing what I was doing, and found myself, not in the great entrance as I had hoped, but in the cold air upon the battlements, looking out on to Plymouth Sound, while away below me, in the cobbled square, the townsfolk danced and sang. My odious companion was with me still, and he stood now, with his hand upon his sword, looking down upon me with that same mocking smile on his face.

'So you are the little maid my sister so much detested,' he said.

'What the devil do you mean?' I asked.

'I would have spanked you for it had I been her,' he said.

Something in the clip of his voice and the droop of his eye struck a chord in my memory. 'Who are you?' I said to him.

'Sir Richard Grenvile,' he replied, 'a Colonel in His Majesty's Army, and knighted some little while ago for extreme gallantry in the field.' He hummed a little, playing with his sash.

'It is a pity', I said, 'that your manners do not match your courage.'

'And that your deportment', he said, 'does not equal your looks.'

This reference to my height – always a sore point, for I had not grown an inch since I was thirteen – stung me to fresh fury. I let fly a string of oaths that Jo and Robin, under the greatest provocation, might have loosed upon the stableman, though certainly not in my presence, and which I had only learnt through my inveterate habit of eavesdropping; but if I hoped to make Richard Grenvile blanch I was wasting my breath. He waited until I had finished, his head cocked as though he were a tutor hearing me repeat a lesson, and then he shook his head.

'There is a certain coarseness about the English tongue that does not do for the occasion,' he said. 'Spanish is more graceful, and far more satisfying to the temper. Listen to this.' And he began to swear in Spanish, loosing upon me a stream of lovely-sounding oaths that would certainly have won my admiration had they come from Jo or Robin. As I listened I looked again for that resemblance to Gartred, but it was gone. He was like his brother Bevil, but with more dash, and certainly more swagger, and I felt he cared not a tinker's curse for anyone's opinion but his own.

'You must admit', he said, breaking off suddenly, 'that I have you beaten.' His smile, no longer sardonic but disarming, had me beaten too, and I felt my anger die within me. 'Come and look at the fleet,' he said, 'a ship at anchor is a lovely thing.'

We went to the battlements and stared out across the Sound. It was still and cloudless and the moon had risen. The ships were motionless upon the water, and they stood out in the moonlight carved and clear. The men were singing, and the sound of their voices was borne to us across the water, distinct from the rough jollity of the crowds in the streets below.

'Were your losses very great at La Rochelle?' I asked him.

'No more than I expected, in an expedition that was bound to be abortive,' he answered, shrugging his shoulders. 'Those ships yonder are filled with wounded men who won't recover. It would be more humane to throw them overboard.' I looked at him in doubt, wondering if this was a further instalment of his peculiar sense of humour. 'The only fellows who distinguished themselves were those in the regiment I have the honour to command,' he continued, 'but as no other officer but myself insists on discipline, it was small wonder that the attack proved a failure.'

His self-assurance was as astounding to me as his former rudeness.

'Do you talk thus to your superiors?' I asked him.

'If you mean superior to me in matters military, such a man does not exist,' he answered, 'but superiors in rank, why yes, invariably. That is why, although I am not yet twenty-nine, I am already the most detested officer in His Majesty's Army.' He looked down at me, smiling, and once again I was at a loss for words.

I thought of my sister Bridget, and how he had trodden upon her dress at Kit's wedding, and I wondered if there was anyone in the world who liked him. 'And the Duke of Buckingham?' I said, 'Do you speak to him in this way too?'

'Oh, George and I are old friends,' he answered. 'He does what he is told. He gives me no trouble. Look at those drunken fellows in the courtyard there. My heaven, if they were under

33

my command I'd hang the bastards.' He pointed down to the square below, where a group of brawling soldiers were squabbling around a cask of ale, accompanied by a pack of squealing women.

'You might excuse them,' I said, 'pent up at sea so long.'

'They may drain the cask dry, and rape every woman in Plymouth, for all I care,' he answered, 'but let them do it like men and not like beasts, and clean their filthy jerkins first.'

He turned away from the battlement in disgust.

'Come now,' he said. 'Let us see if you can curtsy better to me than you did to the Duke. Take your gown in your hands, thus. Bend your right knee, thus. And allow your somewhat insignificant posterior to sink upon your left leg, thus.'

I obeyed him, shaking with laughter, for it seemed to me supremely ridiculous that a colonel in His Majesty's Army should be teaching me deportment upon the battlements of Plymouth Castle.

'I assure you it is no laughing matter,' he said gravely. 'A clumsy woman looks so damnably ill-bred. There now, that is excellent. Once again. Perfection. You can do it if you try. The truth is you are an idle little baggage, and have never been beaten by your brothers.' With appalling coolness, he straightened my gown and rearranged the lace around my shoulders.

'I object to dining with untidy women,' he murmured.

'I have no intention of sitting down with you to dine,' I replied with spirit. 'No one else will ask you, I can vouch for that,' he answered. 'Come, take my arm. I am hungry if you are not.'

He marched me back into the Castle, and to my consternation I found that the guests were already seated at the long tables in the banqueting hall, and the servants were bearing in the dishes. We were conspicuous as we entered, and my usual composure fled from me. It was, it may be remembered, my first venture in the social world. 'Let us go back,' I pleaded, tugging at his arm. 'See, there is no place for us; the seats are all filled.'

'Go back? Not on your life. I want my dinner,' he replied.

He pushed his way past the servants, nearly lifting me from

my feet. I could see hundreds of faces staring up at us, and heard a hum of conversation, and for one brief moment I caught a glimpse of my sister Mary, seated next to Robin, away down in the centre of the hall. I saw the look of horror and astonishment in her eyes, and her mouth frame the word 'Honor' as she whispered to my brother. I could do nothing but hurry forward, tripping over my gown, borne on the relentless arm of Richard Grenvile to the high table at the far end of the hall where the Duke of Buckingham sat beside the Countess of Mount Edgcumbe, and the nobility of Cornwall and Devon, such as they were, feasted with decorum above the common herd. 'You are taking me to the high table,' I protested, dragging at his arm with all my force.

'What of it?' he asked, looking down at me in astonishment. 'I'm damned if I'm going to dine anywhere else. Way there please, for Sir Richard Grenvile.' At his voice the servants flattened themselves against the wall, and heads were turned and I saw the Duke of Buckingham break off from his conversation with the Countess. Chairs were pulled forward, people were squeezed aside, and somehow we were seated at the table a hand's stretch from the Duke himself, while the Lady Mount Edgcumbe peered round at me with stony eyes. Richard Grenvile leant forward with a smile. 'You are perhaps acquainted with Honor Harris, Countess,' he said, 'my sister-in-law. This is her eighteenth birthday.' The Countess bowed, and appeared unmoved. 'You can disregard her,' said Richard Grenvile to me. 'She's as deaf as a post. But for God's sake smile, and take that glassy stare from your eye.' I prayed for death, but it did not come to me. Instead I took the roast swan that was heaped upon my platter.

The Duke of Buckingham turned to me, his glass in his hand. 'I wish you very many happy returns of the day,' he said.

I murmured my thanks, and shook my curls to hide my flaming cheeks.

'Merely a formality,' said Richard Grenvile in my ear. 'Don't let it go to your head. George has a dozen mistresses already, and is in love with the Queen of France.'

He ate with evident enjoyment, vilifying his neighbours with every mouthful, and because he did not trouble to lower his voice I could swear that his words were heard. I tasted nothing of what I ate or drank, but sat like a bewildered fish throughout the long repast. At length the ordeal was over, and I felt myself pulled to my feet by my companion. The wine, which I had swallowed as though it were water, had made jelly of my legs, and I was obliged to lean upon him for support. I have scant memory indeed of what followed next. There was music, and singing, and some Sicilian dancers, strung about with ribbons, performed a tarantella, but their final dizzy whirling was my undoing, and I have shaming recollection of being assisted to some inner apartment of the castle, suitably darkened and discreet, where Nature took her toll of me, and the roast swan knew me no more. I opened my eyes and found myself upon a couch, with Richard Grenvile holding my hand, and dabbing my forehead with his kerchief.

'You must learn to carry your wine,' he said severely.

I felt very ill, and very ashamed, and tears were near the surface.

'Ah, no,' he said, and his voice, hitherto so clipped and harsh, was oddly tender. 'You must not cry. Not on your birthday.'

He continued dabbing at my forehead with the kerchief.

'I have n-never eaten roast swan b-before,' I stammered, closing my eyes in agony at the memory.

'It was not so much the swan as the burgundy,' he murmured. 'Lie still now, you will be easier by and by.'

In truth, my head was still reeling, and I was as grateful for his strong hand as I would have been for my mother's. It seemed to me in no wise strange that I should be lying sick in a darkened unknown room with Richard Grenvile tending me, proving himself so comforting a nurse.

'I hated you at first. I like you better now,' I told him.

'It's hard that I had to make you vomit before I won your approval,' he answered. I laughed, and then fell to groaning again, for the swan was not entirely dissipated. 'Lean against my shoulder, so,' he said to me. 'Poor little one, what an ending to an eighteenth birthday.' I could feel him shake with silent laughter, and yet his voice and hands were strangely tender, and I was happy with him.

'You are like your brother Bevil after all,' I said.

'Not I,' he answered. 'Bevil is a gentleman, and I a scoundrel. I have always been the black sheep of the family.'

'What of Gartred?' I asked.

'Gartred is a law unto herself,' he replied. 'You must have learnt that when you were a little child, and she was wedded to your brother.'

'I hated her with all my heart,' I told him.

'Small blame to you for that,' he answered me.

'And is she content, now that she is wed again?' I asked him.

'Gartred will never be content,' he said. 'She was born greedy, not only for money, but for men too. She had an eye to Antony Denys, her husband now, long before your brother died.'

'And not only Antony Denys,' I said.

'You had long ears for a little maid,' he answered.

I sat up, rearranging my curls, while he helped me with my gown.

'You have been kind to me,' I said, grown suddenly prim, and conscious of my eighteen years. 'I shall not forget this evening.'

'Nor I either,' he replied.

'Perhaps', I said, 'you had better take me to my brothers.'

'Perhaps I had,' he said.

I stumbled out of the little dark chamber to the lighted corridor. 'Where were we all this while?' I asked in doubt, glancing over my shoulder. He laughed, and shook his head.

'The good God only knows,' he answered; 'but I wager it is the closet where Mount Edgcumbe combs his hair.' He looked down at me smiling, and, for one instant, touched my curls with his hands. 'I will tell you one thing,' he said, 'I have never sat with a woman before while she vomited.'

'Nor I so disgraced myself before a man,' I said with dignity.

Then he bent suddenly, and lifted me in his arms like a child. 'Nor have I ever lay hidden in a darkened room with anyone so fair as you, Honor, and not made love to her,' he told me, and, holding me for a moment against his heart, he set me on my feet again.

'And now, if you permit it, I will take you home,' he said.

That is, I think, a very clear and truthful account of my first meeting with Richard Grenvile.

Chapter 4

WITHIN a week of the encounter just recorded I was sent back to my mother at Lanrest, supposedly in disgrace for my ill-behaviour, and once home I had to be admonished all over again, and hear for the twentieth time how a maid of my age and breeding should conduct herself. It seemed that I had done mischief to everyone. I had shamed my brother Jo by that foolish curtsy to the Duke of Buckingham, and further had offended his wife Elizabeth by taking precedence of her and dining at the high table, to which she had not been invited. I had neglected to remain with my sister Mary during the evening, had been observed by sundry persons cavorting oddly on the battlements with an officer, and had finally appeared some time after midnight from the private rooms within the castle in a sad state of disarray.

Such conduct would, my mother said severely, condemn me possibly for all time in the eyes of the world, and had my father been alive he would more than likely have packed me off to the nuns for two or three years, in the hopes that my absence for a space of time would cause the incident to be forgotten. As it was, and here invention failed her, and she was left lamenting that, as both my married sisters Cecilia and Bridget were expecting to lie-in again and could not receive me, I would be obliged to stay at home.

It seemed to me very dull after Radford, for Robin had remained there, and my young brother Percy was still at Oxford. I was therefore alone in my disgrace. I remember it was some weeks after I returned, a day in early spring, and I had gone out to sulk by the apple-tree, that favourite hiding-place of childhood, when I observed a horseman riding up the valley. The trees hid him for a space, and then the sound of horse's hoofs drew nearer, and I realized that he was coming to Lanrest. Thinking it was Robin, I scrambled down from my apple-tree and went to the stables, but when I arrived there I found the servant leading a strange horse to the stall – a fine grey –

and I caught a glimpse of a tall figure passing into the house. I was for following my old trick of eavesdropping at the parlour door, but just as I was about to do so I observed my mother on the stairs.

'You will please go to your chamber, Honor, and remain there until my visitor has gone,' she said gravely.

My first impulse was to demand the visitor's name, but I remembered my manners in time, and, afire with curiosity, went silently upstairs. Once there I rang for Matty, the maid who had served me and my sisters for some years now, and had become my special ally. Her ears were nearly as long as mine, and her nose as keen, and her round, plain face was now alight with mischief. She guessed what I wanted her for before I asked her. 'I'll bide in the hallway when he comes out, and get his name for you,' she said. 'A tall big gentleman he was, a fine man.'

'No one from Bodmin,' I said, with sudden misgiving, for fear my mother should, after all, intend to send me to the nuns.

'Why, bless you, no,' she answered. 'This is a young master, wearing a blue cloak slashed with silver.'

Blue and silver. The Grenvile colours.

'Was his hair red, Matty?' I asked in some excitement.

'You could warm your hands at it,' she answered.

This was an adventure, then, and no more dullness to the day. I sent Matty below, and paced up and down my chamber in great impatience. The interview must have been a short one, for very soon I heard the door of the parlour open, and the clear clipped voice that I remembered well taking leave of my mother, and I heard his footsteps pass away through the hallway to the courtyard. My chamber window looked out on to the garden, and I thus had no glimpse of him, and it seemed eternity before Matty reappeared, her eyes bright with information. She brought forth a screwed-up piece of paper from beneath her apron, and with it a silver piece. 'He told me to give you the note, and keep the crown,' she said.

I unfolded the note, furtive as a criminal.

'Dear Sister,' I read, 'although Gartred has exchanged a Harris for a Denys, I count myself still your brother, and reserve for myself the right of calling upon you. Your good mother, it seems, thinks otherwise, tells me you are indisposed, and has bidden me good-day in no uncertain terms. It is not my custom to ride some ten miles or so to no purpose, therefore you will direct your maid forthwith to conduct me to some part of your domain where we can converse together unobserved, for I dare swear you are no more indisposed than is your brother and servant, Richard Grenvile.'

My first thought was to send no answer, for he took my compliance so much for granted, but curiosity and a beating heart got the better of my pride, and I bade Matty show the visitor the orchard, but that he should not go too directly, for fear of being seen from the house. When she had gone, I listened for my mother's footsteps, and sure enough they sounded up the stairs, and she came into the room. She found me sitting by the window, with a book of prayers open on my knee. 'I am happy to see you so devout, Honor,' she said.

I did not answer, but kept my eyes meekly upon the page.

'Sir Richard Grenvile, with whom you conducted yourself in so unseemly a fashion a week ago in Plymouth, has just departed,' she continued. 'It seems he has left the Army for a while, and intends to reside near to us at Killigarth, standing as Member of Parliament for Fowey. A somewhat sudden decision.'

Still I did not answer. 'I have never heard any good of him,' said my mother. 'He has always caused his family concern, and been a sore trial to his brother Bevil, being constantly in debt. He will hardly make us a pleasant neighbour.'

'He is, at least, a very gallant soldier,' I said warmly.

'I know nothing about that,' she answered, 'but I have no wish for him to ride over here, demanding to see you, when your brothers are from home. It shows great want of delicacy on his part.'

With that she left me, and I heard her pass into her chamber and close the door. In a few moments I had my shoes in my hands and was tiptoeing down the stairs into the garden. Then I flew like the wind to the orchard, and was safe in the apple-tree before many minutes had passed. Presently I heard someone moving about under the trees, and parting the blossom in my hiding-place I saw Richard Grenvile stooping under the low branches. I broke off a piece of twig and threw it at him. He shook his head, and looked about him. I threw another, and this one hit him a sharp crack upon the nose. 'God damn it,' he began, and, looking up, he saw me laughing at him from the apple-tree. In a moment he had swung himself up beside me, and with one arm around my waist had me pinned against the trunk. The branch cracked most ominously.

'Get down at once – the branch will not hold us both,' I said.

'It will, if you keep still,' he told me.

One false move would have seen us both upon the ground, some ten feet below, but to remain still meant that I must continue to lie crushed against his chest, with his arm about me, and his face not six inches away from mine.

'We cannot possibly converse in such a fashion,' I protested.

'Why not? I find it very pleasant,' he answered.

Cautiously he stretched his leg along the full length of the branch to give himself more ease, and pulled me closer.

'Now, what have you to tell me?' he said, for all the world as though it were I who had demanded the interview and not he.

I then recounted my disgrace, and how my brother and sister-in-law had sent me packing home from Plymouth, and it seemed if I must now be treated as a prisoner in my own home.

'And it is no use your coming here again,' I added, 'for my mother will never let me see you. It seems you are a person of ill repute.'

'How so?' he demanded.

'You are constantly in debt – those were her words.'

'The Grenviles are never not in debt. It is the great failing of the family. Even Bevil has to borrow from the Jews.'

'You are a sore trial to him, and to all your relatives.'

'On the contrary, it is they who are a sore trial to me. I can seldom get a penny out of them. What else did your mother say?'

'That it showed want of delicacy to come here asking to see me when my brothers are from home.'

'She is wrong. It showed great cunning, born of long experience.'

41

'And as for your gallantry in the field, she knows nothing about that.'

'I hardly suppose she does. Like all mothers, it is my gallantry in other spheres that concerns her at the present.'

'I don't know what you mean,' I said.

'Then you have less perception than I thought,' he answered, and, loosening his hold upon the branch, he flicked at the collar of my gown. 'You have an earwig running down your bosom,' he said.

I drew back, disconcerted, the abrupt change from the romantic to the prosaic putting me out of countenance.

'I believe my mother to be right,' I said stiffly. 'I think there is very little to be gained from our further acquaintance, and it would be best to put an end to it now.' It was difficult to show dignity in my cramped position, but I made some show of sitting upright, and braced my shoulders.

'You cannot descend unless I let you,' he said, and in truth I was locked there, with his legs across the branch. 'The moment is opportune to teach you Spanish,' he murmured.

'I have no wish to learn it,' I answered.

Then he laughed, and, taking my face in his hands, he kissed me very suddenly, which, being a novelty to me, and strangely pleasant, rendered me, for a few moments, incapable of speech or action. I turned away my head, and began to play with the blossoms. 'You can go now, if you desire it,' he said. I did not desire it, but had too much pride to tell him so. He swung himself to the ground, and lifted me down beside him.

'It is not easy', he said, 'to be gallant in an apple-tree. Perhaps you will tell your mother.' He wore upon his face that same sardonic smile that I had first seen in Plymouth.

'I shall tell my mother nothing,' I said, hurt by this abrupt dismissal. He looked down on me for a moment in silence, and then he said, 'If you bid your gardener trim that upper branch we would do better another time.'

'I am not certain', I answered, 'that I wish for another time.'

'Ah, but you do,' he said, 'and so do I. Besides, my horse needs exercise.' He turned through the trees, making for the gate where he had left his horse, and I followed him silently through the long grass. He reached for the bridle, and climbed into the saddle. 'Ten miles between Lanrest and Killigarth,' he said. 'If I did this twice a week, Daniel would be in a fine condition by the summer. I will come again on Tuesday. Remember those instructions to the gardener.' He waved his gauntlet at me and was gone.

I stood staring after him, telling myself that he was quite as detestable as Gartred, and that I would never see him more; but for all my resolutions I was at the apple-tree again on Tuesday.

There followed then as strange, and to my mind as sweet, a wooing as ever maiden of my generation had. Looking back on it now, after a quarter of a century, when the sequel to it fills my mind with greater clarity, it has the hazy unreality of an elusive dream. Once a week, and sometimes twice, he would ride over to Lanrest from Killigarth, and there, cradled in the apple-tree – with the offending branch lopped as he demanded – he tutored me in love, and I responded. He was but twenty-eight, and I eighteen. Those March and April afternoons, with the bees humming above our heads and the blackcap singing, and the grass in the orchard growing longer day by day, there seemed no end to them and no beginning. Of what we discoursed, when we did not kiss, I have forgotten. He must have told me much about himself, for Richard's thoughts were ever centred about his person, more then than latterly, and I had a picture of a red-haired lad rebellious of authority flaunting his elders, staring out across the storm-tossed Atlantic from the towering, craggy cliffs of his north Cornish coast, so different from our southern shore, with its coves and valleys.

We have, I think, a more happy disposition here in southeast Cornwall, for the very softness of the air, come rain or sun, and the gentle contour of the land, make for a lazy feeling of content. Whereas in the Grenvile country, bare of hedgerow, bereft of tree, exposed to all four winds of heaven – winds laden, as it were, with surf and spray – the mind develops with a quick perception, with more fire to it, more anger, and life itself is hazardous and cruel. Here we have few tragedies at sea, but there the coast is strewn with the bleached bones of vessels wrecked without hope of haven, and about the torn, unburied bodies of the drowned the seals play and the falcons hover. It holds us more than we ever reckon, the few square miles of territory where we are born and bred, and I can understand what devils of unrest surged in the blood of Richard Grenvile.

These thoughts of mine came at a later date, but then, when we were young, they concerned me not, nor he either, and whether he talked to me of soldiering or Stowe, of fighting the French or battling with his own family, it sounded happy in my ears, and all his bitter jests were forgotten when he kissed me and held me close. It seems odd that our hiding-place was not discovered. Maybe in his careless, lavish fashion he showered gold pieces on the servants. Certainly my mother passed her days in placid ignorance.

And then, one day in early April, my brothers rode from Radford, bringing with them young Edward Champernowne, a younger brother of Elizabeth's. I was happy to see Jo and Robin, but in no mood to exchange courtesies with a stranger – besides, his teeth protruded, which seemed to me unpardonable – and also I was filled with furtive fear that my secret meetings would be discovered. After we had dined, Jo and Robin and my mother, with Edward Champernowne, withdrew to the book-room that had been my father's, and I was left alone to entertain Elizabeth. She made no mention of my discourtesy at Plymouth, for which I was grateful, but proceeded to lavish great praise upon her brother Edward, who, she told me, was but a year older than myself, and had recently left Oxford. I listened with but half an ear, my thoughts full of Richard, who, in debt as usual, had talked at our last meeting of selling lands in Killigarth and Tywardreath which he had inherited from his mother, and bearing me off with him to Spain or Naples, where we would live like princes and turn bandit.

Later in the evening I was summoned to my mother's room. Jo was with her, and Robin too, but Edward Champernowne had gone to join his sister. All three of them wore an air of well-being.

My mother drew me to her, and kissed me fondly, and said at once that great happiness was in store for me, that Edward Champernowne had asked for my hand in marriage, that she and my brothers had accepted, the formalities had been settled, my portion agreed to, with Jo adding to it most handsomely, and nothing remained now but to determine upon the date. I believe I stared at them all a moment stupefied, and then broke out wildly in a torrent of protestation, declaring that I would not wed him, that I would wed no man who was not of my own choice, and that sooner than do it I would throw myself from the roof. In vain my mother argued with me, in vain Jo enthused upon the virtues of young Champernowne, of his steadiness, of his noble bearing, and of how my conduct had been such, a few months back, that it was amazing he should have asked for my hand at all. 'You have come to the age, Honor,' he said, 'when we believe marriage to be the only means to settle you, and in this matter Mother and myself are the best judges.' I shook my head, I dug my nails into my hands.

'I tell you I will not marry him,' I said.

Robin had not taken part in the conversation. He sat a little apart, but now he rose and stood beside me.

'I told you, Jo, it would be little use to drive Honor if she had not the inclination,' he said. 'Give her time to accustom herself to the project, and she will think better of it.'

'Edward Champernowne might think better of it too,' replied Jo.

'It were best to settle it now while he is here,' said my mother.

I looked at their worried, indecisive faces – for they all loved me well and were distressed at my obduracy. 'No,' I told them, 'I would sooner die,' and I flounced from the room in feverish anger, and, going to my chamber, thrust the bolt through the door. To my imagination, strained and overwrought, it seemed to me that my brother and my mother had become the wicked parents in a fairy tale, and I the luckless princess whom they were bent on wedding to an ogre, though I believe the inoffensive Edward Champernowne would not have dared lay a finger upon me. I waited till the whole brood of them were abed, and then, changing my gown and wrapping a cloak about me, I stole from the house. For I was bent upon a harebrained scheme, which was no less than walking through the night to Killigarth, and so to Richard. The thunder had passed, and the night was clear enough, and I set off with beating heart down the roadway to the river, which I forded a mile or so below

45

Lanrest. Then I struck westward on the road to Pelynt, but the way was rough, and crossed with intersecting lanes, and my mind misgave me for the fool I was, for without start-lore I had no knowledge of direction. I was ill-used to walking any distance, and my shoes were thin. The night seemed endless and the road interminable, and the sounds and murmurs of the countryside filled me with apprehension, though I pretended to myself I did not care. Dawn found me stranded by another stream, and encompassed about by woods, and, weary and be-draggled, I climbed a further hill and saw at last my first glimpse of the sea, and the hump of Looe Island away to the eastward.

I knew then that some inner sense had led me to the coast, and I was not walking north, as I had feared, but the curl of smoke through the trees and the sound of barking dogs warned me that I was trespassing, and I had no wish to be caught by keepers.

About six o'clock I met a ploughman tramping along the highway, who stared at me amazed and took me for a witch, for I saw him cross his fingers and spit when I had passed, but he pointed out the lane that led to Killigarth. The sun was high now above the sea, and the fishing vessels strung out in a line in Talland Bay. I saw the tall chimneys of the house of Killigarth, and once again my heart misgave me for the sorry figure I should make before Richard. If he was there alone, it would not matter, but what if Bevil was at home, and Grace, his wife, and a whole tribe of Grenviles that I did not know? I came to the house then like a thief, and stood before the windows uncertain what to do. It wore the brisk air of early morning. Servants were astir. I heard a clatter in the kitchens, and the murmur of voices, and I could smell the fatty smell of bacon and smoky ham. Windows were open to the sun, and the sound of laughter came, and men talking.

I wished with all my heart that I was back in my bed-chamber in Lanrest, but there was no returning. I pulled the bell, and heard the clanging echo through the house. Then I drew back, as a servant came into the hall. He wore the Grenvile livery, and had a stern, forbidding air. 'What do you want?' he asked of me.

'I wish to see Sir Richard,' I said.

'Sir Richard and the rest of the gentlemen are at breakfast,' he answered. 'Away with you now – he won't be troubled with you.' The door of the dining-room was open, and I heard more sound of talk and laughter, and Richard's voice topping the rest.

'I must see Sir Richard,' I insisted, desperate now and near to tears, and then, as the fellow was about to lay his hands upon me and thrust me from the door, Richard himself came out into the hall. He was laughing, calling something over his shoulder to the gentlemen within. He was eating still, and had a napkin in his hand.

'Richard,' I called. 'Richard, it is I, Honor,' and he came forward, amazement on his face. 'What the devil –' he began. Then, cursing his servant to be gone, he drew me into a little ante-room beside the hall.

'What is it? What is the matter?' he said swiftly, and I, weak and utterly worn out, fell into his arms and wept upon his shoulder.

'Softly, my little love. Be easy then,' he murmured, and held me close and stroked my hair, until I was calm enough to tell my story. 'They want to marry me to Edward Champernowne,' I stammered – how foolish it sounded to be blurted thus – 'and I have told them I will not do so, and I have wandered all night on the roads to tell you of it.'

I felt him shake with laughter as he had done that first evening weeks ago when I had sickened of the swan.

'Is that all?' he asked. 'And did you tramp twelve miles or more to tell me that? Oh, Honor, my little love, my dear.'

I looked up at him, bewildered that he found so serious a matter food for laughter. 'What am I to do then?' I said.

'Why, tell them to go to the devil, of course,' he answered; 'and if you dare not say it, then I will say it for you. Come in to breakfast.' I tugged at his hand in consternation, for if the ploughman had taken me for a witch, and the servant for a beggar, God only knew what his friends would say to me. He would not listen to my protests, but dragged me in to the dining-room where the gentlemen were breakfasting, and there was I with my bedraggled gown and cloak and my torn slippers, faced with Ranald Mohun, and young Trelawney, Tom Treffry,

47

and Jonathan Rashleigh, and some half-dozen others that I did not know. 'This is Honor Harris of Lanrest,' said Richard. 'I think you gentlemen are possibly acquainted with her.' They one and all stood up and bowed to me, astonishment and embarrassment written plain upon their faces. 'She has run away from home,' said Richard, in no way put out by the situation. 'Would you credit it, Tom, they want to marry her to Edward Champernowne?'

'Indeed,' replied Tom Treffry, quite at a loss, and he bent to stroke his dog's ear to hide his confusion.

'Will you have some bacon, Honor?' said Richard, proffering me a platter heaped with fatty pork, but I was too tired and faint to desire anything more than be taken upstairs and put to rest.

Then Jonathan Rashleigh, a man of family and older than Richard and the others, said quietly: 'Mistress Honor would prefer to withdraw, I fancy. I would summon one of your serving-women, Richard.'

'Damn it, this is a bachelor household,' answered Richard, his mouth crammed with bacon. 'There isn't a woman in the place.'

I heard a snort from Ranald Mohun, who put a handkerchief to his face, and I saw also the baleful eye that Richard cast upon him, and then somehow they one and all made their excuses, and got themselves from the room, and we were alone at last.

'I was a fool to come,' I said. 'Now I have disgraced you before all your friends.'

'I was disgraced long since,' he said, pulling himself another tankard of ale; 'but it was well you came after breakfast rather than before.'

'Why so?' I asked.

He smiled, and drew a document from his breast.

'I have sold Killigarth, and also the lands I hold in Tywardreath,' he answered. 'Rashleigh gave me a fair price for them. Had you blundered in sooner he might have stayed his hand.'

'Will the money pay your debts?' I said.

He laughed derisively. 'A drop in the ocean,' he said; 'but it will suffice for a week or so, until we can borrow elsewhere.'

'Why "we"?' I inquired.

'Well, we shall be together,' he answered. 'You do not think I am going to permit this ridiculous match with Edward Champernowne?' He wiped his mouth, and pushed aside his plate, as though he had not a care in the world. He held out his arms to me, and I went to him. 'Dear love,' I said, feeling in sudden very old and very wise, 'you have told me often that you must marry an heiress, or you could not live.'

'I should have no wish to live if you were wedded to another man,' he answered. Some little time was wasted while he assured me of this.

'But, Richard,' I said presently, 'if I wed you instead of Edward Champernowne, my brother may refuse his sanction.'

'I'll fight him if he does.'

'We shall be penniless,' I protested.

'Not if I know it,' he said. 'I have several relatives as yet unfleeced. Mrs Abbot, my old Aunt Katherine up at Hartland, she has a thousand pounds or so she does not want.'

'But we cannot live thus all our lives,' I said.

'I have never lived anyway else,' he answered.

I thought of the formalities and deeds that went with marriage, the lawyers and the documents.

'I am the youngest daughter, Richard,' I said, hesitating. 'You must bear in mind that my portion will be very small.'

At this he shouted with laughter, and, lifting me in his arms, carried me from the room. 'It's your person I have designs upon,' he said. 'God damn your portion.'

Chapter 5

OH, wild betrothal, startling and swift, decided on in an instant without rhyme or reason, and all objections swept aside like a forest in a fire. My mother was helpless before the onslaught, my brothers powerless to obstruct. The Champernownes, offended, withdrew to Radford, and Jo, washing his hands of me, went with them. His wife would not receive me now, having refused her brother, and I was led to understand that the scandal of my conduct had spread through the whole of Devon. Bridget's husband came posting down from Holberton, and John Pollexefen from Mothercombe, and all the West, it seemed, said I had eloped with Richard Grenville and was to wed him now through dire necessity. He had shamed me in a room at Plymouth – he had carried me by force to Killigarth – I had lived there as his mistress for three months – all these and other tales were spread abroad, and Richard and I, in the gladness of our hearts, did nought but laugh at them. He was for taking horse to London, and giving me refuge with the Duke of Buckingham, who would, he declared, eat out of his hand and give me a dowry into the bargain, but at this moment of folly his brother Bevil came riding to Lanrest, and, with his usual grace and courtesy, insisted that I should go to Stowe and be married from the Grenvile home. Bevil brought law and order into chaos, his approval lent some shadow of decency to the whole proceeding – a quality which had been lacking hitherto; and within a few days of his taking charge my mother and I were safely housed at Stowe, where Kit had gone as a bridegroom nearly eight years before. I was too much in love by then to care a whit for anyone, and, like someone who has feasted too wisely and too well, I swam through the great rooms at Stowe a-glow with confidence, smiling at old Sir Bernard, bowing to all his kinsmen, in no more awe of the grandeur about me than I had been of the familiar, dusty corners in Lanrest. I have small recollection now of what I did, or whom I saw – save that there were Grenviles everywhere and all of them auburn-haired, as Bridget had once told me – but I remember pacing up and down the great gardens while Sir Bernard discoursed solemnly upon the troubles brewing between His Majesty and Parliament, and I remember, too, standing for hours in a chamber – that of the Lady Grace, Bevil's wife – while her women pinned my wedding-gown upon me, and gathered it, and tuckered it, and pinned it yet again, while she and my mother gave advice, and a heap of children, as it seemed to me, played about the floor.

Richard was not much with me. I belonged to the women, he said, during these last days. We would have enough of one another by and by. These last days – what a world of prophecy.

Nothing, then, remains out of the fog of recollection but that final afternoon in May, and the sun that came and went behind the clouds, and a high wind blowing. I can see now the guests assembled on the lawns, and how we all proceeded to the falconry, for an afternoon of sport was to precede a banquet in the evening.

There were the goshawks on their perches, preening their feathers and stretching their wings, the tamer of them permitting our approach; and further removed, solitary upon their blocks in the sand, their larger brethren, the wild-eyed peregrines.

The falconers came to leash and jess the hawks, and hood them ready for the chase, and as they did this the stable men brought the horses for us, and the dogs who were to flush the game yelped and pranced about their heels. Richard mounted me upon the little chestnut mare that was to be mine hereafter, and, as he turned to speak a moment to his falconer about the hooding of his bird, I looked over my shoulder and saw a conclave of horsemen gathered about the gate to welcome a new arrival. 'What now?' said Richard, and the falconer, shading his eyes from the sun, turned to his master with a smile.

'It is Mrs Denys,' he said, 'from Orley Court. Now you can match your red hawk with her tiercel.'

Richard looked up at me and smiled.

'So it has happened after all,' he said, 'and Gartred has chose to visit us.' They were riding down the path towards us, and I wondered how she would seem to me, my childhood enemy, to whom, in so strange a fashion, I was to be related once again. No word had come from her, no message of congratulation, but her natural curiosity had won her in the end. 'Greetings, sister,' called Richard, the old sardonic mockery in his voice. 'So you have come to dance at my wedding after all.'

'Perhaps,' she answered. 'I have not yet decided. Two of the children are not well at home.' She rode abreast of me, that slow smile that I remembered on her face. 'How are you, Honor?'

'Well enough,' I answered.

'I never thought to see you become a Grenvile.'

'Nor I either.'

'The ways of Providence are strange indeed. You have not met my husband.' I bowed to the stranger at her side, a big, bluff, hearty man, a good deal older than herself. So this was the Antony Denys, who had caused poor Kit so much anguish before he died. Maybe it was his weight that had won her. 'Where do we ride?' she asked, turning from me to Richard.

'In the open country, towards the shore,' he answered.

She glanced at the falcon on his wrist. 'A red hawk,' she said, one eyebrow lifted, 'not in her full plumage. Do you think to make anything of her?'

'She has taken kite and bustard, and I propose to put her to a heron today if we can flush one.'

Gartred smiled. 'A red hawk at a heron,' she mocked. 'You will see her check at a magpie and nothing larger.'

'Will you match her with your tiercel?'

'My tiercel will destroy her, and the heron afterwards.'

'That is a matter of opinion.'

They watched each other like duellists about to strike, and I remembered how Richard had told me they had fought with one another from the cradle. I had my first shadow of misgiving that the day would turn in some way to disaster. For a moment I wondered whether I would plead fatigue and stay behind. I rode for pleasure, not for slaughter, and hawking was never my favourite pastime.

Gartred must have observed my hesitation, for she laughed and said: 'Your bride loses her courage. The pace will be too strong for her.'

'What?' said Richard, his face falling. 'You are coming, aren't you?'

'Why, yes,' I said swiftly. 'I will see you kill your heron.'

We rode out to the open country, with the wind blowing in our faces and the sound of the Atlantic coming to us as the long surf rollers spilt themselves with a roar on to the shore far below. At first the sport was poor, for no quarry larger than a woodcock was flushed, and to this the goshawks were flown, who clutch their prey between their claws, and do not kill outright, like the large-winged peregrines. Richard's falcon and Gartred's tiercel were still hooded, and not slipped, for we were not yet come upon the heron's feeding ground. My little mare pawed restlessly at the ground, for up to the present we had had no run and the pace was slow. Near a little copse the falconers flushed three magpies and a cast of goshawks were flown at them, but the cunning magpies, making up for lack of wing power by cunning, scuttled from hedge to hedge, and after some twenty minutes or so of hovering by the hawks, and shouting and driving by the falconers, only one magpie was taken.

'Come. This is poor indeed,' said Gartred scornfully. 'Can we find no better quarry, and so let fly the falcons?'

Richard shaded his eyes from the sun, and looked towards the west. A long strip of moorland lay before us, rough and uneven, and at the far end of it a narrow, soggy marsh, where the duck would fly to feed in stormy weather, and at all seasons of the year, so Richard told me, the sea-birds came, curlews, and gulls, and herons.

There was no bird as yet on passage through the sky, save a small lark high above our heads, and the marsh, where the herons might be found, was still two miles away.

'I'll match my horse to yours, and my red hawk to your tiercel,' said Richard suddenly, and even as he spoke he let fly the hood of his falcon and slipped her, putting spurs to his horse upon the gesture. Within ten seconds Gartred had followed suit, her grey-winged peregrine soaring into the sun, and she and Richard were galloping across the moors towards the marsh, with the two hawks like black specks in the sky above them. My mare, excited by the clattering hoofs of her companions, took charge of me, nearly pulling my arms out of their sockets, and she raced like a mad thing in pursuit of the horses ahead of us, the yelping of the dogs and the cries of the falconers whipping her speed. My last ride. The sun in my eyes, the wind in my face, the movement of the mare beneath me, the thunder of her hooves, the scent of the golden gorse, the sound of the sea. Unforgettable, unforgotten, deep in my soul for all time. I could see Richard and Gartred racing neck to neck, flinging insults at each other as they rode, and in the sky the male and female falcons pitched and hovered. When suddenly away from the marsh ahead of us rose a heron, his great grey wings unfolding, his legs trailing. I heard a shout from

Richard, and an answering cry from Gartred, and in an instant it seemed the hawks had seen their quarry, for they both began, to circle above the heron, climbing higher and still higher, swinging out in rings until they were like black dots against the sun. The watchful heron, rising too, but in a narrower circle, turned down-wind, his queer, ungainly body strangely light and supple, and like a flash the first hawk dived to him – whether it was Richard's young falcon or Gartred's tiercel I could not tell – and missed the heron by a hair's breadth. At once, recovering himself, he began to soar again, in ever higher circles, to recover his lost pitch, and the second hawk swooped, missing in like manner.

I tried to rein in my mare, but could not stop her, and now Gartred and Richard had turned eastward too, following the course of the heron, and we were galloping three abreast, the ground rising steadily towards a circle of stones in the midst of the moor.

'Beware the chasm,' shouted Richard in my ear, pointing with his whip, but he was past me like the wind and I could not call to him.

The heron was now direct above my head, and the falcons lost to view, and I heard Gartred shout in triumph: 'They bind – they bind – my tiercel has her,' and, silhouetted against the sun, I saw one of the falcons locked against the heron and the two come swinging down to earth not twenty yards ahead.

I tried to swerve, but the mare had the mastery, and I shouted to Gartred as she passed me, 'Which way is the chasm?' but she did not answer me. On we flew towards the circle of stones, the sun blinding my eyes, and out of the darkening sky fell the dying heron and the blood-bespattered falcon, straight into the yawning crevice that opened out before me. I heard Richard shout, and a thousand voices singing in my ears as I fell.

It was thus, then, that I, Honor Harris of Lanrest, became a cripple, losing all power in my legs from that day forward until this day on which I write, so that for some twenty-five years now I have been upon my back, or upright in a chair, never walking any more, or feeling the ground beneath my feet. If anyone therefore thinks that a cripple makes an indifferent heroine to a tale, now is the time to close these pages and desist from reading. For you will never see me wed to the man I love, nor become the mother of his children. But you will learn how that love never faltered, for all its strange vicissitudes, becoming to both of us, in later years, more deep and tender than if we had been wed, and you will learn also how, for all my helplessness, I took the leading part in the drama that unfolded, my very immobility sharpening my senses and quickening my perception, while chance itself forced me to my role of judge and witness. The play goes on, then – what you have just read is but the prologue.

Chapter 6

IT is not my purpose to survey, in these after-years, the suffering, bodily and mental, that I underwent during those early months when my life seemed finished. They would make poor reading. And I myself have no inclination to drag from the depths of my being a bitterness that is best forgotten. It is enough to say that they feared at first for my brain, and I lived for many weeks in a state of darkness. As little by little clarity returned, and I was able to understand the full significance of my physical state, I asked for Richard; and I learnt that, after having waited in vain for some sign from me, some thread of hope from the doctors that I might recover, he had been persuaded by his brother Bevil to rejoin his regiment. This was for the best. It was impossible for him to remain inactive. The assassination at Portsmouth of his friend the Duke of Buckingham was an added horror, and he set sail for France with the rest of the expedition in that final half-hearted attack on La Rochelle. By the time he returned I was home again at Lanrest, and had sufficient strength of will to make my decision for the future. This was never to see Richard again. I wrote him a letter, which he disregarded, riding down from London express to see me. I would not see him. He endeavoured to force his way into my room, but my brothers barred the way. It was only when the doctors told him that his presence could but injure me further that he realized the finality of all bonds between us. He rode away without a word. I received from him one last letter, wild, bitter, reproachful – then silence.

In November of that year he married Lady Howard of Fitzford, a rich widow, three times wed already, and four years older than himself. The news came to me indirectly, an incautious word let slip from Matty and at once confusedly covered, and I asked my mother the truth. She had wished to hide it from me, fearing a relapse, and I think my calm acceptance of the fact baffled her understanding.

It was hard for her, and for the rest of them, to realize that I looked upon myself now as a different being. The Honor that was, had died as surely as the heron that afternoon in May, when the falcon slew him.

That she would live for ever in her lover's heart was possible, no doubt, and a lovely fantasy, but the Richard that I knew and loved was made of flesh and blood; he had to endure, even as I had.

I remember smiling, as I lay upon my bed, to think that after all he had found his heiress, and such a notorious one at that. I only hoped that her experience would make him happy, and her wealth insure him some security.

Meanwhile, I had to school myself to a new way of living, and day after day immobility. The mind must atone for the body's helplessness. Percy returned from Oxford about this time, bringing his books of learning, and with his aid I set myself the task of learning Greek and Latin. He made an indifferent though a kindly tutor, and I had not the heart to keep him long from his dogs and his horses, but at least he set me on the road to reading, and I made good progress. The family were all most good and tender. My sisters and their children, tearful and strung with pity as they were at first, soon became easy in my presence, when I laughed and chatted with them, and little by little I – the hitherto spoilt darling – became the guide and mediator in their affairs, and their problems would be brought to me to solve. I am speaking now of years, and not of months, for all this did not happen in a day. Matty, my little maid, became from the first moment my untiring slave and bondswoman. It was she who learnt to read the signs of fatigue about my eyes, and hustled my visitors from the room. It was she who attended to my wants, to my feeding, and my washing, though after some little while I learnt to do this for myself; and after three years, I think it was, my back had so far strengthened that I was able to sit upright and move my body. I was helpless, though in my legs, and during the autumn and the winter months, when the damp settled in the walls of the house, I would feel it also in my bones. It caused me great pain at times, and then I would be hard put to it to keep to the standard of behaviour I had set myself. Self-pity, that most insiduous of poisons, would filter into my veins, and the black devils fill my mind, and then it was that Matty would stand like a sentinel at the door and bar the way to all intruders. Poor Matty, I cursed her often enough when the dark moods had me in thrall, but she bore with me unflinchingly. It was Robin, my dear good Robin, and most constant companion, who first had the thought of making me my chair, and this chair, that was to propel me from room to room, became his pet invention. He took some months in the designing of it, and when it was built, and I was carried to it, and could sit up straight and move the rolling wheels without assistance, his joy I think was even greater than my own.

It made all the difference to my daily life, and in the summer I could even venture to the garden, and propel myself a little distance, up and down before the house, winning some measure of independence. In '32, we had another wedding in the family. My sister Mary, whom we had long teased for her devoutness and sober, gentle ways, accepted the offer of Jonathan Rashleigh of Menabilly, who had lost his first wife in child-bed the year before, and was left with a growing family upon his hands. It was a most suitable match in all respects, Jonathan being then some forty years of age and Mary thirty-two. She was married from Lanrest, and to the wedding, with their father, came his three children, Alice, Elizabeth, and John. Later I was to come to know them well, but even now – as shy and diffident children – they won my affection. To the wedding also came Bevil Grenvile, a close friend to Jonathan as he was to all of us, and it was when the celebrating was over, and Mary departed to her new home the other side of Fowey, that I had a chance to speak with him alone. We spoke for a few moments about his own children, and his life at Stowe, and then I asked him, not without some tremulation, for all my calm assurance, how Richard did.

For a moment he did not answer, and, glancing at him, I saw his brow was troubled. 'I had not wished to speak of it,' he said at length, 'but since you ask me ... all has gone very ill with him, Honor, ever since his marriage.' Some devil of satisfaction rose in my breast, which I could not crush, and 'How so?' I asked. 'Has he not a son?' For I had heard that a boy was born to them a year or so before, on 16 May to be exact – the same date, ironically enough, as that on which I had been crippled. A new life for the one that is wasted, I had thought at the time, when I was told of it, and, like a spoilt child that had learnt no wisdom after all, I remember crying all night upon my pillow, thinking of the boy, who, but for mischance and the workings of destiny, might have been mine. That was a day, if I recollect aright, when Matty kept guard at my door, and I made picture after picture in my mind of Richard's wife propped upon pillows and a baby in her arms, and Richard smiling beside her. The fantasy was one which, for all my disciplined indifference, I found most damnable. But to return to Bevil. 'Yes,' he answered. 'It is true he has a son, and a daughter too, but whether Richard sees them or not I cannot say. The truth is that he has quarrelled with his wife and treated her in barbarous fashion – even laid violent hands upon her, so she says – and she is now petitioning for a divorce against him. Furthermore, he slandered the Earl of Suffolk, his wife's kinsman, who brought an action against him in the Star Chamber and won the case, and Richard, refusing to pay the fine – and in truth he could not, possessing not a penny – is likely to be cast into the Fleet Prison for debt at any moment.' Oh, God, I thought, what a contrast to the life we would have made together. Or was I wrong, and was this symbolic of what might have been? 'He was always violent, even as a lad,' continued Bevil. 'You knew so little of him, Honor; alas! three months of happy wooing is no time in which to judge a man.'

I could not answer this, for reason was on his side. But I thought of the spring days, lost to me for ever, and the apple blossom in the orchard. No maid could have had more tender or more intuitive a lover. 'How was Richard violent?' I asked. 'Irresponsible and wild, perhaps, but nothing worse. His wife must have provoked him.'

'As to that, I know nothing,' answered Bevil, 'but I can well believe it. She is a woman of some malice, and of doubtful morals. She was a close friend to Gartred – perhaps you did not know that – and it was when she was visiting at Orley Court that the match was made between them. Richard – as no one knows better than yourself – could not have been his best self at that time.' I said nothing, feeling, behind Bevil's gentle manner, some faint reproach, unconscious though it was. 'The truth is', said Bevil, 'that Richard married Mary Howard for her money, but once wed found he had no control over her purse or her property, the whole being in the power of trustees who act solely in her interest.'

'Then he is no whit better off than he was before?' I asked.

'Rather worse, if anything,' replied Bevil, 'for the Star Chamber will not release him from his debt for slander, and I have too many claims upon me at this time to help him either.'

It was a sorry picture that he painted, and, though to my jealous fancy it was preferable to the idyllic scene of family bliss that I had in imagination conjured, it was no consolation to learn of his distress. That Richard should ill use his wife because he could not trifle with her property was an ugly fact to face, but, having some inkling of his worse self, I guessed this to be true. He had married her without love, and in much bitterness of heart, and she, suspecting his motive, had taken care to disappoint him. What a rock of mutual trust on which to build a lasting union! I held to my resolve, though, and sent him no word of sympathy or understanding. Nor was it my own pride and self-pity that kept me from it, but a firm belief that such a course was wisest. He must lead his own life, in which I had no further part.

He remained, we heard later, for many months in prison, and then in the autumn of the following year he left England for the Continent, where he saw service with the King of Sweden.

How much I thought of him, and yearned for him, during those intervening years does not matter to this story. I was weakest during the long watches of the night, when my body pained me. During the day I drilled my feelings to obedience, and what with my progress in my studies – I was by way of becoming a fair Greek scholar – and my interest in the lives of my brothers and sisters, the days and the seasons passed with some fair measure of content.

Time heals all wounds, say the complacent, but I think it is not so much time that does it as determination of the spirit. And the spirit can often turn to devil in the darkness.

Five, ten, fifteen years; a large slice out of a woman's life, and a man's too, for that matter. We change from the awakening, questing creatures we were once, afire with wonder and expectancy and doubt, to persons of opinion and authority, our habits formed, our characters moulded in a pattern.

I was a maid, and a rebellious, disorderly one at that, when I was first crippled; but in the year of '42, when the war that was to alter all our lives broke forth, I was a woman of some two and thirty years, the 'good Aunt Honor' to my numerous nephews and nieces, and a figure of some importance to the family at large.

A person who is for ever chair-bound or bed-ridden can become a tyrant if she so desires, and, though I never sought to play the despot, I came to be, after my mother died, the one who made decisions, whose authority was asked for on all occasions, and in some strange fashion it seemed that a legendary quality was wove about my personality, as though my physical helplessness must give me greater wisdom.

I accepted the homage with my tongue in my cheek, but was careful not to destroy the fond illusion. The young people liked me, I think, because they knew me to be a rebel still, and when there was strife within the family I was sure to take their part. Cynical on the surface, I was an incurable romantic underneath, and if there were messages to be given, or meetings to arrange, or secrets to be whispered, my chamber at Lanrest would become trysting-place, rendezvous, and confessional in turn. Mary's stepchildren, the Rashleighs, were my constant visitors, and I found myself involved in many a youthful squabble, defending their escapades with a ready tongue, and soon acting as go-between to their love affairs. Jonathan, my brother-in-law, was a good just man, but stern; a firm believer in the settled marriage as against the impulsive prompting of the heart. No doubt he was right, but there was something distasteful to my mind in the bargaining between parents and the counting of every farthing, so that when Alice, his eldest daughter, turned thin and pale for languishing after that young rake, Peter Courtney – the parents disputing for months whether they should wed or no – I had them both to Lanrest and bade them be happy while the chance was theirs, and no one was a whit the wiser.

They married in due course, and although it ended in a separation (for this I blame the war), at least they had some early happiness together, for which I hold myself responsible.

My godchild Joan was another of my victims. She was, it may be remembered, the child of my sister Cecilia, and some ten years my junior. When John Rashleigh, Mary's stepson, came down from Oxford to visit us, he found Joan at my bedside, and I soon guessed which way the wind was blowing. I had half a thought of sending them to the apple-tree, but some inner sentimentality forbade me, and I suggested the bluebell wood instead. They were betrothed within a week, and married before the bluebells had faded, and not even Jonathan Rashleigh could find fault with the marriage settlement.

But the war years were upon us before we were aware, and Jonathan, like all the county gentlemen, my brothers included, had more anxious problems before them. Trouble had been brewing for a long while now, and we in Cornwall were much divided in opinion, some holding that His Majesty was justified in passing what laws he pleased (though one and all grumbled at the taxes) and others holding to it that Parliament was right in opposing any measure that smacked of despotism. How often I heard my brothers argue the point with Jack Trelawney, Ranald Mohun, Dick Buller, and other of our neighbours – my brothers holding firmly for the King, and Jo already in a position of authority, for his business was to superintend the defences of the coast – and as the months passed tempers became shorter and friendships grew colder, an unpleasing spirit of distrust walking abroad. Civil war was talked of openly, and each gentleman in the county began to look to his weapons, his servants, and his horses, so that he could make some contribution to the cause he favoured when the moment came. The women too were not idle, many – like Cecilia at Mothercombe – tearing strips of bed-linen into bandages, and packing their store-rooms with preserves for fear of siege. Arguments were fiercer then, I do believe, than later when the fighting was amongst us. Friends who had supped with me the week before became of a sudden suspect, and long-forgotten scandals were brought forth to blacken their names, merely because of the present opposition of their views.

The whole business made me sick at heart, and this whipping up of tempers between neighbours who for generations had lived at peace seemed a policy of the devil. I hated to hear Robin, my dearly loved brother, with his tenderness for dogs and horses, slander Dick Buller for upholding Parliament, vowing he took bribes and made spies of his own servants, when Dick and he had gone hawking together not six months before. While Rob Bennett, another of our neighbours and a friend of Buller's, began to spread damning rumours in return about my brother-in-law Jonathan Rashleigh, saying that Jonathan's father and elder brother, who had died very suddenly within a week of one another many years before, during the smallpox scourge, had not succumbed to the disease at all, but had been poisoned. These tales showed how in a few months we had changed from neighbours into wolves at one another's throats.

At the first open rupture between His Majesty and Parliament in '42, my brothers Jo and Robin, and most of our closest friends, including Jonathan Rashleigh, his son-in-law, Peter Courtney, the Trelawneys, the Arundells, and, of course, Bevil Grenvile, declared for the King. There was an end at once to family life and any settled way of living. Robin went off to York to join His Majesty's army, taking Peter Courtney with him, and almost immediately they were both given command of a company. Peter, showing much dash and courage in his first action, was knighted on the field.

My brother Jo and my brother-in-law Jonathan went about the county raising money, troops, and ammunition for the royal cause. The first was no easy matter, for Cornwall was a poor county at the best of times and lately the taxes had well-nigh broken us; but many families, with little ready money to spare, gave their plate to be melted down to silver, a loyal if wasteful gesture. I had qualms about this before following their example, but in the end was obliged to do so as Jonathan Rashleigh was Collector for the district. My attitude to the war was somewhat cynical, for, holding no belief in great causes, and living alone now at Lanrest with only Matty and the servants to tend me, I felt myself curiously detached. The successes of the first year did not go to my head, as they did to the rest of my family, for I could not believe, as they were inclined to, that Parliament would give way so easily. For the Parliamentarians had many powerful men at their command, and much money – all the rich merchants of London were strongly in their favour – besides which I had an uneasy suspicion, which I kept to myself, that their army was incomparably the better of the two. God knows our leaders wanted nothing in courage, but they lacked experience. Equipment, too, was poor, and discipline non-existent in the ranks. By the autumn the war was getting rather too close for comfort, and the two armies were ranged east and west along the Tamar. I had an uneasy Christmas, and in the third week of January I learnt that the worst had happened, and the enemy had crossed the Tamar into Cornwall. I was at breakfast when the news was brought us, and by none other than Peter Courtney, who had ridden hotfoot from Bodmin to warn me that the opposing army was even now on the road to Liskeard. He, with his regiment, which was under the command of Sir Ralph Hopton, was drawn up to oppose them, and Hopton was at the moment holding a council of war at Boconnoc, only a few miles distant. 'With any luck,' he told us, 'the fighting will not touch you, here at Lanrest, but will be between Liskeard and Lostwithiel. If we can break them now and drive them out of Cornwall the war will be as good as won.'

He looked handsome, flushed, and excited, his dark curls falling about his face. 'I have no time to go to Menabilly,' he told me. 'Should I fall in battle, will you tell Alice that I love her well?'

He was gone like a flash, and I and Matty, with the two

elderly men-servants and three lads – all that were left to us – were alone, unarmed and unprepared. There was nothing to do but to get the cattle and the sheep in from pasture and secure them in the farmstead, and bolt and bar ourselves within the house. Then we waited, all gathered round the fireside in my chamber upstairs. Once or twice, opening the casement, we thought we heard the sound of cannon shot, dull and intermittent, strangely distant in the cold clear air of January. Somewhere about three in the afternoon one of the farm lads came running to the house and hammered loud upon the entrance door. 'The enemy are routed,' he called excitedly, 'the whole pack of them scattering like whipped dogs along the road to Liskeard. There's been a great battle fought today on Braddock Down.' More stragglers appeared who had taken refuge in the hedges, and one and all told the same story, that the King's men had won a victory, fighting like furies, and taking nearly a thousand prisoners.

Knowing that rumour was a lying jade, I bade the household bide awhile, and keep the doors fast until the story should be proved, but before nightfall we knew the victory was certain, for Robin himself came riding home to cheer us, covered in dust, with a bloodstained bandage on his arm, and with him the Trelawney brothers and Ranald Mohun. They were all of them laughing and triumphant, for the two Parliament divisions had fled in dire disorder straight for Saltash, and would never, said Jack Trelawney, show their faces more this side the Tamar. 'And this fellow', he said, clapping Robin on the shoulder, 'rode into battle with a hawk on his wrist, which he let fly at Ruthin's musketeers, and, by God, the bird so startled them that the lot of them shot wide, and started taking to their legs before they'd spent their powder.'

'It was a wager I had with Peter,' smiled Robin, 'and if I lost, the forfeit was my spurs, and that I should be godfather to his next baby.'

They rocked with laughter, caring not a whit for the spilt blood and the torn bodies they had trampled, and they sat down, all of them, and drank great jugs of ale, wiping the sweat from their foreheads and discussing every move of the battle they had won like gamesters after a cock-fight.

Bevil Grenvile had been the hero of the day in this, his first engagement, and they described to us how he had led the Cornish foot down one hill and up another in so fierce a charge that the enemy could not withstand them.

'You should have seen him, Honor,' said Robin, 'with his servants and his tenants drawn up in solemn prayer before him, his sword in his hand, his dear honest face lifted to the sky. They were all clad in the blue and silver livery, as if it were high holiday. And down the hill they followed him, shouting "A Grenvile! A Grenvile!" with his servant Tony Paine waving his crimson standard with the three gold rests upon it. My God, I tell you, it made me proud to be a Cornishman.'

'It's in his blood,' said Jack Trelawney. 'Here's Bevil been a country squire for all his life, and you put a weapon in his hand and he turns tiger. The Grenviles are all alike at heart.'

'I wish to heaven', said Ranald Mohun, 'that Richard Grenvile would return from slaughtering the savages in Ireland and come and join his brother.' There was a moment's awkward silence, while some of them remembered the past and recollected my presence in the room, and then Robin rose to his feet and said they must be riding back to Liskeard. Thus, in southeast Cornwall, war touched us for a brief space in '43 and so departed, and many of us who had not even smelt the battle talked very big of what we had heard and seen, while those who had taken part in it, like Robin, boasted that the summer would see the rebels in Parliament laying down their arms for ever.

Alas! his optimism was foolish and ill-judged. Victories we had indeed that year, throughout the west as far as Bristol, with our own Cornishmen covering themselves with glory, but we lost, in that first summer, the flower of our Cornish manhood.

Sydney Godolphin, Jack Trevannion, Nick Slanning, Nick Kendal, one by one their faces come back to me as I review the past, and I remember the sinking feeling in the heart with which I would take up the list of the fallen that would be brought to me from Liskeard. All of them were men of noble conduct and high principle, whom we could ill spare in the county, and whose loss would make its mark upon the army. The worst tragedy of the year, or so it seemed to us, was when

Bevil Grenvile was slain at Lansdowne. Matty came running to my chamber with the tears falling down her cheeks. 'They've killed Sir Bevil,' she said. Bevil, with his grace and courtesy, his sympathy and charm, who was worth all the other Cornish leaders put together. I felt it as if he had been my own brother, but I was too stunned to weep for him. 'They say', said Matty, 'that he was struck down by a pole-axe, just as he and his men had won the day and the enemy were scattering. And big Tony Paine, his servant, mounted young Master Jack upon his father's horse, and the men followed the lad, all of them fighting mad with rage and grief to see their master slain.'

Yes, I could picture it. Bevil killed on an instant, his head split in two by some damned useless rebel, while his boy Jack, barely fourteen, climbed on to Bevil's white charger that I knew so well, and with the tears smarting his eyes brandished a sword that was too big for him. And the men, with the blue and silver colours, following him down the hill, their hearts black with hatred for the enemy. Oh, God, the Grenviles, there was some quality in the race, some white, undaunted spirit bred in their bones and surging through their blood that put them, as Cornishmen and leaders, way ahead above the rest of us. So, outwardly triumphant and inwardly bleeding, we Royalists watched the year draw to its close, and 1644 – that fateful year for Cornwall – opened with His Majesty master of the west, but the large and powerful forces of the Parliament in great strength elsewhere, and still unbeaten.

In the spring of the year, a soldier of fortune, returning from Ireland, rode to London to receive payment for his services. He gave the gentleman in Parliament to understand that in return for this he would join forces with them, and they, pleased to receive so doughty a warrior amongst their ranks, gave him £600 and told him their plans for the spring campaign. He bowed and smiled – a dangerous sign had they but known it – and straightway set forth in a coach and six, with a host of troopers following him and a banner carried in front of him. The banner was a great map of England and Wales on a crimson ground, with the words 'England Bleeding' written across it in letters of gold. When this equipage arrived at Bagshot Heath, the leader of it descended from his coach, and, calling his troopers about him, calmly suggested that they should all now proceed to Oxford and fight for His Majesty, and not against him. The troopers, nothing loath, accepted, and the train proceeded on its way to Oxford, bearing with it a quantity of money, arms, and silver plate, bequeathed by Parliament, and all the minutes of the secret council that had just been held in London.

The name of this soldier of fortune who had hoodwinked the Parliament in so scurrilous a fashion, was Richard Grenvile.

Chapter 7

ONE day towards the end of April '44, Robin came over from Radford to see me, urging me to leave Lanrest and to take up residence, for a time at any rate, with our sister Mary Rashleigh, at Menabilly. Robin was at that time commanding a regiment of foot, for he had been promoted colonel under Sir John Digby, and was taking part in the long-drawn-out siege of Plymouth, which alone among the cities in the west still held out for Parliament.

'Jo and I are both agreed', said Robin, 'that while the war continues you should not continue to live here alone. It is not fit for any woman, let alone one as helpless as yourself. Deserters and stragglers are constantly abroad, robbing on the highway, and the thought of you here, with a few old men and Matty, is a constant disturbance to our peace of mind.'

'There is nothing here to rob,' I protested, 'with the plate gone to the Mint at Truro; and as to harm to my person – a cripple woman can give little satisfaction.'

'That is not the point,' said Robin. 'It is impossible for Jo and Percy and I to do our duty, remembering all the while that you are here alone.'

He argued for half a day before I reluctantly gave way, and then with an ill-grace and much disturbance in my mind.

For fifteen years – ever since I had been crippled – I had not left Lanrest, and to set forth now to another person's house, even though that person was my own sister, filled me with misgiving.

Menabilly was already packed with Rashleigh relatives, who had taken refuge with Jonathan, seizing the war as an excuse, and I had no wish to add to their number. I had a great dislike for strangers, or for conversing with anyone for the sake of courtesy; besides, I was set now in my ways, my days were my own, I followed a personal routine.

'You can live at Menabilly exactly as you do here at Lanrest,' protested Robin, 'save that you will be more comfortable. Matty will attend you, you will have your own apartment and your meals brought to you, if you do not wish to mix with the company. Set on the hill there, with the sea air blowing and the fine gardens for you to be wheeled about in, nothing could be more pleasant, to my opinion.'

I disagreed, but, seeing his anxiety, I said no more; and within a week my few belongings were packed, the house was closed, and I was being carried in a litter to Menabilly.

How disturbing it was, and strange, to be on the road again. To pass through Lostwithiel, to see the people walking in the market-place – the normal daily life of a community from which I had been so long absent, living in my own world at Lanrest. I felt oddly nervous and ill at ease, as I peered through the curtains of my litter; as if I had been suddenly transplanted to a foreign land, where the language and the customs were unknown to me. My spirits rose as we climbed the long hill out of the town, and when we came abreast of the old redoubt at Castledore, and I saw the great blue bay of Tywardreath spread out before me, I thought that maybe after all the change of place and scene might yet be bearable. John Rashleigh came riding along the highway to meet me, waving his hat, a broad smile on his thin, colourless face. He was just twenty-three, and the tragedy of his life was that he had not the health or strength to join the army, but must bide at home and take orders from his father, for he had been cursed from babyhood with a malignant form of ague that kept him shivering and helpless sometimes for days on end. He was a dear, lovable fellow, with a strong sense of duty, yet in great awe of his father; and his wife – my goddaughter Joan – with her merry eyes and mischievous prattle, made him a good foil. Riding with him now was his companion and second cousin, Frank Penrose, a young man of the same age as himself, who was employed by my brother-in-law as secretary and junior agent about the estate.

'All is prepared for you, Honor,' smiled John as he rode beside my litter. 'There are over twenty of us in the house at present, and the lot of them have gathered in the courtyard to greet you. Tonight a dinner is to be given for your reception.'

'Very well, then,' I answered. 'You may tell these fellows to turn back again towards Lostwithiel.'

At this he confessed that Joan had bade him tease me, and all the company were in the east wing of the house, and no one would worry me. 'My stepmother has put you', he said, 'in the gatehouse, for she says you like much light and air, and the chamber there has a window looking both ways, over the outer courtyard to the west, and on to the inner court that surrounds the house. Thus you will see all that goes on about the place, and have your own private peep-show.'

'It sounds', I answered, 'like a garrison, with twenty people crammed within the walls.'

'Nearly fifty altogether, counting the servants,' laughed John, 'but they sleep head to toe in the attics.'

My spirits sank again, and as we turned down from the highway into the park, and I saw the great stone mansion at the end of it, flanked by high walls and outbuildings, I cursed myself for a fool for coming. We turned left into the outer court, surrounded by bakehouses and larders and dairies, and passing under the low archway of the gatehouse – my future dwelling – drew up within the inner court. The house was four-square, built around the court, with a big clock tower or belfry at the northern end, and the entrance to the south. On the steps stood Mary now to greet me, and Alice Courtney, her eldest stepdaughter, and Joan, my godchild, both of them with their babies tugging at their skirts.

'Welcome, dearest Honor, to Menabilly,' said Mary, her dear face puckered already in nervousness that I should hate it. 'The place is full of children, Honor – you must not mind,' smiled Alice, who since her marriage to Peter had produced a baby every year. 'We are thinking out a plan to attach a rope of your own to the bell in the belfry,' said Joan, 'so that if the noise becomes too deafening you can pull it in warning, and the household will be silenced.'

'I am already established, then, as a dragon,' I replied, 'which is all to the good, for I mean to do as I please, as Robin may have warned you.' They carried me in to the dark panelled hall, and, ignoring the long gallery which ran the whole length of the house, and from which I could hear the ominous sound of voices, bore me up the broad staircase and along a passage to the western wing. I was, I must confess, immediately delighted with my apartment, which, though low-ceilinged, was wide and full of light. There were windows at each end, as John had said – the western one looking down over the archway to the outer court and the park beyond, and the eastern one facing the inner court. There was a small room to the right for Matty, and nothing had been forgotten for my comfort.

'You will be bothered by no one,' said Mary. 'The apartments beyond the dressing-room belong to the Sawles – cousins of Jonathan's – who are very sober and retiring and will not worry you. The chamber to your left is never occupied.'

They left me then, and with Matty's aid I undressed and got myself to bed, a good deal exhausted from my journey, and glad to be alone. The first few days passed in becoming accustomed to my new surroundings and settling down, like a hound to a change of kennel.

My chamber was very pleasant, and I had no wish to leave it; also, I liked the chiming of the clock in the belfry, and, once I had told myself firmly that the quietude of Lanrest must be forgotten, I came to listen to the comings and goings that were part of this big house, the bustle in the outer court, the footsteps passing under the arch below me, and even – although I would have denied the accusation – taking a peep from my curtains at the windows opposite that, like mine, looked down upon the inner court, and from which, now and again, people would lean, talking to others within. At intervals during the day the young people would come and converse with me, and I would get a picture of the other inmates of the house, the two families of Sawle and Sparke, cousins to the Rashleighs, between whom there was, it seemed, a perpetual bickering. When my brother-in-law Jonathan was from home, it fell upon his son John to keep the peace, a heavy burden for his none too brawny shoulders, for there is nothing so irritating to a young man as scolding spinsters and short-tempered elderly folk, while Mary, in a fever of unending housekeeping, was from dawn to dusk superintending dairy, store, and still-room to keep her household fed. There were the grandchildren, too, to keep in order – Alice had three small daughters, and Joan a boy and girl, with another baby expected in the autumn – so in one way and another Menabilly was a colony to itself, with a different family in every wing. By the fifth day I was sufficiently at home, and mistress of my nerves, to leave my chamber and take to my chair. With John propelling it, and Joan and Alice on either side, and the children running before, we made a tour of the domain. The gardens were extensive, surrounded by high walls, and laid out to the eastward on rising ground, which, when the summit was reached, looked down over dense woodland across to further hills and the highway that ran down to Fowey, three miles distant. To the south lay pasture land and farm buildings and another pleasure garden, also walled, which had above it a high causeway leading to a summer-house, fashioned like a tower with long leaded windows, commanding a fine view of the sea and the Gribben Head.

'This', said Alice, 'is my father's sanctum. Here he does his writing and accounts, and from the windows can observe every ship that passes, bound for Fowey.' She tried the door to the summer-house, but it was locked. 'We must ask him for the key when he returns,' she said. 'It would be just the place for Honor and her chair when the wind is too fresh up on the causeway.' John did not answer, and it occurred to him perhaps, as it had to me, that his father might not want me for companion. We made a circle of the grounds, returning by the steward's house and the bowling-green, and so through the warren at the back to the outer court. I looked up at the gate-house, already familiar with the vase of flowers set in my window, and noticed for the first time the barred window of the apartment next to mine, and the great buttress that jutted out beside it.

'Why is that apartment never used?' I asked idly. John waited a moment or two before replying. 'My father goes to it at times,' he said. 'He has furniture and valuables shut away.'

'It was my uncle's room,' said Alice, hesitating, with a glance at John. 'He died very suddenly, you know, when we were children.'

Their manner was diffident, and I did not press the question, remembering all at once Jonathan's elder brother, who had died within eight days of his old father, supposedly of small-pox, and about whom the Parliamentarian Rob Bennett had spread his poison rumour.

We then went below the archway, and I schooled myself to an introduction to the Rashleigh cousins. They were all assembled in the long gallery, a great dark panelled chamber with windows looking out on to the court and eastward to the gardens. There were fireplaces at either end, with the Sawles seated before the first and the Sparkes circled round the other, glaring at one another like animals in a cage, while in the centre of the gallery my sister Mary held the balance with her other stepdaughter, Elizabeth, who was twice a Rashleigh, having married her first cousin a mile away at Combe. John propelled me up the gallery and with fitting solemnity presented me to the rival factions.

There were but two Sawles to three Sparkes, and my godchild Joan had made a pun upon their names, saying that what the Sparkes possessed in flame, the Sawles made up in soul. The latter were indeed a dour, forbidding couple, old Nick Sawle doubled up with rheumatics and almost as great a cripple as I was myself, while Temperance, his wife, came of Puritan stock, as her name suggested, and was never without a prayer-book in her hand. She fell to prayer as soon as she observed me – God knows I had never had that effect before on man or woman – and when she had finished asked me if I knew that we were all of us, saving herself, damned to eternity. It was a startling greeting, but I replied cheerfully enough that this was something I had long suspected, whereupon she proceeded to tell me in a rapid whisper, with many spiteful glances at the further fireplace, that Anti-Christ was come into the world. I looked over my shoulder and saw the rounded shoulders of

72

Will Sparke, who was engaged in a harmless game of chequers with his sisters. 'Providence has sent you among us to keep watch,' hissed Temperance Sawle, and while she tore to shreds the characters of her cousins, piece by piece, her husband Nick Sawle droned in my left ear a full account of his rheumatic history, from the first twinge in his left toe some forty years ago to his present dire incapacity to lift either elbow above the perpendicular. Half-stupefied, I made a signal to John, who propelled me to the Sparkes – two sisters and a brother. Will was one of those unfortunate high-voiced old fellows with a woman's mincing ways, whom I felt instinctively must be malformed beneath his clothes. His tongue seemed as two-edged as that of his cousin Temperance, and he fell to jesting with me at once about the habits of the Sawles, as though I were an ally. Deborah made up in masculinity what her brother lacked, being heavily moustached and speaking from her shoes, while Gillian, the younger sister, was all coy prettiness in spite of her forty years, bedecked with rouge and ribbons, and with a high thin laugh that pierced my eardrum like a sword.

'This dread war', said Deborah, in bass tones, 'has brought us all together' – which seemed to me a hollow sentiment, as none of them were on speaking terms with one another, and while Gillian praised my looks and my gown, I saw Will, out of the tail of my eye, making a cheating move upon the chequers board.

The air seemed purer somehow in the gate-house than the gallery, and after I had visited the apartments of Alice and Joan and Elizabeth, and watched the romping of the children, and the kicking of the babies, I was thankful enough to retire to my own chamber and blissful solitude. Matty brought me my dinner – this being a privilege to which I clung – and was full of gossip, as was her nature, about the servants in the house and what they said of their masters. Jonathan, my brother-in-law, was respected, feared, but not much loved. They were all easier when he was from home. He kept an account of every penny spent, and any servant wasting food or produce was instantly dismissed. Mary, my sister, was more liked, though she was said to be a tyrant in the still-room. The young people were all in high favour, especially Alice, whose sweet face and temper would have endeared her to the devil himself, but there was much shaking of heads over her handsome husband, Peter, who had a hot eye for a fine leg, as Matty put it, and was apt to put an arm round the kitchen girls if he had the chance. I could well believe this, having flung a pillow at Peter often enough myself for taking liberties.

'Master John and Mistress Joan are also liked,' said Matty, 'but they say Master John should stand up more to his father.' Her words put me in mind of the afternoon, and I asked her what she knew of the apartment next to mine. 'It is a lumber room, they tell me,' she answered. 'Mr Rashleigh has the key, and has valuables shut away.'

My curiosity was piqued, though, and I bade her search for a crack in the door. She put her face to the keyhole, but saw nothing. I gave her a pair of scissors, both of us giggling like children, and she worked away at the panelling for ten minutes or so until she had scraped a wide enough crack at which to place one eye. She knelt before it for a moment or two, then turned to me in disappointment. 'There's nothing there,' she said. 'It's a plain chamber, much the same as this, with a bed in one corner, and hangings on the wall.' I felt quite aggrieved, having hoped – in my idiotic romantic fashion – for a heap of treasure. I bade her hang a picture over the crack, and turned to my dinner. But later, when Joan came to sit with me at sunset, and the shadows began to fall, she said suddenly, with a shiver, 'You know, Honor, I slept once in this room when John had the ague, and I did not care for it.'

'Why so?' I asked, drinking my wine.

'I thought I heard footsteps in the chamber next door.'

I glanced at the picture over the crack, but it was well hidden.

'What sort of footsteps?' I said.

She shook her head, puzzled. 'Soft ones,' she said, 'like someone walks with slippered soles for fear he shall be heard.'

'How long ago was this?' I asked.

'During the winter,' she said. 'I did not tell anyone.'

'A servant perhaps,' I suggested, 'who had no business to be there.'

'No,' she said, 'none of the servants have a key – no one has but my father-in-law, and he was from home then.' She waited a moment, and then she said, glancing over her shoulder, 'I believe it is a ghost.'

'Why should a ghost walk at Menabilly?' I answered. 'The house has not been built fifty years.'

'People have died here, though,' she said. 'John's old grandfather and his uncle John.' She watched me with bright eyes, and, knowing my Joan, I wagered there was more to come.

'So you too have heard the poison story,' I said, drawing a bow at venture. 'But I don't believe it,' she said, 'it would be wicked, horrible. He is too good and kind a man. But I do think it was a ghost that I heard, the ghost of the elder brother that they called Uncle John.'

'Why should he pace the room with padded soles?' I asked.

She did not answer for a moment, and then, guiltily, she whispered: 'They never speak of it – John made me promise not to tell – but he was mad, a hopeless idiot, and they used to keep him shut up in the chamber there.'

This was something I had never heard before. I found it horrible.

'Are you certain?' I said.

'Oh, yes,' she replied. 'There is a bit about it in old Mr Rashleigh's will – John told me. Old Mr Rashleigh, before he died, made my father-in-law promise to look after the elder brother, give him food and drink, and shelter in the house. They say the chamber there was set aside for him, built in a special way; I don't exactly know. And then he died, you see, very suddenly of the smallpox. John and Alice and Elizabeth don't remember him – they were only babies.'

'What a disagreeable tale,' I said. 'Give me some more wine, and let's forget it.' After a while she went away, and Matty came to draw the curtains. I had no more visitors that night. But as the shadows lengthened, and the owls began to hoot down in the warren, I found my thoughts returning to the idiot Uncle John, shut up in the chamber there, year after year, from the first building of the house, a prisoner of the mind like I was of the body.

But in the morning I heard news that made me forget, for a while, this talk of footsteps in the night.

Chapter 8

THE day being fine, I ventured forth in my chair once more upon the causeway, returning to the house at midday to find that a messenger had ridden to Menabilly, during my absence, bearing letters from Plymouth and elsewhere to members of the household, and the family were now gathered in the gallery discussing the latest information from the war. Alice was seated in one of the long windows overlooking the garden, reading aloud a lengthy epistle from her Peter. 'Sir John Digby has been wounded,' she said, 'and the siege is now to be conducted by a new commander, who has them all by the ears at once. Poor Peter – this will mean an end to hawking excursions and supper parties. They will have to wage the war more seriously.' She turned the page of scrawled writing, shaking her head. 'And who is to command them?' inquired John, who once more was acting as attendant to my chair. 'Sir Richard Grenvile,' answered Alice.

Mary was not in the gallery at the time, and, since she was the only person at Menabilly to know of the romance long finished and forgotten, I was able to hear mention of his name without embarrassment. For it is a strange truth, as I had by then discovered, that we only become aware of hot discomfort when others are made awkward for our sakes.

I knew, from something that Robin had let slip, that Richard was come into the west, his purpose being to raise troops for the King, so I understood, and to be placed now in command of the siege of Plymouth meant promotion. He had already become notorious, of course, for the manner in which he had hoodwinked Parliament and joined His Majesty. 'And what' I heard myself saying, 'does Peter think of his new commander?' Alice folded up her letter. 'As a soldier, he admires him,' she answered, 'but I think he has not a great opinion of him as a man.'

'I have heard,' said John, 'that he hasn't a scruple in the world, and once an injury is done to him he will never forget it or forgive.'

'I believe', said Alice, 'that when in Ireland he inflicted great cruelty on the people – though some say it was no more than they deserved. But I fear he is very different from his brother.'

It made strange hearing to have the lover who had held me once against his heart discussed in so calm and cool a fashion.

At this moment Will Sparke came up to us, also with a letter in his hand. 'So Richard Grenville is commanding now at Plymouth,' he said. 'I have the news here from my kinsman in Tavistock, who is with Prince Maurice. It seems the Prince thinks highly of his ability, but, my heaven – what a scoundrel.'

I began to burn silently, my old love and loyalty rising to the surface.

'We were just talking of him,' said John.

'You heard his first action on coming west, I suppose?' said Will Sparke, warming like all his kind to malicious gossip. 'I had it direct from my kinsman at the time. Grenville rode straight to Fitzford, his wife's property, turned out the caretakers, seized all the contents, had the agent flung into gaol, and took all the money owed by the tenants to his wife for his own use.'

'I thought', said Alice, 'that he had been divorced from his wife.'

'So he is divorced,' replied Will. 'He is not entitled to a penny from the property. But that is Richard Grenville for you.'

'I wonder', I said calmly, 'what has happened to his children?'

'I can tell you that,' said Will. 'The daughter is with the mother in London – whether she has friends in Parliament or not I cannot say. But the lad was at Fitzford with his tutor when Grenville seized the place, and by all accounts is with him now. They say the poor boy is in fear and trembling of his father, and small blame to him.'

'No doubt', I said, 'he was brought up to hate him by his mother.'

'Any woman', retorted Will, 'who had been as ill used as she, unhappy lady, would hardly paint her spouse in pretty colours.'

Logic was with him, as it always was with the persons who

maligned Richard, and presently I bade John carry me upstairs to my apartment. But the day that had started so well when I set forth upon the causeway turned sour on me, and I lay on my bed for the rest of it, telling Matty I would see no visitors.

For fifteen years the Honor that had been lay dead and buried, and here she was struggling beneath the surface once again at the mere mention of a name that was best forgotten. Richard in Germany, Richard in Ireland, was too remote a person to swim into my daily thoughts. When I thought of him, or dreamt of him – which was often – it was always as he had been in the past. And now he must break into the present, a mere thirty miles away, and there would be constant talk of him, criticism, and discussion, and I should be forced to hear his name bandied and besmirched, as Will Sparke had bandied it this morning. 'You know,' he had said, before I went upstairs, 'the Roundheads call him Skellum Grenvile, and have put a price upon his head. The nickname suits him well, and even his own soldiers whisper it behind his back.'

'And what does it signify?' I asked.

'Oh,' he said. 'I thought you were a German scholar, Mistress Harris, as well as learned in the Greek and Latin.' He paused. 'It means a vicious beast,' he sniggered.

Oh, yes, there was much reason for me to lay moodily on my bed, with the memory of a young man smiling at me from the branches of an apple-tree, and the humming of the bees in the blossom.

Fifteen years ... he would be forty-four now, ten years older than myself. 'Matty,' I said, before she lit the candles, 'bring me a mirror.'

She glanced at me suspiciously, her long nose twitching.

'What do you want a mirror for?' she asked.

'God damn you, that's my business,' I answered.

We snapped at one another continually, she and I, but it meant nothing. She brought me the mirror, and I examined my appearance as though seeing myself as a stranger would.

There were my two eyes, my nose, my mouth, much as they had always been, but I was fuller in the face now than I had been as a maid – sluggish from lying on my back, I told myself. There were little lines, too, beneath my eyes, lines that had grown there from pain when my legs hurt me. I had less colour than I had once. My hair was the best point, for this was Matty's special pride, and she would brush it for hours to make it glossy. I handed back the mirror to Matty with a sigh. 'What do you make of it?' she asked.

'In ten years,' I said, 'I'll be an old woman.'

She sniffed and began to fold my garments on a chair.

'I'll tell you one thing,' she said, drawing in her underlip.

'What's that?'

'You're fairer now as a woman than you ever were as a prinking, blushing maid, and I'm not the only one that thinks it.'

This was encouraging, and I had an immediate vision of a long train of suitors all tiptoeing up the stairs to pay me homage. A pretty fancy, but where the devil were they?

'You're like an old hen', I said to Matty, 'who always thinks her poorest chick the loveliest. Go to bed.'

I lay there for some time, thinking of Richard, wondering too about his little son, who must be a lad now of fourteen. Could it be true, as Will Sparke had said, that the boy went in fear of his father? Supposing we had wedded, Richard and I, and this had been our son. Would we have sported with him as a child, danced him upon our knees, gone down with him on all fours on the ground and played at tigers? Would he have come running to me with muddied hands, his hair about his face, laughing? Would he be auburn-haired like Richard?

Would we all three have ridden to the chase, and Richard have shown him how to sit straight in the saddle? Vain, idle supposition, drenched in sentiment, like buttercups by the dew on a wet morning. I was half asleep, muzzy with a dream, when I heard a movement in the next chamber. I raised my head from the pillow, thinking it might be Matty in the dressing-room, but the sound came from the other side. I held my breath and waited. Yes, there it was again. A stealthy footstep padding to and fro. I remembered in a flash the tale that Joan had told me of the mad Rashleigh uncle, confined in there for years. Was it his ghost in truth that stole there in the shadows? The night was pitchy, for it was only quarter moon, and no glimmer came to me from either casement. The clock in the belfry struck one. The footsteps ceased, then proceeded once again, and for the first time too I was aware of a cold current of air coming to my apartment from the chamber beyond.

My own casements were closed, save the one that looked into the inner court, and this was only open to a few inches; besides, the draught did not come from that direction. I remembered then that the closed-up door into the empty chamber did not meet the floor at its base, but was raised two inches or so from the ground, for Matty had tried to look under it before she made the crack with the scissors.

It was from beneath this door that the current of air blew now – and to my certain knowledge there had never been a draught from there before. Something, then, had happened in the empty chamber next to mine to cause the current. The muffled tread continued, stealthy, soft, and with the sweat running down my face I thought of the ghost stories my brothers had recounted to me as a child, of how an earth-bound spirit would haunt the place he hated, bringing with him from the darker regions a whisper of chill dank air. One of the dogs barked from the stables, and this homely sound brought me to my senses. Was it not more likely that a living person was responsible for the cold current that swept beneath the door, and that the cause of it was the opening of the barred window that, like my western one, looked out on to the outer court? The ghost of poor idiot Uncle John would have kept me in my bed for ever, but a living soul, treading furtively in the night hours in a locked chamber, was something to stir the burning curiosity of one who, it may be remembered, had from early childhood shown a propensity to eavesdrop where she was not wanted.

Secretly, stealthily, I reached out my hand to the flint that Matty from long custom left beside my bed, and lit my candle. My chair was also within reach. I pulled it close to me, and, with the labour that years of practice had never mitigated, lowered myself into it. The footsteps ceased abruptly. So I am right, I thought in triumph. No ghost would hesitate at the sound of a creaking chair. I waited perhaps for as long as five minutes, and then the intruder must have recovered himself, for I heard the faint noise of the opening of a drawer. Softly I wheeled myself across the room. Whoever is there, I smiled grimly, is not aware that a cripple can be mobile, granted she has a resourceful brother with a talent for invention. I came abreast the door and waited once again. The picture that Matty had hung over the crack was on a level with my eye. I blew out my candle, trusting to fortune to blunder my way back to bed when my curiosity was satisfied. Then, very softly, holding my breath, I lifted the picture from the nail, and, framing my face with my hands for cover, I peered with one eye into the slit. The chamber was in half darkness, lit by a single candle on a bare table. I could not see to right or left – the crack was not large enough – but the table was in a direct line with my eye. A man was sitting at the table, his back turned to me. He was booted and spurred, and wore a riding-cloak about his shoulders. He had a pen in his hand, and was writing on a long white slip of paper, consulting, now and again, another list propped up before him on the table. Here was flesh and blood indeed, and no ghost; the intruder was writing away as calmly as though he were a clerk on a copying-stool. I watched him come to the end of the long slip of paper, and then he folded it, and, going to the cabinet in the wall, opened the drawer with the same sound I had heard before. The light was murky, as I have said, and, with his back turned to me and his hat upon his head, I could make little of him except that his riding-cloak was a dark crimson. Then he moved out of my line of vision, taking the candle, and walked softly to the far corner of the room. I heard nothing after that, and no further footsteps, and while I waited puzzled, with my eye still to the crack, I became aware suddenly that the draught of air was no longer blowing beneath the door. Yet I had heard no sound of a closing window. I bent down from my chair, testing the bottom of the door with my hand, but no current came. The intruder, therefore, had by some action unperceived by me cut off the draught, making his exit at the same time. He had left the chamber, as he had entered it, by some entrance other than the door that led into the corridor. I blundered back across my room in clumsy fashion, having first replaced the picture on its nail, and knocking into a table on the way, woke that light sleeper, Matty. 'Have you lost your senses?' she scolded, 'circling round your chamber in the pitch-black?' And she lifted me like a child and dumped me in my bed.

'I had a nightmare,' I lied, 'and thought I heard footsteps. Is there anyone moving in the courtyard, Matty?'

She drew aside the curtain. 'Not a soul,' she grumbled, 'not even a cat scratching on the cobbles. Everyone is asleep.'

'You will think me mazed, I don't doubt,' I answered, 'but venture with your candle a moment into the passage, and try the door of the locked apartment next to this.'

'Mazed it is,' she snapped. 'This comes of looking into the mirror on a Friday night.' In a moment she was back again. 'The door is locked as it always is,' she said, 'and, judging by the dust upon the latch, it has not been opened for months, or more.'

'No,' I mused. 'That is just what I supposed.'

She stared at me, and shook her head.

'I'd best brew you a hot cordial,' she said.

'I do not want a hot cordial,' I answered.

'There's nothing like it for putting a stop to bad dreams,' she said. She tucked in my blankets, and, after grumbling a moment or two, went back to her own room. But my mind was far too lively to find sleep for several hours. I kept trying to remember the formation of the house, seen from without, and what it was that struck me as peculiar the day before, when John had wheeled me in my chair towards the gatehouse. It was past four in the morning when the answer came to me. Menabilly was built four-square around the courtyard, with clean, straight lines and no protruding wings. But at the north-west corner of the house, jutting from the wall outside the fastened chamber, was a buttress, running tall and straight from the roof down to the cobbles. Why in the name of heaven, when old John Rashleigh built his house in 1600, did he build the north-west corner with a buttress? And had it some connexion with the fact that the apartment behind was designed for the special use of his idiot eldest son?

Some lunatics are harmless, some are not. But even the worst, the truly animal, are given air and exercise at certain periods of the day, and would hardly be paraded through the corridors of the house itself. I smiled to myself in the darkness, for I had guessed, after three restless hours of tossing on my back, how the intruder had crept into the apartment next to mine without using the locked door into the passage. He had come, and he had gone, as poor Uncle John had doubtless done nearly half a century before, by a hidden stairway in the buttress. But why he had come, and what was his business, I had yet to discover.

Chapter 9

IT turned to rain the next morning, and I was unable to take my usual airing in the grounds. But later in the day the fitful sun peeked through the low clouds and, wrapping my cloak about me, I announced to Matty my intention of going abroad.

John Rashleigh was out riding round the farms on the estate, with the steward Langdon, whose house it was I had observed beyond the bowling-green. Thus I had not my faithful chair attendant. Joan came with me instead, and it was an easy enough matter to persuade her to wheel me first through the archway to the outer court, where I made pretence of looking up to admire my quarters in the gatehouse.

In reality, I was observing the formation of the buttress, which ran, as I thought it did, the whole length of the house on the north-west corner, immediately behind it being the barred chamber.

The width of the buttress was a little over four feet, so I judged, and, if it was hollow behind a false façade of stone, could easily contain a stair. There was, however, no outlet to the court – this was certain. I bade Joan wheel me to the base, on pretence of touching the lichen which already, after only fifty years, was forming on the stone, and I satisfied myself that the outside of the buttress at any rate was solid. If my supposition was correct, then there must be a stairway within the buttress leading underground, far beneath the foundations of the house, and a passage running some distance to an outlet in the grounds. Poor Uncle John. It was significant that there was no portrait of him in the gallery, alongside the rest of the family. If so much trouble was taken by his father that he should not be seen, he must have been an object of either fear or horror. We left the outer court and, traversing the warren, came by the path outside the steward's lodge. The door was open to the parlour, and Mrs Langdon, the steward's wife, was standing in the entrance, a comfortable, homely woman, who, on being introduced to me, insisted that I take a glass of milk. While she was absent, we glanced about the trim room, and Joan, laughing, pointed to a bunch of keys that hung on a nail beside the door. 'Old Langdon is like a gaoler,' she whispered. 'As a rule he is never parted from that bunch, but dangles them at his belt. John tells me he has a duplicate of each key belonging to my father-in-law.'

'Has he been steward long?' I asked.

'Oh, yes,' said Joan. 'He came here as a young man when the house was built. There is no corner of Menabilly that he does not know.'

I wager then, I thought to myself, that he knows too the secret of the buttress, if there is a secret. Joan, with a curiosity much like mine, was examining the labels on the keys. 'Summer-house,' she read, and with a mischievous smile at me, she slipped it from the bunch, and dangled it before my eyes. 'You expressed a wish to peep into the tower on the causeway, did you not?' she teased. At this moment Mrs Langdon returned with the milk, and, fearful of discovery, Joan, like a guilty child, reddened and concealed the key within her gown. We chatted for a few moments, while I drank my milk in haste and Joan gazed with great innocence at the ceiling. Then we bade the good woman farewell and turned into the gardens, through the gate in the high wall.

'Now you have done for yourself,' I said. 'How in the world will you return the key?'

Joan was laughing under her breath. 'I'll give it to John,' she said. 'He must devise some tale or other to satisfy old Langdon. But, seeing that we have the key, Honor, it would be a pity not to make some use of it.' She was an accomplice after my own heart, and a true godchild. 'I make no promise,' I murmured. 'Wheel me along the causeway, and we will see which way the wind is blowing.'

We crossed the gardens, passing the house as we did so, and waved to Alice at the window of her apartment above the gallery. I caught sight, too, of Temperance Sawle, peering like a witch from the side-door, evidently in half a mind to risk the damp ground and join us. 'I am the best off in my chair,' I called to her. 'The walks are wringing wet, and clouds coming up again from the Gribben.'

She bolted like a rabbit within doors again, and I saw her pass into the gallery, while Joan, smothering her laughter, propelled me through the gate on to the causeway.

It was only when mounted thus some ten feet from the ground that the fine view of the sea could be obtained, for down on the level the sloping ground masked all sight of it. Menabilly, though built on a hill, lay therefore in a saucer, and I commented on the fact to Joan as she wheeled me towards the towered summer-house at the far end of the causeway. 'Yes,' she said, 'John has explained to me that the house was so built that no glimpse of it should be sighted from the sea. Old Mr Rashleigh lived in great fear of pirates. But, if the truth be told, he was not above piracy himself, and in the old days, when he was alive, there were bales of silk, and bars of silver, concealed somewhere within the house, stolen from the French and brought hither by his own ships, and then landed down at Pridmouth yonder.'

In which case, I thought privately, a passage known to no one but himself, and perhaps his steward, would prove of great advantage.

But we had reached the summer-house, and Joan, glancing first over her shoulder to see that no one came, produced her key, and turned it in the lock. 'I must tell you,' she confessed, 'that there is nothing great to see. I have been here once or twice, with my father-in-law, and it is nought but a rather musty room, the shelves lined with books and papers, and a fine view from the windows.' She wheeled me through the door, and I glanced about me, half hoping, in a most childish manner, to find traces of piracy. But all was in order. The walls of the summer-house were lined with books, save for the windows, which, even as she said, commanded the whole stretch of the bay to the Gribben and to the east showed the steep coast road that led to Fowey. Anyone, on horse or on foot, approaching Menabilly from the east would be observed by a watcher at the window, likewise a vessel sailing close in-shore. Old Mr Rashleigh had shown great cunning as a builder.

The flagged floor was carpeted, save in one corner by my brother-in-law's writing-table, where a strip of heavy matting served for his feet. It was in keeping with his particular character that the papers on his desk were neatly documented, and filed in order. Joan left me in my chair to browse among the books, while she herself kept watch out on the causeway. There was nothing much to tempt my interest. Books of law, dry as dust, books of accountancy, and many volumes docketed as 'County Affairs', no doubt filed when Jonathan was Sheriff for the Duchy of Cornwall. On a lower shelf, near to his writing-table, were volumes labelled 'My Town House' and another 'Menabilly', while close behind these he had 'Marriage Settlements' and 'Wills'. He was nothing if not methodical in his business. The volume marked 'Wills' was nearest to me, and surprisingly tempting to my hand. I looked over my shoulder and saw through the window that Joan, humming a tune, was busily engaged in picking posies for her children. I reached out my hand and took the volume. Page after page was covered in my brother-in-law's meticulously careful hand. I turned to the entries headed by the words 'My father, John Rashleigh. Born, 1554. Died, 6 May 1624.' Folded close to this – perhaps it had slipped in by accident – was an account of a case brought to the Star Chamber in the year 1616 by one Charles Bennett against the above John Rashleigh. This Charles Bennett, I remembered, was father to Robert Bennett, our neighbour at Looe, who had spread the poison rumour. The case, had I time to peruse it, would have made good reading, for it was of a highly scandalous nature; Charles Bennett accused John Rashleigh of 'leading a most incontinent course of life, lying with divers women, over forty-five in number, uttering blasphemies, etc., etc., and his wife dying through grief at his behaviour, she being a sober virtuous woman'. I was somewhat surprised after this, glancing at the end, to find that John Rashleigh had been acquitted. What a lovely weapon, though, to hold over the head of my self-righteous brother-in-law when he made boast, as he sometimes did, of the high morals of his family. But I turned a page and came to the will I had been seeking.

So old John Rashleigh had not done too badly for his relatives. Nick Sawle had got fifty pounds (which I dare say Temperance had snatched from him) and the Sparkes had benefited to the same extent. The poor of Fowey had some twenty pounds bestowed upon them. It is really most iniquitous, I told myself, that I should be prying thus into matters that concern me not at all, but I read on. All lands in Cornwall, his house in Fowey, his house at Menabilly, and the residue of his estate to his second son Jonathan, his executor. And then the codicil at the end: 'Thirty pounds annuity out of Fowey to the use of my eldest son John's maintenance, to be paid after the death of my second son Jonathan, who during his life will maintain him and allow him a chamber with meat and drink and apparel.' I caught a glimpse of Joan's shadow passing the window, and with a hurried, guilty movement I shut the volume and put it back upon the shelf.

There was no doubt then about the disability of poor Uncle John. I turned my chair from the desk, and as I did so the right wheel stuck against some obstruction on the ground beneath the heavy matting. I bent down from my chair to free the wheel, turning up the edge of the mat as I did so. I saw then that the obstruction was a ring in the flagstone, which, though flat to the ground and unnoticeable possibly to a foot treading upon it, had been enough to obstruct the smooth running of my chair.

I leant from my chair as far as I could, and, seizing the ring with my two hands, succeeded in lifting the stone some three inches from the ground, before the weight of it caused me to drop it once again – but not before I had caught a glimpse of the sharp corner of a step descending into darkness. I replaced the mat just as my godchild came into the summer-house.

'Well, Honor,' she said, 'have you seen all you have a mind to for the present?'

'I rather think I have,' I answered, and in a few moments she had closed the door, turned the key once more in the lock, and we were bowling back along the causeway. She prattled away about this and that, but I paid but scant attention, for my mind was full of my latest discovery. It seemed fairly certain that there was a pit or tunnel underneath the flagstone in the summer-house, and the placing of a mat on top of it, and the position of the desk, suggested that the hiding of it was deliberate. There was no rust about the ring-bolt to show disuse, and the ease with which I, helpless in my chair, had lifted the stone a few inches proved to me that this was no cobwebby corner of concealment long forgotten. The flagstone had been lifted frequently, and recently. I looked over my shoulder down the pathway to the beach, or Pridmouth Cove, as Joan had termed it. It was narrow and steep, flanked with stubby trees, and I thought how easy it would be for an incoming vessel, anchored in deep water, to send a boat ashore with some half-dozen men, who could climb up the path to where it ended beneath the summer-house on the causeway, and for a watcher at the window of the summer-house to relieve the men of any burden they should bear upon their backs. Was this what old John Rashleigh had foreseen when he built his tower, and did bales of silk and bars of silver lie stacked beneath the flagstone some forty years before? It seemed very probable, but whether the step beneath the flagstone had any connexion with my suspicion of the buttress it was difficult to say. One thing was certain. There was a secret entrance to Menabilly through the chamber next to mine, and someone had passed that way only the night before, for I had seen him with my own eyes.

'You are silent, Honor,' said Joan, breaking in upon my thoughts. 'What are you thinking of?'

'I have just come to the opinion', I answered, 'that I was somewhat rash to leave Lanrest, where each day was alike, and come amongst you all at Menabilly, where something different happens every day.'

'I wish I thought as you did,' she replied. 'To me the days and weeks seem much the same, with the Sawles backbiting at the Sparkes, and the children fretful, and my dear John grousing all the while that he cannot go fighting with Peter and the rest.'

We came to the end of the causeway, and were about to turn in through the gate into the walled gardens when her little son Jonathan, a child of barely three years, came running across the path to greet us. 'Uncle Peter is come,' he cried, 'and another gentleman, and many soldiers. We have been stroking the horses.'

I smiled up at his mother. 'What did I tell you?' I said. 'Not a day passes but there is some excitement at Menabilly.'

I had no wish to run the gauntlet of the long windows in the gallery, where the company would be assembled, and bade Joan wheel me to the entrance in the front of the house, which was usually deserted at this time of the day, when no one was within the dining-chamber. Once indoors, one of the servants could carry me to my apartment in the gate-house, and later I could send for Peter, always a favourite with me, and have his news of Robin. We passed in then through the door, little Jonathan running in front, and at once we heard laughter and talk coming from the gallery. The wide arched door to the inner courtyard was open, and we could see some half-dozen troopers with their horses watering at the well beneath the belfry. There was much bustle and clatter, a pleasant, lively sound, and I saw one of the troopers look up to a casement in the attic and wave his hand in greeting to a blushing kitchen-girl. He was a big, strong-looking fellow with a broad grin on his face, and then he turned, and signalled to his companions to follow him, which they did, each one leading his horse away from the well and following him through the archway beneath my gate-house to the outer courtyard and the stables.

It was when they turned thus and clattered through the court that I noticed how each fellow wore upon his shoulder a scarlet shield with three gold rests upon it. For a moment I thought my heart would stop beating, and I was seized with sudden panic.

'Find one of the servants quickly,' I said to Joan. 'I wish to be carried straightway to my room.'

But it was too late. Even as she sent little Jonathan scampering hurriedly towards the servants' quarters, Peter Courtney came out into the hall, his arm about his Alice, in company with two or three brother officers. 'Why, Honor,' he cried. 'This is a joy indeed. Knowing your habits, I feared to find you hiding in your apartment, with Matty standing like a dragon at the door. Gentlemen, I present to you Mistress Honor Harris, who has not the slightest desire to make your acquaintance.' I could have slain him for his lack of discretion, but he was one of those gay light-hearted creatures with a love of jesting and poking fun, and no more true perception than a bumble-bee. In a moment his friends were bowing before my chair and exchanging introductions, and Peter, still laughing and talking in his haphazard strident way, was pushing my chair through to the gallery. Alice, who made up in intuition all he lacked, would have stopped him had I caught her eye, but she was too glad to have a glimpse of him to do anything but smile and hold his arm. The gallery seemed full of people – Sawles, and Sparkes, and Rashleighs all chatting at the top of their voices, and at the far end by the window I caught sight of Mary in conversation with someone whose tall back and broad shoulders were painfully, almost terrifyingly familiar. Mary's expression, preoccupied and distrait, told me that she was at that moment wondering if I had returned from my promenade, for I saw her eyes search the gardens; and then she saw me, and her brow wrinkled in a well-known way and she began talking sixteen to the dozen. Her loss of composure gave me back my own. What in hell's name do I care, after fifteen years, I told myself? There is no need to swoon at an encounter. God knows I have breeding enough to be mistress of the situation, here in Mary's house at Menabilly, with nigh a score of people in the room.

Peter, impervious to any doubtful atmosphere, propelled me slowly towards the window, and out of the corner of my eye I saw my sister Mary, overcome by cowardice, do something that I dare swear I might have done myself had I been her, and that was to murmur a hasty excuse to her companion about summoning the servants to bring further refreshment, before she fled from the gallery without looking once in my direction. Richard turned and saw me. And as he looked at me it was as if my whole heart moved over in my body and was mine no longer.

'Sir,' said Peter, 'I am pleased to present to you my dearly loved kinswoman, Mistress Honor Harris of Lanrest.'

'My kinswoman also,' said Richard – and then he bent forward and kissed my hand.

'Oh, is that so, sir?' said Peter vaguely, looking from one to the other of us. 'I suppose all we Cornish families are in some way near related. Let me fill your glass, sir. Honor, will you drink with us?'

'I will,' I answered. In truth, a glass of wine seemed to me my only salvation at the moment. While Peter filled the glasses I had my first long look at Richard. He had altered. There was no doubt of it. He had grown much broader, for one thing, not only in the body, but about the neck and shoulders. His face was somewhat heavier than it had been. There was a brown, weather-beaten air about him that was not there before, and lines beneath his eyes. It was after all, fifteen years. And then he turned to me, giving me my glass, and I saw that there was only one white streak in his auburn hair, high above the temple, and the eyes that looked at me were quite unchanged.

'Your health and fortune,' he said quietly, and draining his glass, he held it out, with mine, to be refilled. I saw the little tell-tale pulse beating on his right temple, and I knew then that the encounter was as startling and as moving to him as it was to me.

'I did not know', he said, 'that you were at Menabilly.'

I saw Peter glance at him curiously, and I wondered if this was the first time he had ever seen his commanding officer show any sign of nervousness or strain. The hand that held the glass trembled very slightly, and the voice that spoke was hard, queerly abrupt.

'I came here a few days since from Lanrest,' I answered, my voice perhaps as oddly flat as his. 'My brothers said I must not live alone while the war continues.'

'They showed wisdom,' he replied. 'Essex is moving westward all the time. It is very probable we shall see fighting once again this side of the Tamar.' At this moment Peter's small daughters came running to his knees, shrieking with joy to see their father, and Peter, laughing an apology, was swept into family life upon the instant, taking one apiece upon his shoulder and moving down the gallery in triumph. Richard and I were thus left alone beside the window. I looked out on to the garden, noting the trim yew hedges and the smooth lawns, while a score of trivial observations ran insanely through my head.

'How green the grass is after the morning rain', and 'It is something chilly for the time of year' were phrases I had never yet used in my life, even to a stranger, but they seemed, at that moment, to be what was needed to the occasion. Yet though they rose unbidden to my tongue, I did not frame them, but continued looking out upon the garden in silence, with Richard as dumb as myself. And then in a low voice, clipped and hard, he said:

'If I am silent you must forgive me. I had not thought, after fifteen years, to find you so damnably unchanged.'

This streak back from the indifferent present to the intimate past was a new shock to be borne, but a curiously exciting one.

'Why damnably?' I said, watching him over the rim of my glass.

'I had become used, over a long period, to a very different picture,' he said. 'I thought of you as an invalid, wan and pale, a sort of shadow without substance, hedged about with doctors and attendants. And instead I find – this.' He looked me then full in the face with a directness and a lack of reserve that I remembered well.

'I am sorry', I answered, 'to disappoint you.'

'You misinterpret me,' he said. 'I have not said I was disappointed. I am merely speechless.' He drained his glass once more and put it back on the table. 'I shall recover', he said, 'in a moment or two. Where can we talk?'

'Talk?' I asked. 'Why, we can talk here, I suppose, if you wish to.'

'Amidst a host of babbling fools and screaming children – not on your life,' he answered. 'Have you not your own apartments?'

'I have,' I replied with some small attempt at dignity, 'but it would be considered somewhat odd if we retired there.'

'You were not used to quibble at similar suggestions in the past,' he said.

This was something of a blow beneath the belt, and I had no answer for him.

'I would have you remember', I said, with lameness, 'that we have been strangers to one another for fifteen years.'

'Do you think', he said, 'that I forget it for a moment?'

At this juncture we were interrupted by Temperance Sawle, who, with baleful eyes, had been watching us from a distance, and now moved within our orbit. 'Sir Richard Grenvile, I believe,' she said.

'Your servant, ma'am,' replied Richard with a look that would have slain anyone less soul-absorbed than Temperance.

'The Evil One seeks you for his own,' she announced. 'Even at this moment I see his talons at your throat, and his jaws open to devour you. Repent, repent, before it is too late.'

'What the devil does she mean?' said Richard.

I shook my head, and pointed to the heavens, but Temperance, warming to her theme, continued:

'The mark of the Beast is on your forehead,' she declared. 'The men you lead are become as ravening wolves. You will all perish, every one of you, in the bottomless pit.'

'Tell the old fool to go to hell,' said Richard.

I offered Mistress Sawle a glass of wine, but she flinched as if it had been boiling oil. 'There shall be a weeping and a gnashing of teeth,' she continued.

'My God, you're right,' said Richard, and, taking her by the shoulders, he twisted her round like a top, and walked her across the room to the fireplace and her husband.

'Keep this woman under control,' he ordered, and there was an immediate silence, followed by a little flutter of embarrassed conversation. Peter Courtney, very red about the neck, hurried forward with a brimming decanter. 'Some more wine, sir?' he said.

'Thank you, no, I've had about as much as I can stand,' said Richard. I noticed the young officers, all with their backs turned, examining the portraits on the walls with amazing interest. Will Sparke was one of the little crowd about the fireplace, staring hard at the King's general, his mouth wide open.

'A good day for catching flies, sir,' said Richard pleasantly.

A little ripple of laughter came from Joan, hastily suppressed as Richard turned his eyes upon her.

Will Sparke pressed forward. 'I have a young kinsman under your command,' he said, 'an ensign of the Twenty-third Regiment of Foot.'

'Very probably,' said Richard. 'I never speak to ensigns.'

He beckoned to John Rashleigh, who had returned but a few moments ago from his day's ride, and was now hovering at the entrance to the gallery somewhat mud-stained and splashed, bewildered by the unexpected company. 'Hi, you,' called Richard, 'Will you summon one of your fellow servants, and carry Mistress Harris's chair to her apartment? She has had enough of the company downstairs.'

'That is John Rashleigh, sir,' whispered Peter hurriedly, 'the son of the house, and your host in his father's absence.'

'Ha! My apologies,' said Richard, walking forward with a smile. 'Your dress being somewhat in disorder, I mistook you for a menial. My own young officers lose their rank if they appear so before me. How is your father?'

'Well, sir, I believe,' stammered John in great nervousness.

'I am delighted to hear it,' said Richard. 'Tell him so, when you see him. And tell him too that now I am come into the west I propose to visit here very frequently – the course of the war permitting it.'

'Yes, sir.'

'You have accommodation for my officers, I suppose, and for a number of men out in the park, should we wish to bivouac at any time.'

'Yes, indeed, sir.'

'Excellent. And now I propose to dine upstairs with Mistress Harris, who is a close kinswoman of mine, a fact of which you may not be aware. What is the usual method with her chair?'

'We carry it, sir – it is quite a simple matter.' John gave a nod to Peter, who, astonishingly subdued for him, came forward, and the pair of them seized an arm of my chair on either side.

'It would be an easier matter', said Richard, 'if the occupant were bodily removed, and carried separately.' And before I could protest he had placed his arms about me and had lifted me from the chair. 'Lead on, gentlemen,' commanded Richard.

The strange procession proceeded up the stairs, watched by the company in the gallery and by some of the servants too, who, with their backs straight against the wall, and their eyes lowered, permitted us to pass. John and Peter tramped on ahead, with the chair between them, step by step, both of them red about the neck; while I, with my head on Richard's shoulder, and my arms tight about him for fear of falling, thought the way seemed over long.

'I was in error just now,' said Richard in my ear. 'You have changed after all.'

'In what way?' I asked.

'You are two stone heavier,' he answered.

And so we came to my chamber in the gate-house.

Chapter 10

I CAN recollect that supper as if it were yesterday. I lay on my bed with the pillows packed behind me, and Richard was seated on the end of it, with the low table in front of us both.

It might have been a day since we had parted, instead of fifteen years. When Matty came into the room bearing the platters, her mouth pursed and disapproving – for she had never understood how we came to lose one another, but imagined he had deserted me because of my crippled state – Richard burst out laughing on the instant, calling her 'old go-between', which had been his nickname for her in those distant days, and asked her how many hearts she had broken since he saw her last. She was for replying to him shortly, but it was no use. He would have none of it, and, taking the platters from her and putting them on the table, he soon had her reconciled – blushing from head to toe – while he poked fun at her broadening figure and the frizzed curl on her forehead. 'There are some half-dozen troopers in the court,' he told her, 'waiting to make your acquaintance. Go and prove to them that Cornish women are better than the frousts in Devon,' and she went off, closing the door behind her, guessing no doubt that for the first time in fifteen years I had no need of her services. He fell to eating right away, for he was always a good trencher-man, and soon cleared all that had been put before us, while I – still weak with the shock of seeing him – toyed with the wishbone of a chicken. He started walking about the chamber before he had finished,

95

a habit I remembered well, with a great bone in one hand and a pie in the other, talking all the while about the defences at Plymouth, which his predecessor had allowed to become formidable instead of razing them to the ground on first setting siege to the place. 'You'd hardly credit it, Honor,' he said, 'but there's that fat idiot Digby been sitting on his arse nine months before the walls of Plymouth, allowing the garrison to sortie as they please, fetch food and firewood and build up barricades, while he played cards with his junior officers. Thank God a bullet in his head will keep him to his bed a month or two, and allow me to conduct the siege instead.'

'And what do you propose to do?' I asked.

'My first two tasks were simple,' he replied, 'and should have been done last October. I threw up a new earthwork at Mount Batten, and the guns I have placed there so damage the shipping which endeavours to pass through the Sound that the garrison are hard put to it for supplies. Secondly, I have cut off their water-power, and the mills within the city can no longer grind flour for the inhabitants. Give me a month or two to play with, and I'll have 'em starved.' He took a great bite out of his pie, and winked at me.

'And the blockade by land, is that effective now?' I questioned.

'It will be, when I've had time to organize it,' he answered. 'The trouble is that I've arrived to find that most of the officers in my command are worse than useless — I've sacked more than half of them already. I have a good fellow in charge at Saltash, who sent the rebels flying back to Plymouth with several fleas in their ears when they tried a sortie a week or two back — a sharp engagement in which my nephew Jack — Bevil's eldest boy, you remember him — did very well. Last week we sprang a little surprise on one of their outposts close to Maudlyn. We beat them out of their position there, and took a hundred prisoners. I rather think the gentlemen of Plymouth sleep not entirely easy in their beds.'

'Prisoners must be something of a problem,' I said. 'It is hard enough to find forage in the country for your own men. You are obliged to feed them, I suppose?'

'Feed them be damned,' he answered. 'I send the lot to

Lydford Castle, where they are hanged without trial for high treason.' He threw his drumstick out of the window, and tore the other from the carcase.

'But, Richard,' I said, hesitating, 'that is hardly justice, is it? I mean – they are only fighting for what they believe to be a better cause than ours?'

'I don't give a fig for justice,' he replied. 'The method is effective, and that's the only thing that matters.'

'I am told the Parliament has put a price upon your head already,' I said. 'I am told you are much feared and hated by the rebels.'

'What would you have them do, kiss my backside?' he asked. He smiled, and came and sat beside me on the bed.

'The war is too much with us; let us talk about ourselves,' he said. I had not wished for that, but hoped to keep him busy with his siege of Plymouth.

'Where are you living at the moment?' I parried. 'In tents about the fields?'

'What would I be doing in a tent,' he mocked, 'with the best houses in Devon at my disposal? Nay, my headquarters are at Buckland Abbey, which my grandfather sold to Francis Drake half a century ago, and I do not mind telling you that I live there very well. I have seized all the sheep and cattle upon the estate, and the tenants pay their rents to me, or else are hanged. They call me the Red Fox behind my back, and the women, I understand, use the name as a threat to their children when they misbehave, saying "Grenvile is coming. The Red Fox will have you." '

He laughed, as if this was a fine jest, but I was watching the line of his jaw, which was heavier than before, and the curve of his mouth that narrowed at the corners.

'It was not thus', I said softly, 'that your brother Bevil's reputation spread throughout the West.'

'No,' he said, 'and I have not a wife like Bevil had, nor a home I love, nor a great brood of happy children.'

His voice was harsh suddenly, and strangely bitter. I turned my face away, and lay back on my pillows.

'Do you have your son with you at Buckland?' I asked quietly.

'My spawn?' he said. 'Yes, he is somewhere about the place with his tutor.'

'What is he like?'

'Dick? Oh, he's a little handful of a chap, with mournful eyes. I call him "whelp" and make him sing to me at supper. But there's no sign of Grenvile in him – he's the spit of his God-damned mother.'

The boy we would have played with, and taught, and loved. I felt suddenly sad, and oddly depressed, that his father should dismiss him with this careless shrug of a shoulder.

'It went wrong with you then, Richard, from the beginning,' I said.

'It did,' he answered.

There was a long silence, for we had entered upon dangerous ground.

'Did you never try,' I asked, 'to make some life of happiness?'

'Happiness was not in question,' he said. 'That went with you, a factor you refused to recognize.'

'I am sorry,' I said.

'So am I,' he answered.

The shadows were creeping across the floor. Soon Matty would come to light the candles.

'When you refused to see me, that last time,' he said, 'I knew that nothing mattered any more but bare existence. You have heard the story of my marriage, with much embellishment, no doubt, but the bones of it are true.'

'Had you no affection for her?'

'None whatever. I wanted her money, that was all.'

'Which you did not get.'

'Not then. I have it now. And her property, and her son – whom I fathered in a moment of black insensibility. The girl is with her mother up in London. I shall get her too one day, when she can be of use to me.'

'You are very altered, Richard, from the man I loved.'

'If I am so, you know the reason why.'

The sun had gone from the windows, the chamber seemed bleak and bare. Every bit of those fifteen years was now be-tween us. Suddenly he reached out his hand to mine, and, taking it, held it against his lips. The touch I so well remembered was very hard to bear.

'Why in the name of God', he said, rising to his feet, 'were you and I marked down for such tragedy?'

'It is no use being angry,' I said. 'I gave that up long ago. At first, yes, but not now. Not for many years. Lying on my back has taught me some discipline – but not the kind you engender in your troops.'

He came and stood beside my bed, looking down upon me.

'Has no one told you', he said, 'that you are more lovely now than you were then?'

I smiled, thinking of Matty and the mirror.

'I think you flatter me,' I answered, 'or maybe I have more time now I lie idle, to play with paint and powder.'

No doubt he thought me cool and at my ease, and had no knowledge that his tone of voice ripped wide the dusty years and sent them scattering.

'There is no part of you', he said, 'that I do not now remember. You had a mole in the small of your back which gave you much distress. You thought it ugly – but I liked it well.'

'Is it not time', I said, 'that you went downstairs to join your officers? I heard one of them say you were to sleep this night at Grampound.'

'There was a bruise on your left thigh,' he said, 'caused by that confounded branch that protruded halfway up the apple-tree. I compared it to a dark-sized plum, and you were much offended.'

'I can hear the horses in the courtyard,' I said. 'Your troopers are preparing for the journey. You will never reach your destination before morning.'

'You lie there,' he said, 'so smug and so complacent on your bed, very certain of yourself now you are thirty-four. I tell you, Honor, I care not two straws for your civility.'

And he knelt then at my bed with his arms about me and the fifteen years went whistling down the wind.

'Are you still queasy when you eat roast swan?' he whispered.

He wiped away the silly childish tears that pricked my eyes, and laughed at me, and smoothed my hair.

'Beloved half-wit, with your God-damned pride,' he said, 'do you understand now that you blighted both our lives?'

'I understood that at the time,' I told him.

'Why then, in the name of heaven, did you do it?'

'Had I not done so, you would soon have hated me, as you hated Mary Howard.'

'That is a lie, Honor.'

'Perhaps. What does it matter? There is no reason now to harp back on the past.'

'There I agree with you. The past is over. But we have the future with us. My marriage is annulled; you know that, I suppose. I am free to wed again.'

'Then do so, to another heiress.'

'I have no need of an heiress now, with all the estates in Devon to my plunder. I have become a gentleman of fortune to be looked upon with favour by the spinsters of the west.'

'There are many you might choose from, all agog for husbands.'

'In all probability. But I want one spinster only, and that yourself.'

I put my two hands on his shoulders and stared straight at him. The auburn hair, the hazel eyes, the little pulse that beat in his right temple. He was not the only one with recollections. I had my memories too, and could – had I the mind and lack of modesty – have reminded him of a patch of freckles that had been as much a matter for discussion as the mole upon my back.

'No, Richard.'

'Why?'

'Because I will not have you wedded to a cripple.'

'You will never change your mind?'

'Never.'

'And if I carry you by force to Buckland?'

'Do so, if you will, I can't prevent you. But I shall still be a cripple.' I leant back on my pillows, faint suddenly, and exhausted. It had not been a light thing to bear, this strain of seeing him, of beating down the years. Very gently he released me, and smoothed my blankets, and when I asked for a glass of water he gave me one in silence. It was nearly dark, and the clock in the belfry had struck eight a long while since. I could hear the jingling of harness from the courtyard, and the scraping sound of horses.

'I must ride to Grampound,' he said at length.

'Yes,' I said.

He stood for a moment looking down on to the court. The candles were lighted now throughout the house. The west windows of the gallery were open, sending a beam of light into my chamber. There was sound of music. Alice was playing her lute, and Peter singing.

Richard came once more and knelt beside my bed.

'I understand', he said, 'what you have tried so hard to tell me. There can never be, between us, what there was once. Is that it?'

'Yes,' I said.

'I knew that all along, but it would make no difference,' he said.

'It would,' I said, 'after a little while.'

Peter had a young voice, clear and gay, and his song was happy. I thought how Alice would be looking at him over her lute.

'I shall always love you,' said Richard, 'and you will love me too. We cannot lose each other now, not since I have found you again. May I come and see you often, that we may be together?'

'Whenever you wish,' I answered.

There came a burst of clapping from the gallery, and the voices of the officers and the rest of the company asking for more. Alice struck up a lively jiggling air upon her lute – a soldier's drinking song, much whistled at the moment by our men – and they one and all chimed in upon the chorus, with the troopers in the courtyard making echo to the song.

'Do you have as much pain now as when you were first hurt?' he said.

'Sometimes,' I answered, 'when the air is damp. Matty calls me her weather-glass.'

'Can nothing be done for it?'

'She rubs my legs and my back with lotion that the doctors

gave her. But it is of little use. You see, the bones were all smashed and twisted, and they cannot knit together.'

'Will you show me, Honor?'

'It is not a pretty sight, Richard.'

'I have seen worse in battle.'

I pulled aside my blanket and let him look upon the crumpled limbs that he had once known whole and clean. He was thus the only person in the world to see me so, except Matty and the doctors. I put my hands over my eyes, for I did not care to see his face.

'There is no need for that,' he said. 'Whatever you suffer, you shall share with me, from this day forward.' He bent then, and kissed my ugly twisted legs, and after a moment covered me again with the blanket. 'Will you promise', he said, 'never to send me from you again?'

'I promise,' I said.

'Farewell, then, sweetheart, and sleep sound this night.'

He stood for a moment, his figure carved clear against the beam of light from the windows opposite, and then turned and went away down the passage. Presently I heard them all come out into the courtyard and mount their horses; there was the sound of leave-taking and laughter, Richard's voice high above the others telling John Rashleigh he would come again. Suddenly clipt and curt, he called an order to his men, and they went riding through the archway beneath the gate-house where I lay, and I heard the sound of the hoof-beats echo across the park.

Chapter 11

THAT Richard Grenvile should become suddenly, within a few hours, part of my life again was a mental shock that for a day or two threw me out of balance. The first excitement over and the stimulation of his presence that evening fading away, reaction swung me to a low ebb. It was all too late. No good could come of it. Memory of what had been, nostalgia of the past coupled with sentiment, had stirred us both to passion for a moment; but reason came with daylight. There could never be a life for us together, only the doubtful pleasure of brief meetings which the hazards of war might at any time render quite impracticable. What then? For me a lifetime of lying on my back, waiting for a chance encounter, for a message, for a word of greeting; and for him, after a space, a nagging irritation that I existed in the background of his life, that he had not visited me for three months and must make some effort to do so, that I expected some message from him which he found difficult to send – in short, a friendship that would become as wearisome to him as it would be painful to me.

Although his physical presence, his ways, his tenderness – however momentary – had been enough to engender in me once again all the old love and yearning in my heart, cold criticism told me he had altered for the worse.

Faults that I had caught glimpses of in youth were now increased tenfold. His pride, his arrogance, his contempt for anyone's opinion but his own – these were more glaring than they had ever been. His knowledge of military matters was great, that I well believed, but I doubted if he would ever work in harmony with the other leaders, and his quick temper was such that he would have every royalist leader by the ears, and in the end give offence to His Majesty himself.

The callous attitude to prisoners – dumped within Lydford Castle and hanged without trial – showed me that streak of cruelty I had always known was in his nature; and his contemptuous dismissal of his little son, who must, I felt sure, be baffled and bewildered at the sudden change in his existence, betrayed a deliberate want of understanding that was almost vile. That suffering and bitterness had turned him hard, I granted. Mine was the fault, perhaps; mine was the blame.

But the hardness had bitten into his nature now, and it was too late to alter it. Richard Grenvile at forty-four was what Fate, and circumstance, and his own will, had made him.

So I judged him without mercy, in those first days after our encounter, and was within half a mind of writing to him once again, putting an end to all further meetings. Then I remembered how he had knelt beside my bed, and I had shared with him my terrible disfigurement, and he, more tender than any father, more understanding than any brother, had kissed me and bade me sleep.

If he had this gentleness and intuition with me, a woman, how was it that he showed to others, even to his son, a character at once so proud and cruel, so deliberately disdainful?

I felt torn between two courses, lying there on my bed in the gate-house. One was to see him no more, never, at any time. Leave him to carve his own future, as I had done before. And the other was to ignore the great probability of my own personal suffering, spurn my own weak body that would be tortured incessantly by his physical presence, and give to him wholeheartedly and without any reservation all the small wisdom I had learnt, all the love, all the understanding that might yet bring him some measure of peace.

This second course seemed to me more positive than the first, for if I renounced him now, as I had done before, it would be through cowardice, a sneaking fear of being hurt in more intolerable a fashion, if it were possible, than I had been fifteen years ago.

Strange how all arguments in solitude, sorted, sifted, and thrashed in the quietude of one's own chamber, shrivel to nothing when the subject of them is close once more instead of separated by distance. And so it was with Richard, for when he rode to Menabilly on his return from Grampound to Plymouth, and, coming out on to the causeway to seek me, found me in my chair looking out towards the Gribben, and kissed my hand with all the old fire, and love, and ardour – haranguing me straightforth upon the gross inefficiency of every Cornishman he had so far encountered except those under his immediate command – I knew that we were bound together for all time, and I could not send him from me. His faults were my faults, his arrogance my burden, and he stood there, Richard Grenvile, what my tragedy had made him.

'I cannot stay long,' he said to me. 'I have word from Saltash that those damned rebels have made a sortie in my absence, effected a landing at Cawsand, and taken the fort at Inceworth. The sentries were asleep, of course, and if the enemy haven't shot them, I will. I'll have my army purged before I'm finished.'

'And no one left to fight for you, Richard,' I said.

'I'd sooner have hired mercenaries from Germany or France than own these soft-bellied fools,' he answered. And he was gone in a flash, leaving me half-happy, half-bewildered, with an ache in my heart that I knew now was to be for ever part of my existence.

That evening my brother-in-law, Jonathan Rashleigh, returned to Menabilly, having been some little while in Exeter on the King's affairs. He had come by way of Fowey, having spent, so he informed us, the last few days at his town house there on the quay, where he had found much business to transact, and some loss amongst his shipping, for the Parliament had at this time command of the sea and seized every vessel they could find, and it was hard for any unarmed merchant ship to run the gauntlet.

Some feeling of constraint came upon the place at his return, of which even I, secure in my gate-house, could not but be aware.

The servants were more prompt about their business, but less willing. The grandchildren, who had run about the passages in his absence, were closeted in their quarters with the doors well shut. The voices in the gallery were more subdued. It was indeed obvious that the master had returned. Alice, and John, and Joan found their way more often to the gate-house, as if it had become in some way a sanctuary. John looked harassed and preoccupied, and Joan whispered to me in confidence that his father found fault with his running of the estate and said he had no head for figures.

I could see that Joan was burning to inquire about my friendship with Richard Grenvile, which they must have thought strangely sudden, and I saw Alice look at me, though she said nothing, with a new warm glance of understanding. 'I knew him well long ago, when I was eighteen,' I told them, but to plunge back into the whole history was not my wish. I think Mary had given them a hint or two, in private. She herself said little of the visit, beyond remarking he had grown much stouter, a true sisterly remark, and then she showed me the letter he had left for Jonathan, which ended with these words:

'I here conclude, praying you to present once more my best

respects to your good wife, being truly glad she is yours, for a more likely good wife was in former time hardly to be found, and I wish my fortune had been as good – but patience is a virtue, and so I am your ready servant and kinsman, Richard Grenvile.'

Patience is a virtue. I saw Mary glance at me as I read the lines.

'You do not intend, Honor,' she said in a low voice, 'to take up with him again?'

'In what way, Mary?'

'Why, wed with him, to be blunt. This letter is somewhat significant.'

'Rest easy, sister. I shall never marry Richard Grenvile or any man.'

'I should not be comfortable, nor Jonathan either, if Sir Richard should come here and give an impression of intimacy. He may be a fine soldier, but his reputation is anything but that.'

'I know, Mary.'

'Jo writes from Radford that they say hard things of him in Devon.'

'I can well believe it.'

'I know it is not my business, but it would sadden me much, it would greatly grieve us all, if – if you bound yourself to him in some way.'

'Being a cripple, Mary, makes one strangely free of bonds.'

She looked at me doubtfully, and then said no more, but I think the bitterness was lost on her.

Presently Jonathan himself came up to pay his respects to me. He hoped I was comfortable, that I had everything I needed, and did not find the place too noisy after the quiet of Lanrest.

'And you sleep well, I trust, and are not disturbed at all?'

His manner, when he asked this, was somewhat odd, a trifle evasive, which was strange for him, who was so self-possessed a person.

'I am not a heavy sleeper,' I told him. 'A creaking board or a hooting owl is enough to waken me.'

'I rather feared so,' he said abruptly. 'It was foolish of Mary

106

to put you in this room, facing as it does a court on either side. You would have been better in the south front, next to our own apartments. Would you prefer this?'

'Indeed, no. I am very happy here.'

I noticed that he stared hard at the picture on the door, hiding the crack, and once or twice seemed as if he would ask a question, but could not bring himself to the point; then, after chat upon no subject in particular, he took his leave of me.

That night, between twelve and one, since I was wakeful, I sat up in bed to drink a glass of water. I did not light my candle, for the glass was within my reach. But as I replaced it on the table I became aware of a cold draught of air blowing beneath the door of the empty room. That same chill draught I had noticed once before. I waited, motionless, for the sound of footsteps, but none came. And then, faint and hesitating, came a little scratching sound upon the panel of the door where I had hung the picture. Someone, then, was in the empty room, clad in his stockinged feet, with his hands upon the door.

The sound continued for five minutes, certainly not longer, and then ceased as suddenly as it had started, and once again the tell-tale draught of air was cut in a trice, and all was as before. A horrid suspicion formed then in my mind, which in the morning became certainty. When I was dressed, and in my chair and Matty busy in the dressing-room, I wheeled myself to the door and lifted the picture from the nail. It was as I thought. The crack had been filled in. I knew then that my presence in the gate-house had been a blunder on the part of my sister, and that I caused annoyance to that unknown visitor who prowled by night in the adjoining chamber.

The secret was Jonathan Rashleigh's, and not mine to know. Suspecting my prying eyes, he had given orders for my peephole to be covered. I pondered then upon the possibility, which had entered my head earlier, that Jonathan's elder brother had not died of the smallpox some twenty years before, but was still alive – in some horrid state of preservation, blind and dumb – living in animal fashion in a lair beneath the buttress, and that the only person to know of this were my brother-in-law and his steward Langdon, and some stranger – a keeper possibly – clad in a crimson cloak.

If it were indeed so, and my sister Mary and her stepchildren were in ignorance of the fact, while I, a stranger, had stumbled upon it, then I knew I must make some excuse and return home to Lanrest, for to live day by day with a secret of this kind upon my conscience was something I could not do. It was too sinister, too horrible.

I wondered if I should confide my fears to Richard, when he next came, or whether, in his ruthless fashion, he would immediately give orders to his men to break open the room and force the buttress, so bringing ruin perhaps to my brother-in-law and host.

Fortunately, the problem was solved for me in a very different way, which I will now disclose. It will be remembered that on the day of Richard's first visit my godchild Joan had mischievously borrowed the key of the summer-house, belonging to the steward, and allowed me to explore the interior. The flurry and excitement of receiving visitors had put all thoughts of the key from her little scatter-brained head, and it was not until two days after my brother-in-law's return that she remembered the key's existence.

She came to me with it in her hand, in great perturbation, for, she said, John was already so much out of favour with his father for some neglect on the estate that she was loath now to tell him of her theft of the key, for fear it should bring him into greater trouble. As for herself, she had not the courage to take the key back to Langdon's house and confess the foolery. What was she then to do?

'You mean,' I said, 'what am I to do? For you wish to absolve yourself of all responsibility, isn't that so?'

'You are so clever, Honor,' she pleaded, 'and I so ignorant. Let me leave the key with you, and so forget it. Baby Mary has a cough, and poor John a touch of his ague. I really have so much on my mind.'

'Very well, then,' I answered, 'we will see what can be done.'

I had some idea of taking Matty into my confidence, and weaving a talk by which Matty would visit Mrs Langdon and say she had found the key thrown down on a path in the Warren, which would be plausible enough, and while I turned this over in my mind I dangled the key between my fingers. It was of medium size, not larger, in fact, than the one in my own door. I compared the two, and found them very similar. A sudden thought then struck me, and, wheeling my chair into the passage I listened for a moment, to discover who stirred about the house. It was a little before nine o'clock, with the servants all at their dinner and the rest of the household either talking in the gallery or already retired to their rooms for the night. The moment seemed well-chosen for a very daring gamble, which might, or might not, prove nothing to me. I turned down the passage and halted outside the door of the locked chamber. I listened again, but no one stirred. Then very stealthily I pushed the key into the rusty lock. It fitted. It turned. And the door creaked open. I was so carried away for a moment by the success of my own scheme that I was non-plussed. I sat in my chair, uncertain what to do. But that there was a link between this chamber and the summer-house now seemed definite, for the key turned both locks.

The chance to examine the room might never come again, and, for all my fear, I was devoured with horrid curiosity. I edged my chair within the room, and kindling my candle – for it was of course in darkness, with the windows barred – I looked about me. The chamber was simple enough. Two windows, one to the north and the other to the west, both with iron bars across them. A bed in the far corner, a few pieces of heavy furniture, and the table and chair I had already seen from the crack. The walls were hung about with a heavy arras, rather old, and worn in many parts. It was indeed a disappointing room, with little that seemed strange in its appointments. It had the faded musty smell that always clings about disused apartments. I laid the candle on the table, and wheeled myself to the corner that gave upon the buttress. This too had an arras hanging from the ceilings, which I lifted – and found nothing but bare stone behind it. I ran my hands over the surface, but could find no join. The wall seemed smooth to my touch. But it was murky, and I could not see, so I returned to the table to fetch my candle, first listening at the door to make certain that the servants were still at supper. It was while I waited there, with an eye to the passage that turned at right angles, running beneath the belfry, that I felt a sudden breath of cold air on the back of my head.

I looked swiftly over my shoulder, and noticed that the arras on the wall beside the buttress was blowing to and fro, as though a cavity had opened, letting through a blast of air, and even as I watched, I saw, to my great horror, a hand appear from behind a slit in the arras and lift it to one side. There was no time to wheel my chair into the passage, no time even to reach my hand out to the table and blow the candle. Someone came into the room with a crimson cloak about his shoulders, and stood for a moment, with the arras pushed aside and a great black hole in the wall behind him. He considered me a moment, and then spoke. 'Close the door gently, Honor,' he said, 'and leave the candle. Since you are here it is best that we should have an explanation, and no further mischief.'

He advanced into the room, letting the arras drop behind him, and I saw then that the man was my brother-in-law, Jonathan Rashleigh.

Chapter 12

I FELT like a child caught out in some misdemeanour, and was hot with shame and sick embarrassment. If he then was the stranger in the crimson cloak, walking his house in the small hours, it was not for me to question it. To be discovered thus, prying in his secrets, with the key not only of this door, but of his summer-house as well, was surely something he could never pardon.

'Forgive me,' I said. 'I have acted very ill.'

He did not answer at once, but first made certain that the door was closed. Then he lit further candles, and, laying aside his cloak, drew a chair up to the table.

'It was you,' he said, 'who made a crack there in the panel? It was not there before you came to Menabilly.'

His blunt question showed me what a shrewd grasp he had of my gaping curiosity, and I confessed that I was indeed the culprit. 'I will not attempt to defend myself,' I said. 'I know

110

I had no right to tamper with your walls. There was some talk of ghosts, otherwise I would not have done it. And one night during last week I heard footsteps.'

'Yes,' he said. 'I had not thought to find your chamber occupied. I heard you stir, and guessed then what had happened. We are somewhat pushed for room, as you no doubt realize, otherwise you would not have been put into the gate-house.'

He waited a moment, and then, looking closely at me, he said: 'You have understood, then, that there is a secret entry to this chamber.'

'Yes.'

'And the reason you are here this evening is that you wished to find whither it led?'

'I knew it must be within the buttress.'

'How did you come upon that key?'

This was the very devil, but there was nothing for it but to tell him the whole story, putting the blame heavily upon myself and saying little of Joan's share in the matter. I said that I had looked about the summer-house, and admired the view, but as to my peering at his books, and his father's will and lifting the heavy mat and finding the flagstone – nay, he would have to put me on the rack before I confessed to that.

He listened in silence, regarding me coldly all the while, and I knew what an interfering fool he must consider me.

'And what do you make of it, now you know that the nightly intruder is none other than myself?' he questioned.

Here was a stumbling-block. For I could make nothing of it. And I did not dare voice that secret very fearful supposition that I kept hidden at the back of my mind.

'I cannot tell, Jonathan,' I answered, 'except that you use this entry for some purpose of your own, and that your family know nothing of it.' At this he was silent, considering me slowly, and then, after a long pause, he said to me: 'John has some knowledge of the subject, but no one else, except my steward Langdon. Indeed, the success of the royal cause we have at heart would gravely suffer should the truth become known.'

This last surprised me. I did not see that his family secrets could be of any concern to His Majesty. But I said nothing.

'Since you already know something of the truth,' he said, 'I will acquaint you further, desiring you first to keep all knowledge of it to yourself.'

I promised, after a moment's hesitation, being uncertain what dire secret I might now be asked to share.

'You know', he said, 'that at the beginning of hostilities I, with certain other gentlemen, was appointed by His Majesty's Council to collect and receive the plate given to the royal cause in Cornwall, and arrange for it to be taken to the Mint at Truro and there melted down?'

'I knew you were Collector, Jonathan – no more than that.'

'Last year another Mint was erected at Exeter, under the supervision of my kinsman, Sir Richard Vyvyan, hence my constant business with that city. You will appreciate, Honor, that to receive a great quantity of very valuable plate, and be responsible for its safety until it reaches the Mint, is a heavy burden upon my shoulders.'

'Yes, Jonathan.'

'Spies abound, as you are well aware. Neighbours have long ears, and even a close friend can turn informer. If some member of the rebel army could but lay his hands upon the treasure that so frequently passes into my keeping, the Parliament would be ten times the richer, and His Majesty ten times the poorer. Therefore all cartage of the plate has to be done at night, when the roads are quiet. Also it is necessary to have depots throughout the county, where the plate can be stored until the necessary transport can be arranged. You have followed me so far?'

'Yes, Jonathan, and with interest.'

'Very well, then. These depots must be secret. As few people as possible must know their whereabouts. It is therefore imperative that the houses or buildings that serve as depots should contain hiding-places, known only to their owners. Menabilly, as you have already discovered, has such a hiding-place.'

I found myself getting hot under the skin, not at the implied sarcasm of his words, but because his revelation was so very different from what I – with excess of imagination – had supposed.

'The buttress against the far corner of this room', he continued, 'is hollow in the centre. A flight of narrow steps leads to a small room, built in the thickness of the wall and beneath the courtyard, where it is possible for a man to stand, and sit, though it is but five feet square. This room is connected with a passage, or rather tunnel, which runs under the house and so beneath the causeway to an outlet in the summer-house. It is in this small buttress room that I have been accustomed, during the past year, to hide the plate. You understand me?'

I nodded, gripped by his story, and deeply interested.

'When the plate is brought to this depot, or taken away, we work by night, my steward, John Langdon, and I. The wagons wait down at Pridmouth, and we bring the plate from the buttress room, along the tunnel to the summer-house, and so down to the cove in one of my hand-carts, where it is placed in the wagons. The men who conduct the procession from here to Exeter are all trustworthy, but none of them, naturally, know whereabouts at Menabilly I have kept the plate hidden. That is not their business. No one knows that but myself and Langdon, and now you, Honor, who – I regret to say – have really no right at all to share the secret.'

I said nothing, for there was no possible defence.

'John knows the plate has been concealed in the house, but has never inquired where. He is, as yet, ignorant of the room beneath the buttress, as well as the tunnel to the summer-house.'

Here I risked offence by interrupting him.

'It was providential', I said, 'that Menabilly possessed so excellent a hiding-place.'

'Very providential,' he agreed. 'Had it not been so I could hardly have set about the business. You wonder, no doubt, why the house should have been so constructed?'

I confessed to some small wonder on the subject.

'My father', he said briefly, 'had certain – how shall I put it? – shipping transactions, which necessitated privacy. The tunnel was therefore useful in many ways.'

In other words, I said to myself, your father, dear Jonathan, was nothing more or less than a pirate of the first order, whatever his standing and reputation in Fowey and the county.

'It happened also', he said in a lower tone, 'that my unfortunate eldest brother was not in full possession of his faculties.

This was his chamber, from the time the house was built in 1600 until his death, poor fellow, twenty-four years later. At times he was violent, hence the reason for the little cell beneath the buttress, where lack of air and close confinement soon rendered him unconscious and easy then to handle.'

He spoke naturally, and without restraint, but the picture that his words conjured up turned me sick. I saw the wretched, shivering maniac choking for air in the dark room beneath the buttress, with the four walls closing in upon him. And now this same room stacked with silver plate like a treasure-house in a fairy-tale.

Jonathan must have seen my change of face, for he looked kindly at me and rose from his chair.

'I know', he said, 'it is not a pretty story. It was a relief to me, I must admit, when the smallpox that carried off my father took my brother too. It was not a happy business caring for him, with young children in the house. You have heard, no doubt, the malicious tales that Robert Bennett spread abroad?'

I mentioned vaguely that some rumour had come to my ears.

'He took the disease some five days after my father,' said Jonathan. 'Why he should have taken it, while my wife and I escaped, we shall never know. But so he did, and, becoming violent at the same time with one of his periodic fits, stood not a chance. It was over very quickly.'

There were sounds of the servants moving from the kitchens.

'You will return now to your apartment,' he said, 'and I will go back the way I came. You may give me John Langdon's key. If in future you hear me come to this apartment, you will understand what I am about. I keep accounts here of the plate temporarily in my possession, which I refer to from time to time. I need hardly tell you that not a word of what has this night passed between us must be spoken about to any other person.'

'I give you my solemn promise, Jonathan.'

'Good night, then, Honor.'

He helped me turn my chair into the passage, and then, very softly, closed the door behind me. I got to my own room a few moments before Matty came upstairs to draw the curtains.

Chapter 13

ALTHOUGH there were never any ties of affection between me and my brother-in-law, I certainly held him in greater respect and regard after our encounter of that evening. I knew now that 'the King's business' on which he travelled to and fro was no light matter, and it was small wonder he was often short-tempered with his family. Men with less sense of duty would long since have shelved the responsibility on to other shoulders. I respected him too for having taken me into his confidence, after my unwarrantable intrusion into his locked chamber. I was left only with a sneaking regret that he had not shown me the staircase in the buttress or the cell beneath it, but this would have been too much to expect. I had a vivid picture, though, of the flapping arras and the black gulf behind. Meanwhile, the progress of the war was causing each one of us no small concern. Our western army was under the supreme command of the King's nephew, Prince Maurice, who was in great need of reinforcements, especially of cavalry, if he was ever to strike a decisive blow against the enemy. But the plan of the summer campaign appeared unsettled, and although Maurice's brother, Prince Rupert, endeavoured to persuade the King to send some two thousand horse into the west there was the usual obstruction from the Council, and the cavalry were not forthcoming. This, of course, we heard from Richard, who, fuming with impatience because he had as yet none of the guns that had been promised him, told us with grim candour that our western army was anyhow worn with sickness, and quite useless, and that Prince Maurice himself had but one bee in his bonnet, which was to sit before Lyme Regis, waiting for the place to open up to him. 'If Essex and the rebel army choose to march west,' said Richard, 'there is nothing to stop him, except a mob of sick men all lying on their backs, and a handful of drunken generals. I can do nothing, with my miserable two men and a boy squatting before Plymouth.' Essex did choose

115

to march west, and was in Weymouth and Bridport by the third week of June, and Prince Maurice, with great loss of prestige, retreated in haste to Exeter.

Here he found his aunt, the Queen, who had arrived in a litter from Bristol, being fearful of the approaching enemy, and it was here at Exeter that she gave birth to her youngest child, which did not lessen the responsibilities of Prince Maurice and his staff. He decided that the wisest course was to get her away to France as speedily as possible, and she set forth for Falmouth, very weak and nervous, two weeks after the baby had been born.

My brother-in-law Jonathan was among those who waited on her as she passed through Bodmin on her way south, and came back telling a very pitiful tale of her appearance, for she was much worn and shaken by her ordeal. 'She may have advised His Majesty ill on many an occasion,' said Jonathan, 'but at least she is a woman, and I tremble to think of her fate if she fell into the hands of the rebels.' It was a great relief to all the Royalists in Cornwall when she reached Falmouth without mishap, and embarked for France.

But Essex and the rebel army were gathering in numbers all the while, and we felt it was but a matter of weeks before he passed through Dorset into Devon, with nothing but the Tamar then between him and Cornwall. The only one who viewed the approaching struggle with relish was Richard. 'If we can but draw the beggar into Cornwall,' he said, 'a county of which he knows nothing, and whose narrow lanes and high hedges would befog him completely, then, with the King's and Rupert's army coming up in the rear and cutting off all retreat, we will have him surrounded and destroyed.'

I remember him rubbing his hands gleefully, and laughing at the prospect like a boy on holiday, but the idea did not much appeal to Jonathan and other gentlemen, who were dining at Menabilly on that day. 'If we have fighting in Cornwall, the country will be devastated,' said Francis Bassett, who with my brother-in-law was engaged at that time in trying to raise troops for the King's service, and finding it mighty hard. 'The land is too poor to feed an army – we cannot do it. The fighting must be kept the other side of the Tamar, and we look to you and your troops, Grenvile, to engage the enemy in Devon and keep us from invasion.'

'My good fool,' said Richard – at which Francis Bassett coloured, and we all felt uncomfortable – 'you are a country squire, and I respect your knowledge of cattle and pigs. But for God's sake leave the art of war to professional soldiers like myself. Our aim at present is to destroy the enemy, which we cannot do in Devon, where there is no hope of encirclement. Once across the Tamar he will run his head into a noose. My only fear is that he will not do so, but will use his superior cavalry on the open Devon moors against Maurice and his hopeless team of half-wits, in which case we shall have lost one of the greatest chances this war has yet produced.'

'You are prepared, then,' said Jonathan, 'to see Cornwall laid waste, people homeless, and much sickness and suffering spread abroad? It does not appear to be a prospect of much comfort.'

'Damn your comfort,' said Richard. 'It will do my fellow countrymen a world of good to see a spot of bloodshed. If you cannot suffer that for the King's cause, then we may as well treat with the enemy forthwith.'

There was some atmosphere of strain in the dining-chamber when he had spoken, and shortly afterwards my brother-in-law gave the host's signal for dispersal. It was an oddity I could not explain even to myself that since Richard had come back into my life I could face company with greater equanimity than I had done before, and had now formed the habit of eating downstairs rather than in my chamber. Solitude was no longer my one aim. After dining, since it was still light, he took a turn with me upon the causeway, making himself attendant to my chair.

'If Essex draws near to Tavistock', he said, 'and I am forced to raise the siege of Plymouth and retreat, can I send the whelp to you?'

I was puzzled for a moment, thinking he alluded to his dog.

'What whelp?' I asked. 'I did not know you possessed one.'

'The south-west makes you slow of brain,' he said. 'My spawn, I mean – my pup, my son and heir. Will you have him here under your wing and put some sense into his frightened head?'

'Why, yes, indeed, if you think he would be happy with me.'

'I think he would be happier with you than with any other person in the world. My aunt Abbot at Hartland is too old, and Bevil's wife at Stowe is so slung about with her own brood that I do not care to ask her. Besides, she has never thought much of me.'

'Have you spoken to Jonathan?'

'Yes. He is willing. But I wonder what you will make of Dick. He is a scrubby object.'

'I will love him, Richard, because he is your son.'

'I doubt that sometimes when I look at him. He has a shrinking, timid way with him, and his tutor tells me that he cries for a finger scratch. I would exchange him any day for young Joe Grenvile, a kinsman, whom I have as aide-de-camp at Buckland. He is up to any daring scheme, that lad, and a fellow after my own heart, like Bevil's eldest boy.'

'Dick is barely turned fourteen,' I said to him. 'You must not expect too much. Give him a year or two to learn confidence.'

'If he has taken after his mother, then I'll turn him off and let him starve,' said Richard. 'I won't have frog's spawn about me.'

'Perhaps', I said, 'your example does not greatly encourage him to take after yourself. Were I a child I would not want a red fox for a father.'

'He is the wrong age for me,' said Richard: 'too big to dandle, and too small to talk to. He is yours, Honor, from this day forward. I declare I will bring him over to you this day week.'

And so it was arranged, with Jonathan's permission, that Dick Grenvile, and his tutor, Herbert Ashley, should add to the numbers at Menabilly. I was strangely happy and excited the day they were expected, and went with my sister Mary to inspect the room that had been put to their service beneath the clock-tower.

I took pains with my toilet, wearing my blue gown that was my favourite, and bidding Matty brush my hair for half the morning. And all the while I told myself what a sentimental fool I was to waste such time and trouble for a little lad who would not look at me. It was about one o'clock that I heard the horses trotting across the park, and I called in a fever to Matty to fetch the servants to carry me downstairs, for I wished to be in the garden when I greeted them, for I have a firm belief that it is always easier to become acquainted with anyone out of doors, in the sun, than shut fast within four walls.

I was seated, then, in the walled garden beneath the causeway, when the gate opened and a lad came walking across the lawn towards me. He was taller than I had imagined, with the flaming Grenvile locks, and an impudent snub-nose, and a swagger about him that reminded me instantly of Richard. And then, as he spoke, I realized my mistake. 'My name is Joe Grenvile,' he said. 'They have sent me from the house to bring you back. There has been a slight mishap. Poor Dick tumbled from his horse as we drew rein in the courtyard – the stones were somewhat slippery – and he has cut his head. They have taken him to your chamber, and your maid is washing off the blood.'

This was very different from the picture I had painted, and I was at once distressed that the arrival should have gone awry.

'Is Sir Richard with you?' I asked as he wheeled me down the path. 'Yes,' said young Joe, 'and in a great state of irritation, cursing poor Dick for incompetence, which made the little fellow worse. We have to leave again within the hour. Essex has reached Tiverton, you know, and Taunton Castle is also in the rebel's hands. Prince Maurice has withdrawn several units from our command, and there is to be a conference at Okehampton, which Sir Richard must attend. Ours are the only troops that are now left outside Plymouth.'

'And you find all this greatly stirring, do you, Joe?' I asked.

'Yes, madam. I can hardly wait to have a crack at the enemy myself.'

We turned in at the garden entrance, and found Richard pacing up and down the hall. 'You would hardly believe it possible,' he said, 'but the whelp must go and tumble from his horse, right on the very doorstep. Sometimes I think he has softening of the brain, to act in so boobish a fashion. What do you think of Joe?' He clapped the youngster on the shoulder, who looked up at him with pride and devotion. 'We shall make a soldier of this chap, anyway,' he said. 'Go and draw me some ale, Joe, and a tankard for yourself. I'm as thirsty as a drowning man.'

'What of Dick?' I asked. 'Shall I not go to him?'

'Leave him to the women and his useless tutor,' said Richard. 'You'll soon have enough of him. I have one hour to spend at Menabilly, and I want you to myself.' We went to the little ante-room beyond the gallery, and there he sat with me while he drank his ale, and told me that Essex would be at Tavistock before the week was out.

'If he marches on Cornwall, then we have him trapped,' said Richard, 'and if the King will only follow fast enough on his heels the game is ours. It will be unpleasant while it lasts, my sweetheart, but it will not be for long, that I can promise you.'

'Shall we see fighting in this district?' I asked, with some misgiving.

'Impossible to answer. It depends on Essex, whether he strikes north or south. He will make for Liskeard and Bodmin, where we shall try to hold him. Pray for a dirty August, Honor, and they will be up to their eyes in mud. I must go. I sleep tonight in Launceston, if I can make it.' He put his tankard on the table, and first closing the door, knelt beside my chair. 'Look after the little whelp,' he said, 'and teach him manners. If the worst should happen and there be fighting in the neighbourhood, hide him under your bed. Essex would take any son of mine as hostage. Do you love me still?'

'I love you always.'

'Then cease listening for footsteps in the gallery, and kiss me as though you meant it.'

It was easy for him, no doubt, to hold me close for five minutes and have me in a turmoil with his love-making, and then ride away to Launceston, his mind aflame with other matters; but for me, left with my hair and gown in disarray, and no method of escape, and long hours stretching before me to think about it all, it was rather more disturbing. I had chosen the course, though – I had let him come back into my life, and I must put up with the fever he engendered in me which could never more be stilled.

So, calling to his aide-de-camp, he waved his hand to me and rode away to Launceston, where, I told myself with nagging jealousy, he and young Joe would in all probability dine over-well and find some momentary distraction before the more serious business of tomorrow, for I knew my Richard too well to believe he lived a life of austerity simply because he loved me.

I patted my curls, and smoothed my lace collar, then pulled the bellrope for a servant, who, with the aid of another, bore me in my chair to my apartments. I did not pass through the front of the house, as was my custom, but through the back rooms beneath the belfry, and here in a passage I found Frank Penrose, my brother-in-law's cousin and dependant, engaged in earnest conversation with a young man of about his own age who had a sallow complexion and retreating chin, and who appeared to be recounting the story of his life.

'This is Mr Ashley, Mistress Honor,' said Frank with the smarming manner peculiar to him. 'He has left his charge resting in your apartment. Mr Ashley is about to take refreshment with me below.'

Mr Ashley bowed and scraped his heels.

'Sir Richard informed me you are the boy's godmother, madam,' he said, 'and that I am to take my commands from you. It is, of course, rather irregular, but I will endeavour to adapt myself to the circumstances.' You are a fool, I thought, and a prig, and I don't think I am going to like you, but aloud I said: 'Please continue, Mr Ashley, as you have been accustomed to at Buckland. I have no intention of interfering in any way, except to see that the boy is happy.' I left them both bowing and scraping, and ready to pull me to pieces as soon as my back was turned, and so was brought to the gate-house. I met Matty coming forth with a basin of water, and strips of bandage on her arm.

'Is he much hurt?' I asked.

Her lips were drawn in the tight line that I knew meant disapproval of the whole proceeding.

'More frightened than anything else,' she said, 'He'll fall to pieces if you look at him.'

The servants set me down in the room and withdrew, closing the door. He was sitting hunched up in a chair beside the hearth, a white shrimp of a boy with great dark eyes and tight

121

black locks, his pallor worsened by the bandage on his head. He watched me nervously, biting his nails all the while.

'Are you better?' I said gently.

He stared at me for a moment, and then said, with a queer jerk of his head: 'Has he gone?'

'Has who gone?' I asked.

'My father.'

'Yes. He has ridden away to Launceston with your cousin.' He considered this a moment.

'When will he be back?' he asked.

'He will not be back. He has to attend a meeting at Okehampton tomorrow or the following day. You are to stay here for the present. Did he not tell you who I am?'

'I think you must be Honor. He said I was to be with a lady who was beautiful. Why do you sit in that chair?'

'Because I cannot walk. I am a cripple.'

'Does it hurt?'

'No. Not very much. I am used to it. Does your head hurt you?'

He touched the bandage warily. 'It bled,' he said. 'There is blood under the bandage.'

'Never mind, it will soon heal.'

'I will keep the bandage on or it will bleed afresh,' he said. 'You must tell the servant who washed it not to move the bandage.'

'Very well,' I said, 'I will tell her.'

I took a piece of tapestry and began to work on it so that he should not think I watched him, and would grow accustomed to my presence.

'My mother used to work at tapestry,' he said after a lengthy pause. 'She worked a forest scene with stags running.'

'That was pretty,' I said.

'She made three covers for her chairs,' he went on. 'They were much admired at Fitzford. You never came to Fitzford, I believe?'

'No, Dick.'

'My mother had many friends, but I did not hear her speak of you.'

'I do not know your mother, Dick. I only know your father.'

122

'Do you like him?' The question was suspicious, sharply put.

'Why do you ask?' I said, evading it.

'Because I don't. I hate him. I wish he would be killed in battle.' The tone was savage, venomous. I stole a glance at him, and saw him once more biting at the back of his hand.

'Why do you hate him?' I asked quietly.

'He is a devil, that's why. He tried to kill my mother. He tried to steal her house and money, and then kill her.'

'Why do you think that?'

'My mother told me.'

'Do you love her very much?'

'I don't know. I think so. She was beautiful. More beautiful than you. She is in London now, with my sister. I wish I could be with her.'

'Perhaps', I said, 'when the war is finished with, you will go back to her.'

'I would run away,' he said, 'but for London being so far, and that I might get caught in the fighting. There is fighting everywhere. There is no talk of anything at Buckland but the fighting. I will tell you something.'

'What is that?'

'Last week I saw a wounded man brought in to the house upon a stretcher. There was blood upon him.'

The way he said this puzzled me, his manner was so shrinking.

'Why', I asked, 'are you so much afraid of blood?'

The colour flamed into his pale face.

'I did not say I was afraid,' he answered quickly.

'No, but you do not like it. Neither do I. It is most unpleasant. But I am not fearful if I see it spilt.'

'I cannot bear to see it spilt at all,' he said, after a moment. 'I have always been thus, since I was a little child. It is not my fault.'

'Perhaps you were frightened as a baby.'

'That's what my mother brought me up to understand. She told me that when she had me in her arms once my father came into the room and quarrelled violently with her upon some matter, and that he struck her on the face, and she bled. The blood ran on to my hands. I cannot remember it, but that is how it was.'

I began to feel very sick at heart, and despondent, but was careful that he should not notice it.

'We won't talk about it any more then, Dick, unless you want to. What shall we discuss instead?'

'Tell me what you did when you were my age, how you looked, and what you said; and had you brothers and sisters?'

And so I wove him a tale about the past, thus making him forget his own, while he sat watching me; and by the time that Matty came, bringing us refreshment, he had lost enough of his nervousness to chat with her too, and make big eyes at the pasties, which soon disappeared, while I sat and looked at his little chiselled features, so unlike his father's, and the close black curls upon his head. Afterwards I read to him for a while, and he left his chair and came and curled on the floor beside my chair, like a small dog who would make friends in a strange house, and when I closed the book he looked up at me and smiled — and the smile for the first time was Richard's smile and not his mother's.

Chapter 14

FROM that day forward Dick became my shadow. He arrived early, with my breakfast, never my best moment of the day, but because he was Richard's son I suffered him. He then left to do his lessons with the sallow Mr Ashley while I made my toilet, and later in the morning came to walk beside my chair upon the causeway.

He sat beside me in the dining-chamber, and brought a stool to the gallery when I went there after dinner; seldom speaking, always watchful, he hovered continually about me like a small phantom.

'Why do you not run and play in the gardens?' I asked. 'Or ask Mr Ashley to take you down to Pridmouth? There are fine shells there on the beach, and as the weather is warm you could swim if you had the mind. There's a young cob, too, in the stables you could ride across the park.'

'I would rather stay with you,' he said.

And he was firm on this, and would not be dissuaded. Even Alice, who had the warmest way with children I ever saw, failed with him, for he would shake his head and take his stool behind my chair.

'He has certainly taken a fancy to you, madam,' said the tutor, relieved, I am sure, to find his charge so little trouble. 'I have found it very hard to interest him.'

'He is your conquest,' said Joan, 'and you will never more be rid of him. Poor Honor. What a burden to the end of your days!'

But it did not worry me. If Dick was happy with me, that was all that mattered, and if I could bring some feeling of security to his poor lonely little heart and puzzled mind I should not feel my days were wasted. Meanwhile, the news worsened, and some five days after Dick's arrival word came from Fowey that Essex had reached Tavistock, and the siege of Plymouth had been raised, with Richard withdrawing his troops from Saltash, Mount Stampford, and Plympton, and retreating to the Tamar bridges.

That evening a council was held at Tywardreath amongst the gentry in the district, at which my brother-in-law presided, and one and all decided to muster what men and arms and ammunition they could, and ride to Launceston to help defend the county.

We were at once in a state of consternation, and the following morning saw the preparations for departure. All those on the estate who were able-bodied and fit to carry arms paraded before my brother-in-law with their horses, their kit packed on the saddles, and amongst them were the youngest of the house-servants who could be spared and all the grooms. Jonathan, and his son-in-law, John Rashleigh of Coombe, and Oliver Sawle from Penrice – brother to old Nick Sawle – and many other gentlemen from round about Fowey and St Austell, gathered at Menabilly before setting forth, while my poor sister Mary went from one to the other with her face set in a smile I knew was sadly forced, handing them cake and fruit and pasties to cheer them on their way. John was left with many long instructions, which I could swear he would never carry in his head, and then we watched them set off across the park, a strange, pathetic little band full of ignorance and high courage, the tenants wielding their muskets as though they were hayforks, and with considerable more danger to themselves than to the enemy they might encounter. It was '43 all over again, with the rebels not thirty miles away, and although Richard might declare that Essex and his army were running into a trap, I was disloyal enough to wish they might keep out of it.

Those last days of July were clammy warm. A sticky breeze blew from the south-west that threatened rain and never brought it, while a tumbled sea rolled past the Gribben white and grey. At Menabilly we made a pretence of continuing as though all were as usual, and nothing untoward likely to happen, and even forced a little gaiety when dining that we must wait upon ourselves, now that there were none but womenfolk to serve us. But for all this deception, intended to convey a sense of courage, we were tense and watchful – our ears always pricked for the rumble of cannon or the sound of horses. I can remember how we all sat beside the long table in the dining-chamber, the portrait of His Majesty gazing calmly down upon us from the dark panelling above the open hearth, and how at the end of a strained, tedious meal Nick Sawle, who was the eldest amongst us, conquered his rheumatics and rose to his feet in great solemnity, saying, 'It were well that, in this time of stress and trouble, we should give a toast unto His Majesty. Let us drink to our beloved King, and may God protect him, and all who have gone forth from this house to fight for him.'

They all then rose to their feet too, except myself, and looked up at his portrait – those melancholy eyes, that small obstinate mouth – and I saw the tears run down Alice's cheeks as she thought of Peter, and sad resignation come to Mary's face, her thoughts with Jonathan. Yet none of them, gazing at the King's portrait, dreamed of blaming him for the trouble that had come upon them. God knows I had no sympathy for the rebels, who each one of them was out for feathering his own nest and building up a fortune, caring nothing for the common people whose lot they pretended would be bettered by their victory, but nor could I, in my heart, recognize the King as the fountain of all truth, but thought of him always as a stiff, proud man, small in intelligence as he was in stature, yet commanding, by his grace of manner, his dignity, and his moral virtue, a wild devotion in his followers that sprang from their warm hearts and not their reason.

We were a quiet, subdued party who sat in the long gallery that evening. Even the sharp tongue of Temperance Sawle was stilled, her thin features were pinched and anxious, while the Sparkes forwent their usual game of chequers and sat talking in low voices, Will the rumour-monger without much heart now for his hobby. 'Have the rebels crossed the Tamar?' This was, I think, the thought in all our minds, and while Mary, Alice, and Joan worked at their tapestry, and I read in a soft voice to Dick, my brain was busy all the while reckoning the shortest distance that the enemy would take, and whether they would cross by Saltash or by Gunnislake. John had left the dining-chamber as soon as the King's health had been drunk, saying he could stand this waiting about no longer, but must ride to Fowey for news. He returned about nine o'clock, saying that the town was well-nigh empty, with so many ridden to north to join the army, but that those who were left were standing at their doors, glum and despondent, saying that word had come that Grenvile and his troops had been defeated at New-bridge below Gunnislake, while Essex and some ten thousand men were riding towards Launceston. I remember Will Sparke leaping to his feet at hearing this, and breaking out into a tirade against Richard, his shrill voice sharp and nervous. 'What have I been saying all along?' he cried. 'When it comes to a test like this, the fellow is no commander. The pass at Gunnislake should be easy to defend, no matter the strength of the op-ponent, and here is Grenvile pulled out and in full retreat with-out having struck a blow to defend Cornwall. Heaven, what a contrast to his brother.'

'It is only rumour, cousin Will,' said John with an uncom-fortable glance in my direction. 'There was no one in Fowey able to swear to the truth of it.'

'I tell you, everything is lost,' said Will. 'Cornwall will be ruined and overrun, even as Sir Francis Bassett said the other day. And if it is so, then Richard Grenvile will be to blame for it.'

I watched young Dick swallow the words with eager eyes, and, pulling at my arm, he whispered, 'What is it he says? What has happened?'

'John Rashleigh hears that the Earl of Essex has passed into Cornwall,' I told him softly, 'finding little opposition. We must wait until the tale is verified.'

'Then my father has been slain in battle?'

'No, Dick. Nothing has been said of that. Do you wish me to continue reading?'

'Yes, please, if you will do so.'

And I went on with the tale, taking no notice of his biting of his hand, for my anxiety was such that I could have done the same myself. Anything might have happened during these past forty-eight hours. Richard left for slain upon the steep road down from Gunnislake and his men fled in all directions, or taken prisoner perhaps and at this moment being put to torture in Launceston Castle that he might betray the plan of battle. It was always my fault to let imagination do its worst, and although I guessed enough of Richard's strategy to know that a retreat on the Tamar bank was probably his intention from the first, in order to lure Essex into Cornwall, yet I longed to hear the opposite, and that a victory had been gained that day and the rebels pushed back into Devon.

I slept but ill that night, for to be ignorant of the truth is, I shall always believe, the worst sort of mental torture, and to a powerless woman, who cannot forget her fears in taking action, there is no remedy. The next day was as hot and airless as the one preceding, and when I came down after breakfast I wondered if I looked as haggard and careworn to the rest of the company as they looked to me. And still no news. Everything was strangely silent – even the jackdaws who usually clustered in the trees down in the warren had flown and settled elsewhere. Shortly before noon, when some of us were assembled in the dining-chamber to take cold meat, Mary, coming from her sun parlour across the hall, cried, 'There is a horseman riding through the park towards the house.' Everyone began talking at once and pushing to the windows, and John, something white about the lips, went to the courtyard to receive whomever it should be.

The rider clattered into the inner court, with all of us watching from the windows, and though he was covered from head to foot with dust, and had a great slash across his boot, I recognized him as young Joe Grenvile.

'I have a message for Mistress Harris,' he said, flinging himself from his horse. My throat went dry, and my hands wet. He is dead, I thought, for certain.

'But the battle? How goes the battle?' and 'What of the rebels?' 'What has happened?' Questions on all sides were put to him, with Nick Sawle on one side, and Will Sparke on the other, so that he had to push his way through them to reach me in the hall.

'Essex will be in Bodmin by nightfall,' he said briefly. 'We have just had a brush above Lostwithiel with Lord Robartes and his brigade, who have now turned back to meet him. We ourselves are in hot retreat to Truro, where Sir Richard plans to raise more troops. I am come from the road but to bring this message to Mistress Harris.'

'Essex at Bodmin?' A cry of alarm went up from all the company, and Temperance Sawle went straightway on her knees and called upon her Maker. But I was busy tearing open Richard's letter.

'My sweet love,' I read, 'the hook is nicely baited, and the poor misguided fish gapes at it with his mouth wide open. He will be in Bodmin at night, and most probably in Fowey tomorrow. His chief adviser in the business is that crass idiot, Jack Robartes, whose mansion at Lanhydrock I have just had infinite pleasure in pillaging. They will swallow the bait hook, line, and sinker. We shall come up on them from Truro, and His Majesty, Maurice, and Ralph Hopton from the east. The King has already advanced as far as Tavistock, so the fish will be most prettily landed. Your immediate future at Menabilly being somewhat unpleasant, it will be best if you return the whelp to me, with his tutor. I have given Joe instructions on the matter. Keep to your chamber, my dear love, and have no fear. We will come to your succour as soon as may be. My respects to your sister and the company.

Your devoted servant
Richard Grenvile

I placed the letter in my gown, and turned to Joe.

'Is the General well?' I asked.

'Never better,' he grinned. 'I have just left him eating roast pork on the road to Grampound, while his servant cleaned his boots. We seized a score of pigs from Lord Robartes's park, and a herd of sheep, and some twenty head of cattle – the troops are in high fettle. If you hear rumours of our losses at Newbridge, pay no attention to them; the higher the figure they are put at by the enemy, the better pleased will be Sir Richard.'

I motioned then that I would like to speak with him apart, and he withdrew alone with me to the sun-parlour.

'What is the plan for Dick?' I asked.

'Sir Richard thinks it best if the boy and Mr Ashley embark by fishing-boat for St Mawes, if arrangements can be made with one of the fellows at Polkerris. They can keep close inshore, and once around the Dodman the passage will not be long. I have money here to pay the fishermen, and pay them well, for their trouble.'

'When should they depart?'

'As soon as possible. I will see to it, and go with them to the beach. Then I shall return to join Sir Richard, and with any luck catch up with him on the Grampound-Truro road. The trouble is that the roads are already choked with people in headlong flight from Essex, all making for the west, and it will not be long now before the rebel cavalry reach the district.'

'There is, then, no time to lose,' I answered. 'I will ask Mr John Rashleigh to go with you to Polkerris – he will know the men there who are most likely to be trusted.'

I called John to come to me, and hurriedly explained the plan, whereupon he set forth straightway to Polkerris with Joe Grenvile, while I sent word to Herbert Ashley that I wished to speak to him. He arrived looking very white about the gills, for rumour had run riot in the place that the Grenvile troops were flying in disorder with the rebels on their heels and the war was irrevocably lost. He looked much relieved when I told him that he and Dick were to depart upon the instant, by sea and not by road, and went immediately to pack their things, promising to be ready within the hour. The task then fell upon me to break the news to my shadow. He was standing by the side-door, looking out on to the garden, and I beckoned him to my side.

'Dick,' I said to him, 'I want you to be brave and sensible. The neighbourhood is likely to be surrounded by the enemy before another day, and Menabilly will be seized. Your father thinks it better you should not be found here, and I have arranged, therefore, with Mr Rashleigh, that you and your tutor should go by boat to St Mawes, where you will be safe.'

'Are you coming too?' he asked.

'No, Dick. This is a very sudden plan, made only for yourselves. I, and the rest of the company, will remain at Menabilly.'

'Then so will I.'

'No, Dick. You must let me judge for you. And it is best for you to go.'

'Does it mean that I must join my father?'

'That I cannot tell. All I know is that the fishing-boat is to take you to St Mawes.'

He said nothing, but looked queerly sulky and strange, and after a moment or two went up to join his tutor.

I had a pain at the pit of my stomach all the while, for there is nothing so contagious as panic, and the atmosphere of sharp anxiety was rife in the air. In the gallery little groups of people were gathered, all with strained eyes and drawn faces, and Alice's children, aware of tension, chose – poor dears – this moment to be fretful, and were clinging to her skirts crying bitterly.

'There is time yet to reach Truro if only we had conveyance,' I heard Will say, his face grey with fear, 'but Jonathan took all the horses with him, and the farm wagons would be too slow. Where has John gone? Is it not possible for him to arrange in some manner that we be conducted to Truro?'

His sisters watched him with anxious eyes, and I saw Gillian whisper hurriedly to Deborah that none of their things were ready and it would take her till evening to sort out what was necessary for travel. Then Nick Sawle, drawing himself up proudly, said in a loud voice: 'My wife and I propose to stay at Menabilly. If cowards care to clatter on the roads as fugitives, they are welcome to do so, but I find it a poor return to our Cousin Jonathan to desert his house like rats in a time of trouble.'

My sister Mary looked towards me in distress

'What do you counsel, Honor?' she said. 'Should we set forth, or should we stay? Jonathan gave me no commands. He assured me that the enemy would not cross the Tamar, or, at the worst, be turned back after a few miles.'

'My God,' I said, 'if you care to hide in the ditches with the driven cattle, then by all means go, but I swear you will fare worse upon the road than you are likely to do at home. Better to starve under your own roof than in the hedges.'

'We have plenty of provisions,' said Mary, snatching a ray of hope. 'We are not likely to want for anything, unless the siege be long.' She turned in consultation to her stepdaughters, who were all of them still occupied in calming the children, and I thought it wisest not to spread further consternation by telling her that once the rebels held the house they would make short work of her provisions.

The clock in the belfry had just struck three when Dick and his tutor came down ready for departure. The lad was still sulky, and turned his head from me when I would say goodbye. This was better than the rebellious tears I had expected, and with a cheerful voice I wished him a speedy journey, and assured him that a week or less would see the end of all our troubles. He did not answer, and I signed to Herbert Ashley to take his arm and to start walking across the park with Frank Penrose, who would conduct them to Polkerris, and there fall in with John Rashleigh and Joe Grenvile, who must by this time have matters well arranged.

Anxiety and strain had brought an aching back upon me, and I desired nothing so much as to retire to the gate-house and lie upon my bed. I sent for Matty, and she, with the help of Joan and Alice, carried me upstairs. The sun was coming strongly through my western casement, and the room was hot and airless. I lay upon my bed, sticky wet, wishing with all my heart that I were a man and could ride with Joe Grenvile on the road to Truro, instead of lying there, a woman and a cripple, waiting for the relentless tramp of enemy feet. I had been there but an hour, I suppose, snatching brief oblivion, when I heard once more the sound of a horse galloping across the park, and, calling to Matty, I inquired who it should be. She went to the casement and looked out.

'It's Mr John,' she said, 'in great distress by his expression. Something has gone amiss.' My heart sank at her words. Perhaps, after all, the fishermen at Polkerris could not be tempted to set sail. In a moment or two I heard his footstep on the stairs and he flung into my room, forgetting even to knock upon the door.

'We have lost Dick,' he said. 'He has vanished, and is nowhere to be found.' He stood staring at me, the sweat pouring down his face, and I could see that his whole frame was trembling.

'What do you mean? What has happened?' I asked swiftly, raising myself in my bed.

'We were all assembled on the beach,' he said, his breath coming quickly, 'and the boat was launched. There was a little cuddy below deck, and with my own eyes I saw Dick descend to it, his bundle under his arm. There was no trouble to engage the boat, and the men – both of them stout fellows, well known to me – were willing. Just before they drew anchor we heard a clatter on the cobbles beside the cottages, and some lads came running down in great alarm to tell us that the first body of rebel horse had cut the road from Castledore to Tywardreath, and that Polmear Hill was already blocked with troops. At this the men began to make sail, and young Joe Grenvile turned to me with a wink and said, 'It looks as if I must go by water too.' Before I could answer him, he had urged his horse into the sea and was making for the sand flats half a mile away to the westward. It was half tide, but he had reached them, and turned in his saddle to wave to us, within five and twenty minutes. He'll be on Gosmoor by now, and halfway to St Austell.'

'But Dick?' I said. 'You say you have lost Dick?'

'He was in the boat,' he said stubbornly. 'I swear he was in the boat. But we turned to listen to the lads and their tale of the troops at Tywardreath, and then with one accord we watched young Joe put his horse to the water and swim for it. By heaven, Honor, it was the boldest thing I have ever seen a youngster do, for the tide can run swiftly between Polkerris and the flats. And then Ashley the tutor, looking about him, called for Dick, but could not find him. We searched the vessel from stem to stern, but he wasn't there. He was not on the beach. He was not anywhere. For God's sake, Honor, what are we to do now?'

I felt as helpless as he did, and sick with anxiety, for here was I having failed utterly in my trust, and the rebel troops were not two miles away.

'Where is the boat now?' I asked.

'Lying off the Gribben, waiting for a signal from me,' said John, 'with that useless tutor aboard, with no other thought in his mind but getting to St Mawes. But even if we find the boy, Honor, I fear it will be too late.'

'Search the cliffs in all directions,' I said, 'and the grounds, and the park and pasture. Was anything said to the lad upon the way?'

'I cannot say. I think not. I only heard Frank Penrose tell him that by nightfall he would be with his father.'

So that was it, I thought. A moment's indiscretion, but enough to turn Dick from his journey, and make him play truant like a child from school. I could do nothing in the search, but bade John set forth once more with Frank Penrose, saying no word to anyone of what had happened. And, calling to Matty, I bade her take me to the causeway.

Chapter 15

ONCE on the high ground, I had as good a view of the surrounding country as I could wish, and I saw Frank Penrose and John Rashleigh strike out across the park to the beacon fields, and then divide. All the while I had a fear in my heart that the boy had drowned himself, and would be found with the rising tide floating face downwards in the wash below Polkerris cliffs. There was no sign of the boat, and I judged it to be to the westward, beyond Polkerris and the Gribben.

Back and forth we went along the causeway, with Matty pushing my chair, and still no sign of a living soul, nothing but the cattle grazing on the farther hills, and the ripple of a breeze blowing the corn upon the skyline.

Presently I sent Matty within doors for a cloak, for the breeze was freshening, and on her return she told me that stragglers, were already pouring into the park from the roads, women, and children, and old men, all with makeshift bundles on their backs, begging for shelter, for the route was cut to Truro and the rebels were everywhere. My sister Mary was at her wits' ends to know what to say to them, and many of them were already kindling fires down in the Warren and making rough shelter for the night.

'As I came out just now,' said Matty, 'a litter borne by four horses came to rest in the courtyard, and a lady within demanded harbourage for herself and her young daughters. I heard the servant say they had been nine hours upon the road.'

I thanked God in my heart that we had remained at Menabilly and not lost our heads like these other poor unfortunates.

'Go back, Matty,' I said, 'and see what you can do to help my sister. None of the servants have any sense left in their heads.'

She had not been gone more than ten minutes before I saw two figures coming across the fields towards me. One of them, seeing me upon the causeway, waved his arm, while with the other he held fast to his companion.

It was John Rashleigh, and he had Dick with him.

When they reached me I saw the boy was dripping wet, and scratched about the face and hands by brambles, but for once he was not bothered by the sight of blood, but stared at me defiantly.

'I will not go,' he said. 'You cannot make me go.'

John Rashleigh shook his head at me, and shrugged his shoulders in resignation. 'It's no use, Honor,' he said. 'We shall have to keep him. There's a wash on the beaches now, and I've signalled to the boat to make sail and take the tutor across the bay to Mevagissey or Gorrau, where he must make shift for himself. As for this lad, I found him halfway up the cliff, a mile from Polkerris – he had been waist-deep in water for the past three hours. God only knows what Sir Richard will say to the bungle we have made.'

'Never mind Sir Richard. I will take care of him,' I said, 'when – and if – we ever clap eyes on him again. That boy must return to the house with me and be shifted into dry clothes before anything else is done with him.'

Now, the causeway at Menabilly is set high, as I have said, commanding a fine view both to east and to west, and at this moment, I know not why, I turned my head towards the coast road that descended down to Pridmouth from Coombe and Fowey, and I saw, silhouetted on the skyline above the valley, a single horseman. In a moment he was joined by others, who paused an instant on the hill, and then, following their leader, plunged down the narrow roadway to the cove. John saw them too, for our eyes met, and we looked at one another long and silently, while Dick stood between us, his eyes downcast, his teeth chattering.

Richard in the old days was wont to tease me for my south-coast blood, so sluggish, he averred, compared with that which ran through his own north-coast veins, but I swear I thought, in the next few seconds, as rapidly as he had ever done or was likely yet to do.

'Have you your father's keys?' I said to John.

'Yes,' he said.

'All of them?'

'All of them.'

'On your person now?'

'Yes.'

'Then open the door of the summer-house.'

He obeyed me without question – thank God his stern father had taught him discipline – and in an instant we stood at the threshold with the door flung open.

'Lift the mat from beneath the desk there,' I said, 'and raise the flagstone.' He looked at me then in wonder, but went without a word to do as I had bidden him. In a moment the mat was lifted, and the flagstone too and the flight of steps betrayed to view. 'Don't ask me any questions, John,' I said. 'There is no time. A passage runs underground from those steps to the house. Take Dick with you now, first replacing the flagstone above your heads, and crawl with him along the passage to the further end. You will come to a small room, like a cell, and another flight of steps. At the top of the steps is a door, which opens, I believe, from the passage end. But do not try to open it until I give you warning from the house.'

I could read the sense of what I said go slowly to his mind, and a dawn of comprehension come into his eyes.

'The chamber next to yours?' he said. 'My uncle John?'

'Yes,' I said. 'Give me the keys. Go quickly.'

There was no trouble now with Dick. He had gathered from my manner that danger was deadly near and the time for truancy over. He bolted down into the hole like a frightened rabbit. I watched John settle the mat over the flagstone, and then, descending after Dick he lowered the stone above his head and disappeared. The summer-house was as it had been, empty, and untouched. I leant over in my chair and turned the key in the lock, and then put the keys inside my gown. I looked out to the eastward and saw that the skyline was empty. The troopers would have reached the cove by now, and, after they had watered their horses at the mill, would climb up the further side and be at Menabilly within ten minutes. The sweat was running down my forehead clammy cold, and as I waited for Matty to fetch me – and God only knew how much longer she would be – I thought how I would give all I possessed in the world at that moment for one good swig of brandy.

Far out on the beacon hills I could see Frank Penrose still searching hopelessly for Dick, while in the meadows to the west one of the women from the farm went calling to the cows, all oblivious of the troopers who were riding up the lane.

And at that moment my godchild Joan came hurrying along the causeway to fetch me, her pretty face all strained and anxious, her soft dark hair blowing in the wind.

'They are coming,' she said. 'We have seen them from the windows. Scores of them, on horseback, riding now across the park.'

Her breath caught in a sob, and she began running with me

along the causeway, so that I too was caught in a sudden panic and could think of nothing but the wide door of Menabilly still open to enfold me. 'I have searched everywhere for John,' she faltered, 'but I cannot find him. One of the servants said they saw him walking out towards the Gribben. Oh, Honor – the children – what will become of us? What is going to happen?'

I could hear shouting from the park, and out on the hard ground beyond the gates came the steady rhythmic beat of horses trotting; not the light clatter of a company, but line upon line of them, the relentless measure of a regiment, the jingle of harness, the thin alien sound of a bugle.

They were waiting for us by the windows of the gallery, Alice, and Mary, the Sawles, the Sparkes, a little tremulous gathering of frightened people, united now in danger, and two other faces that I did not know, the peaky, startled faces of strange children with lace caps upon their heads and wide lace collars. I remembered then the unknown lady who had flung herself upon my sister's mercy, and as we turned into the hall, slamming the door behind us, I saw the horses that had drawn the litter still standing untended in the courtyard, save that the grooms had thrown blankets upon them, coloured white and crimson, and stamped at the corners with a dragon's head. A dragon's head ... but even as my memory swung back into the past I heard her voice, cold and clear, rising above the others in the gallery. 'If only it can be Lord Robartes, I can assure you all no harm will come to us. I have known him well these many years, and am quite prepared to speak on your behalf.'

'I forgot to tell you,' whispered Joan. 'She came with her two daughters, scarce an hour ago. The road was held, and they could not pass St Blazey. It is Mrs Denys of Orley Court.'

Her eyes swung round to me. Those same eyes, narrow, heavy-lidded, that I had seen often in my more troubled dreams, and her gold hair, golder than it had been in the past, for art had taken counsel with Nature and outstripped it. She stared at the sight of me, and for a second I caught a flash of odd discomfort like a flicker in her eyes, and then she smiled her slow, false, well-remembered smile, and, stretching out her hands, she said, 'Why, Honor this is indeed a pleasure. Mary did not tell me that you too were here at Menabilly.'

I ignored the proffered hand, for a cripple in a chair can be as ill-mannered as she pleases, and as I stared back at her in my own fashion, with suspicion and foreboding in my heart, we heard the horses ride into the courtyard and the bugles blow. Poor Temperance Sawle went down upon her knees, the children whimpered, and my sister Mary, with her arm about Joan and Alice, stood very white and still. Only Gartred watched with cool eyes, her hands playing gently with her girdle.

'Pray hard and pray fast, Mrs Sawle,' I said. 'The vultures are gathering.'

And, since there was no brandy in the room, I poured myself some water from a jug, and raised my glass to Gartred.

Chapter 16

IT was Will Sparke, I remember, who went to unbar the door – though he had been the first to bolt it earlier – and as he did so he excused himself in his high-pitched, shaking voice, saying, 'It is useless to start by offending them. Our only hope lies in placating them.'

We could see through the windows how the troopers dismounted, staring about them with confident, hard faces beneath their close-fitting skull helmets, and it seemed to me that one and all they looked the same, with their cropped heads and their drab brown leather jerkins, and this ruthless similarity was both startling and grim. There were more of them on the eastward side now, in the gardens, the horses' hoofs trampling the green lawns and the little yew trees as a first symbol of destruction, and all the while the thin, high note of the bugle sounded, like a huntsman summoning his hounds to slaughter. In a moment we heard their heavy footsteps in the house, clamping through the dining-chamber and up the stairs, and into the gallery returned Will Sparke, a nervous smile on his face, which was drained of all colour. Behind him came three officers, the first a big, burly man with a long nose and heavy jaw, wearing a green sash about his waist. I recognized him at once as Lord Robartes, the owner of Lanhydrock, a big estate on the Bodmin road, who in former days had gone riding and hawking with my brother Kit, but was not much known to the rest of us. He was now our enemy, and could dispose of us as he wished. 'Where is the owner of the house?' he asked, and looked towards old Nick Sawle, who turned his back.

'My husband is from home,' said Mary, coming forward, 'and my stepson somewhere in the grounds.'

'Is everyone living in the place assembled here?'

'All except the servants.'

'You have no malignants in hiding?'

'None.'

Lord Robartes turned to the staff officer at his side.

'Make a thorough search of the house and grounds,' he said. 'Break down any door you find locked, and test the panelling for places of concealment. Give orders to the farm-people to round up all sheep and cattle and other livestock, and place men in charge of them, and the granaries. We will take over this gallery and all other rooms on the ground-floor for our personal use. Troops to bivouac in the park.'

'Very good, sir.' The officer stood to attention, and then departed about his business. Lord Robartes drew up a chair to the table and the remaining officer gave him paper and a quill.

'Now, madam,' he said to Mary, 'give me your full name and the name and occupation of each member of your household.'

One by one he had us documented, looking at each victim keenly as though the very admission of name and age betrayed some sign of guilt. Only when he came to Gartred did his manner relax something of its hard suspicion. 'A foolish time to journey, Mrs Denys,' he said. 'You would have done better to remain at Orley Court.'

'There are so many soldiery abroad of little discipline and small respect,' said Gartred languidly. 'It is not very pleasant for a widow with young daughters to live alone, as I do. I hoped by travelling south to escape the fighting.'

'You thought wrong,' he answered, 'and I am afraid you must abide by the consequences of such an error. You will have to remain here in custody with Mrs Rashleigh and her household.'

Gartred bowed, and did not answer. Lord Robartes rose to his feet. 'When the apartments above have been searched you may go to them,' he said, addressing Mary and the rest of us, 'and I must request you to remain in them until further orders. Exercise once a day will be permitted in the garden here, under close escort. You must prepare your food as, and how, you are able. We shall take command of the kitchens, and certain stores will be allotted to you. Your keys, madam.'

I saw Mary falter, and then, slowly and reluctantly, she unfastened the string from her girdle. 'Can I not have entry there myself?' she asked. 'No, madam. The stores are no longer yours, but the possession of the Parliament, like everything pertaining to this estate.'

I thought of the jars of preserves upon Mary's shelves, the honeys, and the jams, and the salted pilchards in the larder, and the smoked hams, and the sides of salted mutton. I thought of the bread in the bakeries, the flour in the bins, the grain in the granaries, the young fruit setting in the orchards. And all the while I thought of this, the sound of heavy feet came tramping from above, and out in the grounds came the bugle's cry.

'I thank you, madam. I must warn you, and the rest of the company, that any attempt at escape, any contravention of my orders, will be punished with extreme severity.'

'What about milk for the children?' said Joan, her cheeks very flushed, her head high. 'We must have milk, and butter, and eggs. My little son is delicate, and inclined to croup.'

'Certain stores will be given you daily, madam – I have already said so,' said Lord Robartes. 'If the children need more nourishment, you must do without yourselves. I have some five hundred men to quarter here, and their needs come before yours, or your children's. Now you may go to your apartments.'

This was the moment I had waited for, and, catching Joan's eye, I summoned her to my side. 'You must give up your apartment to Mrs Denys,' I murmured, 'and come to me in the gatehouse. I shall move my bed into the adjoining chamber.' Her lips framed a question, but I shook my head. She had sense enough to accept it, for all her agitation, and went at once to

Mary with the proposition, who was so bewildered by the loss of her keys that her natural hospitality had deserted her.

'I beg of you to make no move because of me,' said Gartred, smiling, her arms about her children. 'May and Gertie and I can fit in anywhere. The house is something like a warren – I remember it of old.'

I looked at her thoughtfully, and remembered then how Kit had been at Oxford at the same time as my brother-in-law, when old Mr Rashleigh was still alive, and that during the days of Jonathan's first marriage Kit had ridden over to Menabilly often from Lanrest.

'You have been here before then?' I said to Gartred, speaking to her for the first time since I had come into the gallery.

'Why, bless me, yes,' she yawned. 'Some five-and-twenty years ago Kit and I came for a harvest supper, and lost ourselves about the passages.' But at this moment Lord Robartes, who had been conferring with his officer, turned from the door.

'You will now, please,' he said, 'retire to your apartments.'

We went out the farther door, where the servants were huddled like a flock of startled sheep, and Matty and two others seized the arms of my chair. Already the troopers were in the kitchens, in full command, and the round of beef that had been roasting for our dinner was being cut into great slices and served out amongst them, while down the stairs came three more of them, two fellows and a non-commissioned officer, bearing loads of Mary's precious stores in their arms.

Another had a great pile of blankets, and a rich embroidered cover that had been put aside until winter in the linen room.

'Oh, but they cannot have that,' said Mary. 'Where is an officer? I must speak to someone of authority.'

'I have authority', replied the sergeant, 'to remove all linen, blankets, and covers that we find. So keep a cool temper, lady, for you'll find no redress.' They stared us coolly in the face, and one of them favoured Alice with a bold, familiar stare, and then whispered something in the ear of his companion.

Oh, God, how I hated them upon the instant. I, who had regarded the war with irony and cynicism hitherto, and a bitter shrug of the shoulder, was now filled with burning anger when it touched me close. Their muddied boots had trampled the floors, and upstairs wanton damage could at once be seen where they had thrust their pikes into the panelling and stripped the hangings from the walls. In Alice's apartments the presses had been overturned and the contents spilled upon the floor, and already a broken casement hung upon its hinge with the glass shattered. Alice's nurse was standing in the centre of the room, crying and wringing her hands, for the troopers had carried off some of the children's bedding, and one clumsy oaf had trodden his heel upon the children's favourite doll and smashed its head to pieces. At the sight of this, their precious toy, the little girls burst into torrents of crying, and I knew then the idiot rage that surges within a man in wartime and compels him to commit murder. In the gardens the troopers were tramping down the formal beds, and with their horses had flattened the growing flowers, whose strewn petals lay crumpled now and muddied by the horses' hoofs.

I took one glance, and then bade Matty and her companions bear me to my room. It had suffered like disturbance, with the bed tumbled and the stuffing ripped from the chairs for no rhyme or reason, and they had saved me the trouble of unlocking the barred chamber, for the door was broken in and pieces of planking strewn about the floor. The arras was torn in places, but the arras that hung before the buttress was still and undisturbed.

I thanked God in my heart for the cunning of old John Rashleigh, and desiring Matty to set me down beside the window I looked out into the courtyard, and saw the soldiers all gathered below, line upon line of them, with their horses tethered, and the tents gleaming white already in process of erection in the park, with the camp-fires burning, and the cattle lowing as they were driven by the soldiers to a pen, and all the while that God-damned bugle blowing, high-pitched and insistent, in a single key. I turned from the window, and told Matty that Joan and her children would now be coming to the gate-house, and I would remain here, in the chamber that had been barred.

'The troopers have made short work of mystery,' said Matty, looking about her, and at the broken door. 'There was nothing put away here after all, then.' I did not answer, and while she busied herself with moving my bed and my own belongings I wheeled myself to the cabinet and saw that Jonathan had taken the precaution of removing his papers before he went, leaving the cabinet bare.

When the two rooms were in order, and the servants had helped Matty to repair the door, thus giving me my privacy from Joan, I sent them from me to give assistance to Joan in making place for Gartred in the southern front. All was now quiet, save for the constant tramping of soldiers in the court below, and the coming and going beneath me in the kitchens. Very cautiously I drew near the north-east corner of my new apartment, and lifted the arras. I ran my hands over the stone wall, as I had done that time before in the darkness when Jonathan had discovered me, and once again I could find no outlet, no division in the stone.

I realized then that the means for entry must be from without only, a great handicap to us, who used it now, but no doubt cunningly intended by the builder of the house, who had no desire for his idiot eldest son to come and go at pleasure. I knocked with my fists against the wall, but they sounded not at all. I called 'John' in a low voice, expecting no answer; nor did I receive one.

This, then, was a new and hideous dilemma, for I had warned John not to attempt an entry to the chamber before I warned him, since I was confident at the time that I would be able to find the entrance from inside. This I could not do, and John and Dick were in the meantime waiting in the cell below the buttress for a signal from me. I placed my face against the wall, crying 'John ... John ...' as loudly as I dared, but I guessed, with failing heart, that the sound of my voice would never carry through the implacable stone. Hearing footsteps in the corridor I let the arras fall and returned to the window, where I made a pretence of looking down into the court. I heard movements in my old apartment in the gate-house, and a moment later a loud knocking on the door between. 'Please enter,' I called, and the roughly-repaired door was pushed aside, tottering on its hinge, and Lord Robartes himself came into the room, accompanied by one of his officers and Frank Penrose with his arms bound tight behind him.

'I regret my sudden intrusion,' said Lord Robartes, 'but we have just found this man in the grounds. He volunteered information I find interesting, which you may add to, if you please.'

I glanced at Frank Penrose, who, half frightened out of his wits, stared about him like a hare, passing his tongue over his lips.

I did not answer, but waited for Lord Robartes to continue.

'It seems you have had living here, until today, the son of Skellum Grenvile,' he said, watching me intently, 'as well as his tutor. They were to have left by fishing-boat for St Mawes a few hours since. You were the boy's godmother and had the care of him, I understand. Where are they now?'

'Somewhere off the Dodman, I hope,' I answered.

'I am told that as the boat set sail from Polkerris the boy could not be found,' he replied, 'and Penrose here and John Rashleigh went in search of him. My men have not yet come upon John Rashleigh or the boy. Do you know what has become of them.'

'I do not,' I answered. 'I only trust they are aboard the boat.'

'You realize', he said harshly, 'that there is a heavy price upon the head of Skellum Grenvile, and to harbour him or any of his family would count as treason to Parliament. The Earl of Essex has given me strict orders as to this.'

'That being the case,' I said, 'you had better take Mrs Denys into closer custody. She is Sir Richard's sister, as you no doubt know.'

I had caught him off guard with this, and he looked at me nonplussed. Then he began tapping on the table in sudden irritation. 'Mrs Denys has, I understand, little or no friendship with her brother,' he said stiffly. 'Her late husband, Mr Antony Denys, was known to be a good friend to Parliament and an opposer of Charles Stuart. Have you nothing further to tell me about your godson?'

'Nothing at all,' I said, 'except that I have every belief that he is upon that fishing-boat, and with the wind in the right quarter he will be, by this time, nearly halfway to St Mawes.'

He turned his back on me at that and left the room, with the luckless Frank Penrose shuffling at his heels, and I realized, with relief, that the agent was ignorant as to Dick's whereabouts, like everybody else in Menabilly, and for all he knew my tale might be quite true and both Dick and John some ten miles out at sea. Not one soul, then, in the place knew the secret of the buttress but myself, for Langdon the steward had accompanied my brother-in-law to Launceston. This was a great advantage, making betrayal an impossibility. But I still could not solve the problem of how to get food and drink and reassurance to the two fugitives I had myself imprisoned. And another fear began to nag at me, with recollection of brother-in-law's words: 'Lack of air and close confinement soon rendered him unconscious and easy to handle.' Uncle John, gasping for breath in the little cell beneath the buttress. How much air, then, came through to the cell from the tunnel beyond? *Enough for how many hours?*

Once again, as earlier in the day, the sweat began to trickle down my face, and half-unconsciously I wiped it away with my hand. I felt myself defeated. There was no course for me to take. A little bustle from the adjoining room, and a child's cry, told me that Joan and her babies had come to my old apartment, and in a moment she came through, with little Mary whimpering in her arms and small Jonathan clinging to her skirts.

'Why did you move, Honor dear?' she said. 'There was no need.' And like Matty she gazed about the room in curiosity. 'It is very plain and bare,' she added; 'nothing valuable at all. I am much relieved, for those brutes would have got it. Come back in your own chamber, Honor, if you can bear with the babies.'

'No,' I said. 'I am well enough.'

'You look so tired and drawn,' she said, 'but I dare swear I do the same. I feel I have aged ten years these last two hours. What will they do to us?'

'Nothing,' I said, 'if we keep to our rooms.'

'If only John would return,' she said, tears rising to her eyes. 'Supposing he has had some skirmish on the road, and has been hurt? I cannot understand what can have become of him.'

The children began to whimper, hearing the anxiety in her voice, and then Matty, who loved children, came and coaxed the baby, and proceeded to undress her for her cot, while little Jonathan, with a small boy's sharp nervous way, began to plague us all with questions: Why did they come to their Aunt Honor's room? And who were all the soldiers? And how long would they stay?

The hours wore on with horrid dragging tedium, and the sun began to sink behind the trees at the far end of the park, while the air was thick with smoke from the fires lit by the troopers.

All the time there was tramping below, and orders called, and the pacing to and fro of horses, with the insistent bugle sometimes far distant in the park, echoed by a fellow bugle, and sometimes directly beneath the windows. The children were restless, turning continually in their cots and calling for either Matty or their mother, and when Joan was not hushing them she was gazing from my window, reporting fresh actions of destruction, her cheeks aflame with indignation. 'They have rounded up all the cattle from the beef park and the beacon fields, and driven them into the park here, with a pen about them,' she said, 'and they are dividing up the steers now into another pen.' Suddenly she gave a little cry of dismay. 'They have slaughtered three of them,' she said. 'The men are quartering them already by the fires. Now they are driving the sheep.' We could hear the anxious baaing of the ewes to the sturdy lambs, and the lowing of the cattle. I thought of the five hundred men encamped there in the park, and the many hundreds more between us and Lostwithiel, and how they and their horses must be fed, but I said nothing. Joan shut the window, for the smoke from the camp-fires blew thick about the room and the noise of the men shouting and calling orders made a vile and sickening clamour. The sun set in a dull crimson sky, and the shadows lengthened.

About half past eight Matty brought us a small portion of a pie upon one plate, with a carafe of water. Her lips were grimly set.

'This for the two of you,' she said. 'Mrs Rashleigh and Lady Courtney fare no better. Lady Courtney is making a little broth for the children's breakfast, in case they give us no eggs.'

Joan ate my piece of pie as well as hers, for I had no appetite.

I could think of one thing only, and that was that it was now nearly five hours since her husband and Richard's son had lain hidden in the buttress. Matty brought candles, and presently Alice and Mary came to say good night, poor Mary looking suddenly like an old woman from anxiety and shock, with great shadows under her eyes.

'They're axing the trees in the orchard,' she said. 'I saw them myself, sawing the branches, and stripping the young fruit that has scarce formed. I sent down a message to Lord Robartes, but he returned no answer. The servants have been told by the soldiers that tomorrow they are going to cut the corn, strip all the barley from Eighteen Acres, and the wheat from the Great Meadow. And it wants three weeks to harvest.'

The tears began to course down her cheeks, and she turned to Joan.

'Why does John not come?' she said in useless reproach. 'Why is he not here to stand up for his father's home?'

'If John was here he could do nothing,' I said swiftly before Joan could lash back in anger. 'Don't you understand, Mary, that this is war? This is what has been happening all over England, and we in Cornwall are having our first taste of it.'

Even as I spoke there came a great burst of laughter from the courtyard, and a tongue of flame shot up to the windows. The troopers were roasting an ox in the clearing above the Warren, and because they were too idle to search for firewood they had broken down the doors from the dairy and the bakery, and were piling them upon the fire.

'There must have been thirty officers or more at dinner in the gallery,' said Alice quietly. 'We saw them from our windows afterwards walk up and down the terrace before the house. One or two were Cornish – I remember meeting them before the war – but most of them were strangers.'

'They say the Earl of Essex is in Fowey,' said Joan, 'and has set up his headquarters at Place. Whether it is true or not I do not know.'

'The Treffrys will not suffer,' said Mary bitterly. 'They have too many relatives fighting for the rebels. You won't find Bridget has her stores pillaged, and her larders ransacked.'

'Come to bed, Mother,' said Alice gently. 'Honor is right – it does no good to worry. We have been spared so happily until now. If my father and Peter are safe somewhere, with the King's army, nothing else can matter.'

They went to their own apartments, and Joan to the children next door, while Matty – all oblivious of my own hidden fears – helped me undress for bed.

'There's one discovery I've made this night, anyway,' she said grimly, as she brushed my hair.

'What is that, Matty?'

'Mrs Denys hasn't lost her taste for gentlemen.'

I said nothing, waiting for what would follow.

'You and the others, and Mrs Sawle, and Mistress Sparke, had pie for your supper,' she said, 'but there was roast beef and burgundy taken up to Mrs Denys, and places set for two upon the tray. Her children were put together in the dressing-room, and had a chicken between them.'

I realized that Matty's partiality for eavesdropping and her nose for gossip might stand us in good stead in the immediate future.

'And who was the fortunate who dined with Mrs Denys?' I asked.

'Lord Robartes himself,' said Matty with sour triumph.

My first suspicion became a certainty. It was not mere chance that had so strangely brought Gartred to Menabilly after five-and-twenty years. She was here for a purpose.

'Lord Robartes is not an ill-looking man,' I said. 'I might invite him to share cold pie with me another evening.'

Matty snorted, and lifted me to bed. 'I'd like to see Sir Richard's face if you did,' she snapped.

'Sir Richard would not mind,' I answered. 'Not if there was something to be gained from it.'

I feigned a lightness I was far from feeling, and when she had blown the candles and was gone I lay back in my bed with my nerves tense and strained. The flames outside my window died away, and slowly the shouting and the laughter ceased, and the tramping of feet, and the movement of the horses, and the calling bugles. I heard the clock in the belfry strike ten, then eleven, and then midnight. The people within the house were

149

still and silent, and so was the alien enemy. At a quarter after midnight a dog howled in the far distance, and as though it were a signal I felt suddenly upon my cheek a current of cold chill air. I sat up in bed and waited. The draught continued, blowing straight from the torn arras on the wall. 'John,' I whispered, and 'John,' I whispered again. I heard a movement from behind the arras, like a scratching mouse. Slowly, stealthily, I saw the hand come from behind the arras, lifting it aside, and a figure step out, dropping on all fours and creeping to my bed. 'It is I, Honor,' I said, and the cold, froggy hand touched me, icy cold, and the hands clutched me and the dark figure climbed on to my bed, and lay trembling beside me.

It was Dick, the clothes still dank and chill upon him, and he began to weep, long and silently, from exhaustion and from fear.

I held him close, warming him as best I could, and when he was still I whispered, 'Where is John?'

'In the little room,' he said, 'below the steps. We sat there, waiting, hour after hour, and you did not come. I wanted to turn back, but Mr Rashleigh would not let me.' He began to sob again, and I drew the covers over his head.

'He has fainted, down there on the steps,' he said. 'He's lying there now, his head between his hands. I got hold of the long rope that hangs there, above the steps, and pulled at it, and the hinged stone gave way, and I came up into this room. I did not care – I could not stay there longer, Honor. It's black as pitch, and closer than a grave.' He was still trembling, his head buried in my shoulder. I went on lying there, wondering what to do, whether to summon Joan and thus betray the secret to another, or wait until Dick was calmer and then send him back there with a candle to John's aid. And as I waited, my heart thumping, my ears strained to all sounds, I heard from without the tiptoe of a footstep in the passage, the noise of the latch of the door gently lifted and then let fall again as the door was seen to be fastened, and a moment's pause; then the footsteps tiptoeing gently away once more, and the soft, departing rustle of a gown. Someone had crept to the chamber in the stillness of the night, and that someone was a woman.

I went on lying there with my arms wrapped close about the sleeping boy and the clock in the belfry struck one, then two, then three. . . .

Chapter 17

As the first grey chinks of light came through the casement I roused Dick, who lay sleeping with his head upon my shoulder like a baby, and when he had blinked a moment, and got his wits restored to him, I bade him light the candle and creep back again to the cell. The fear that gripped me was that lack of air had caused John to faint, and since he was by nature far from strong anything might have happened. Never, in all the fifteen years I had been crippled, had I so needed the use of my legs as now, but I was helpless. In a few moments Dick was back again, his little ghost's face looking more pallid than ever in the grey morning light. 'He is awake,' he said, 'but very ill, I think. Shaking all over, and seeming not to know what has been happening. His head is burning hot, but his limbs are cold.'

At least he was alive, and a wave of thankfulness swept over me. But from Dick's description I realized what had happened. The ague, that was his legacy from birth, had attacked John once again with its usual ferocity, and small wonder, after more than ten hours crouching beneath the buttress. I made up my mind swiftly. I bade Dick bring the chair beside my bed, and with his assistance I lowered myself into it. Then I went to the door communicating with the gate-house chamber, and very gently called for Matty. Joan answered sleepily, and one of the children stirred.

'It is nothing,' I said, 'it is only Matty that I want.'

In a moment or two she came from the little dressing-room, her round plain face yawning beneath her night-cap, and would have chided me for rising had I not placed my finger on my lips. The urgency of the situation was such that my promise to my brother-in-law must finally be broken, though little of it held as it was. And without Matty it would be impossible to act. She came in, then, her eyes round with wonder when she saw Dick. 'You love me, Matty, I believe,' I said to her. 'Now I ask you to prove that love as never before. This boy's safety and life is in our hands.' She nodded, saying nothing.

'Dick and Mr John have been hiding since last evening,' I said. 'There is a staircase and a little room built within the thickness of these walls. Mr John is ill. I want you to go to him and bring him here. Dick will show you the way.'

He pulled aside the arras, and now for the first time I saw how the entrance was effected. A block of stone, about four feet square, worked on a hinge, moved by a lever and a rope, if pulled from beneath the narrow stair. This gave an opening just wide enough for a man to crawl through. When it was shut the stone was so closely fitting that it was impossible to find it from within the chamber, nor could it be pushed open, for the lever held it. The little stairway, set inside the buttress, twisted steeply to the cell below, which had height enough for a man to stand upright. More I could not see, craning from my chair, save for a dark heap, that must be John, lying on the lower step.

There was something weird and fearful in the scene, with the grey light of morning coming through the casement, and Matty, a fantastic figure in her nightclothes and cap, edging her way through the gap in the buttress. As she disappeared with Dick I heard the first high call of the bugle from the park, and I knew that for the rebel army the day had now begun. Soon the soldiers within the house would also be astir, and we had little time in hand. It was, I believe, some fifteen minutes before they were all three within the chamber, though it seemed an hour, and in those fifteen minutes the daylight had filled the room and the troopers were moving in the courtyard down below. John was quite conscious, thank God, and his mind lucid, but he was trembling all over and in a high fever, fit for nothing but his own bed and his wife's care. We took rapid consultation, in which I held firmly to one thing, and that was that no further person, not even Joan his wife nor Mary his stepmother, should be told how he had come into the house, or that Dick was with us still.

John's story, then, was to be that the fishing-boat came in to one of the coves beneath the Gribben, where he put Dick aboard, and that on returning across the fields he had seen the arrival of the troopers, and hid until nightfall. But, his fever coming upon him, he decided to return, and therefore climbed in by the lead piping and the creeper that ran along the south front of the house outside his father's window. For corroboration of this John must go at once to his father's room, where his stepmother was sleeping, and waken her, and win her acceptance of the story. And this immediately, before the household were awake. It was like a nightmare to arrange, with Joan his wife in the adjoining chamber, through which he must pass to gain the southern portion of the house. For if he went by passage beneath the belfry he might risk encounter with the servants or the troopers. Matty went first, and since there was no question from Joan, or any movement from the children, we judged them to be sleeping, and poor John, his body on fire with fever, crept swiftly after her. I thought of the games of hide-and-seek I had played with my brothers and sisters at Lanrest as children, and how now that it was played in earnest there was no excitement but a sickening strain, which brought sweat to the forehead and a pain to the belly. When Matty returned, and reported John in safety in his father's rooms, the first stage of the proceeding was completed. The next I had to break to Dick with great misgiving and an assumption of sternness and authority I was far from feeling. It was that he could remain with me, in my apartment, but must be prepared to stay, perhaps for long hours at a time, within the secret cell beneath the buttress, and have a palliasse there to sleep upon if need be, should there be visitors to my room.

He fell to crying at once, as I had expected, beseeching me not to let him stay alone in the dark cell. He would go mad, he said – he could not stand it, he would rather die.

I was well-nigh desperate, now that the house was beginning to stir, and the children to talk in the adjoining chamber.

'Very well, then,' I said. 'Open the door, Matty. Call the troopers. Tell them that Richard Grenvile's son is here and wishes to surrender himself to their mercy. They have sharp swords, and the pain will soon be over.' God forgive me that I could find it in my heart so to terrify the lad, but it was his only salvation.

The mention of the swords, bringing the thought of blood, sent the colour draining from his face, as I knew it would, and he turned to me, his dark eyes desperate, and said, 'Very well. I will do as you ask me.' It is those same dark eyes that haunt me still, and will always do so, to the day I die.

I bade Matty take the mattress from my bed, and the stool beside the window, and some blankets, and bundle them through the open gap on to the stair. 'When it is safe for you to come, I will let you know,' I said. 'But how can you,' said Dick, 'when the gap is closed?' Here I was forced back again into the old dilemma of the night before. I could have wept with strain and weariness, and looked at Matty in despair. 'If you do not quite close the gap,' she said, 'but let it stay open three inches, Master Dick, with his ear put close to it, will hear your voice.'

We tried it, and although I was not happy with the plan it seemed the one solution. We found, too, that with a gap of two or three inches he could hear me strike with a stick upon the floor, once, twice, or thrice, which we arranged as signals. Thrice meant real danger, and then the stone must be pulled flush to the wall.

He had gone to his cell, with his mattress and his blankets and half a loaf that Matty had found for him, as the clock in the belfry struck six, and almost immediately little Jonathan from the adjoining room came pushing through the door, his toys under his arm, calling in loud tones for me to play with him. The day had started. When I look back now, to the intolerable strain and anguish of that time, I wonder how in God's name I had the power to endure it. For I had to be on guard, not only against the rebels, but against my friends too, and those I loved. Mary, Alice, and Joan, must all three remain in ignorance of what was happening, and their visits to my chamber, which should have been a comfort and a consolation in this time of strain, merely added to my anxiety.

What I would have done without Matty I do not know. It was she, acting sentinel as she had done in the past, who kept them from the door when Dick was with me, and, poor lad, I had to have him often, for the best part of the day. Luckily, my crippled state served as a good excuse, for it was known that often in the past I had 'bad days', and had to be alone, and this lie was now my only safeguard. John's story had been accepted as full truth, and since he was quite obviously ill, and in high fever, he was allowed to remain in his father's rooms with Joan to care for him and was not removed to closer custody under guard. Severe questioning from Lord Robartes could not shake John from his story, and, thank heaven, Robartes had too many other cares gathering fast upon his shoulders to worry any further about what had happened to Skellum Grenvile's son.

I remember Matty saying to me on that first day, Friday, the second of August: 'How long will they be here, Miss Honor? When will the Royalist army come to relieve us?'

And I, thinking of Richard down at Truro, and His Majesty already, so the rumour ran, entering Launceston, told her four days at the longest. But I was wrong. For four whole weeks the rebels were our masters.

It is nearly ten years since that August of '44, but every day of that age-long month is printed firm upon my memory.

The first week was hot and stifling, with a glazed blue sky and not a cloud upon it, and in my nostrils now I can recapture the smell of horse-flesh, and the stink of sweating soldiery, borne upwards to my open casement from the fetid court below.

Day in, day out, came the jingle of harness, the clattering of hoofs, the march of tramping feet, and the grinding sound of wagon wheels, and ever insistent, above the shouting of orders and the voices of the men, the bugle call, hammering its single note.

The children, Alice's and Joan's, unused to being within doors at high summer, hung fretful from the windows, adding to the babel, and Alice, who had the care of all of them whilst Joan nursed John in the greater quietude of the south front, would take them from room to room to distract them. Imprisonment made cronies of us all, and no sooner had Alice and the brood departed than the Sparke sisters, who hitherto had preferred chequers to my company, would come inquiring for me with some wild rumour to unfold, gleaned from the frightened servants, of how the house was to be burnt down with all its inmates when Essex gave the order – but not till the women had been ravaged. I dare say I was the only woman in the house to be unmoved by such a threat, for God knows I could not be more bruised and broken than I was already. But for Deborah and Gillian it was another matter, and Deborah, whom I judged to be even safer from assault than I was myself, showed me with trembling hands the silver bodkin with which she would defend her honour. Their brother Will was become a sort of toady to the officers, thinking that by smiling and wishing them good morning he would win their favour and his safety, but as soon as their backs were turned he was whispering some slander about their persons, and repeating snatches of conversation he had overheard, bits and pieces that were no use to anyone. Once or twice Nick Sawle came tapping slowly to my room, leaning on his two sticks, a look of lost bewilderment and muddled resentment in his eye because the rebels had not been flung from Menabilly within four-and-twenty hours of their arrival, and I was forced to listen to his theories that His Majesty must be now at Launceston, now at Liskeard, now back again at Exeter – suppositions which brought our release no nearer. While he argued his poor wife Temperance stared at him dully, in a kind of trance, her religious eloquence pent up at last from shock and fear so that she could do no more than clutch her Prayer Book without quoting from it.

Once a day we were allowed within the garden, for some thirty minutes, and I would leave Matty in my room on an excuse and had Alice push my chair, while her nurse walked with the children. The poor gardens were laid waste already, with the yew trees broken and the flower-beds trampled, and up and down the muddied paths we went, stared at by the sentries at the gate and by the officers gathered at the long windows in the gallery. Their appraising, hostile eyes burnt through our backs, but must be endured for the sake of the fresh air we craved, and sometimes their laughter came to us. Their voices were hard and ugly, for they were mostly from London and the eastern counties, except the staff officers of Lord Robartes – and I never could abide the London twang, made doubly alien now through enmity. Never once did we see Gartred when we took our exercise, though her two daughters, reserved and unfriendly, played in the far corner of the garden, watching us and the children with blank eyes. They had neither of them inherited her beauty, but were brown-haired and heavy-looking, like their dead father, Antony Denys.

'I don't know what to make of it,' said Alice, in my ear. 'She is supposed to be a prisoner like us, but she is not treated so. I have watched her, from my window, walk in the walled garden beneath the summer-house, talking and smiling to Lord Robartes, and the servants say he dines with her most evenings.'

'She only does what many other women do in wartime,' I said, 'and turns the stress of the day to her advantage.'

'You mean she is for the Parliament?' asked Alice.

'Neither for the Parliament, nor for the King, but for Gartred Denys,' I answered. 'Do you not know the saying – to race with the hare and to run with the hounds? She will smile on Lord Robartes, and sleep with him too if she has a mind, just as long as it suits her. He would let her leave tomorrow, if she asked him.'

'Why, then,' said Alice, 'does she not do so, and return in safety to Orley Court?'

'That', I answered 'is what I would give a great deal to find out.' And as we paced up and down, up and down, before the staring, hostile eyes of the London officers, I thought of the footstep I had heard at midnight in the passage, the soft hand on the latch, and the rustle of a gown. Why should Gartred, while the house slept, find her way to my apartment in the north-east corner of the building and try my door, unless she knew her way already. And granting that she knew her way, what then was her motive?

It was ten days before I had my answer.

On Sunday, August the eleventh, came the first break in the weather. The sun shone watery in a mackerel sky, and a bank of cloud gathered in the south-west. There had been much coming and going all the day, with fresh regiments of troopers riding to the park, bringing with them many carts of wounded, who were carried to the farm buildings before the house. Their cries of distress were very real and terrible, and gave to us, who were their enemies, a sick dread and apprehension. The shouting and calling of orders was persistent on that day, and the bugle never ceased from dawn to sundown.

For the first time we were given soup only for our dinner, and a portion of stale bread, and this, we were told, would be the best we could hope for from henceforward. No reason was given, but Matty, with her ears pricked, had hung about the kitchens with her tray under her arm, and gleaned some gossip from the courtyard.

'There was a battle yesterday on Braddock Down,' she said. 'They've lost a lot of men.' She spoke softly, for with our enemies about us we had grown to speak in whispers, our eyes upon the door.

I poured half my soup into Dick's bowl, and watched him drink it greedily, running his tongue round the rim like a hungry dog. 'The King is only three miles from Lostwithiel,' she said. 'He and Prince Maurice have joined forces, and set up their headquarters at Boconnoc. Sir Richard has advanced, with nigh a thousand men from Truro, and is coming up on Bodmin from the west. "Your fellows are trying to squeeze us dry," said the trooper in the kitchen, "like a bloody orange. But they won't do it." '

'And what did you answer him?' I said to Matty.

She smiled grimly, and cut Dick the largest slice of bread.

'I told him I'd pray for him, when Sir Richard got him,' she answered.

After eating, I sat in my chair looking out across the park and watching the clouds gathering thick and fast. There were scarce a dozen bullocks left in the pen, out of the fine herd there had been the week before, and only a small flock of sheep. The rest had all been slaughtered. These remaining few would be gone within the next eight-and-forty hours. Not a stem of corn remained in the far meadows. The whole had been cut and ground, and the ricks pulled. The grass in the park was now bare earth where the horses had grazed upon it. Not a tree stood in the orchard beyond the Warren. If Matty's tale was true, and the King and Richard were to east and west of Lostwithiel, then the Earl of Essex and ten thousand men were pent up in a narrow strip of land some nine miles long, with no way of escape except the sea.

Ten thousand men, with provisions getting low, and only the bare land to live on, while three armies waited in their rear.

There was no laughter tonight from the courtyard, no shouting, and no chatter; only a blazing fire as they heaped the cut trees and kitchen benches upon it, the doors torn from the larder and the tables from the stewards' room, and I could see their sullen faces lit by the leaping flames.

The sky darkened, and slowly, silently, the rain began to fall. And as I listened to it, remembering Richard's words, I heard the rustle of a gown and a tap upon my door.

Chapter 18

DICK was gone in a flash to his hiding-place, and Matty clearing his bowl and platter. I sat still in my chair, with my back to the arras, and bade them enter who knocked upon the door.

It was Gartred. She was wearing, if I remember right, a gown of emerald green, and there were emeralds round her throat and in her ears. She stood a moment within the doorway, a half smile on her face. 'The good Matty,' she said, 'always so devoted. What ease of mind a faithful servant brings.'

I saw Matty sniff, and rattle the plates upon her tray, while her lips tightened in ominous fashion.

'Am I disturbing you, Honor?' said Gartred, that same smile still on her face. 'The hour is possibly inconvenient – you go early no doubt to bed?'

All meaning is in the inflexion of the voice, and when rendered on paper words seem plain and harmless enough. I give the remarks as Gartred phrased them, but the veiled contempt, the mockery, the suggestion that, because I was crippled, I must be tucked down and in the dark by half past nine, this was in her voice, and in her eyes as they swept over me.

'My going to bed depends upon my mood, as doubtless it

does with you,' I answered. 'Also it depends upon my company.'

'You must find the hours most horribly tedious,' she said, 'but then no doubt you are used to it by now. You have lived in custody so long that to be made prisoner is no new experience. I must confess I find it unamusing.' She came closer in the room, looking about her, although I had given her no invitation.

'You have heard the news, I suppose?' she said.

'That the King is at Boconnoc, and a skirmish was fought yesterday in which the rebels got the worst of it? Yes, I have heard that,' I answered. The last of the fruit, picked before the rebels came, was standing on a platter in the window. Gartred took a fig and began to eat it, still looking about her in the room. Matty gave a snort of indignation which passed unnoticed, and taking her tray went from the chamber with a glance at Gartred's back that would have slain her had it been perceived.

'If this business continues long,' said Gartred, 'we none of us here will find it very pleasant. The men are already in an ugly mood. Defeat may turn them into brutes.'

'Very probably,' I said.

She threw away the skin of her fig and took another.

'Richard is at Lanhydrock,' she said. 'Word came today through a captured prisoner. It is rather ironic that we have the owner of Lanhydrock in possession here. Richard will leave little of it for him by the time this campaign is settled, whichever way the battle goes. Jack Robartes is black as thunder.'

'It is his own fault,' I said, 'for advising the Earl of Essex to come into Cornwall and run ten thousand men into a trap.'

'So it is a trap?' she said. 'And my unscrupulous brother the baiter of it? I rather thought it must be.'

I did not answer. I had said too much already. And Gartred was in quest of information. 'Well, we shall see,' she said, eating her fig with relish, 'but if the process lasts much longer the rebels will turn cannibal. They have the country stripped already between here and Lostwithiel, and Fowey is without provisions. I shudder to think what Jack Robartes would do to Richard if he could get hold of him.'

'The reverse holds equally good,' I told her.

She laughed, and squeezed the last drop of juice into her mouth.

'All men are idiots,' she said, 'and more especially in wartime. They lose all sense of values.'

'It depends', I said, 'upon the meaning of values.'

'I value one thing only,' she said. 'My own security.'

'In that case,' I said, 'you showed neglect of it when you travelled upon the road ten days ago.'

She watched me under heavy lids and smiled.

'Your tongue hasn't blunted with the years,' she said, 'nor tribulation softened you. Tell me, do you still care for Richard?'

'That is my affair,' I said.

'He is detested by his brother officers. I suppose you know that,' she said, 'and loathed equally in Cornwall as in Devon. In fact, the only creatures he can count his friends are sprigs of boys, who daren't be rude to him. He has a little train of them, nosing his shadow.'

Oh, God, I thought, you bloody woman, seizing upon the one insinuation in the world to make me mad. I watched her play with her rings.

'Poor Mary Howard,' she said; 'what she endured. You were spared intolerable indignities, you know, Honor, by not being his wife. I suppose Richard has made great play lately of loving you the same, and no doubt he does, in his curious vicious fashion. Rather a rare new pastime, a woman who can't respond.'

She yawned and strolled over to the window. 'His treatment of Dick is really most distressing,' she said. 'The poor boy adored his mother, and now I understand Richard intends to rear him as a freak, just to spite her. What did you think of him when he was here?'

'He was young, and sensitive, like many other children,' I said.

'It was a wonder to me he was ever born at all,' said Gartred, 'when I think of the revolting story Mary told me. However, I will spare your feelings, if you still put Richard on a pedestal. I am glad, for the lad's sake, that Jack Robartes did not find

161

him here at Menabilly. He has sworn an oath to hang any relative of Richard's.'

'Except yourself,' I said.

'Ah, I don't count,' she answered. 'Mrs Denys of Orley Court is not the same as Gartred Grenvile.' Once more she looked up at the walls, and then again into the courtyard.

'This is the room, isn't it,' she said, 'where they used to keep the idiot? I can remember him mouthing down at Kit when we rode here five-and-twenty years ago.'

'I have no idea,' I said. 'The subject is not discussed among the family.'

'There was something odd about the formation of the house,' she said carelessly. 'I cannot recollect exactly what it was. Some cupboard, I believe, where they used to shut him up when he grew violent, so Kit told me. Have you discovered it?'

'There are no cupboards here,' I said, 'except the cabinet over yonder.'

'I am so sorry', she said, 'that my coming here forced you to give your room to Joan Rashleigh. I could so easily have made do with this one, which one of the servants told me was never used until you took it over.'

'It was much simpler', I said, 'to place you and your daughters in a larger room, where you can entertain visitors to dinner.'

'You always did like servants' gossip, did you not?' she answered. 'The hobby of all old maids. It whips their appetite to imagine what goes on behind closed doors.'

'I don't know,' I said. 'I hardly think my broth tastes any better for picturing you hip to hip with Lord Robartes.'

She looked down at me, her gown in her hands, and I wondered who had the greatest capacity for hatred, she or I.

'My being here', she said, 'has at least spared you all, so far, from worse unpleasantness. I have known Jack Robartes for many years.'

'Keep him busy, then,' I said. 'That's all we ask of you.'

I was beginning to enjoy myself at last, and, realizing it, she turned towards the door. 'I cannot guarantee', she said, 'that his good temper will continue. He was in a filthy mood tonight at dinner, when he heard of Richard at Lanhydrock, and has gone off now to a conference at Fowey with Essex and the chiefs of staff.'

'I look to you, then,' I said, 'to have him mellow by the morning.' She stood with her hand on the door, her eyes sweeping the hangings on the wall. 'If they lose the campaign,' she said, 'they will lose their tempers too. A defeated soldier is a dangerous animal. Jack Robartes will give orders to sack Menabilly, and destroy inside and without.'

'Yes,' I said. 'We are all aware of that.'

'Everything will be taken,' she said, 'clothes, jewels, furniture, food – and not much left of the inhabitants. He must be a curious man, your brother-in-law, Jonathan Rashleigh, to desert his home, knowing full well what must happen to it in the end.'

I shrugged my shoulders. And then, as she left, she gave herself away. 'Does he still act as Collector for the Mint?' she said. Then for the first time I smiled, for I had my answer to the problem of her presence.

'I cannot tell you,' I said. 'I have no idea. But if you wait long enough for the house to be ransacked, you may come upon the plate you think he has concealed. Good night, Gartred.'

She stared at me a moment, and then went from the room. At last I knew her business, and had I been less preoccupied with my own problem of concealing Dick, I might have guessed it sooner. Whoever won or lost the campaign in the west, it would not matter much to Gartred, she would see to it that she had a footing on the winning side. She could play the spy for both. Like Temperance Sawle, I was in a mood to quote the Scriptures and declaim, 'Where the body lies, there will the eagles be gathered together.' If there were pickings to be scavenged in the aftermath of battle, Gartred Denys would not stay at home in Orley Court. I remembered her grip upon the marriage settlement with Kit. I remembered that last feverish search for a lost trinket on the morning she left Lanrest, a widow, and I remembered too the rumours I had heard since she was widowed for the second time, how Orley Court was much burdened with debt and must be settled among her daughters when they came of age. Gartred had not yet found a third husband to her liking, but in the meantime she must live. The silver plate of Cornwall would be a prize indeed, could she lay hands on it.

This, then, was her motive, with suspicion already centred on my room. She did not know the secret of the buttress, but memory had reminded her that there was, within the walls of Menabilly, some such hiding-place. And with sharp guesswork, she had reached the conclusion that my brother-in-law would make a wartime use of it. That the hiding-place might also conceal her nephew had, I was certain, never entered her head. Nor – and this was supposition on my part – was she working in partnership with Lord Robartes. She was playing her own game, and if the game was likely to be advanced by letting him make love to her, that was only by the way. It was far pleasanter to eat roast meat than watered broth; besides, she had a taste for burly men. But if she found she could not get what she wanted by playing a lone hand – then she would lay her cards upon the table and damn the consequences.

This, then, was what we had to fear, and no one in the house knew of it but myself. So Sunday, August the eleventh, came and went, and we woke next morning to another problematical week in which anything might happen, with the three Royalist armies squeezing the rebels tighter hour by hour, the strip of country left to them becoming daily more bare and devastated, and a steady, sweeping rain turning all the roads to mud.

Gone was the hot weather, the glazed sky, and the sun. No longer did the children hang from the windows, and listen to the bugles, and watch the troopers come and go. No more did we take our daily exercise before the windows of the gallery. A high, blustering wind broke across the park, and from my tightly shut casement I could see the closed, dripping tents, the horses tethered line upon line beneath the trees at the far end, their heads disconsolate, while the men stood about in huddled, melancholy groups, their fires dead as soon as kindled. Many of the wounded died in the farm buildings. Mary saw the burial parties go forth at dawn, a silent, grey procession in the early morning mist, and we heard they took them to the Long Mead, the valley beneath the woods at Pridmouth.

No more wounded came to the farm buildings, and we

guessed from this that the heavy weather had put a stop to fighting. But we heard also that His Majesty's army now held the east bank of the Fowey River, from St Veep down to the fortress at Polruan, which commanded the harbour entrance. The rebels in Fowey were thus cut off from their shipping in the Channel and could receive no supplies by sea, except from such small boats as could land at Pridmouth or Polkerris or on the sand flats at Tywardreath, which the heavy run from the south-west now made impossible. There was little laughter or chatter now from the mess-room in the gallery, so Alice said, and the officers, with grim faces, clamped back and forth from the dining-chamber, which Lord Robartes had taken for his own use, while every now and then his voice would be raised in irritation and anger, as a messenger would ride through the pouring rain bearing some counter-order from the Earl of Essex in Lostwithiel or some fresh item of disaster. Whether Gartred moved about the house or not I do not know. Alice said she thought she kept to her own chamber. I saw little of Joan, for poor John's ague was still unabated, but Mary came from time to time to visit me, her face each day more drawn and agonized as she learnt of further devastation to the estate. More than three hundred of the sheep had already been slaughtered, thirty fatted bullocks, and sixty store bullocks. All the draught oxen taken, and all the farm horses, some forty of them in number. A dozen or so hogs were left out of the eighty there had been, and these would all be gone before the week was out. The last year's corn had vanished the first week of the rebel occupation, and now they had stripped the new, leaving no single blade to be harvested. There was nothing left, of course, of the farm wagons, or carts, or farming tools – these had all been taken. And the sheds where the winter fuel had been stored were as bare as the granaries. There was, in fact – so the servants in fear and trembling reported to Mary – scarcely anything remaining of the great estate that Jonathan Rashleigh had left in her keeping a fortnight since. The gardens spoilt, the orchards ruined, the timber felled, the livestock eaten. Whichever way the war in the west should go, my brother-in-law would be a bankrupt man.

And they had not yet started upon the house or the inhabitants. Our feeding was already a sore problem. At midday we all gathered to the main meal of the day. This was served to us in Alice's apartment in the east wing, while John lay ill in his father's chamber, and there some twenty of us herded side by side, the children clamouring and fretful, while we dipped stale bread in the mess of watery soup provided, helped sometimes by swollen beans and cabbage. The children had their milk, but no more than two cupfuls for the day, and already I noticed a staring look about them, their eyes over-large in the pale faces, while their play had become listless, and they yawned often. Young Jonathan started his croup, bringing fresh anxiety to Joan, and Alice had to go below to the kitchen and beg for rhubarb sticks to broil for him – a favour which was only granted her because her gentle ways won sympathy from the trooper in charge. The old people suffered like the children, and complained fretfully with the same misunderstanding of what war brings. Nick Sawle would stare long at his empty bowl when he had finished and mutter 'Disgraceful! Quite unpardonable!' into his beard, and look malevolently about him as though it were the fault of someone present, while Will Sparke with sly cunning would seat himself among the younger children and under pretence of making friends sneak crumbs from them when Alice and her nurse turned their backs. The women were less selfish, and Deborah, whom I had thought as great a freak in her own way as her brother was in his, showed great tenderness, on a sudden, for all those about her who seemed helpless, nor did her deep voice and incipient moustache discourage the smallest children.

It was solely with Matty's aid that I was able to feed Dick at all. By some means, fair or foul, which I did not inquire into, she had made an ally of the second scullion, to whom she pulled a long story about her ailing, crippled mistress, with the result that further soup was smuggled to my chamber beneath Matty's apron and no one the wiser for it. It was this same scullion who fed us with rumours, too – most of them disastrous to his own side – which made me wonder if a bribe would make him a deserter. At mid-week we heard that Richard had seized Restormel Castle by Lostwithiel, and that Lord Goring, who commanded the King's horse, held the bridge and the road below St Blazey. Essex was now pinned up in our peninsula, some seven miles long and two broad, with ten thousand men to feed, and the guns from Polruan trained on Fowey Harbour. It could not last much longer. Either Essex and the rebels must be relieved by a further force marching to him from the east, or he must stand and make a fight of it. And we would sit, day after day, with cold hearts and empty bellies, staring out upon the sullen soldiery as they stood huddled in the rain outside their tents, while their leaders within the house held councils of despondency. Another Sunday came, and with it a whisper of alarm among the rebels that the country people were stealing forth at night and doing murder. Sentries were found strangled at their posts, men woke to find their comrades with cut throats, others would stagger to headquarters from the high road, their hands lopped from their wrists, their eyes blinded. The Cornish were rising.

On Tuesday, the twenty-seventh, there was no soup for our midday dinner, only half a dozen loaves amongst the twenty of us. On Wednesday one jugful of milk for the children, instead of three, and the milk much watered.

On Thursday Alice and Joan and Mary, and the two Sparke sisters and I, divided our bread amongst the children, and made for ourselves a brew of herb tea with scalding water. We were not hungry. Desire for food left us when we saw the children tear at the stale bread and cram it in their mouths, then turn and ask for more which we could not give to them. And all the while the south-west wind tore and blustered in the teeming sky, and the rebel bugle that had haunted us so long sounded across the park like a challenge of despair.

Chapter 19

ON Friday, the thirtieth of August, I lay all day upon my bed, for to gather with the others now would be a farce, and in any case I had not the strength to do so. My cowardly soul forbade me watch the children beg and cry for their one crust of bread.

167

Matty brewed me a cup of tea, and it seemed wrong to swallow even that. Hunger had made me listless, and, heedless of danger, I let Dick come and lie upon his mattress by my bed, while he knawed a bone that Matty had scavanged for him. His eyes looked larger than ever in his pale face, and his black curls were lank and lustreless. It seemed to me that in his hunger he grew more like his mother, and sometimes, looking down on him, I would fancy she had stepped into his place and it was Mary Howard I fed and sheltered from the enemy, and she who licked the bones with little pointed teeth and tore at the strips of flesh with small, eager paws.

Matty herself was hollow-eyed and sallow. Gone were the buxom hips and the apple cheeks. Whatever food she could purloin from her friend the scullion – and there was precious little now for the men themselves – she smuggled to Dick or to the children.

During the day, while I slipped from one racking dream into another, with Dick curled at my feet like a puppy, Matty leant up against the window, staring at the mist that had followed now upon the rain, and hid the tents and horses from us.

The hoof-beats woke me shortly after two, and Matty, opening the window, peered down into the outer court and watched them pass under the gate-house to the courtyard. Some dozen officers, she said, with an escort of troopers, and the leader on a great black horse wearing a dark grey cloak. She slipped from the room to watch them descend from their horses in the inner court, and came back to say that Lord Robartes had stood himself on the steps to receive them, and they had all passed into the dining-chamber with sentries before the doors.

Even my tired brain seized the salient possibility – that this was the last council to be held, and that the Earl of Essex had come to it in person. I pressed my hands over my eyes to still my aching head. 'Go find your scullion,' I said to Matty. 'Do what you will to him, but make him talk.' She nodded, tightening her lips, and before she went she brought another bone to Dick, from some lair within her own small room, and, luring him with it like a dog to his kennel, got him to his cell beneath the buttress.

Three, four, five, and it was already murky, the evening

drawing in early because of the mist and rain, when I heard the horses pass beneath the archway once again, and so out across the park. At half-past five Matty returned. What she had been doing those intervening hours I never asked her from that day to this, but she told me the scullion was without, and wished to speak to me. She lit the candles, for I was in darkness, and as I raised myself upon my elbow I questioned her with my eyes, and she gave a jerk of her head towards the passage.

'If you give him money,' she whispered, 'he will do anything you ask him.' I bade her fetch my purse, which she did, and then, going to the door, she beckoned him within.

He stood blinking in the dim light, a sheepish grin on his face – but that face, like ours, was lean and hungry.

I beckoned him to my bed, and he came near, with a furtive glance over his shoulder. I gave him a gold piece, which he pocketed instantly. 'What news have you?' I asked.

He looked at Matty, and she nodded. He ran his tongue over his lips.

' 'Tis only rumour,' he said, 'but it's what they're saying in the courtyard.' He paused, and looked again towards the door.

'The retreat begins tonight,' he said. 'There'll be five thousand of them marching through darkness to the beaches. You'll hear them, if you listen. They'll come this way, down to Pridmouth and Polkerris. The boats will take them off when the wind eases.'

'Horses can't embark in small boats,' I said. 'What will your generals do with their two thousand horse?'

He shook his head, and glanced at Matty. I gave him another gold piece.

'I had but a word with Sir William Balfour's groom,' he said. 'There's talk of breaking through the Royalist lines tonight, when the foot retreat. I can't answer for the truth of it, nor could he.'

'What will happen to you and the other cooks?' I asked.

'We'll go by sea, same as the rest,' he said.

'Not likely,' I said. 'Listen to the wind.'

It was soughing through the trees in the Warren, and the rain spattered against my casement.

'I can tell you what will happen to you,' I said. 'The morning will come, and there won't be any boats to take you from the beaches. You will huddle there, in the driving wind and rain with a thundering great south-west sea breaking down at Pridmouth and the country people coming down on you all from the cliffs with pitch-forks in their hands. Cornish folk are not pleasant when they are hungry.'

The man was silent, and passed his tongue over his lips once again.

'Why don't you desert?' I said. 'Go off tonight, before worse can happen to you. I can give you a note to a Royalist leader.'

'That's what I told him,' said Matty. 'A word from you to Sir Richard Grenvile would see him through to our lines.'

The man looked from one to the other of us, foolish, doubtful, greedy. I gave him a third gold piece. 'If you break through to the King's army', I said, 'within an hour, and tell them there what you have just told me – about the horse trying to run for it before morning – they'll give you plenty more of these gold pieces, and a full supper into the bargain.' He scratched his head, and looked again at Matty. 'If the worst comes to the worst and you're held prisoner,' I told him, 'it would be better than having the bowels torn out of you by Cornishmen.'

It was this last word that settled him. 'I'll go,' he said, 'if you'll write a word for me.'

I scribbled a few words to Richard, which were as like as not never to reach his hands (nor did they do so, as I afterward discovered), and bade the fellow find his way through the woods to Fowey if he could, and in the growing darkness get a boat to Bodinnick, which was held by the Royalists, and there give warning of the rebel plan.

It would be too late, no doubt, to do much good, but it was at least a venture worth the trying. When he had gone, with Matty to speed him on his way, I lay back on my bed and listened to the rain, and as it fell I heard in the far distance, from the high road beyond the park, the tramp of marching feet. Hour after hour they sounded, tramp, tramp, without a pause, through the long hours of the night, with the bugle crying thin and clear above the moaning of the wind. When the morning broke, misty, and wet, and grey, they were still marching there upon the high road, bedraggled, damp, and dirty, hundred upon hundred straggling in broken lines across the park and making for the beaches.

Order was gone by midday on Saturday, discipline was broken, for as a watery sun gleamed through the scurrying clouds we heard the first sounds of gun-fire from Lostwithiel, as Richard's army broke upon them from the rear. We sat at our windows, hunger at last forgotten, with the rain blowing in our weary faces, and all day long they trudged across the park, a hopeless tangle now of men and horses and wagons; voices yelling orders that were not once obeyed, men falling to the ground in weariness and refusing to move further, horses, carts, and the few cattle that remained all jammed and bogged together in the sea of mud that once had been a park. The sound of the gun-fire drew nearer, and the rattle of musket-shots, and one of the servants, climbing to the belfry, reported that the high ground near Castledore was black with troops and smoke and flame, while down from the fields came little running figures, first a score, then fifty, then a hundred, then a hundred more, to join the swelling throng about the lanes and in the park.

And the rain went on, and the retreat continued.

At five o'clock word went round the house that we were every one of us to descend to the gallery. Even John, from his sick-bed, must obey the order. The rest had little strength to drag their feet, and I found difficulty in holding to my chair. Nothing had passed our lips now but weak herb tea for two whole days. Alice looked like a ghost, for I think she had denied herself entirely for the sake of her three little girls. Her sister Elizabeth was scarcely better, and her year-old baby in her arms was as still as a waxen doll. Before I left my chamber I saw that Dick was safe within his cell, and this time, in spite of protestations, I closed the stone that formed the entrance.

A strange band we were, huddled there together in the gallery, with wan faces; the children strangely quiet, and an ominously heavy look about their hollow eyes. It was the first time I had seen John since that morning a month ago, and he seemed most wretchedly ill, his skin a dull yellow colour, and shaking still in every limb. He looked across at me as though to ask a question, and I nodded to him, summoning a smile.

171

We sat there waiting, no one with the heart or strength to speak. A little apart from us, near the centre window, sat Gartred with her daughters. They too were thinner and paler than before, and I think had not tasted chicken now for many days, but, compared to the poor Rashleigh and Courtney babies, they were not ill-nourished.

I noticed that Gartred wore no jewels and was very plainly dressed, and somehow the sight of this gave me a strange foreboding. She took no notice of us, beyond a few words to Mary on her entrance, and seated beside the little table in the window she proceeded to play patience. She turned the cards with faces uppermost, considering them with great intentness. This, I thought, is the moment she has been waiting for for over thirty days.

Suddenly there was a tramping in the hall and into the gallery came Lord Robartes, his boots splashed with mud, the rain running from his coat. His staff officers stood beside him, and one and all wore faces grim and purposeful.

'Is everybody in the household here?' he called harshly.

Some sort of murmur rose from amongst us, which he took to be assent.

'Very well, then,' he said, and, walking towards my sister Mary and her stepson John, he stood confronting them.

'It has come to my knowledge', he said, 'that your malignant husband, madam, and your father, sir, have concealed upon the premises large quantities of silver, which should by right belong to Parliament. The time has ended for any trifling or protestation. Pressure is being brought to bear upon our armies at this moment, forcing us to a temporary withdrawal. The Parliament needs every ounce of silver in the land, to bring this war to a successful conclusion. I ask you, madam, therefore, to tell me where the silver is concealed.'

Mary, God bless her ignorance, turned up her bewildered face to him.

'I know nothing of any silver,' she said, 'except the few pieces of plate we have kept of our own, which you now possess, having my keys.'

'I talk of great quantities, madam, stored in some place of hiding, until it can be transported by your husband to the Mint.'

'My husband was Collector for Cornwall, that is true, my lord. But he has never said a word to me about concealing it at Menabilly.'

He turned from her to John.

'And you sir? No doubt your father told you all his affairs?'

'No,' said John firmly. 'I know nothing of my father's business, nor have I any knowledge of a hiding-place. My father's only confidant is his steward, Langdon, who is with him at present. No one here at Menabilly can tell you anything at all.'

For a moment Lord Robartes stared down at John, then, turning away, he called to his three officers. 'Sack the house,' he said briefly. 'Strip the hangings and all furnishings. Destroy everything you find. Take all jewels, clothes, and valuables. Leave nothing of Menabilly but the bare walls.'

At this poor John struggled to his feet. 'You cannot do this,' he said. 'What authority has Parliament given you to commit such wanton damage? I protest, my lord, in the name of common decency and humanity.' And my sister Mary, coming forward, threw herself upon her knees. 'My Lord Robartes,' she said, 'I swear to you by all I hold most dear that there is nothing concealed within my house. If it were so I would have known of it. I do implore you to show mercy to my home.'

Lord Robartes stared down at her, his eyes hard.

'Madam,' he said, 'why should I show your house mercy, when none was shown to mine? Both victor and loser pay the penalty in civil war. Be thankful that I have heart enough to spare your lives.' And with that he turned on his heel and went from us, taking his officers with him and leaving two sentries at the door.

Once again he mounted his horse in the courtyard and rode away, back to the useless rearguard action that was being fought in the hedges and ditches up at Castledore, with the mizzle rain falling thick and fast. We heard the major he had left in charge snap forth an order to his men – and straightway they started tearing at the panelling in the dining-chamber. We could hear the woodwork rip, and the glass shatter as they smashed the mullioned windows. At this first warning of destruction Mary turned to John, the tears ravaging her face. 'For God's sake,' she said, 'if you know of any hiding-place, tell them of it, so that we save the house. I will take full blame upon myself when your father comes.' John did not answer. He looked at me. And no one of the company there present saw the look save Gartred, who at that moment raised her head, I made no motion of my lips. I stared back at him, as hard and merciless as Lord Robartes. He waited a moment, then answered very slowly, 'I know nought of any hiding-place.'

I think had the rebels gone about their work with shouts and merriment, or even drunken laughter, the destruction of the house would have been less hard to bear. But because they were defeated troops, and knew it well, they had cold savage murder in their hearts, and did what they had to do in silence.

The door of the gallery was open, with the two sentries standing on guard beside it, and no voices were uplifted, no words spoken. There was only the sound of the ripping wood, the breaking of the furniture, the hacking to pieces of the great dining-table, and the grunts of the men as they lifted their axes. The first thing that was thrown down to us across the hall, torn and split, was the portrait of the King, and even the muddied heel that had been ground upon the features, and the great crack across the mouth, had not distorted those melancholy eyes that stared up at us without complaint from the wrecked canvas.

We heard them climb the stairs and break into the south rooms, and as they tore down the door of Mary's chamber she began to weep long and silently, and Alice took her in her arms and hushed her like a child. The rest of us did nothing, but sat like spectres, inarticulate. Then Gartred looked towards me from her window. 'You and I, Honor, being the only members of the company without a drop of Rashleigh blood, must pass the time somehow. Tell me, do you play piquet?'

'I haven't played it since your brother taught me, sixteen years ago,' I answered.

'The odds are in my favour, then,' she said. 'Will you risk a *partie*?' As she spoke she smiled, shuffling her cards, and I guessed the double meaning she would bring to it.

'Perhaps,' I said, 'there is more at stake than a few pieces of silver.'

We heard them tramping overhead, and the sound of the

splitting axe, while the shivering glass from the casements fell to the terrace outside.

'You are afraid to match your cards against mine?' said Gartred.

'No,' I said. 'No, I am not afraid.'

I pushed my chair towards her and sat opposite her at the table. She handed the cards for me to cut and shuffle, and when I had done so, I returned them to her for the dealing, twelve apiece. There started then the strangest *partie* of piquet that I have ever played, before or since, for while Gartred risked a fortune I wagered for Richard's son, and no one knew it but myself. The rest of the company, dumb and apathetic, were too weak even to wonder at us, and if they did it was with shocked distaste and shuddering dislike, that we – because we did not belong to Menabilly – could show ourselves so heartless.

'Five cards,' called Gartred.

'What do they make?' I said.

'Making nine.'

'Good.'

'Five.'

'A quart major, nine. Three knaves.'

'Not good.'

She led with the ace of hearts, to which I played the ten, and as she took the trick we heard the rebels wrenching the tapestry from the bedroom walls above. There was a dull smouldering smell, and a wisp of smoke blew past the windows of the gallery.

'They are setting fire', said John quietly, 'to the stables and the farm-buildings before the house.'

'The rain will surely quench the flames,' whispered Joan. 'They cannot burn fiercely, not in the rain.'

One of the children began to wail, and I saw gruff Deborah take her on her knee and murmur to her. The smoke of the burning buildings was rank and bitter in the steady rain, and the sound of the axes overhead and the tramping of the men was as though they were felling trees in a thick forest, instead of breaking to pieces the great four-poster bed where Alice had borne her babies. They threw the glass mirror out on to the terrace, where it splintered to a thousand fragments, and with it came the broken candle-sticks, the tall vases, and the tapestried chairs.

'Fifteen,' said Gartred, leading the king of diamonds, and 'Eighteen,' I answered, trumping it with my ace.

Some of the rebels, with a sergeant in charge of them, came down the staircase, and they had with them all the clothing they had found in Jonathan's and Mary's bedroom, and her jewels too, and combs, and the fine figured arras that had hung upon the walls. This they loaded in bundles upon the pack-horses that waited in the courtyard. When they were fully laden a trooper led them through the archway, and two more took their place. Through the broken windows of the wrecked dining-chamber we could see the disordered rebel bands still straggling past the smouldering farm buildings towards the meadows and the beach, and as they gazed up at the house, grinning, their fellows at the house windows, warming to their work and growing reckless, shouted down to them with jeers and cat-calls, throwing out the mattresses, the chairs, the tables – all they could lay hands upon which would make fodder for the flames that rose reluctantly in the slow drizzle from the blackened farm buildings.

There was one fellow making a bundle of all the clothing and the linen. Alice's wedding-gown, and the little frocks she had embroidered for her children, and all Peter's rich apparel that she had kept with such care in her press till he should need it. The tramping ceased from overhead, and we heard them pass into the rooms beneath the belfry. Some fellow, in mockery, began to toll the bell, and the mournful clanging made a new sound in our ears, mingling with the shouting and yelling and rumble of wagon wheels that still came to us from the park, and the ever-increasing bark of cannon-shot, now barely two miles distant.

'They will be in the gate-house now,' said Joan. 'All your books and your possessions, Honor, they will not spare them any more than ours.' There was reproach in her voice, and disillusion, that her favourite aunt and godmother should show no sign of grief. 'My cousin Jonathan would never have permitted this,' said Will Sparke, his voice high with hysteria. 'Had there been plate concealed about the premises he would have given it, and willingly, rather than have his whole house robbed, and we, his relatives, lose everything.' Still the bell tolled and the ceilings shook with heavy, murderous feet, and down into the inner court now they threw the debris from the west part of the building, portraits, and benches, rugs and hangings, all piled on top of one another in hideous confusion, while those below discarded the less valuable, and fed them to the flames.

We started upon the third hand of the *partie*. 'A tierce to a king,' called Gartred, and 'Good,' I replied, following her lead of spades. And all the while I knew that the rebels had now come to the last room of the house, and were tearing down the arras before the buttress. I saw Mary raise her grief-stricken face and look toward us. 'If you would say one word to the officer,' she said to Gartred, 'he might prevent the men from further damage. You are a friend of Lord Robartes, and have some sway with him. Is there nothing you can do?'

'I could do much,' said Gartred, 'if I were permitted. But Honor tells me it is better for the house to fall about our ears. Fifteen, sixteen, seventeen, and eighteen. My trick, I fancy.'

She wrote her score on the tablets by her side.

'Honor,' said Mary, 'you know that it will break Jonathan's heart to see his home laid desolate. All that he has toiled and lived for, and his father before him, for nearly fifty years. If Gartred can in some way save us, and you are trying to prevent her, I can never forgive you, nor will Jonathan, when he knows of it.'

'Gartred can save no one, unless she likes to save herself,' I answered, and began to deal for the fourth hand.

'Five cards,' called Gartred.

'*Equalë*,' I answered.

'A quart to a king.'

'A quart to a knave.'

We were in our fifth and last game, each winning two apiece, when we heard them tramping down the stairs, with the major in the lead. The terrace and the courtyard were heaped high with wreckage, the loved possessions and treasures of nearly fifty years, even as Mary had said, and what had not been packed upon the horses was left now to destroy. They set fire to the remainder, and watched it burn, the men leaning upon their axes and breathing hard now that the work was over. When the pile was well alight the major turned his back upon it, and coming into the gallery clicked his heels and bowed derisively to John.

'The orders given my by Lord Robartes have been carried out with implicit fidelity,' he announced. 'There is nothing left within Menabilly House but yourselves, ladies and gentlemen, and the bare walls.'

'And you found no silver hidden?' asked Mary.

'None, madam, but your own – now happily in our possession.'

'Then this wanton damage, this wicked destruction, has been for nothing?'

'A brave blow has been struck for Parliament, madam, and that is all that we, her soldiers and her servants, need consider.'

He bowed and left us, and in a moment we heard him call further orders, and horses were brought, and he mounted and rode away even as Lord Robartes had done an hour before. The flames licked the rubble in the courtyard, and save for their dull hissing, and the patter of the rain, there was suddenly no other sound. A strange silence had fallen upon the place. Even the sentries stood no longer by the door. Will Sparke crept to the hall.

'They've gone,' he said. 'They've all ridden away. The house is bare, deserted.'

I looked up at Gartred, and this time it was I who smiled, and I who spread my cards upon the table.

'Discard for *carte blanche*,' I said softly, and, adding ten thus to my score, I led her for the first time, and with my next hand drew three aces to her one, and gained the *partie*.

She rose then from the table without a word, save for one mock curtsy to me, and calling her daughters to her, went upstairs. I sat alone, shuffling the cards as she had done, while out into the hall faltered the poor weak members of our company to gaze about them, stricken at the sight that met their eyes.

The panels ripped, the floors torn open, the windows shattered from their frames, and all the while the driving rain, that had neither doors nor windows now to bar it, blew in upon their faces, soft and silent, with great flakes of charred timber and dull soot from the burning rubble in the courtyard. The last rebels had retreated to the beaches, save for the few who still made the stand at Castledore, and there was no trace of them left now at Menabilly but the devastation they had wrought, and the black, churning slough that once was road and park. As I sat there, listening, still shuffling the cards in my hands, I heard, for the first time, a new note above the cannon and the musket shot and the steady pattering rain. Not clamouring or insistent, like the bugle that had haunted me so long, but quick, triumphant, coming ever nearer, the sharp, brisk tattoo of the Royalist drums.

Chapter 20

THE rebel army capitulated to the King in the early hours of Sunday morning. There was no escape by sea for the hundreds of men herded on the beaches. Only one fishing-boat put forth from Fowey bound for Plymouth, in the dim light before dawn, and she carried in her cabin the Lord General the Earl of Essex, and his adviser, Lord Robartes. So much we learnt later, and we learnt too that Matty's scullion had proved faithful to his promise and borne his message to Sir Jacob Astley at Bodinnick on the Friday evening. But by the time word had reached His Majesty, the out-posts upon the road were warned and the Parliament horse had successfully broken through the Royalist lines, and made good their escape to Saltash. So, by a lag in time, over two thousand rebel horse got clean away to fight another day, a serious mishap which was glossed over by our forces in the heat and excitement of the big surrender, and I think the only one of our commanders to go nearly hopping mad at the escape was Richard Grenvile.

It was, I think, most typical of his character that when he sent a regiment of his foot to come to our succour on that Sunday morning, bringing us food from their own wagons, he did not come himself, but forwarded me this brief message, stopping not to consider whether I lived or died, or whether his son was with me still:

'You will soon learn', he wrote, 'that my plan has only partially succeeded. The horse have got away, all owing to that besotted idiot Goring lying in a stupor at his headquarters, and permitting – you will scarcely credit it – the rebels to slip through his lines without as much as a musket-shot at their backsides. May God preserve us from our own commanders. I go now in haste to Saltash in pursuit, but have little hope of overtaking the sods, if Goring, with his cavalry, has already failed.'

First a soldier, last a lover, my Richard had no time to waste over a starving household and a crippled woman who had let a whole house be laid waste about her for the sake of the son he did not love. So it was not the father after all who carried the fainting lad into my chamber once again, and laid him down, but poor sick John Rashleigh, who crawling for the second time into the tunnel beneath the summer-house, found Dick unconscious in the buttress cell, tugged at the rope, and so opened the hinged stone into the room.

This was about nine o'clock on the Saturday night, after the house had been abandoned by the rebels, and we were all too weak to do much more than smile at the Royalist foot when they beat their drums under our gaping windows on the Sunday morning.

The first necessity was milk for the children and bread for ourselves, and later in the day, when we had regained a little measure of our strength and the soldiers had kindled a fire for us in the gallery – the only room left liveable – we heard once more the sound of horses, but this time heartening and welcome, for they were our own men coming home. I suppose I had been through a deal of strain those past four weeks, something harder than the others because of the secret I had guarded; and so, when it was over, I suffered a strange relapse, accentuated, maybe, by natural weakness, and had not the strength for several days to lift my head. The scenes of joy and reunion, then, were not for me. Alice had her Peter, Elizabeth her John of Coombe, Mary had her Jonathan, and there was kissing, and crying, and kissing again, and all the horrors of our past days to be described, and the desolation to be witnessed. But I had no shoulder on which to lean my head, and no breast to weep upon. A truckle-bed from the attic served me for support, this being one of the few things found that the rebels had not destroyed. I recollect that my brother-in-law bent over me when he returned, and praised me for my courage, saying that John had told him everything and I had acted as he would have done himself, had he been home. But I did not want my brother-in-law. I wanted Richard. And Richard had gone to Saltash, chasing rebels. All the rejoicing came as an anticlimax. The bells pealing in Fowey Church, echoed by the bells at Tywardreath, and His Majesty summoning the gentlemen of the county to his headquarters at Boconnoc and thanking them for their support – he presented Jonathan with his own lace handkerchief and Prayer Book – and a sudden wild thanksgiving for deliverance and for victory, seemed premature to me, and strangely sour. Perhaps it was some fault in my own character, some cripple quality, but I turned my face to the wall, and my heart was heavy. The war was not over, for all the triumphs in the west. Only Essex had been defeated, and his eight thousand men. There were many thousands in the north and east of England who had yet to show their heels. 'And what is it all for?' I thought. 'Why can they not make peace? Is it to continue thus, with the land laid waste, and houses devastated, until we are all grown old?'

Victory had a hollow sound, with our enemy Lord Robartes in command at Plymouth, still stubbornly defended, and there was something narrow and parochial in thinking the war over because Cornwall was now free. It was the second day of our release, when the menfolk had ridden off to Boconnoc to take leave of His Majesty, that I heard the sound of wheels in the outer court, and preparation for departure, and then those wheels creaking over the cobbles and disappearing through the park. I was too tired then to question it, but later in the day, when Matty came to me, I asked her who it was that went away from Menabilly in so confident a fashion. 'Who else could it be', Matty answered, 'but Mrs Denys?' So Gartred, like a true gambler, had thought best to cut her losses and be quit of us.

'How did she find the transport?' I inquired.

Matty sniffed as she wrung out a piece of cloth to bathe my back. 'There was a gentleman she knew, it seems, amongst the Royalist party who rode hither yesterday with Mr Rashleigh. A Mr Ambrose Manaton. And it's he who has provided her the escort for today.'

I smiled, in spite of myself. However much I hated Gartred I had to bow to the fashion in which she landed on her feet in all and every circumstance.

'Did she see Dick', I asked, 'before she left?'

'Aye,' said Matty. 'He went up to her at breakfast and saluted her. She stared at him amazed – I watched her. And then she asked him, "Did you come in the morning with the infantry?" and he grinned like a little imp, and answered: "I have been here all the time."'

'Imprudent lad,' I said. 'What did she say to him?'

'She did not answer for a moment, Miss Honor, and then she smiled – you know her way – and said, "I might have known it. You may tell your gaoler you are not worth one bar of silver."'

'And that was all?'

'That was all. She went soon after. She'll never come again to Menabilly.' And Matty rubbed my sore back with her hard, familiar hands. But Matty was wrong, for Gartred did come again to Menabilly, as you shall hear, and the man who brought her was my own brother. But I run ahead of my story, for we are still in September '44.

That first week, while we recovered our strength, my brother-in-law and his steward set to work to find out what it would cost to make good the damage that had been wrought upon his house and his estate. The figure was collossal, and beyond his means. I can see him now, seated in one corner of the gallery, reading from his great account book, every penny he had lost meticulously counted and entered in the margin. It would take months, nay years, he said, to restore the house and bring back the estate to its original condition. While the war lasted no redress would be forthcoming. After the war, so he was told, the Crown would see that he was not the loser. I think Jonathan knew the value of such promises, and, like me, he thought the

182

rejoicings in the west were premature. One day the rebels might return again, and next time the scales be turned.

In the meantime, all that could be done was to save what was left of the harvest – and that but one meadow of fourteen acres which the rebels had left uncut but the rain had well-nigh ruined.

Since his house in Fowey had been left bare in the same miserable fashion as Menabilly, his family, in their turn, were homeless, and the decision was now made amongst us to divide. The Sawles went to their brother at Penrice, and the Sparkes to other relatives at Tavistock. The Rashleighs themselves, with children, split up among near neighbours until a wing of Menabilly should be repaired. I was for returning to Lanrest until I learnt, with a sick heart, that the whole house had suffered a worse fate than Menabilly and was wrecked beyond hope of restoration.

There was nothing for it but to take shelter for the time being with my brother Jo at Radford, for although Plymouth was still held by Parliament the surrounding country was safe in Royalist hands, and the subduing of the garrison and harbour was only, according to our optimists, a matter of three months at the most.

I would have preferred, had the choice been offered me, to live alone in one bare room at Menabilly than repair to Radford and the stiff household of my brother, but alas! I had become in a few summer months but another of the vast number of homeless people, turned wanderer through war, and must swallow pride and be grateful for hospitality, from whatever direction it might come.

I might have gone to my sister Cecilia at Mothercombe or my sister Bridget at Holberton, both of whom were pleasanter companions than my brother Jo, whose official position in the county of Devon had turned him somewhat cold and proud, but I chose Radford for the reason that it was close to Plymouth – and Richard was once more Commander of the Siege. What hopes I had of seeing him, God only knew, but I was sunk deep now in the mesh I had made for myself, and waiting for a word from him, or a visit of an hour had become my sole reason for existence.

'Why cannot you come with me to Buckland?' pleaded Dick, for the tutor, Herbert Ashley, had been sent to fetch him home. 'I would be content at Buckland, and not mind my father, if you could come too and stand between us.'

'Your father', I answered him, 'has enough work on his hands without keeping house for a crippled woman.'

'You are not crippled,' declared the boy with passion. 'You are only weak about the legs, and so must sit confined to your chair. I would tend you, and wait upon you, hour by hour with Matty, if you would but come with me to Buckland.'

I smiled, and ran my hand through his dark curls.

'You shall come and visit me at Radford,' I said, 'and tell me of your lessons. How you fence, and how you dance, and what progress you make in speaking French.'

'It will not be the same', he said, 'as living here with you in the house. Shall I tell you something? I like you best of all the people that I know – next to my own mother.'

Ah, well, it was an achievement to be second once again to Mary Howard. The next day he rode away in company with his tutor, turning back to wave to me all the way across the park, and I shed a useless, sentimental tear when he was gone from me.

What might have been – what could have been. These are the saddest phrases in our English tongue. And back again, pell-mell would come the fantasies; the baby I had never borne, the husband I would never hold. The sickly figures in an old maid's dream, so Gartred would have told me.

Yes, I was thirty-four, an old maid and a cripple; but sixteen years ago I had had my moment, which was with me still, vivid and enduring, and by God I swear I was happier with my one lover than Gartred ever had been with her twenty.

So I set forth upon the road again and turned my back on Menabilly, little thinking that the final drama of the house must yet be played with blood and tears, and I kissed my dear Rashleighs one and all and vowed I would return to them as soon as they could have me.

Jonathan escorted me in my litter as far as Saltash, where Robin came to meet me. I was much shaken, not by the roughness of the journey, but by the sights I had witnessed on the road. The aftermath of war was not a pleasant sight to the beholder.

The country was laid waste, for one thing and that was the fault of the enemy. The corn was ruined, the orchards devastated, the houses smoking. And in return for this the Cornish people had taken toll upon the rebel prisoners. There were many of them still lying in the ditches, with the dust and flies upon them. Some without hands and feet, some hanging downwards from the trees. And there were stragglers who had died upon the road, in the last retreat, too faint to march from Cornwall – and these had been set upon and stripped of their clothing and left for the hungry dogs to lick.

I knew then, as I peered forth from the curtains of my litter, that war can make beasts of every one of us, and that the men and women of my own breed could act even worse in warfare than the men and women of the eastern counties. We had, each one of us, because of the civil war, streaked back two centuries in time, and were become like those half savages of the fourteen hundreds who, during the Wars of the Roses, slit each other's throats without compunction.

At Saltash there were gibbets in the market square, with the bodies of rebel troopers hanging upon them scarcely cold, and as I turned my sickened eyes away from them I heard Jonathan inquire of a passing soldier what faults they had committed.

He grinned, a fine tall fellow, with the Grenvile shield on his shoulder. 'No fault,' he said, 'except that they are rebels, and so must be hanged, like the dogs they are.'

'Who gave the order, then?'

'Our General, of course. Sir Richard Grenvile.'

Jonathan said nothing, but I saw that he looked grave, and I leant back upon my cushions, feeling, because it was Richard's doing and I loved him, that the fault was somehow mine and I was responsible. We halted there that night, and in the morning Robin came, with an escort, to conduct me across the Tamar and so through the Royalist lines outside the Plymouth defences, round to Radford.

Robin looked well and bronzed, and I thought again with cynicism how men, in spite of protestations about peace, are really bred to war and thrive upon it. He was not under Richard's command, but was colonel of foot under Sir John Berkeley, in the army of Prince Maurice, and he told us that the King had decided not to make a determined and immediate assault upon Plymouth after all, but leave it to Grenvile to subdue by slow starvation, while he and Prince Maurice marched east out of Devon towards Somerset and Wiltshire, there to join forces with Prince Rupert and engage the Parliament forces which were still unsubdued. I thought to myself that Richard would reckon this bad strategy, for Plymouth was no pooping little town, but the finest harbour in all England next to Portsmouth, and for His Majesty to gain the garrison, and have command also of the sea, was of very great importance. Slow starvation had not conquered it before; why then should it do so now? What Richard needed for assault was guns and men. But I was a woman, and not supposed to have knowledge of these matters. I watched Robin and Jonathan in conversation and caught a murmur of the word 'Grenvile', and Robin say something about 'harsh treatment of the prisoners' and 'Irish methods not suiting Devon men', and I guessed that Richard was already getting up against the county. No doubt I would hear more of this at Radford.

No one hated cruelty more than I did, nor deplored the streak of it in Richard with greater sickness of heart, but as we travelled towards Radford, making a great circuit of the forts around Plymouth, I noticed with secret pride that the only men who carried themselves like soldiers were those who wore the Grenvile shields on their shoulders. Some of Goring's horse were quartered by St Budeaux and they were lolling about the village, drinking with the inhabitants, while a sentry squatted on a stool, his great mouth gaping in a yawn, his musket lying at his feet. From the nearby inn came a group of officers, laughing and very flushed, but the sentry did not leap to his feet when he observed them. Robin joined the officers a moment, exchanging greetings, and as we passed through the village he told me that the most flushed of the group was Lord Goring himself, a very good fellow, and a most excellent judge of horses.

'Does that make him a good commander?' I asked.

'He is full of courage,' said Robin, 'and will ride at anything.

That is all that matters.' And he proceeded to tell me about a race which had been run the day before, under the very nose of the rebels, and how Lord Goring's chestnut had beaten Lord Wentworth's roan by half a neck. 'Is that how Prince Maurice's army conducts its war?' I asked. Robin laughed – he too thought it all very fine sport.

But the next post we passed was held by Grenvile men. And here there was a barrier across the road, with armed sentries standing by it, and Robin had to show his piece of paper, signed by Sir John Berkeley, before we could pass through. An officer barked an order to the men, and they removed the barrier. There were perhaps a score of them standing by the postern, cleaning their equipment; they looked lean and tough, with an indefinable quality about them that stamped them Grenvile men. I would have known them on the instant had I not seen the scarlet pennant by the postern door, with the three golden rests staring from the centre, capped by a laughing gryphon.

We came at length by Plymstock to Radford, and my brother's house, and as I was shown to my apartments looking north over the river towards the Cattwater and Plymouth I thought of my eighteenth birthday long ago, and how Richard had sailed into the Sound with the Duke of Buckingham. It seemed a world ago, and I another woman. My brother was now a widower, for Elizabeth Champernowne had died a few years before the war in childbed, and my youngest brother Percy, with his wife Phillipa, had come to live with him and look after Jo's son, John, a child of seven, since they themselves were childless. I had never cared much for Radford, even as a girl, and now within its austere barrack precincts I found myself homesick, not so much for Lanrest and the days that were gone, but for my last few months at Menabilly. The danger I had known there, and the tension I had shared, had, in some strange fashion, rendered the place dear to me. The gate-house between the courtyards, the long gallery, the causeway that looked out to the Gribben and the sea, seemed to me now, in retrospect, my own possession, and even Temperance Sawle with her prayers and Will Sparke with his high-pitched voice were people for whom I felt affection because of the siege we had each of us endured. The fighting did not touch them here at Radford, for all its proximity to Plymouth, and the talk was of the discomfort they had to bear by living within military control.

Straight from a sacked house and starvation, I wondered that they should think themselves ill-used, with plenty of food upon the table; but no sooner had we sat down to dinner (I had not the face to demand it, the first evening, in my room) than Jo began to hold forth, with great heat, upon the dictatorial manners of the army. 'His Majesty has thought fit', he said, 'to confer upon Richard Grenvile the designation of General in the West. Very good. I have no word to say against the appointment. But when Grenvile trades upon the title to commandeer all the cattle within a radius of thirty miles or more to feed his army, and rides roughshod over the feelings of the county gentry with the one sentence "Military necessities come first", it is time that we all protested.'

If Jo remembered my old alliance with Richard, the excitement of the moment had made him conveniently forget it. Nor did he know that young Dick had been in my care at Menabilly the past weeks. Robin, too, full of his own commander, Berkeley, was pleased to agree with Jo. 'The trouble with Grenvile', said Robin, 'is that he insists upon his fellows being paid. The men in his command are like hired mercenaries. No free quarter, no looting, no foraging as they please, and all this comes very hard upon the pockets of people like yourself, who must provide the money.'

'Do you know', continued Jo, 'that the Commissioners of Devon have been obliged to allot him one thousand pounds a week for the maintenance of his troops? I tell you, it hits us very hard.'

'It would hit you harder', I said, 'if your house was burnt down by the Parliament.'

They stared at me in surprise, and I saw young Phillipa look at me in wonder for my boldness. Woman's talk was not encouraged at Radford. 'That my dear Honor', said Jo coldly, 'is not likely to happen.' And, turning his shoulder to me, he harped on the outraged Devon gentry, and how this new-styled General in the West had coolly told them he had need of all their horses and their muskets in this siege of Plymouth, and if they did not give them to him voluntarily he would send a company of his soldiers to collect them.

'The fellow is entirely without scruples, no doubt of that,' said Percy, 'but in fairness to him I must say that all the country people tell me they would rather have Grenvile's men in their villages than Goring's. If Grenvile finds one of his own fellows looting, he is shot upon the instant. But Goring's men are quite out of control, and drunk from dawn to dusk.'

'Oh, come,' frowned Robin, 'Goring and his cavalry are entitled to a little relaxation, now that the worst is over. No sense in keeping fellows standing to attention all day long.'

'Robin is right,' said Jo. 'A certain amount of licence must be permitted, to keep the men in heart. We shall never win the war otherwise.'

'You are more likely to lose it', I said, 'by letting them loll about the villages with their tunics all undone.'

The statement was rendered the more unfortunate by a servant entering the room upon this instant and announcing Sir Richard Grenvile. He strode in with his boots ringing on the stone flags, in that brisk way I knew so well, totally unconscious of himself or the effect he might produce, and with a cool nod to Jo, the master of the house, he came at once to me and kissed my hand.

'Why the devil', he said, 'did you come here and not to Buckland?' That he at once put me at a disadvantage amongst my relatives did not worry him. I murmured something about my brother's invitation, and attempted to introduce him to the company. He bowed to Phillipa, but turned back immediately to me.

'You've lost that weight that so improved your person,' he said. 'You're as thin as a church mouse.'

'So would you be', I answered, 'if you'd been held prisoner by the rebels for four weeks.'

'The whelp is asking for you all day long,' said Richard. 'He dins your praises in my ears till I am sick of them. I have him outside, with Joseph. Hi! spawn!' He turned on his heels, bawling for his son. I think I never knew of any man, save Richard, who could in so brief a moment fill a room with his presence and become, as it were, the master of a house that was in no

189

way his. Jo stood at his own table, his napkin in his hand, and
Robin too, and Percy, and they were like dumb servants waiting for the occasion, while Richard took command. Dick crept
in cautiously, timid and scared as ever, his dark eyes lighting at
the sight of me, and behind him strode young Joseph Grenvile,
Richard's kinsman and aide-de-camp, his features and his
colouring so like his General's as to make me wonder and not
for the first time, God forgive my prying mind, whether
Richard had been purposely vague about the relationship between them, and whether he was not as much his son as Dick
was. God damn you, I thought, begetting sons about the
countryside before I was even crippled. 'Have you all dined?'
said Richard, reaching for a plum. 'These lads and I could eat
another dinner.' Jo, with heightened colour and a flea in his
ear, as the saying goes, called the servants to bring back the
mutton. Dick squeezed himself beside me, like a small dog
regaining his lost mistress, and while they ate Richard de-
claimed upon the ill-advisability of the King having marched
east without first seeing Plymouth was subdued.

'It's like talking to a brick wall, God bless him,' said Richard,
his mouth full of mutton. 'He knows no more of warfare than
this dead sheep I swallow.' I saw my brothers look at one another in askance, that a general should dare to criticize his king.
'I'll fight in his service until there's no breath left in my body,'
said Richard, 'but it would make it so much simpler for the
country if he would ask advice of soldiers. Put some food into
your belly, spawn. Don't you want to grow as fine a man as Jo
here?' I saw Dick glance under his eyes at Joseph with a flicker
of jealousy. Jo then was the favourite, no doubt about that.
What a world of difference between them, too – the one so
broad-shouldered, big, and auburn-haired; the other little, with
black hair and eyes. I wonder, I thought grudgingly, what
buxom country girl was Joseph's mother, and if she still lived,
and what had happened to her? But while I pondered the
question, as jealous as young Dick, Richard continued talking.
'It's that damned lawyer who's to blame,' he said; 'that fellow
Hyde, an upstart from God knows what snivelling country
town, and now jumped into favour as Chancellor of the Exchequer. His Majesty won't move a finger without asking his

190

advice. I hear Rupert has all but chucked his hand in, and returned to Germany. Depend upon it, it's fellows like this one who will lose the war for us.'

'I have met Sir Edward Hyde,' said my brother. 'He seemed to me a very able man.'

'Able my arse,' said Richard. 'Anyone who jiggles with the Treasury must be double-faced to start with. I've never met a lawyer yet who didn't line his own pockets before he fleeced his clients.' He tapped young Joseph on the shoulder. 'Give me some tobacco,' he said. The youngster produced a pipe and pouch from his coat. 'Yes, I hate the breed,' said Richard, blowing a cloud of smoke across the table, 'and nothing affords me greater pleasure than to see them trounced. There was a fellow called Braband, who acted as attorney for my wife against me in the Star Chamber in the year '33 – a neighbour of yours, Harris, I believe?'

'Yes,' said my brother coldly, 'and a man of great integrity devoted to the King's cause in this war.'

'Well, he'll never prove that now,' said Richard. 'I found him creeping about the Devon lanes disguised the other day, and seized the occasion to arrest him as a spy. I've waited eleven years to catch that blackguard.'

'What have you done to him, sir?' asked Robin.

'He was disposed of', said Richard, 'in the usual fashion. No doubt he is doing comfortably in the next world.'

I saw young Joseph hide his laughter in his wine-glass, but my three brothers gazed steadfastly at their plates.

'I dare say', said my eldest brother slowly, 'that I should be very ill-advised if I attempted to address to you, General, a single word of criticism, but . . .'

'You would, sir,' said Richard, 'be extremely ill-advised.' And, laying his hand a moment on Joseph's shoulder he rose from the table. 'Go on, lads, and get your horses. Honor, I will conduct you to your apartment. Good evening, gentlemen.'

I felt that whatever reputation I might have for dignity in the eyes of my family was gone to the winds for ever as he swept me to my room. Matty was sent packing to the kitchen, and he lay me on my bed and sat beside me.

'You had far better', he said, 'return with me to Buckland.

Your brothers are all asses. As for the Champernownes, I have a couple of them on my staff, and both are useless. You remember Edward, the one they wanted you to marry? Dead from the neck upwards.'

'And what would I do at Buckland,' I said, 'among a mass of soldiers. What would be thought of me?'

'You could look after the whelp,' he said, 'and minister to me in the evening. I get very tired of soldiers' company.'

'There are plenty of women', I said, 'who could give you satisfaction.'

'I have not met any,' he said.

'Bring them in from the hedgerows,' I said, 'and send them back again in the morning. It would be far less trouble than having me upon your hands from dawn till dusk.'

'My God,' he said, 'if you think I want to bounce about with some fat female after a hard day's work sweating my guts out before the walls of Plymouth, you flatter my powers of resilience. Keep still, can't you, while I kiss you?'

Below the window, in the drive, Jo and Dick paced the horses up and down. 'Someone', I said, 'will come into the room.'

'Let them,' he answered. 'What the hell do I care?'

I wished that I could have the same contempt for my brother's house as he had. It was dark and by the time he left, and I felt as furtive as I had done at eighteen when slipping from the apple-tree.

'I did not come to Radford', I said weakly, 'to behave like this.'

'I have a very poor opinion', he answered, 'of whatever else you came for.'

I thought of Jo and Robin, Percy and Phillipa, all sitting in the hall below, and the two lads pacing their horses under the stars.

'You have placed me', I said, 'in a most embarrassing position.'

'Don't worry, sweetheart,' he said. 'I did that to you sixteen years ago.' As he stood there, laughing at me, with his hand upon the door, I had half a mind to throw my pillow at him.

'You and your double-faced attorneys,' I said. 'What about

your own two faces? That boy out there – your precious Joseph
– you told me he was your kinsman?'

'So he is,' he grinned.

'Who was his mother?'

'A dairy-maid at Killigarth. A most obliging soul. Married
now to a farmer, and mother of his twelve sturdy children.'

'When did you discover Joseph?'

'A year or so ago, on returning from Germany, and before
I went to Ireland. The likeness was unmistakable. I took some
cheeses and a bowl of cream off his mother, and she recalled
the incident, laughing with me, in her kitchen. She bore no
malice. The boy was a fine boy. The least I could do was to
take him off her hands. Now I wouldn't be without him for the
world.'

'It is the sort of tale', I said sulkily, 'that leaves a sour taste
in the mouth.'

'In yours, perhaps,' he said, 'but not in mine. Don't be so
mealy-mouthed my loved one.'

'You lived at Killigarth,' I said, 'when you were courting me.'

'God damn it,' he said, 'I didn't ride to see you every day.'

I heard them all in a moment laughing beneath my window,
and then mount their horses and gallop away down the avenue,
and as I lay upon my bed, staring at the ceiling, I thought how
the blossom of my apple-tree, so long dazzling and fragrant
white, had a little lost its sheen and was become, after all, a
common apple-tree; but that the realization of this, instead of
driving me to torments as it would have done in the past,
could now, because of my four-and-thirty years, be borne with
equanimity.

Chapter 21

I was fully prepared, the following morning, to have my
brother call upon me at an early hour and inform me icily that
he could not have his home treated as a bawdy house for
soldiery. I knew so well the form of such a discourse. The

honour of his position, the welfare of his young son, the delicate feelings of Phillipa, our sister-in-law, and although the times were strange and war had done odd things to conduct, certain standards of behaviour were necessary for people of our standing. I was in fact already planning to throw myself upon my sister Cecilia's mercy over at Mothercombe, and had my excuses already framed, when I heard the familiar sound of tramping feet. I bid Matty look from the window, and she told me that a company of infantry was marching up the drive, wearing the Grenvile shields. This, I felt, would add fuel to the flames that must already be burning in my brother's breast.

Curiosity, however, was too much for me, and instead of remaining in my apartment like a child who had misbehaved, I bade the servants carry me downstairs to the hall. Here I discovered my brother Jo in heated argument with a fresh-faced young officer, who declared coolly, and with no sign of perturbation, that his General, having decided that Radford was most excellently placed for keeping close observation on the enemy battery at Mount Batten, wished to commandeer certain rooms of the house for himself as a temporary headquarters, and would Mr John Harris be good enough to show the officer a suite of rooms commanding a north-western view?

Mr Harris, added the officer, would be put to no inconvenience, as the General would be bringing his own servants, cooks, and provisions. 'I must protest', I heard my brother say, 'that this is a highly irregular proceeding. There are no facilities here for soldiers, I myself am hard-pressed with work about the county, and ...'

'The General told me', said the young officer, cutting him short, 'that he had a warrant from His Majesty authorizing him to take over any place of residence in Devon or Cornwall that should please him. He already has a headquarters at Buckland, Werrington, and Fitzford, and there the inhabitants were not permitted to remain, but were forced to find room elsewhere. Of course, he does not propose to deal thus summarily with you, sir. May I see the rooms?'

My brother stared at him tight-lipped for a moment, then, turning on his heel, escorted him up the stairs which I had just descended. I was very careful to avoid his eye.

During the morning the company of foot proceeded to establish themselves in the north wing of the mansion, and, watching from the long window in the hall, I saw the cooks and pantry boys stagger towards the kitchen entrance bearing plucked fowls, and ducks, and sides of bacon, besides crate after crate of wine. Phillipa sat at my side, stitching her sampler.

'The King's General', she said meekly, 'believes in doing himself well. I have not seen such fare since the siege of Plymouth started. Where do you suppose he obtains all his supplies?'

I examined my nails, which were in need of trimming, and so did not have to look her in the face.

'From the many houses', I answered, 'that he commandeers.'

'But I thought', said Phillipa, with maddening persistency, 'that Percy told us Sir Richard never permitted his men to loot.'

'Possibly', I said with great detachment, 'Sir Richard looks upon ducks and burgundy as perquisites of war.'

She went to her room soon after, and I was alone when my brother Jo came down the stairs.

'Well,' he said grimly, 'I suppose I have you to thank for this invasion.'

'I know nothing about it,' I answered.

'Nonsense. You planned it together last night.'

'Indeed we did not.'

'What were you doing then, closeted with him in your chamber?'

'The time seemed to pass', I said, 'in reviving old memories.'

'I thought', he said, after a moment's pause, 'that your present condition, my dear Honor, would make talk of your former intimacy quite intolerable, and any renewal of it beyond question.'

'So did I,' I answered.

He looked down at me, his lips pursed.

'You were always shameless as a girl,' he said. 'We spoilt you most abominably, Robin, your sisters, and I. And now at thirty-four you behave like a dairy-maid.'

He could not have chosen an epithet, to my mind, more unfortunate.

'My behaviour last night', I said, 'was very different from a dairy-maid.'

'I am glad to hear it. But the impression, upon us here below, was to the contrary. Sir Richard's reputation is notorious, and for him to remain within a closed apartment for nearly an hour and three-quarters alone with a woman can conjure up, to my mind, one thing and one thing only.'

'To my mind', I answered, 'it can conjure up at least a dozen.'

After that I knew I must be damned for ever, and was not surprised when he left me without further argument, except to express a wish that I might have some respect for his roof, though 'ceiling' would have been the apter word, in my opinion.

I felt brazen and unrepentant all the day, and when Richard appeared that evening, in tearing spirits, commanding dinner for two in the apartment his soldiers had prepared for him, I had a glow of wicked satisfaction that my relatives sat below in gloomy silence, while I ate roast duck with the General overhead.

'Since you would not come to Buckland,' he said, 'I had perforce to come to you.'

'It is always a mistake', I said, 'to fall out with a woman's brothers.'

'Your brother Robin has ridden off with Berkeley's horse to Tavistock,' he answered, 'and Percy I am sending on a delegation to the King. That leaves only Jo to be disposed of. It might be possible to get him over to the Queen of France.'

He tied a knot in his handkerchief as a reminder.

'And how long', I asked, 'will it take before Plymouth falls before you?' He shook his head, and looked dubious.

'They have the whole place strengthened', he said, 'since our campaign in Cornwall, and that's the devil of it. Had His Majesty abided by my advice, and tarried here a fortnight only with his army, we would have the place today. But no. He must listen to Hyde and march to Dorset, and here I am, back again where I was last Easter, with less than a thousand men to do the job.'

'You'll never take it then', I asked, 'by direct assault?'

'Not unless I can increase my force', he said, 'by nearly another thousand. I'm already recruiting hard up and down the county. Rounding up deserters, and enlisting new levies. But the fellows must be paid. They won't fight otherwise, and I don't blame 'em. Why the devil should they?'

'Where', I said, 'did you get this burgundy?'

'From Lanhydrock,' he answered. 'I had no idea Jack Robartes had laid down so good a cellar. I've had every bottle of it removed to Buckland.' He held his goblet to the candle-light, and smiled.

'You know that Lord Robartes sacked Menabilly simply and solely because you had pillaged his estate?'

'He is an extremely dull-witted fellow.'

'There is not a pin to choose between you where pillaging is concerned. A Royalist does as much damage as a rebel. I suppose Dick told you that Gartred was one of us at Menabilly?'

'What was she after?'

'The Duchy silver plate.'

'More power to her. I could do with some of it myself, to pay my troops.'

'She was very friendly with Lord Robartes.'

'I have yet to meet a man that she dislikes.'

'I think it very probable that she acts spy for Parliament.'

'There you misjudge her. She would do anything to gain her own ends but that. You forget the old saying: that, of the three families in Cornwall, a Godolphin was never wanting in wit, a Trelawney in courage, or a Grenvile in loyalty. Gartred was born and bred a Grenvile, no matter if she beds with every fellow in the Duchy.'

A brother, I thought, will always hold a brief for a sister. Perhaps Robin at this moment was doing the same thing for me.

Richard had risen and was looking through the window towards the distant Cattwater and Plymouth.

'Tonight', he said quietly, 'I've made a gambler's throw. It may come off. It may be hopeless. If it succeeds, Plymouth can be ours by daybreak.'

'What do you mean?'

He continued looking through the window to where the lights of Plymouth flickered.

'I am in touch with the second in command in the garrison,' he said softly, 'a certain Colonel Searle. There is a possibility that for the sum of three thousand pounds he will surrender the city. Before wasting further lives, I thought it worth my while to assay bribery.'

I was silent. The prospect was hazardous, and somehow smelt unclean.

'How have you set about it?' I asked at length.

'Young Jo slipped through the lines tonight at sunset,' he answered, 'and will, by now, be hidden in the town. He bears upon him my message to the colonel, and a firm promise of three thousand pounds.'

'I don't like it,' I said. 'No good will come of it.'

'Maybe not,' he said indifferently, 'but at least it was worth trying. I don't relish the prospect of battering my head against the gates of Plymouth the whole winter.'

I thought of young Jo and his impudent brown eyes.

'Supposing', I said slowly, 'that they catch your Joseph?'

Richard smiled. 'The lad', he answered, 'is quite capable of looking after himself.'

But I thought of Lord Robartes as I had seen him last, with muddied boots, and the rain upon his shoulders, sour and surly in defeat, and I knew how much he must detest the name of Grenvile.

'I shall be rising early,' said Richard, 'before you are awake. If, by midday, you hear a salvo from every gun inside the garrison, you will know that I have entered Plymouth, after one swift and very bloody battle.' He took my face in his, and kissed it, and then bade me good night. But I found it hard to sleep. The excitement of his presence in the house had turned to anxiety and strain. I knew, with all the intuition in my body, that he had gambled wrong.

I heard him ride off, with his staff, about 5.30 in the morning, and then dead tired, my brain chasing itself in circles, I fell into a heavy sleep.

When I awoke it was past ten o'clock. A grey day, with a nip of autumn in the air. I had no wish for breakfast, nor even to get up, but stayed there in my bed. I heard the noises of the house, and the coming and going of the soldiers in their wing, and at twelve o'clock I raised myself upon my elbow and looked towards the river. Five past twelve. A quarter past. Half past twelve. There was no salvo from the guns. There was not even a musket shot. It rained at two, then cleared, then rained again. The day dragged on, dull, interminable. I had a sick feeling of suspense all the while. At five o'clock Matty brought me my dinner on a tray, which I picked at with faint appetite. I asked her if she had heard any news, but she said she knew of none. But later, when she had taken away my tray, and come to draw my curtains, her face was troubled.

'What is the matter?' I asked.

'It's what one of Sir Richard's men was saying, down there to the sentry,' she answered, 'some trouble today in Plymouth. One of their best young officers taken prisoner by Lord Robartes, and condemned to death by Council of War. Sir Richard has been endeavouring all day to ransom him, but has not succeeded.'

'Who is it?'

'I don't know.'

'What will happen to the officer?'

'The soldier did not say.'

I lay back again on my bed, my hands over my eyes, to dim the candle. Foreboding never played me wrong, not when I was seized with it for a whole night and day. Maybe perception was a cripple quality. Later I heard the horses coming up the drive and the sentries standing to attention. Footsteps climbed the stairs, slowly, heavily, and passed along to the rooms in the northern wing. A door slammed, and there was silence. It was a long while that I waited there, lying on my back. Just before midnight I heard him walk along the passage and his hand fumbled a moment on the latch of my door. The candles were blown, and it was darkness. The household slept. He came to my side, and knelt before the bed. I put my hand on his head, and held him close to me. He knelt thus for many moments without speaking.'

'Tell me,' I whispered, 'if it will help you.'

'They hanged him,' he said, 'above the gates of the town where we could see him. I sent a company to cut him down, but they were mown down by gunfire. They hanged him, before

199

my eyes.' Now that suspense was broken, and the long day of strain behind me, I was aware of the feeling of detachment that possesses all of us when a crisis has been passed, and the suffering is not one's own.

This was Richard's battle. I could not fight it for him. I could only hold him in the darkness.

'That rat Searle', he said, his voice broken, strangely unlike my Richard, 'betrayed the scheme, and so they caught the lad. I went myself beneath the walls of the garrison to parley with Robartes. I offered him any terms of ransom or exchange. He gave me no answer. And while I stood there, waiting, they strung him up above the gate . . .'

He could not continue. He lay his head upon me, and I held his hands that clutched so fiercely at the patchwork quilt upon the bed.

'Tomorrow', I said, 'it might have been the same. A bullet through the head. A thrust from a pike. An unlucky stumble from his horse. This happens every day. An act of war. Look upon it in that way. Jo died in your service, as he would wish to do.'

'No,' he said, his voice muffled. 'It was my fault. On me the blame, now, tonight, for all eternity. An error in judgement. The wrong decision.'

'Jo would forgive you. Jo would understand.'

'I can't forgive myself. That's where the torture lies.'

I thought then of all the things that I would want to bring before him. How he was not infallible, and never had been, and that this stroke of fate was but a grim reminder of the fact. His own harsh measures to the enemy had been repaid, measure for measure. Cruelty begat cruelty, betrayal gave birth to treachery, the qualities that he had fostered in himself these past years were now recoiled upon him.

The men of Parliament had not forgotten his act of perfidy in the spring, when, feigning to be their friend, he had deserted to the King, bearing their secrets. They had not forgotten the executions without trial, the prisoners condemned to death in Lydford Castle, nor the long line of troopers hanging from the gibbets in the market-square of Saltash. And Lord Robartes, with his home Lanhydrock ravaged and laid waste, his goods seized, had seen rough justice and revenge in taking the life of the messenger who bore an offer of bribery and corruption in his pocket.

It was the irony of the Devil, or Almighty God, that the messenger should have been no distant kinsman, but Richard Grenvile's son. All this came before me in that moment when I held Richard in my arms. And now, I thought, we have come to a crisis in his life. The dividing of the ways. Either to learn from this single tragedy of a boy's death that cruelty was not the answer, that dishonesty dealt a returning blow, that accepting no other judgement but his own would in a space of time make every friend an enemy; or to learn nothing, to continue through the months and years deaf to all counsel, unscrupulous, embittered, the Skellum Grenvile with a price upon his head, the red fox who would be pointed to for evermore as lacking chivalry, a hated contrast to his well-beloved brother.

'Richard...' I whispered. 'Richard, my dear and only love ...' but he rose to his feet, he went slowly to the window, and, pulling aside the curtains, stood there with the moonlight on his hands that held the sword, but his face in shadow.

'I shall avenge him', he said, 'with every life I take. No quarter any more. No pardons. Not one of them shall be spared. From this moment I shall have one aim only in my life, to kill rebels. And to do it as I wish I must have command of the army; otherwise I fail. I will brook no dispute with my equals, I will tolerate no orders from those senior to me. His Majesty made me General in the West, and by God, I swear that the whole world shall know it.'

I knew then that his worse self possessed him, soul and body, and that nothing that I could say or do could help him in the future. Had we been man and wife, or truly lovers, I might, through the close day-by-day intimacy, have learnt to soften him; but Fate and circumstance had made me no more than a shadow in his life, a phantom of what might have been. He had come to me tonight because he needed me, but neither tears nor protestations nor assurances of my love and tenderness to all eternity would stay him now from the pursuit of the dim and evil star that beckoned to him.

Chapter 22

RICHARD was constantly at Radford during the six months that followed. Although his main headquarters were at Buckland, and he rode frequently through both Devon and Cornwall raising new recruits to his command, a company of his men was kept at my brother's house throughout, and his rooms always in preparation.

The reason given that watch must be kept upon the fortresses of Mount Batten and Mount Stamford was true enough, but I could tell from my brother's tightened lips, and Percy and Phillipa's determined discussion upon other matters when the General's name was mentioned, that my presence in the house was considered to be the reason for the somewhat singular choice of residence. And when Richard with his staff arrived to spend a night or two, and I was bidden to a dinner *tête-à-tête* immediately upon his coming into the house, havoc at once was played with what shred of reputation might be left to me. The friendship was considered odd, unfortunate; I think, had I thrown my cap over the mills and gone to live with him at Buckland, it might have been better for the lot of us. But this I steadfastly refused to do, and even now, in retrospect, I cannot give the reason, for it will not formulate itself in words. Always, at the back of my mind, was the fear that by sharing his life with too great intimacy, I would become a burden to him, and the love we bore for one another slip to disenchantment. Here at Radford he could seek me out upon his visits, and being with me would bring him peace and relaxation, tonic and stimulation; whatever mood he would be in, weary or high-spirited, I could attune myself accordingly. But had I made myself persistently available, in some corner of his house, little by little he would have felt the tug of an invisible chain, the claim that a wife brings to bear upon a husband, and the lovely freedom that there was between us would exist no more. The knowledge of my crippled state, so happily glossed over and indeed forgotten when he came to me at Radford, would have nagged me, a perpetual reproach, had I lived beneath his roof at Buckland. The sense of helplessness, of ugly inferiority, would have worked like a maggot in my mind, and even when he was most gentle and most tender I should have thought, with some devil flash of intuition: 'This is not what he is wanting.'

That was my greatest fault; I lacked humility. Though sixteen years of discipline had taught me to accept crippledom and become resigned to it, I was too proud to share the stigma of it with my lover. Oh, God, what I would have given to have walked with him and ridden, to move and turn before him, to have liveliness and grace.

Even a gipsy in the hedges, a beggar-woman in the gutters, had more dignity than I. He would say to me, smiling over his wine, 'Next week you shall come to me at Buckland. There is a chamber, high up in the tower, looking out across the valley to the hills. This was once my grandfather's, who fought in the *Revenge*, and when Drake purchased Buckland he used the chamber as his own, and hung maps upon the wall. You could lie there, Honor, dreaming of the past, and the Armada. And in the evening I would come to you, and kneel beside your bed, and we would make believe that the apple-tree at Lanrest was still in bloom, and you eighteen.'

I could see the room as he described it. And the window looking to the hills. And the tents of the soldiers below. And the pennant flying from the tower, scarlet and gold. I could see too the other Honor, walking by his side upon the terrace, who might have been his lady.

And I smiled at him, and shook my head. 'No, Richard,' I said, 'I will not come to Buckland.'

And so the autumn passed, and a new year came upon us once again. The whole of the west country was held firmly for the King, save Plymouth, Lyme, and Taunton, which stubbornly defied all attempts at subjugation, and the two seaports, relieved constantly by the Parliament shipping, were still in no great danger of starvation. So long as these garrisons were unsubdued the west could not be counted truly safe for His Majesty, and although the Royalist leaders were of good heart, and expressed great confidence, the people throughout the whole country were already sick and tired of war, which had brought them nothing but loss and high taxation. I believe it was the same for Parliament, and that troops deserted from the army every day. Men wanted to be home again, upon their rightful business. The quarrel was not theirs. They had no wish to fight for King or Parliament. 'A plague on both your houses' was the common cry. In January Richard became Sheriff for Devon, and with this additional authority he could raise fresh troops and levies, but the way he set about it was never pleasing to the Commissioners of the county. He rode roughshod over their feelings, demanding men and money as a right, and for the smallest pretext he would have a gentleman arrested and clapped into gaol, until such time as a ransom would be paid.

This would not be hearsay from my brother, but frank admissions on the part of Richard himself. Always unscrupulous where money was concerned, now that he had an army to pay, any sense of caution flew to the winds. Again and again I would hear his justification: 'The country is at war. I am a professional soldier, and I will not command men who are not paid. While I hold this appointment from His Majesty, I will undertake to feed, clothe, and arm the forces at my disposal, so that they hold themselves like men and warriors and do not roam the countryside, raping and looting and in rags, like the disorderly rabble under the so-called command of Berkeley, Goring, and the rest. To do this I must have money. And to get money I must demand it from the pockets of the merchants and the gentry of Cornwall and Devon.' I think he became more hated by them every day, but by the common people more respected. His troops won such credit for high discipline that their fame spread far abroad to the eastern counties, and it was, I believe, because of this that the first seeds of jealousy began to sow themselves in the hearts and minds of his brother commanders. None of them were professionals like himself, but men of estate and fortune, who by their rank had immediately, upon the outbreak of the war, been given high commands, and expected to lead newly-raised armies into battle. They were gentlemen of leisure, of no experience, and, though many of them were gallant and courageous, warfare to them consisted of a furious charge upon blood horses, dangerous and exciting, with more speed to it than a day's hawking, and, when the fray was over, a return to their quarters to eat, and drink, and play cards, while the men they had led could fend for themselves. Let them loot the villages, and strip the poor inhabitants – it saved the leaders a vast amount of unpleasantness, and the trouble that must come from organization. But it was irritating, I imagine, to hear how Grenvile's men were praised, and how Grenvile's men were paid and fed and clothed, and Sir John Berkeley, who commanded the troops at Exeter, and was for ever hearing complaints from the common people about Lord Goring's cavalry, and Lord Wentworth's foot, was glad enough, I imagine, to report to his supreme commander, Prince Maurice, that even if Grenvile's men were disciplined, the Commissioners of Devon and Cornwall had no good word to say of Grenvile himself, and that, in spite of all the fire-eating and hanging of rebel prisoners, Plymouth was still not taken.

In the despatches that passed between John Berkeley and Richard, which from time to time he quoted to me with a laugh, I could read the veiled hint that Berkeley at Exeter, with nothing much to do, would think it far preferable for himself and for the royal cause if he should change commands with Richard.

'They expect me', Richard would say, 'to hurl my fellows at the defences without any regard for their lives, and, having lost three-quarters of them in one assault, recruit another five hundred the following week. Had I command of unlimited forces, and of God's quantity of ammunition, a bombardment of three days would reduce Plymouth to ashes. But with the little I have at my disposal I cannot hope to reduce the garrison before the spring. In the meanwhile, I can keep the swine harassed night and day, which is more than Digby ever did.'

His blockade of Plymouth was complete by land, but, the rebels having command of the Sound, provisions and relief could be brought to them by sea, and this was the real secret of their success. All that Richard, as commander of the siege could do was to wear out the defenders by constant surprise attack upon the outward positions, in the hope that in time they would, from very weariness, surrender.

It was a hopeless, gruelling task, and the only people to win glory and praise for their stout hearts, were the men who were besieged within the city.

It was shortly after Christmas that Richard decided to send Dick to Normandy, with his tutor, Herbert Ashley.

'It's no life for him at Buckland,' he said. 'Ever since Jo went I've had a guard to watch him, day and night, and the thought of him, so close to the enemy should they try a sally, becomes a constant anxiety. He can go to Caen, or Rouen; and when the business is well over I shall send for him again.'

'Would you never', I said with diffidence, 'consider returning him to London, to his mother?'

He stared at me as though I had lost my senses.

'Let him go back to that bitch-faced hag,' he said, astounded, 'and become more of a little reptile than he is already? I would sooner send him this moment to Robartes, and let him hang.'

'He loves her,' I said. 'She is his mother.'

'So does a pup snuggle to the cur that suckled him,' he answered, 'but soon forgets her smell, once he is weaned. I have but one son, Honor, and if he can't be a credit to me and become the man I want, I have no use for him.'

He changed the subject abruptly, and I was reminded once again how I had chosen to be friend, not wife, companion and not mistress, and to meddle with his child was not my business. So Dick rode to Radford to bid me good-bye, and put his arms about me, and said he loved me well. 'If only', he said, 'you could have come with me to Normandy.'

'Perhaps', I said, 'you will not remain there long. And, anyway, it will be fresh and new to you, and you will make friends there, and be happy.'

'My father does not wish me to make friends,' he said. 'I heard him say as much to Mr Ashley. He said that in Caen there were few English, and therefore it would be better to go there than to Rouen, and that I was to speak to no one, and go nowhere, without Mr Ashley's knowledge or permission. I know what it is. He is afraid that I might fall in with some person who should be friendly to my mother.'

I had no answer to this argument, for I felt it to be true. 'I shall not know you', I said, summoning a smile, 'the next time that I lay eyes upon you. I know how boys grow, once they are turned fifteen. I saw it with my brother Percy. You will be a young man, with lovelocks on your shoulders, and a turn for poetry, in six months' time.'

'Fine poetry I shall write,' he sulked, 'conversing in French day by day with Mr Ashley.'

If I were in truth his stepmother, I thought, I could prevent this; and if I were in truth his stepmother, he would have hated me. So whichever way I looked upon the matter, there was no solution to Dick's problem. He had to face the future, like his father. And so Dick and the timid, unconvincing Herbert Ashley set sail for Normandy, the last day of December, taking with them a bill in exchange for twenty pounds, which was all that the General in the West could spare them, Dick taking besides my love and blessing, which would not help at all. And while they rocked upon the Channel between Falmouth and St Malo, Richard launched an attack upon Plymouth which this time, so he promised, would not fail. I can see him now, in his room in that north block at Radford, poring over his map of the Plymouth defences. When I asked to look at it he tossed it to me with a laugh, saying no woman could make head or tail of his marks and crosses.

And he was right, for never had I seen a chart more scribbled upon with dots and scratches. But even my unpractised eye could note that the network of defences was formidable indeed, for before the town and the garrison could be attacked a chain of outer forts, or 'works' as he termed them, had first to be breached. He came and stood beside me, and with his pen pointed to the scarlet crosses on the map.

'There are four works here to the north, in line abreast,' he said, 'the Pennycomequick, the Maudlyn, the Holiwell, and the Lipson forts. I propose to seize them all. Once established there, we shall turn the guns against the garrison itself. My main strength will fall upon the Maudlyn works, the others being more in the nature of a feint to draw their fire.' He was in high spirits, as always before a big engagement, and, suddenly, folding his map, he said to me: 'You have never seen my fellows, have you, in their full war-paint, prior to a battle? Would you like to do so?'

I smiled. 'Do you propose to make me your aide-de-camp?'

'No, I am going to take you round the posts.'

It was three o'clock, a cold fine afternoon in January. One of the wagons was fitted as a litter for my person, and, with Richard riding at my side, we set forth to view his army.

It was a sight that even now, when all is over and done with and the Siege of Plymouth a forgotten thing except for the official records in the archives of the town, I can call before me with wonder and with pride. The main body of his army was drawn up in the fields behind the little parish of Egg Buckland (not to be confused with the Buckland Monachorum, where Richard had his headquarters) and since there had been no warning of our coming, the men were not summoned to parade, but were going about their business in preparation for the attack ahead.

The first signal that the General had come in person was a springing to attention of the guards before the camp, and straightway there came a roll upon the drums from within, followed by a second more distant, and then a third, and then a fourth, so that in the space of a few moments, so it seemed to me, the air around me rang with a tattoo, as the drums of every company sounded the alert. And swiftly, unfolding in the crisp cold air, the scarlet pennant broke from the pole-head, with the golden rests staring from the centre.

Two officers approached and, saluting with their swords, stood before us. This Richard acknowledged with a half gesture of his hand, and then my chair was lifted from the wagon, and, with a stalwart young corporal to propel me, we proceeded round the camp.

I can smell now the wood smoke from the fires as the blue rings rose into the air, and I can see the men, bending over their washtubs, or kneeling before the cooking-pots, straightening themselves with a jerk as we approached, and standing to attention like steel rods. The foot were quartered separately from the horse, and these we inspected first, great brawny fellows of five foot ten or more, for Richard had disdain for little men and would not recruit them. They had a bronzed, clean look about them, the result, so Richard said, of living in the open. 'No billeting in cottages amongst the village folk for

Grenvile troops,' he said. 'The result is always the same – slackness and loss of discipline.'

I had fresh in my mind a picture of the rebel regiment who had taken Menabilly. Although they had worn a formidable air upon first sight, with their close helmets and uniform jerkins, they had soon lost their sheen, and as the weeks wore on they became dirty-looking and rough, and with the threat of defeat had one and all reverted to a London mob in panic.

Richard's men had another stamp upon them, and, though they were drawn mostly from the farms and moors of Cornwall and of Devon, rustic in speech and origin, they had become knit, in the few months of his command, into a professional body of soldiers, quick of thought and swift of limb, with an admiration for their leader that showed at once in the upward tilt of their heads as he addressed them and the flash of pride in their eyes. A strange review. I in my chair, a hooded cloak about my shoulders, and Richard walking by my side; the camp-fires burning, the white frost gleaming on the clipped turf, the drums beating their tattoo as we approached each different company.

The horse were drawn up on the further field, and we watched them being groomed and watered for the night, fine sleek animals – many of them seized from rebel estates, as I was fully aware – and they stamped on the hard ground, the harness jingling, their breath rising in the cold air like the smoke from the fires.

The sun was setting, fiery red, beyond the Tamar into Cornwall, and as it sank beyond the hills it threw a last dull sullen glow upon the forts of Plymouth to the south of us.

We could see the tiny figures of the rebel sentries, like black dots, upon the outer defences, and I wondered how many of the Grenvile men about me would make themselves a sacrifice to the spitting thunder of the rebel guns. Lastly, as evening fell, we visited the forward posts, and here there was no more cleaning of equipment, no grooming of horses, but men stripped bare for battle, silent, motionless, and we talked in whispers, for we were scarce two hundred yards from the enemy defences.

The silence was grim, uncanny. The assault force seemed

dim figures in the gathering darkness, for they had blackened their faces to make themselves less visible, and I could make out nothing of them but white eyes, gleaming, and the show of teeth when they smiled.

Their breastplates were discarded for a night attack, and in their hands they carried pikes, steely sharp. I felt the edge of one of them and shuddered.

At the last post we visited the men were not so prompt to challenge us as hitherto, and I heard Richard administer a sharp reproof to the young officer in charge. The colonel of the regiment of foot, in command of the post, came forth to excuse himself, and I saw that it was my old suitor of the past, Jo's brother-in-law, Edward Champernowne. He bowed to me, somewhat stiffly, and then turning to Richard, I heard him stammer several attempts at explanation, and the two withdrew to a little distance. On his return Richard was silent, and we straightway turned back towards my wagon and the escort, and I knew that the review was finished.

'You must return alone to Radford,' he said. 'I will send the escort with you. There will be no danger.'

'And the coming battle?' I asked. 'Are you confident, and pleased?'

He paused a moment before replying. 'Yes,' he answered, 'yes, I am hopeful. The plan is sound, and there is nothing wanting in the men. If only my seconds were more dependable.' He jerked his head toward the post from which we had just lately come. 'Your old lover, Edward Champernowne,' he said. 'I sometimes think he would do better to command a squad of ducks. He has a flickering reason when his long nose is glued upon a map, ten miles from the enemy, but give him a piece of work to do upon the field a hundred yards away, and he is lost.'

'Can you not replace him with some other?' I questioned.

'Not at this juncture,' he said. 'I have to risk him now.'

He kissed my hand and smiled, and it was not until he had turned his back on me and vanished that I remembered I had never asked him whether the reason for his not returning with me to Radford was because he proposed to lead the assault in person.

I jogged back in the wagon to my brother's house, my spirits sinking. Shortly before daybreak, next morning, the attack began. The first we heard of it at Radford was the echo of the guns across the Cattwater – whether from within the garrison or from the outer defences, we could not tell – but by midday we had the news that three of the Works had been seized and held by the Royalist troops, and the most formidable of the forts, the Maudlyn, stormed by the commanding General in person. The guns were turned, and the men of Plymouth felt for the first time their own fire fall upon the walls of the city. I could see nothing from my window but a pall of smoke hanging like a curtain in the sky, and now and again, the wind being northerly, I thought I heard the sound of distant shouting from the besieged within the garrison.

At three o'clock, with barely three hours of daylight left, the news was not so good. The rebels had counter-attacked, and two of the forts had been recaptured. The fate of Plymouth now depended upon the rebels gaining back the ground they had lost and driving the Royalists from their foothold all along the line, and most especially from the Maudlyn Works. I watched the setting sun, as I had done the day before, and I thought of all those, both rebel men and Royalist, whose lives had been held forfeit within these past four-and-twenty hours. We dined in the hall at half past five, with my brother Jo seated at the head of his table, as was his custom, and Phillipa at his right hand and his little motherless son, young John, upon his left. We ate in silence, none of us having much heart for conversation, while the battle only a few miles away hung thus in the balance. We were nearly finished when my brother Percy, who had ridden down to Plymouth to get news, came bursting in upon us.

'The rebels have gained the day,' he said grimly, 'and driven off Grenvile with the loss of three hundred men. They stormed the fort on all sides, and finally recaptured it, barely an hour ago. It seems that Grenvile's covering troops, who should have come to his support and turned the scale to success, failed to reach him. A tremendous blunder on the part of someone.'

'No doubt the fault of the General himself,' said Jo drily, 'in having too much confidence.'

'They say, down in Plymstock, that the officer responsible has been shot by Grenvile for contravention of orders,' said Percy, 'and is lying now in his tent with a bullet through his head. Who it is they could not tell me, but we shall hear anon.'

I could think of nothing but those three hundred men who were lying now upon their faces under the stars, and I was filled with a great war-sickness, a loathing for guns and pikes and blood and battle-cries. The brave fellows who had smiled at me the night before, so strong, so young and confident, were now carrion for the sea-gulls who swooped and dived in Plymouth Sound, and it was Richard, my Richard, who had led them to their death. I could not blame him. He had only, by attacking, done his duty. He was a soldier. . . .

As I turned away to call a servant for my chair, a young secretary, employed by my elder brother on the Devon Commission, came into the room, much agitated, with a request to speak to him.

'What is the matter?' said Jo tersely. 'There is no one but my family present.'

'Colonel Champernowne lies at Egg Buckland, mortally wounded,' said the secretary. 'He was not hurt in battle, but pistolled by the General himself on returning to headquarters.'

There was a moment of great silence. Jo rose slowly from his chair, very white and tense, and I saw him turn round and look at me, as did my brother Percy. In a moment of perception I knew what they were thinking. Jo's brother-in-law, Edward Champernowne, had been my suitor seventeen years before, and they both saw, in this sudden terrible dispute after the heat of battle, no military cause, but some private jealous wrangle, the settling of a feud.

'This', said my elder brother slowly, 'is the beginning of the end for Richard Grenvile.'

His words fell upon my ear cold as steel, and, calling softly to the servant, I bade him take me to my room.

The next day I left for Mothercombe, to my sister Cecilia, for to remain under my brother's roof one moment longer would have been impossible. The vendetta had begun.

My eldest brother, with the vast family of Champernowne behind him, and supported by the leading families in the county of Devon, most of them members of the Commission, pressed for the removal of Sir Richard Grenvile from his position as Sheriff and commander of the King's forces in the west. Richard retaliated by turning my brother out of Radford and using the house and estate as a jumping-ground for a fresh assault upon Plymouth.

Snowed-up in Mothercombe with the Pollexefens, I knew little of what was happening, and Cecilia, with consummate tact and delicacy, avoided the subject. I myself had had no word from Richard since the night I had bidden him good-bye before the battle, and now that he was engaged in a struggle with foe and former friends as well I thought it best to keep silent. He knew my whereabouts, for I had sent word of it, and should he want me he would come to me.

The thaw burst at the end of March, and we had the first tidings of the outside world for many weeks.

The peace moves between King and Parliament had come to nothing, for the Treaty of Uxbridge had failed, and the war, it seemed, was to be carried on more ruthlessly than ever.

The Parliament, we heard, was forming a New Model army, likely to sweep all before it, in the opinion of the judges, while His Majesty had sent forth an edict to his enemies saying that unless the rebels repented their end must be damnation, ruin, and infamy. The young Prince of Wales, it seemed, was now to bear the title of supreme commander of all the forces in the west, and was gone to Bristol, but since he was a lad of only fifteen years or so the real authority would be vested in his Advisory Council, at the head of whom was Hyde, the Chancellor of the Exchequer.

I remember John Pollexefen shaking his head as he heard the news. 'There will be nothing but wrangles now between the Prince's Council and the Generals,' he said. 'Each will countermand the orders of the other. Lawyers and soldiers never agree. And while they wrangle the King's cause will suffer. I do not like it.'

I thought of Richard and how he had once vouchsafed the same opinion. 'What is happening at Plymouth?' asked my sister. 'Stalemate,' said her husband. 'A token force of less than a thousand men left to blockade the garrison, and Grenvile with the remainder gone to join Goring in Somerset and lay siege to Taunton. The spring campaign has started.'

Soon a year would have come and gone since I had left Lanrest for Menabilly. The snow melted down in the Devon valley where Cecilia had her home, and the crocus and daffodil appeared. I made no plans. I sat and waited. Someone brought a rumour that there was great disaffection in the High Command, and that Grenvile, Goring, and Berkeley were all at loggerheads.

March turned to April. The golden gorse was in full bloom. And on Easter Day a horseman came riding down the valley, wearing the Grenvile badge. He asked at once for Mistress Harris, and, saluting gravely, handed me a letter.

'What is it?' I asked before I broke the seal. 'Has something happened?' My throat felt dry and strange, and my hands trembled. 'The General has been gravely wounded', replied the soldier, 'in a battle before Wellington House at Taunton. They fear for his life.' I tore open the letter, and read Richard's shaky scrawl.

'Dear Heart,' he said, 'this is the very devil. I am like to lose my leg, if not my life, with a great gaping hole in my thigh, below the groin. I know now what you suffer. Come teach me patience. I love you.'

I folded the letter, and, turning to the messenger, asked him where the General lay.

'They were bringing him from Taunton down to Exeter when I left,' he answered. 'His Majesty had dispatched his own chirurgeon to attend upon Sir Richard. He was very weak, and bade me ride without delay to bring you this.'

I looked at Cecilia, who was standing by the window. 'Would you summon Matty to pack my clothes,' I said, 'and ask John if he would arrange for a litter, and for horses? I am going to Exeter.'

Chapter 23

WE took the southern route to Exeter, and at every halt upon the journey I thought to hear the news of Richard's death.

Totnes, Newton Abbot, Ashburton, each delay seemed longer than the last, and when at length after six days I reached the capital of Devon, and saw the great cathedral rising high above the city and the river, it seemed to me I had been weeks upon the road.

Richard still lived. This was my first inquiry, and the only thing that mattered. He was lodging at the hostelry in the Cathedral square, where I immediately repaired. He had taken the whole building for his personal use, and had a sentry before the door.

When I gave my name a young officer immediately appeared from within, and something ruddy about his colouring, and familiar in his bearing, made me pause a moment before addressing him correctly. Then his courteous smile gave me the clue.

'You are Jack Grenvile, Bevil's boy,' I said, and he reminded me of how he had come once with his father to Lanrest in the days before the war. I remembered too how I had washed him as a baby on that memorable visit to Stowe in '28, but this I did not tell him.

'My uncle will be most heartily glad to see you,' he said as I was lifted from my litter. 'He has talked of little else since writing to you. He has sent at least ten women flying from his side since coming here, swearing they were rough and did not know their business, nor how to dress his wound. Matty shall do it, he said, while Honor talks to me.' I saw Matty colour up with pleasure at these words, and assume at once an air of authority before the corporal who shouldered our trunks.

'And how is he?' I asked, as I was set down within the great inn parlour, which had been, judging by the long table in the centre, turned into a mess-room for the General's staff.

'Better these last three days than hitherto,' replied his nephew, 'but at first we thought to lose him. Directly he was wounded I applied to the Prince of Wales to wait on him, and I attended him here from Taunton. Now he declares he will not send me back. Nor have I any wish to go.'

'Your uncle', I said, 'likes to have a Grenvile by his side.'

'I know one thing,' said the young man. 'He finds fellows of my age better company than his contemporaries, which I take as a great compliment.' At this moment Richard's servant came down the stairs saying the General wished to see Mistress Harris upon the instant. I went first to my room, where Matty washed me and changed my gown, and then, with Jack Grenvile to escort me, I went along the corridor, in my wheeled chair, to Richard's room.

It looked out upon the cobbled square, and as we entered the great bell from the Cathedral chimed four o'clock.

'God confound that blasted bell,' said a familiar voice, sounding stronger than I had dared to hope, from the dark-curtained bed in the far corner. 'A dozen times I have asked the Mayor of this damned city to have it silenced, and nothing has been done. Harry, for God's sake make a note of it."

'Sir,' answered hurriedly a tall youth at the foot of the bed, scribbling a word upon his tablets.

'And move these pillows, can't you? Not that way, you clumsy lout; behind my head, thus. Where the devil is Jack? Jack is the only lad who knows how I like them placed.'

'Here I am, Uncle,' said his nephew, 'but you will not need me now. I have brought you someone with gentler hands than I.'

He pushed my chair towards the bed, smiling, and I saw Richard's hand reach out to pull back the curtains.

'Ah!' he said, sighing deeply. 'You have come at last.' He was deathly white. And his eyes had grown larger, perhaps in contrast to the pallor of his face. His auburn locks were clipped short, giving him a strangely youthful look. For the first time I noticed in him a resemblance to Dick. I took his hand and held it.

'I did not wait,' I said, 'once I had read your letter.'

He turned to the two lads standing at the foot of the bed, his nephew and the one he had named Harry.

216

'Get out, both of you,' he said, 'and if that damned chirurgeon shows his face, tell him to go to the devil.'

'Sir,' they replied, clicking their heels, and I could swear that as they left the room young Jack Grenvile winked an eye at his companion.

Richard lifted my hand to his lips, and then cradled it beside his cheek. 'This is a good jest', he said, 'on the part of the Almighty. You and I both smitten in the thigh.'

'Does it pain you much?' I asked.

'Pain me? My God, splinters from a cannon-ball, striking below the groin, burn something fiercer than a woman's kiss. Of course it pains me.'

'Who has seen the wound?'

'Every chirurgeon in the army, and each one makes more mess of it than his fellow.'

I called for Matty, who was waiting outside the door, and she came in at once with a basin of warm water and bandages and towels.

'Good day to you, mutton-face,' said Richard. 'How many corporals have you bedded with *en route*?'

'No time to bed with anyone,' snapped Matty, 'carried at the rate we were, with Miss Honor delaying only to sleep a few snatched hours every night. Now we've come here to be insulted.'

'I'll not insult you, unless you tie my bandages too tight.'

'Come, then,' she said. 'Let's see what they have done to you.'

She unfolded the bandages with expert fingers, and exposed the wound. It was deep, in truth, the splinters having penetrated the bone and lodged there. With every probe of her fingers he winced and groaned, calling her every name under the sun, which did not worry her.

'It's clean, that's one thing,' she said. 'I fully expected to find it gangrenous. But you'll have some of those splinters to the end of your days, unless you let them take your leg off.'

'They'll not do that,' he answered. 'I'd rather keep the splinters and bear the pain.'

'It will give you an excuse, at any rate, for your bad temper,' she replied. She washed the wound, and dressed it once again, and all the while he held my hand as Dick might do. Then she finished, and he thumbed his finger to his nose as she left the room.

'Over three months', he said, 'since I have seen you. Are the Pollexefens as unpleasant as the rest of your family?'

'My family were not unpleasant till you made them so.'

'They disliked me from the first. Now they pursue their dislike across the county. You know the Commissioners of Devon are in Exeter at this moment, with a list of complaints a mile long to launch at me?'

'I did not know.'

'It's all a plot, hatched by your brother. Three members of the Prince's Council are to come down from Bristol and discuss the business with the Commissioners; and as soon as I am fit enough to move I am to go before them. Jack Berkeley, commanding here at Exeter, is up to his neck in the intrigue.'

'And what exactly is the intrigue?'

'Why, to have me shifted from my command, of course, and for Berkeley to take my place.'

'Would you mind so very much? The blockade of Plymouth has not brought you much satisfaction.'

'Jack Berkeley is welcome to Plymouth. But I'm not going to lie down and accept some secondary command, dished out to me by the Prince's Council while I hold authority from His Majesty himself.'

'His Majesty', I said, 'appears by all accounts to have his own troubles. Who is this General Cromwell we hear so much about?'

'Another God-damned Puritan with a mission,' said Richard. 'They say he talks with the Almighty every evening, but I think it far more likely that he drinks. He's a good soldier, though. So is Fairfax. Their new Model Army will make mincemeat of our disorganized rabble.'

'And, knowing this, you choose to quarrel with your friends?'

'They are not my friends. They are a set of low, back-biting blackguards. And I have told them all so, to their faces.'

It was useless to argue with him. And his wound had made him more sensitive on every point. I asked if he had news of Dick, and he showed me a stilted letter from the tutor, as well as copies of instructions that he had sent to Herbert Ashley.

There was nothing very friendly or encouraging amongst them. I caught a glimpse of the words, 'For his education I desire he may constantly and diligently be kept to the learning of the French tongue; reading, writing, and arithmetic, also riding, fencing, and dancing. All this I shall expect of him, which, if he follow according to my desire for his own good, he shall not want anything. But if I understand that he neglects in any kind what I have herein commanded him to do, truly I will neither allow him a penny to maintain him, nor look on him again as my son.' I folded the instructions, and put them back into the case, which he locked and kept beside him.

'Do you think', I said, 'to win his affection in that way?'

'I don't ask for his affection,' he said. 'I ask for his obedience.'

'You were not harsh thus with Jo. Nor are you so unrelenting to your nephew Jack.'

'Jo was one in a million, and Jack has some likeness to him. That lad fought at Lansdown like a tiger, when poor Bevil fell. And he was but fifteen, as Dick is now. All these lads I have affection for because they hold themselves like men. But Dick, my son and heir, shudders when I speak to him, and whimpers at the sight of blood. It does not make for pride in his father.'

An argument. A blow. A baby's cry. And fifteen years of poison seeping through a child's blood. There was no panacea that I could think of to staunch the flood of resentment. Time and distance might bring a measure of healing that close contact only served to wound. Once again Richard kissed my hand. 'Never mind young Dick,' he said. 'It is not he who has a dozen splinters through his thigh.'

No man, I think, was ever a worse patient than Richard Grenvile, and no nurse more impervious to his threats and groans and curses than was Matty. My role, if less exacting, called for great equanimity of temperament. Being a woman, I did not have his spurs hurled at my head, as did his luckless officers, but I suffered many a bitter accusation because my name was Harris, and he liked to taunt me too because I had been born and bred in south-east Cornwall, where the women all were hags and scolds, so he averred, and the men cowards and deserters. 'Nothing good came out of Cornwall yet,' he said, 'save from the north coast.' And seeing that this failed to rouse me he sought by other means to make me rankle, a strange and unprofitable pastime for a sick man, but one I could understand in full measure, for I had often wished so to indulge myself some seventeen years before, but had never the courage of my moods.

He kept his bed for some five weeks, and then, by the end of May, was sufficiently recovered to walk in his chamber with a stick, and at the same time curse his harassed staff for idleness.

The feathers flew when he first came downstairs, for all the world like a turkey-fight, and I never saw high-ranking officers more red about the ears than the colonels and the majors he addressed that May morning. They looked at the door with longing eyes, like schoolboys, with but one thought in their mind, to win freedom from his lashing tongue, or so I judged from their expressions. But when, after I had taken my airing in the square, I conversed with them, sympathy on the tip of my tongue, they one and all remarked upon the excellence of the General's health and spirits.

'It does one good', said a colonel of foot, 'to see the General himself again. I hardly dared to hope for it, a month since.'

'Do you bear no malice then,' I said, 'for his words to you this morning?'

'Malice?' said the colonel, looking puzzled. 'Why should I bear malice? The General was merely taking exercise.'

The ways of professional soldiers were beyond me.

'It is a splendid sign', said Richard's nephew Jack, 'when my uncle gives vent to frowns and curses. It mostly means he is well pleased. But see him smile, and speak with courtesy, and you may well reckon that the luckless receiver of his favours is halfway to the guard-room. I once saw him curse a fellow for fifteen minutes without respite, and that evening promote him to the rank of captain. The next day he received a prisoner, a country squire, I think, from Barnstaple, who owed him money, and my uncle plied him with wine, and smiles, and favours. He was hanging from a tree at Buckland two hours afterwards.'

I remember asking Richard if these tales were true. He laughed. 'It pleases my staff', he said, 'to weave a legend about my person.' But he did not deny them.

Meanwhile, the Prince's Council had come to Exeter to have discussion with the Devon Commissioners and to hear the complaints they had to make against Sir Richard Grenvile. It was unfortunate, I felt, that the head of the Prince's Council was that same Sir Edward Hyde whom Richard had described to me at Radford as a jumped-up lawyer. I think the remark had been repeated to him, for when he arrived at the hostelry to call upon Richard, accompanied by Lords Culpepper and Capel, I thought his manner very cold and formal, and I could see he bore little cordiality towards the general who had so scornfully dubbed him upstart. I was presented to them, and immediately withdrew. What they thought of me I neither knew nor cared. It would be but another scandalous tale to spread, that Sir Richard Grenvile had a crippled mistress.

What in truth transpired behind those closed doors I never discovered. As soon as the three members of the Prince's Council tried to speak they would be drowned by Richard, with a tirade of accusations against the Governor of the city, Sir John Berkeley, who, so he avowed, had done nothing for nine months now but put obstructions in his path. As to the Commissioners of Devon, they were traitors, one and all, and tried to keep their money in their pockets rather than pay the army that defended them.

'Let Berkeley take over Plymouth, if he so desires it,' Richard declared. (This he told me afterwards.) 'God knows it troubles me to be confined to blocking up a place, when there is likely to be action in the field. Give me power to raise men in Cornwall and in Devon, without fear of obstruction, and I will place an army at the disposal of the Prince of Wales that will be a match for Cromwell's Puritans.' Whereupon he formally handed over his resignation as commander of the Siege of Plymouth, and sent the lords of the Council packing off back to Bristol to receive the Prince's authority sanctioning him to a new command. 'I handled them', he said to me gleefully, 'with silken gloves. Let Jack Berkeley stew at Plymouth, and good luck to him.' And he drank a bottle and a half of burgundy at supper, which played havoc with his wound next morning.

I have forgotten how many days we waited for the royal warrant to arrive, confirming him in the appointment to raise troops, but it must have been ten days or more. At last Richard declared that he would not kick his heels waiting for a piece of paper that few people would take the trouble to read, and he proceeded to raise recruits for the new army. His staff were dispatched about the countryside rounding up the men who had been idle, or had deserted and gone home, during his illness. All were promised pay and clothing. And as Sheriff of Devon (for this post he had not resigned with his command) Richard ordered his old enemies, the Commissioners, to raise fresh money for the purpose. I guessed this would bring a hornet's nest about his ears again, but I was only a woman, and it was not my business.

I sat one day beside my window, looking out on to the Cathedral, and I saw Sir John Berkeley, who had not yet gone to Plymouth, ride away from the hostelry looking like a thundercloud. There had been a stormy meeting down below, and, according to young Jack, Sir John had got the worst of it.

'I yield to no man', said Richard's nephew, 'in my admiration for my uncle. He has the better of his opponents every time. But I wish he would guard his tongue.'

'What', I asked wearily, 'are they disputing now?'

'It is always the same story,' said Jack. 'My uncle says that as Sheriff of the county he can compel the Commissioners to pay his troops. Sir John declares the contrary. That it is to him, as Governor of the city and commander before Plymouth, to whom the money should be paid. They'll fight a duel about it before they have finished.' Shortly afterwards Richard came to my room white with passion. 'My God,' he said, 'I cannot stand this hopeless mess an instant longer. I shall ride at once to Bristol to see the Prince. When in doubt, go to the highest authority. That has always been my rule. Unless I can get satisfaction out of His Highness I shall chuck the whole affair.'

'You are not well enough to ride,' I said.

'I can't help that. I won't stay here and have that hopeless nincompoop Jack Berkeley obstruct every move I make. He is hand-in-glove with your blasted brother, that's the trouble.'

'You began the trouble,' I said, 'by making an enemy of my

brother. All this has come about because you shot Edward Champernowne.'

'What would you have had me do – promote the sod?' he stormed. 'A weak-bellied rat who caused the death of three hundred of my finest troops because he was too lily-livered to face the rebel guns and come to my support? Shooting was too good for him. A hundred years ago he would have been drawn and quartered.'

The next day he left for Barnstaple, where the Prince of Wales had gone to escape the plague at Bristol, and I was thankful that he took his nephew Jack as aide-de-camp. He had three men to hoist him into the saddle, and he still looked most damnably unwell. He smiled up at me as I leant from my window in the hostelry, and saluted with his sword. 'Have no fear,' he said, 'I'll return within a fortnight. Keep well. Be happy.'

But he never did return, and that was the end of my sojourn as a nurse and comforter at Exeter. On the eighteenth of June the King and Prince Rupert were heavily defeated by General Cromwell at Naseby, and the rebel army, under the supreme command of General Fairfax, was marching once again towards the west. The whole of the Royalist strategy had now to be changed to meet this new menace, and, while rumours ran rife that Fairfax was coming upon Taunton, I had a message from Richard to say that he had been ordered by the Prince of Wales to besiege Lyme and had the commission of field-marshal in his pocket.

'I will send for you', he said, 'when I have fixed my headquarters. In the meantime, rest where you are. I think it very likely that we shall all of us, before the summer is out, be on the run again.' This news was hardly pleasant hearing, and I bethought me of the relentless marching feet that I had heard a year ago at Menabilly. Was the whole horror of invasion to be endured once again? I did as he bade me, and stayed at Exeter. I had no home, and one roof was as good to me now as another. If I lacked humility, I also had no pride. I was nothing more nor less, by this time, than a camp-follower. A pursuivant of the drum.

On the last day of June Jack Grenvile came for me, with a

troop of horse to bear my litter. Matty and I were already packed and ready. We had been waiting since the message a fortnight before.

'Where are we bound?' I said gaily. 'For Lyme or London?'

'For neither,' he said grimly. 'For a tumbled-down residence in Ottery St Mary. The General has thrown up his commission.'

He could tell me little of what had happened, except that the bulk of the new forces that had been assigned to Richard's new command, and were to rendezvous at Tiverton, had suddenly been withdrawn by the orders of the Prince's Council and diverted to the defence of Barnstaple, without a word of explanation to the General. We came to Ottery St Mary, a sleepy Devon village where the inhabitants stared at the strange equipage that drew up before the manor house as though the world were suddenly grown crazy – in which they showed good reason. In the meadows behind the village were drawn Richard's own horse and foot, who had followed him from the beginning. Richard himself was seated in the dining-chamber of his headquarters, his wounded leg propped upon a chair before him.

'Greetings', he said maliciously, 'from one cripple to another. Let us retire to bed and see who has the greatest talent for invention.'

'If that', I said, 'is your mood, we will discuss it presently. At the moment I am tired, hungry, and thirsty. But would you care to tell me what the devil you are doing in Ottery St Mary?'

'I am become a free man,' he answered, smiling, 'beholden to neither man nor beast. Let them fight the New Model Army in their own fashion. If they won't give me the troops, I do not propose to ride alone with nephew Jack against Fairfax and some twenty thousand men.'

'I thought', I said, 'that you were become field-marshal.'

'An empty honour,' he said, 'signifying nothing. I have just returned the commission to the Prince of Wales in an empty envelope, desiring him to place it up a certain portion of his person. What shall we drink for supper, hock or burgundy?'

Chapter 24

THAT was, I think, the most fantastic fortnight I have ever known. Richard, with no command and no commission, lived like a royal prince in the humble village of Ottery St Mary, the people for miles around bringing their produce to the camp, their corn, their cattle, in the firm belief that he was the supreme commander of His Majesty's troops from Lyme to Land's End. For payment he referred them graciously to the Commissioners of Devon. The first Sunday after his arrival he caused an edict to be read in the Church of Ottery St Mary and other churches in the neighbouring parishes, desiring that all those persons who had been plundered by the Governor of Exeter, Sir John Berkeley, when quartering troops upon them, should bring to him, Sir Richard Grenvile, the King's General in the West, an account of their losses, and he would see that they were righted.

The humble village folk, thinking that a saviour had come to dwell amongst them, came on foot from a distance of twenty miles or more, each one bearing in his hands a list of crimes and excesses committed, according to them, by Lord Goring's troopers and Sir John Berkeley's men, and I can see Richard now, standing in the village place before the church, distributing largesse in princely fashion from a sum of money he had discovered behind a panel in his headquarters, a house belonging to an unfortunate squire with vague Parliamentary tendencies, whom Richard had immediately arrested. On the Wednesday, since it was fine, he held a review of his troops – the sight being free to the villagers – and the drums sounded, and the church bells pealed, and in the evening bonfires were lit and a great supper was served at the headquarters to the officers, at which I presided like a queen.

'We may as well be merry,' said Richard, 'while the money lasts.' I thought of that letter to the Prince of Wales, which must by now have reached the Prince's Council, and I pictured the Chancellor of the Exchequer, Edward Hyde, opening the paper before the assembly.

I thought also of Sir John Berkeley, and what he would say when he heard about the edict in the churches, and it seemed to me that my rash and indiscreet lover would be wiser if he struck his camp and hid in the mists of Dartmoor, for he could not bluff the world much longer in Ottery St Mary.

The bluff was superb while it lasted, and, since the Parliamentary squire whom we had superseded kept a well-stocked cellar, we soon had every bottle sampled, and Richard drank perdition to the supporters of both Parliament and Crown.

'What will you do', I asked, 'if the Council sends for you?'

'Exactly nothing,' he answered, 'unless I have a letter, in his own handwriting, from the Prince of Wales himself.'

And, with a smile that his nephew would call ominous, he opened yet another bottle.

'If we continue thus,' I said, turning my glass down upon the table, 'you will become as great a sot as Goring.'

'Goring cannot stand after five glasses,' said Richard. 'I can drill a whole division after twelve.' And, rising from the table, he called to the orderly who stood without the door. 'Summon Sir John Grenvile,' he said. In a moment Jack appeared, also a little flushed and gay about the eyes.

'My compliments', said Richard, 'to Colonels Roscarrock and Arundell. I wish the troops to be paraded on the green. I intend to drill them.'

His nephew did not flicker an eyelid, but I saw his lips quiver.

'Sir,' he said, 'it is past eight o'clock. The men have been dismissed to their quarters.'

'I am well aware of the fact,' replied his uncle. 'It was for the purpose of rousing them that drums were first bestowed upon the army. My compliments to Colonels Roscarrock and Arundell.'

Jack clicked his heels and left the room. Richard walked slowly, and very solemnly, towards the chair where lay his sling and sword. He proceeded to buckle them about his waist.

'The sling', I said softly, 'is upside down.'

He bowed gravely in acknowledgement, and made the necessary adjustment. And from without the drums began to beat, sharp and alert, in the gathering twilight.

I was, I must confess, only a trifle less dazed about the head than I had been on that memorable occasion long before, when I had indulged too heavily in burgundy and swan. This time – and it was my only safeguard – I had my chair to sit in, and I can remember, through a sort of haze, being propelled towards the village green with the drums sounding in my ears and the soldiers running from all directions to form lines upon the grass sward. Villagers leant from their casements, and I remember one old fellow in a nightcap shrieking out that Fairfax was come upon them and they would all be murdered in their beds.

It was, I dare swear, the one and only occasion in the annals of His Majesty's army when two regiments have been drawn up and drilled by their commanding general in the dusk after too good a dinner.

'My God,' I heard Jack Grenvile choke behind me, whether in laughter or emotion I never discovered, 'this is magnificent. This will live for ever.' And when the drums were silent I heard Richard's voice, loud and clear, ring out across the village green.

It was a fitting climax to a crazy fourteen days. . . .

At breakfast the next morning a messenger came riding to the door of the headquarters with the news that Bridgwater had been stormed and captured by Fairfax and his rebel forces, that the Prince's Council had fled to Launceston, and that the Prince of Wales bade Sir Richard Grenvile depart instantly with what troops he had and come to him in Cornwall.

'Is the message a request or a command?' asked my general.

'A command, sir,' replied the officer, handing him a document, 'not from the Council, but from the Prince himself.'

Once again the drums were sounded, but this time for the march, and as the long line of troops wound their way through the village and on to the highway to Okehampton I wondered how many years would pass before the people of Ottery St Mary forgot Sir Richard Grenvile and his men. We followed, Matty and I, within a day or two, with an escort to our litter and orders to proceed to Werrington Park, near Launceston, which was yet another property that Richard had seized, without a scruple, from the owner of Buckland Monachorum, Francis Drake. We arrived to find Richard, in fair spirits, restored to the Prince's favour, after a very awkward three hours before the Council. It might have been more awkward, had not the Council been in so immediate a need of his services.

'And what has been decided?' I asked.

'Goring is to go north, to intercept the rebels,' he said, 'while I remain in Cornwall and endeavour to raise a force of some three thousand foot. It would have been better if they had sent me to deal with Fairfax, as Goring is certain to make a hash of it.'

'There is no one but you', I said, 'who can raise troops in Cornwall. Men will rally to a Grenvile, but none other. Be thankful that the Council sent for you at all, after your impudence.'

'They cannot afford', said Richard, 'to do without me. And anyway, I don't give a fig for the Council and that snake, Hyde. I am only doing this business to oblige the Prince. He's a lad after my own heart. If His Majesty continues to haver as he does at present, with no coherent plan of strategy, I am not at all sure that the best move would not be to hold all Cornwall for the Prince, live within it like a fortress, and let the rest of England go to blazes.'

'You have only to phrase that a little differently,' I said, 'and a malicious friend who wished you ill would call it treason.'

'Treason be damned,' he said. 'It is but sound common sense. No man has greater loyalty to His Majesty than I, but he does more to wreck his own cause than any who serve under him.'

While Matty and I remained at Werrington, Richard travelled the length and breadth of Cornwall, recruiting troops for the Prince's army. It was no easy business. The last invasion had been enough for Cornishmen. Men wished only to be left alone to tend their land and business. Money was as hard to raise as it had been in Devon, and with some misgiving I watched Richard use the same high-handed measures with the Commissioners of the Duchy as he had with those of the sister county. Those who might have yielded with some grace to tact gave way grudgingly to pressure, and Richard during that summer and early autumn of 1645 made as many enemies amongst the Cornish landowners as he had done in Devon.

On the north coast men rallied to his call because of his link with Stowe; the very name of Grenvile sounding like a clarion.

They came to him from beyond the border even, from Apple-dore and Bideford, and down the length of that storm-bound Atlantic coast from Hartland point to Padstowe. They were his best recruits. Clear-eyed, long-limbed, wearing with pride the scarlet shield with the three gold rests upon their shoulders. Men from Bude and Stratton and Tintagel, men from Boscastle and Camelford. And with great cunning Richard introduced his prince as Duke of Cornwall, who had come into the west to save them from the savage rebel hordes beyond the Tamar.

But farther south he met with rebuffs. Danger seemed more remote to people west of Truro, and even the fall of Bristol to Fairfax and the Parliament, which came like a clap of doom on 10 September, failed to rouse them from their lethargy.

'Truro, Helston, and St Ives', said Richard, 'are the three rottenest towns in Cornwall,' and he rode down, I remember, with some six hundred horse to quell a rising of the townsfolk, who had protested against a levy he had raised the week before.

He hanged at least three men, while the remainder were either fined or imprisoned. He took the opportunity, too, of visiting the Castle at St Mawes, and severely reprimanded its com-mander, Major Bonython, because he had failed to pay the soldiers under his command within the garrison.

'Whoever I find half-hearted in the Prince's cause must change his tune or suffer disciplinary action,' declared Richard. 'Whoever fails to pay his men shall contribute from his own pocket, and whoever shows one flicker of disloyalty to me, as commander, or to the Prince I serve, shall answer for it with his life.'

I heard him say this myself, in the market-place at Launces-ton before a great crowd assembled there, the last day of Sep-tember, and, while his own men cheered so that the echo came ringing back to us from the walls of the house, I saw few smiles upon the faces of the townsfolk gathered there.

'You forget', I said that night to him at Werrington, 'that Cornishmen are independent, and love freedom better than their fellows.'

'I remember one thing,' he answered, with that thin, bitter smile of his which I knew too well, 'that Cornishmen are cowards, and love their comfort better than their King.'

As autumn drew on, I began to wonder if either freedom or comfort would belong to any of us by the end of the year.

Chard, Crediton, Lyme, and finally Tiverton fell before Fairfax in October, and Lord Goring had done nothing to stop them. Many of his men deserted and came flocking to join Richard's army, for they had greater faith in him as a commander. This led to further jealousy, further recriminations, and it looked as though Richard would fall as foul with Goring as he had done with Sir John Berkeley three months earlier. There was constant fault-finding, too, by the Prince's Council in Launceston, and scarcely a day would pass without some interfering measure from the Chancellor, Edward Hyde.

'If they would but leave me alone', stormed Richard, 'to recruit my army and to train my troops, instead of flooding my headquarters day by day with dispatches written by lawyers with smudged fingers who have never so much as smelt gunpowder, there would be greater likelihood of my being able to withstand Fairfax when he comes.'

Money was getting scarce again, and the equipping of the army for winter another nightmare for my General.

Boots and stockings were worn through and hard to replace, while the most vital necessity of all, ammunition, was very low in stock, the chief reason for this being that the Royalist magazine for the western forces had been captured at the beginning of the autumn by the rebels, when they took Bristol, and all that Richard had at his disposal were the small reserves at Bodmin and Truro.

Then suddenly, without any warning, Lord Goring threw up his command and went to France, giving as the reason that his health had cracked and he could no longer shoulder any responsibility.

'The rats', said Richard slowly, 'are beginning, one by one, to desert the sinking ship.' Goring took several of his best officers with him, and the command in Devon was given to Lord Wentworth, an officer with little experience, whose ideas of discipline were even worse than Goring's. He immediately went into winter quarters at Bovey Tracey, and declared that nothing could be done against the enemy until the spring. It

As autumn drew on, I began to wonder if either freedom or comfort would belong to any of us by the end of the year.

Chard, Crediton, Lyme, and finally Tiverton fell before Fairfax in October, and Lord Goring had done nothing to stop them. Many of his men deserted and came flocking to join Richard's army, for they had greater faith in him as a commander. This led to further jealousy, further recriminations, and it looked as though Richard would fall as foul with Goring as he had done with Sir John Berkeley three months earlier. There was constant fault-finding, too, by the Prince's Council in Launceston, and scarcely a day would pass without some interfering measure from the Chancellor, Edward Hyde.

'If they would but leave me alone', stormed Richard, 'to recruit my army and to train my troops, instead of flooding my headquarters day by day with dispatches written by lawyers with smudged fingers who have never so much as smelt gunpowder, there would be greater likelihood of my being able to withstand Fairfax when he comes.'

Money was getting scarce again, and the equipping of the army for winter another nightmare for my General.

Boots and stockings were worn through and hard to replace, while the most vital necessity of all, ammunition, was very low in stock, the chief reason for this being that the Royalist magazine for the western forces had been captured at the beginning of the autumn by the rebels, when they took Bristol, and all that Richard had at his disposal were the small reserves at Bodmin and Truro.

Then suddenly, without any warning, Lord Goring threw up his command and went to France, giving as the reason that his health had cracked and he could no longer shoulder any responsibility.

'The rats', said Richard slowly, 'are beginning, one by one, to desert the sinking ship.' Goring took several of his best officers with him, and the command in Devon was given to Lord Wentworth, an officer with little experience, whose ideas of discipline were even worse than Goring's. He immediately went into winter quarters at Bovey Tracey, and declared that nothing could be done against the enemy until the spring. It

They came to him from beyond the border even, from Apple-
dore and Bideford, and down the length of that storm-bound
Atlantic coast from Hartland point to Padstowe. They were his
best recruits. Clear-eyed, long-limbed, wearing with pride the
scarlet shield with the three gold rests upon their shoulders.
Men from Bude and Stratton and Tintagel, men from Boscastle
and Camelford. And with great cunning Richard introduced
his prince as Duke of Cornwall, who had come into the west
to save them from the savage rebel hordes beyond the Tamar.

But farther south he met with rebuffs. Danger seemed more
remote to people west of Truro, and even the fall of Bristol to
Fairfax and the Parliament, which came like a clap of doom on
10 September, failed to rouse them from their lethargy.

'Truro, Helston, and St Ives', said Richard, 'are the three
rottenest towns in Cornwall,' and he rode down, I remember,
with some six hundred horse to quell a rising of the townsfolk,
who had protested against a levy he had raised the week before.

He hanged at least three men, while the remainder were either
fined or imprisoned. He took the opportunity, too, of visiting
the Castle at St Mawes, and severely reprimanded its commander, Major Bonython, because he had failed to pay the
soldiers under his command within the garrison.

'Whoever I find half-hearted in the Prince's cause must
change his tune or suffer disciplinary action,' declared Richard.
'Whoever fails to pay his men shall contribute from his own
pocket, and whoever shows one flicker of disloyalty to me, as
commander, or to the Prince I serve, shall answer for it with his
life.'

I heard him say this myself, in the market-place at Launceston before a great crowd assembled there, the last day of September, and, while his own men cheered so that the echo came
ringing back to us from the walls of the house, I saw few smiles
upon the faces of the townsfolk gathered there.

'You forget', I said that night to him at Werrington, 'that
Cornishmen are independent, and love freedom better than
their fellows.'

'I remember one thing,' he answered, with that thin, bitter
smile of his which I knew too well, 'that Cornishmen are
cowards, and love their comfort better than their King.'

He did not answer them at once, but the next day, in his lodgings, he composed a letter to the Secretary-at-War, and gave full details of the plan, so far only breathed to me in confidence, of what he believed imperative to be done. He showed me the draft of it on his return, and much of what he proposed filled me with misgiving; not because of its impracticability, but because the kernel of it was so likely to be misconstrued. He proposed, in short, to make a treaty with the Parliament, by which Cornwall would become separate from the remainder of the country and be ruled by the Prince of Wales, as Duke of the Duchy. The Duchy would contain its own army and its own fortifications, and control its own shipping. In return, the Cornish would give a guarantee not to attack the forces of the Parliament. Thus gaining a respite, the people of Cornwall, and especially the western army, would become so strong that in the space of a year or more they would be in ripe condition to give effective aid unto His Majesty once more. (This last, it may be realized, was not to be one of the clauses in the treaty.) Failing an agreement with Parliament, then Richard advised that a line be held from Barnstaple to the English Channel, and ditches dug from the north coast to the Tamar, so that the whole of Cornwall become virtually an island. On this river bank would be the first line of defence, and all the bridges would be destroyed. This line, he averred, could be held for an indefinite period, and any attempt at an invasion be immediately repulsed. When he had finished his report, and sent it to the Council, he returned to me at Werrington, to await an answer. Five days, a week, and no reply. And then at last a cold message from the Chancellor and the Secretary-at-War, to say that the plan had been considered, but had not found approval. The Prince's Council would thus consider other measures, and acquaint Sir Richard Grenville when his services would be required.

'So,' said Richard, throwing the letter on to my lap, 'a smack in the eye for Grenvile, and a warning not to rise above his station. The Council prefers to lose the war in their own fashion. Let them do so. Time is getting short, and if I judge Fairfax rightly neither snow nor hail nor frost will hamper him in Devon. It would be wise, my Honor, if you sent word of warning to Mary Rashleigh, and told her that you would spend Christmas with her.'

The sands were running out. I could tell it by his easy manner, his shrugging of his shoulders.

'And you?' I said, with that old sick twist of foreboding in my heart.

'I will come later,' he said, 'and we will see the New Year in together, in that room above the gate-house.'

And so, on the third morning of December, I set forth once again, after eighteen months, for my brother-in-law's house of Menabilly.

Chapter 25

MY second coming was very different from my first. Then it had been spring, with the golden gorse in bloom and young John Rashleigh coming to meet me on the highway before the park. War had not touched the neighbourhood, and in the park were cattle grazing, and flocks of sheep with their young lambs, and the last of the blossom falling from the fruit trees in the orchards. Now it was December, a biting wind cutting across the hills and valleys, and no young, laughing cavalier came out to greet me. As we turned in at the park gates I saw at once that the walls were still tumbled, and had not been repaired since the destruction wrought there by the rebels. Where the acres dipped to the sea above Polkerris a labourer with a team of oxen ploughed a single narrow enclosure, but about it to east and west the land was left uncultivated. What should be rich brown ploughland was left to thistle. A few lean cattle grazed within the park, and even now, after a full year or more had come and gone, I noticed the great bare patches of grassland where the rebel tents had stood, and the blackened roots of the trees they had felled for firewood. As we climbed the hill towards the house, I could see the reassuring curl of smoke rise from the chimneys and could hear the barking of the stable dogs, and I wondered, with a strange feeling of sadness and regret, whether I should be as welcome now as I had been eighteen months before. Once again my litter passed into the outer court, and, glancing up at my old apartment in the gate-house, I saw that it was shuttered and untenanted, even as the barred room beside it, and that the whole west wing wore the same forlorn appearance. Mary had warned me in her letter that only the eastern portion of the house had as yet been put in order, and they were living in some half a dozen rooms, for which they had found hangings and the bare necessities of furniture. Once more into the inner court, with a glance upward at the belfry and the tall weather-vane, and then – reminiscent of my former visit – came my sister Mary out upon the steps, and I noticed, with a shock, that her hair had gone quite white. Yet she greeted me with her same grave smile and gentle kiss, and I was taken straightway to the gallery, where I found my dear Alice strung about as always with her mob of babies, and the newest of the brood, just turned twelve months, clutching at her knee in her first steps. This was now all our party. The Sawles had returned to Penrice, and the Sparkes to Devon, and my goddaughter Joan, with John and the children, were living in the Rashleigh town house at Fowey. My brother-in-law, it seemed, was somewhere about the grounds, and at once, as they plied me with refreshment, I had to hear all the news of the past year – of how Jonathan had not yet received one penny piece from the Crown to help him in the restoration of his property, and how whatever had been done he had done him-self, with the aid of his servants and tenants.

'Cornwall is become totally impoverished,' said my sister sadly, 'and everyone dissatisfied. The harvest of this summer could not make up for all we lost last year, and each man with an estate to foster says the same. Unless the war ends swiftly we shall all be ruined.'

'It may end swiftly,' I answered, 'but not as you would wish it.'

I saw Mary glance quickly at Alice, and Alice made as though to say something, and then desisted. And I realized that as yet no mention had been made of Richard, my relationship to him being something that the Rashleighs possibly preferred should be ignored. I had not been questioned once about the past twelve months.

'They say, who know about these things,' said Mary, 'that His Majesty is very hopeful, and will soon send an army to the west to help us drive Fairfax out of Devon.'

'His Majesty is too preoccupied in keeping his own troops together in the Midlands,' I answered, 'to concern himself about the west.'

'You do not think', said Alice anxiously, 'that Cornwall is likely to suffer invasion once again?'

'I do not see how we are to avoid it.'

'But ... we have plenty of troops, have we not?' said Mary, still shying from mention of their General. 'I know we have been taxed hard enough to provide for them.'

'Troops without boots or stockings make poor fighters,' I said, 'especially if they have no powder for their muskets.'

'Jonathan says everything has been mismanaged,' said Mary. 'There is no supreme authority in the west to take command. The Prince's Council say one thing – the commanders say another. I, for my part, understand nothing of it. I only wish it were well over.'

I could tell from their expressions – even Alice's, usually so fair and generous – that Sir Richard Grenvile had been as badly blamed at Menabilly as elsewhere for his high-handed ways and indiscretions, and that unless I broached his name now there would be an uneasy silence on the subject for the whole duration of my visit. Not one of them would take the first step, and there would be an awkward barrier between us all, making for discomfort. 'Perhaps,' I said, 'having dwelt with Richard Grenvile for the past eight months, ever since he was wounded, I am prejudiced in his favour. I know he has many faults, but he is the best soldier that we have in the whole of His Majesty's army. The Prince's Council would do well to listen to his advice, on military matters if on nothing else.'

They neither of them said anything for a moment, and then Alice, colouring a little, said, 'Peter is with your brother Robin, you know, under Sir John Digby, before Plymouth. He told us, when he was last here, that Sir Richard constantly sent orders to Sir John, which he has no right to do.'

'What sort of orders, good or bad?' I asked.

'I hardly think the orders themselves were points of dispute,' said Alice. 'They were possibly quite necessary. But the very fact that he gave them to Sir John, who is not a subordinate, caused irritation.'

At this juncture my brother-in-law came to the gallery and the discussion broke, but I wondered, with a heavy heart, how many friends were now left to my Richard among those who had at first sworn fealty to his leadership. After I had been at Menabilly a few days, my brother-in-law himself put the case more bluntly. There was no discreet avoidance, on his part, of Richard's name. He asked me straight out if he had recovered from his wound, as he had heard report from Truro that on the last visit to the Council the general had looked far from well, and very tired.

'I think he is tired,' I said, 'and unwell. And the present situation gives him little cause for confidence or good spirits.'

'He has done himself irreparable harm here in Cornwall,' said my brother-in-law, 'by commanding assistance rather than requesting it.'

'Hard times require hard measures,' I said. 'It is no moment to go cap in hand for money to pay troops when the enemy is in the next county.'

'He would have won far better response had he gone about his business with courtesy and an understanding of the general poverty of all of us. The whole Duchy would have rallied to his side had he but half the understanding that was his brother Bevil's.'

And to this I could give no answer, for I knew it to be true. ...

The weather was cold and dreary, and I spent much of my time within my chamber, which was the same that Gartred had been given eighteen months before. It had suffered little in the general damage, for which, I suppose, thanks had to be rendered to her. It was a pleasant room, with one window to the gardens, still shorn of their glory, and the new grass seeds that had been sown very clipped yet and thin, and two windows to the south, from where I could see the causeway sloping to rising ground and the view upon the Bay. I was content enough, yet strangely empty; for it comes hard to be alone again after eight months in company with the man you love. I had shared

237

his troubles and misfortunes, and his follies too. His moods were become familiar, loved, and understood. The cruel quip, the swift malicious answer to a question, and the sudden, fleeting tenderness, so unaccountable, so warming, that would change him in one moment from a ruthless soldier to a lover.

When I was with him the days were momentous and full; now they had all the chill drabness of December, when as I took my breakfast the candles must be lit, and for my brief outing on the causeway I must be wrapped in cloak and coverture. The fall of the year, always to me a moment of regret, was now become a period of tension and foreboding.

At Christmas came John and Joan from Fowey, and Peter Courtney, given a few days' grace from Sir John Digby in the watch on Plymouth, and we all made merry for the children's sake, and maybe for our own as well. Fairfax was forgotten, and Cromwell too, the doughty second-in-command who led his men to battle, so we were told, with a prayer upon his lips. We roasted chestnuts before the two fires in the gallery, and burnt our fingers snatching sugar plums from the flames, and I remember too an old blind harper who was given shelter for the night on Christmas Eve, and came and played to us in the soft candlelight. Since the wars there were many such wanderers upon the road, calling no home their own, straggling from village to village, receiving curses more often than silver pieces. Maybe the season had made Jonathan more generous, for this old fellow was not turned away, and I can see him now, in his threadbare jerkin and torn hose, with a black shade over his eyes, sitting in the far corner of the gallery, his nimble fingers drumming the strings of his harp, his quavering old voice strangely sweet and true. I asked Jonathan if he were not afraid of thieves in these difficult times, and, shaking his head, he gestured grimly to the faded tapestries on the panels, and the worn chairs. 'I have nothing left of value,' he said. 'You yourself saw it all destroyed a year since.' And then, with a half-smile and a lowered voice: 'Even the secret chamber and the tunnel contain nothing now but rats and cobwebs.'

I shuddered, thinking suddenly of all I had been through when Dick had hidden there, and I turned with relief to the sight of Peter Courtney playing leap-frog with his children, the sound of their merry laughter rising above the melancholy strains of the harper's lament. The servants came to fasten the shutters, and for a moment my brother-in-law stood before the window looking out upon the lead sky, so soon to darken, and together we watched the first pale snowflakes fall. 'The gulls are flying inland,' he said. 'We shall have a hard winter.' There was something ominous in his words, harmless in themselves, that rang like a premonition of disaster. Even as he spoke the wind began to rise, echoing in the chimneys and circling above the gardens wheeled the crying gulls, who came so seldom from their ledges in the cliffs, and with them the scattered flocks of redwing from the north, birds of passage seeking sanctuary.

Next morning we woke to a white world, strangely still, and a sunless sky teeming with further snow to come, while clear and compelling through the silence came the Christmas bells from the church at Tywardreath.

I thought of Richard, alone with his staff at Werrington, and I feared that he would never keep his promise now, with the weather broken and snowdrifts maybe ten feet deep upon the Bodmin moors.

But he did come, at midday on the ninth of January, when for four and twenty hours a thaw had made a slush of the frozen snow and the road from Launceston to Bodmin was just passable to an intrepid horseman. He brought Jack Grenvile with him, and Jack's younger brother, Bunny, a youngster of about the age of Dick, with a pugnacious jaw and merry eyes, who had spent Christmas with his uncle and now never left his side, vowing he would not return to Stowe again to his mother and his tutor, but would join the army and kill rebels. As I watched Richard tweak his ear, and laugh and jest with him, I felt a pang of sorrow in my heart for Dick, lonely and unloved, save for that dreary Herbert Ashley, across the sea in Normandy, and I wondered if it must always be that Richard should show himself so considerate and kind to other lads, winning their devotion, and remain a stranger to his own son.

My brother-in-law, who had known Bevil well, bade welcome Bevil's boys, and after a first fleeting moment of constraint –

for the visit was unexpected – he welcomed Richard, too, with courtesy. Richard looked better, I thought – the hard weather suited him – and after five minutes his was the only voice we heard in the long gallery, a sort of hush coming upon the Rashleigh family with his presence, and my conscience told me that his coming had put an end to their festivity. Peter Courtney, the jester-in-chief, was stricken dumb upon the instant, and I saw him frown to Alice to chide their eldest little girl, who, unafraid, ventured to Richard's side and pulled his sash.

None of them were natural any more because of the General, and, glancing at my sister Mary, I saw the well-known frown upon her face as she wondered about her larder, and what fare she could provide, and I guessed too that she was puzzling as to which apartment could be given to him, for we were all crammed into one wing as it was. 'You are on your way to Truro, I suppose?' she said to him, thinking he would be gone by morning. 'No,' he answered. 'I thought, while the hard weather lasted, I might bide with you a week at Menabilly, and shoot duck instead of rebels.'

I saw her dart a look of consternation at Jonathan, and there was a silence, which Richard found not at all unusual, as he was unused to other voices but his own, and he continued cursing with great heartiness, the irritating slowness of the Cornish people. 'On the north coast,' he said, 'where these lads and myself were born and bred, response is swift and sudden, as it should be. But the Duchy falls to pieces south of Bodmin, and the men become like snails.' The fact that the Rashleighs had been born in south-east Cornwall did not worry him at all. 'I could never', he continued, 'have resided long at Killigarth. Give a fellow a command at Polperro or at Looe on Christmas Day, and with a slice of luck it will be obeyed by midsummer.'

Jonathan Rashleigh, who owned land in both places, stared steadily before him. 'But whistle a fellow overnight at Stratton,' said Richard, 'or from Morwenstowe, or Bude, and he is at your side by morning. I tell you frankly that had I none other but Atlantic men in my army I would face Fairfax tomorrow with composure. But the first sight of cold steel, the rats from Truro and beyond will turn and run.'

'I think you underestimate your fellow countrymen and mine,' said Jonathan quietly.

'Not a bit of it. I know them all too well.'

If, I considered, the conversation of the week was to continue in this strain, the atmosphere of Menabilly would be far from easy. But Jack Grenvile, with a discretion born of long practice, tapped his uncle on the shoulder. 'Look, sir,' he said. 'There are your duck.' Pointing to the sky above the garden, still grey and heavy with unfallen snow, he showed the teal in flight, heading to the Gribben. Richard was at once a boy again, laughing, jesting, clapping his hands upon his nephew's shoulders, and in a moment the men of the household fell under the spell of his change of mood, and John, and Peter, and even my brother-in-law, were making for the shore. We women wrapped ourselves in cloaks and went out upon the causeway to watch the sport, and it seemed to me that the years had rolled away, as I saw Richard, with Peter's goshawk on his wrist, turn to laugh at me. The boys were running across the thistle park to the long mead in the Pridmouth valley, shouting and calling to one another, and the dogs were barking.

The snow still lay upon the fields, and the cattle in the beef park nosed hungrily for fodder. The flocks of lapwing, growing tame and bold, wheeled screaming round our heads. For a brief moment the sun came from the white sky and shone upon us, and the world was dazzling. 'This', I thought, 'is an interlude, lasting a single second. I have my Richard, Alice has her Peter, Joan her John. Nothing can touch us for today. There is no war. The enemy are not in Devon, waiting for the word to march.'

In retrospect, the events of '44 seemed but an evil dream that could never be repeated, and as I looked across the valley to the further hill, and saw the coast road winding down the fields of Tregares and Culver Close to the beach at Pridmouth, I remembered the troopers who had appeared there, on the skyline, on that fateful August day. Surely Richard was mistaken? They could not come again? There was a shouting from the valley, and up from the marshes rose the duck, with the hawks above them, circling, and I suddenly shivered for no reason. Then the sun went blank, and a cat's paw rippled the sea, while a great shadow passed across the Gribben hill. Something fell upon my cheek, soft and clammy white. It was snowing once again.

That night we made a circle by the fire in the gallery, while Jonathan and Mary retired early to their room.

The blind harper had departed with the New Year, so there was none to make music for us save Alice and her lute, and Peter with his singing, while the two Grenvile brothers, Jack and Bunny, whistled softly together – a schoolboy trick learnt from their father Bevil long ago, when the great house at Stowe had rung with singing and with music. John heaped logs upon the fire, and blew the candles, and the flames lit the long room from end to end, shining on the panelling and on the faces of us, one and all, as we sat around the hearth.

I can see Alice as she was that night fingering her lute, looking up adoringly at her Peter, who was to prove, alas! so faithless in the years to come, while he, with his constraint before his General melting with the firelight and the late hour, threw back his head and sang to us:

'And wilt thou leave me thus?
Say nay, say nay, for shame.
To save thee from the blame
Of all my grief and grame,
And wilt thou leave me thus?
Say nay! Say nay!'

I saw Joan and John hold hands and smile; John, with his dear honest face, who would never be unfaithful and a deserter to his Joan, as Peter would to Alice, but was destined to slip away from her for all that, to the land from which no one of us returns, in barely six years' time.

'And wilt thou leave me thus,
And have no more pity
Of him that loveth thee?
Alas! thy cruelty.
And wilt thou leave me thus?
Say nay! Say nay!'

Plaintive and gentle were Alice's fingers upon the lute, and Jack and Bunny, cupping their mouths with their hands, whistled softly to her lead. I stole a glance at Richard. He was staring into the flames, his wounded leg propped on a stool before him. The flickering firelight cast shadows on his features, distorting them to a grimace, and I could not tell whether he smiled or wept.

'You used to sing that once, long ago,' I whispered, but if he heard me he made no move; he only waited for the last verse of Peter's song. Then he laid aside his pipe, blowing a long ribbon of smoke into the air, and reached across the circle for Alice's lute.

'We are all lovers here, are we not?' he said. 'Each in our own fashion, except for these sprigs of boys.' He smiled maliciously, and began to drum the strings of the lute:

> 'Your most beautiful bride who with garlands is crowned
> And kills with each glance as she treads on the ground,
> Whose lightness and brightness doth shine in such splendour,
>   That none but the stars
>   Are thought fit to attend her,
> Though now she be pleasant and sweet to the sense,
> Will be damnably mouldy a hundred years hence.'

He paused, cocking an eye at them, and I saw Alice shrink back in her chair, glancing uncertainly at Peter. Joan was picking at her gown, biting her lips. Oh, God, I thought, why do you break the spell? Why do you hurt them? They are none of them much more than children.

> 'Then why should we turmoil in cares and in fears,
> Turn all our tranquill'ty to sighs and to tears?
> Let's eat, drink, and play till the worms do corrupt us,
>   'Tis certain, Post Mortem,
>   Nulla voluptas,
> For health, wealth, and beauty, wit, learning and sense,
> Must all come to nothing a hundred years hence.'

He rippled a final chord upon the strings, and, rising to his feet, handed the lute to Alice with a bow.

'Your turn again, Lady Courtney,' he said. 'Or would you prefer to play at spillikins?'

Someone – Peter, I think it was – forced a laugh, and then John rose to light the candles. Joan leant forward and raked apart the fire, so that the logs no longer burnt a flame. They flickered dully, and went dark. The spell was broken.

'It is snowing still,' said Jack Grenvile, opening a shutter. 'Let us hope it falls twenty foot in depth in Devon, and stifles Fairfax and his merry men.'

'It will more likely stifle Wentworth,' said Richard, 'sitting on his arse in Bovey Tracey.'

'Why does everyone stand up?' asked young Bunny. 'Is there to be no more music?' But no one answered. The war was upon us once again, the fear, the doubt, the nagging insecurity, and all the quiet had vanished from the evening.

Chapter 26

I SLEPT uneasily that night, passing from one troubled dream into another, and at one moment I thought to hear the sound of horses' hoofs riding across the park. Yet my windows faced east, and I told myself it was but fancy, and the wind stirring in the snow-laden trees. But when Matty came to me with breakfast she bore a note in her hands from Richard, and I learnt that my fancy was in truth reality, and that he, and the two Grenviles and Peter Courtney, had all ridden from the house shortly after daybreak.

A messenger had come to Menabilly with the news that Cromwell had made a night attack on Lord Wentworth in Bovey Tracey, and, finding the Royalist army asleep, had captured four hundred of the horse, while the remainder of the foot who had not been captured had fled to Tavistock in complete disorder and confusion. 'Wentworth has been caught napping,' Richard had scribbled on a torn sheet of paper, 'which is exactly what I feared would happen. What might have been a small reverse is likely to turn into disaster if a general order is given to retreat. I propose riding forthwith to the Prince's Council, and offering my services. Unless they appoint a supreme commander to take over Wentworth's rabble, we shall have Fairfax and Cromwell across the Tamar.' Mary need not have worried after all. Sir Richard Grenvile had passed but a single night under her roof, and not the week that she had dreaded. ... I rose that morning with a heavy heart, and, going downstairs to the gallery, found Alice in tears, for she knew that Peter would be foremost in the fighting when the moment came. My brother-in-law looked grave, and departed at mid-day, also bound for Launceston, to discover what help might be needed from the landowners and gentry in the event of invasion. John, with Frank Penrose, set forth to warn the tenants on the estate that once again their services might be needed, and the day was wretchedly reminiscent of that other day in August, nearly eighteen months before. But now it was not midsummer, but midwinter. And there was no strong Cornish army to lure the rebels into a trap, with another Royalist army marching in the rear.

Our men stood alone – with His Majesty three hundred miles away or more, and General Fairfax was a very different leader from the Earl of Essex. He would walk into no trap, but if he came would cross the Tamar with a certainty.

In the afternoon Elizabeth from Coombe came to join us, her husband having gone, and told us that the rumour ran in Fowey that the siege of Plymouth had been raised and that Digby's troops, along with Wentworth's, were retreating fast to the Tamar bridges.

We sat before the smouldering fire in the gallery, a little group of wretched women, and I stared at that same branch of ash that had burnt so brightly the preceding night, when our men were with us, and was now a blackened log amongst the ashes.

We had faced invasion before, had endured the brief horrors of enemy occupation, but we had never known defeat. Alice and Mary were talking of the children, the necessity this time of husbanding supplies beneath the floor-boards of the rooms, as though a siege was all that was before us. But I said nothing, only stared into the fire. And I wondered who would suffer most, the men who died swiftly in battle or those who would remain to face imprisonment and torture. I knew then that I would rather Richard fought and died than stayed to fall into the hands of Parliament. It did not bear much thinking what they would do to Skellum Grenvile if they caught him.

'The King will march west, of course,' Elizabeth was saying. 'He could not leave Cornwall in the lurch. They say he is raising a great body of men in Oxfordshire, this moment. When the thaw breaks ...'

'Our defences will withstand the rebels,' Joan said. 'John was talking to a man in Tywardreath. Much has been accomplished since last time. They say we have a new musket – with a longer barrel – I do not know exactly, but the rebels will not face it, so John says. ...'

'They have no money,' said Mary. 'Jonathan tells me the Parliament is desperate for money. In London the people are starving. They have no bread. The Parliament are bound to seek terms from the King, for they will be unable to continue the war. When the spring comes ...'

I wanted to put my fingers in my ears and muffle the sound of their voices. On and on, one against the other, the old false tales that had been told so often. It cannot go on. ... They must give in. ... They are worse off than we. ... When the thaw breaks, when the spring comes. ... And suddenly I saw Elizabeth look towards me – she had less reserve than Alice, and I did not know her so well – and ask, 'What does Sir Richard Grenvile say? You must hear everything of what goes on. Will he attack and drive the rebels back to Dorset?'

Her ignorance, and theirs, was so supreme that I had not the heart nor the will to enlighten her.

'Attack?' I said. 'With what forces do you suggest that he attacks?'

'Why, with those at his disposal,' she answered. 'We have many able-bodied men in Cornwall.'

I thought of the sullen bands I had seen sulking in the square at Launceston, and the handful of brawny fellows in the fields below Werrington, wearing the Grenvile shield on their shoulders.

246

'A little force of pressed men', I said, 'and volunteers, against some fifty thousand trained soldiers?'

'But man for man we are superior,' urged Elizabeth. 'Everyone says that. The rebels are well equipped, no doubt, but when our fellows meet them face to face, in fair fight, in open country ...'

'Have you not heard', I said softly, 'of Cromwell, and the New Model Army? Do you not realize, that never in England, until now, has there been raised an army like it?'

They stared at me, nonplussed, and Elizabeth, shrugging her shoulders, said I had greatly altered since the year before, and was now become defeatist. 'If we all talked in that fashion,' she said, 'we would have been beaten long ago. I suppose you have caught it from Sir Richard. I do not wonder that he is unpopular.'

Alice looked embarrassed, and I saw Mary nudge Elizabeth with her foot.

'Don't worry,' I said. 'I know his faults far better than you all. But I think if the Council of the Prince would only listen to him this time, we might save Cornwall from invasion.'

That evening, on going to my room, I looked out on the weather, and saw that the night was clear and the stars were shining. There would be no more snow, not yet awhile. I called Matty to me, and told her my resolve. This was to follow Richard back to Werrington, if transport could be got for me at Tywardreath, and to set forth at noon the following day, passing the night at Bodmin, and so to Werrington the day after. By doing this I would disobey his last instructions, but I had, in my heart, a premonition that unless I saw him now I would never see him more. What I thought, what I feared, I cannot tell. But it came to me that he might fall in battle, and that by following him I would be with him at the last.

The next morning was fine, as I expected, and I rose early, and went down to breakfast, and informed the Rashleigh family of my plan. They one and all begged me to remain, saying it was folly to travel the roads at such a season, but I was firm; and at length John Rashleigh, dear, faithful friend, arranged matters for me, and accompanied me as far as Bodmin.

It was bitter cold upon the moors, and I had little stomach

for my journey, as, with Matty at my side, I left the hostelry at Bodmin at daybreak. The long road to Launceston stretched before us, bleak and dreary, with great snow-drifts on either side of us, and one false step of our horses would send the litter to destruction. Although we were wrapped about with blankets, the nipping, nagging wind penetrated the curtains, freezing our faces, and when we halted at Five Lanes for hot soup and wine to warm us I had half a mind to go no further, but find lodging for the night at Altarnun. The man at the inn put an end to my hesitation. 'We have had soldiers here these past two days,' he said, 'deserters from the army before Plymouth. Some of Sir John Digby's men. They were making for their homes in west Cornwall. They were not going to stay on the Tamar banks to be butchered, so they told me.'

'What news had they?' I asked, my heart heavy.

'Nothing good,' he answered. 'Confusion everywhere. Orders, and counter-orders. Sir Richard Grenvile was down on Tamar-side, inspecting bridges, giving instructions to blow them when the need arose, and a colonel of foot refused to take the order, saying he would obey none other than Sir John Digby. What is to become of us if the generals start fighting amongst themselves?'

I felt sick, and turned away. There would be no biding for me this night at Altarnun. I must reach Werrington by night-fall.

On, then, across the snow-covered moors, wind-swept and desolate, and every now and then we would pass straggling figures making for the west, their apparel proclaiming to the world that once they were King's men, but now deserters. They were blue from cold and hunger, and yet they wore a brazen, sullen look, as though they cared no longer what became of them, and some of them shouted as we passed, 'To hell with the war. We're going home,' and shook their fists at my litter, jeering, 'You're driving to the devil.'

The short winter afternoon soon closed in, and by the time we came to Launceston, and turned out of the town to St Stephens, it was grown pitch-dark, and snowing once again. An hour or so later I would have been snow-bound on the road, with nothing but waste moorland on either side of me. At last we came to Werrington, which I had not thought to see again, and when the startled sentry at the gates recognized me, and let the horses pass through the park, I thought that even he, a Grenvile man, had lost his look of certainty and pride, and would become, granted ill-fortune, no better than the deserters on the road.

We drew up into the cobbled court, and an officer came forth whose face was new to me. His expression was blank when I gave him my name, and he told me that the General was in conference and could not be disturbed. I thought that Jack might help me, and asked therefore if Sir John Grenvile, or his brother Mr Bernard, could see Mistress Honor Harris on a matter of great urgency.

'Sir John is no longer with the General,' answered the officer. 'The Prince of Wales recalled him to his entourage yesterday. And Bernard Grenvile has returned to Stowe. I am the General's aide-de-camp at present.' This was not hopeful, for he did not know me, and as I watched the figures of the soldiers, passing backwards and forwards in the hall within the house, and heard the tattoo of a drum in the far distance. I thought how ill-timed and crazy was my visit, for what could they do with me, a woman and a cripple, in this moment of great stress and urgency?

I heard a murmur of voices. 'They are coming out now,' said the officer. 'The conference is over.' I caught sight of Colonel Roscarrock, whom I knew well, a loyal friend of Richard's, and in desperation I leant from my litter and called to him. He came to my side at once, in great astonishment, but at once, with true courtesy, covered his consternation and gave orders for me to be carried into the house. 'Ask me no questions,' I said. 'I have come at a bad moment. I can guess that. Can I see him?' He hesitated for a fraction of a minute. 'Why, of course,' he said, 'he will want to see you. But I must warn you, things are not going well for him. We are all concerned ...' He broke off in confusion, looking most desperately embarrassed and unhappy.

'Please,' I said, avoiding his eyes, 'please tell him I am here.' He went at once into the room that Richard used as his own, and where we had sat together, night after night, for over seven months. He stayed a moment, and then came for me. My chair

249

had been lifted from the litter, and he took me to the room, then closed the door. Richard was standing by the table. His face was hard, set in the firm lines that I knew well. I could tell that of all things in the world I was, at that moment, the farthest from his thoughts.

'What the devil', he said wearily, 'are you doing here?'

It was not the welcome that I yearned for, but was that which I deserved.

'I am sorry,' I said. 'I could not rest, once you were gone. If anything is going to happen – which I know it must – I want to share it with you. The danger, I mean. And the aftermath.'

He laughed shortly, and tossed a paper on to my lap.

'There'll be no danger,' he said, 'not for you, or I. Perhaps, after all, it is as well you came. We can travel west together.'

'What do you mean?' I said.

'That letter – you can read it,' he said. 'It is a copy of a message I have just sent to the Prince's Council, resigning from His Majesty's Army. They wil have it in an hour's time.'

I did not answer for a moment. I sat quite cold and still.

'What do you mean?' I asked at length. 'What has happened?' He went to the fire and stood with his hands behind his back. 'I went to them', he said, 'as soon as I returned from Menabilly. I told them that, if they wished to save Cornwall and the Prince, they must appoint a supreme commander. Men are deserting in hundreds, discipline is non-existent. This would be the only hope, the last and final chance. They thanked me. They said they would consider the matter. I went away. I rode next morning to Gunnislake and Callington. I inspected the defences. There I commanded a certain colonel of foot to blow a bridge when need arose. He disputed my authority, saying his orders were to the contrary. Would you like to know his name?'

I said nothing. Some inner sense had told me.

'It was your brother, Robin Harris,' he said. 'He even dared to bring your name into a military matter. "I cannot take orders from a man", he said, "who has ruined the life and reputation of my sister. Sir John Digby is my commander, and Sir John has bidden me to leave this bridge intact." '

Richard stared at me an instant, and then began to pace up and down the strip of carpet by the fire.

250

'You would hardly credit it,' he said; 'such lunacy, such gross incompetence. It matters not that he is your brother, that he drags a private quarrel into the King's business. But to leave the bridge for Fairfax, to have the impertinence to tell me, a Grenvile, that John Digby knows his business best . . .'

I could see Robin, very red about the neck, with beating heart and swelling anger, thinking, dear damned idiot, that by defying his commander he was somehow defending me and downing, in some bewildering hothead fashion, the seducer of his sister.

'What then?' I asked. 'Did you see Digby?'

'No,' he answered. 'What would be the use, if he defied me, as your brother did? I returned here to Launceston, to take my commission from the Council as supreme commander, and thus show my powers to the whole army, and be damned to them.'

'And you have the commission?'

He leant to the table, and, seizing a small piece of parchment, held it before my eyes. 'The Council of the Prince', he read, 'appoints Lord Hopton in supreme command of His Majesty's forces in the West, and desires that Sir Richard Grenvile should serve under him as Lieutenant-General of the foot.'

He read slowly, with deadly emphasis and scorn; and then tore the document to tiny shreds and threw the pieces in the fire. 'That is my answer to them,' he said. 'They may do as they please. Tomorrow you and I will return to shoot duck at Menabilly.' He pulled the bell beside the fire, and his new aide-de-camp appeared. 'Bid the servants bring some supper,' he said. 'Mistress Harris has travelled long, and has not dined.'

When the officer had gone I put out my hand to Richard.

'You can't do this,' I said. 'You must do as they tell you.'

He turned round on me in anger. 'Must?' he said. 'There is no must. Do you think that I shall truckle to that damned lawyer at this juncture? It is he who is at the bottom of this, he who is to blame. I can see him, with his bland attorney's manner, talking to the members of the Council. "This man is dangerous," he says to them, "this soldier, this Grenvile. If we give him the supreme command he will take precedence of us, and send us about our business. We will give Hopton the com-

251

mand. Hopton will not dare to disobey. And when the enemy cross the Tamar, Hopton will withstand them just long enough for us to slip across to Guernsey with the Prince." That is how the lawyer talks; that is what he has in mind. The traitor, the damned disloyal coward.'

He faced me, white with anger.

'But, Richard,' I persisted, 'don't you understand, my love, my dear, that it is you they will call disloyal at this moment? To refuse to serve under another man, with the enemy in Devon? It is you who will be pointed at, reviled? You, and not Hyde?'

He would not listen; he brushed me away with his hand.

'This is not a question of pride, but concerns my honour,' he said. 'They do not trust me. Therefore I resign. Now, for God's sake, let us dine, and say no more. Tell me, was it snowing still at Menabilly?'

I failed him that last evening. Failed him miserably. I made no effort once to enter in his mood, that switched now so suddenly from black anger to forced jollity. I wanted to talk about the future, about what he proposed to do, but he would have none of it. I asked what his officers thought, what Colonel Roscarrock had said, and Colonels Arundell and Fortiscue. Did they too uphold him in his grave, unorthodox decision? But he would not speak of it. He bade the servants open another bottle of wine, and with a smile he drained it all, as he had done seven months before at Ottery St Mary. It was nearly midnight when the new aide-de-camp knocked upon the door, bearing a letter in his hand.

Richard took it, and read the message; then with a laugh threw it in the fire. 'A summons from the Council,' he said, 'to appear before them at ten tomorrow, in the Castle court at Launceston. Perchance they plan some simple ceremony, and will dub me Earl. That is the customary reward for soldiers who have failed.'

'Will you go?' I asked.

'I shall go,' he said, 'and then proceed with you to Menabilly.'

'You will not relent?' I asked. 'Not swallow your pride, or honour, as you call it, and consent to do as they demand of you?'

He looked at me a moment, and he did not smile.

'No,' he said slowly. 'I shall not relent.'

I went to bed, to my old room, next to his, and left the door open between our chambers, should he be restless, and wish to come to me. But at past three in the morning I heard his footstep on the stair, and he did not speak or call to me.

I slept one hour perhaps, or two. I do not remember. It was still snowing when I woke, and dull and grey. I bade Matty dress me in great haste, and sent word to Richard, asking if he would see me.

He came instead to my room, and with great tenderness told me to stay abed, at any rate until he should return from Launceston.

'I will be gone an hour,' he said; 'two at the utmost. I shall but delay to tell the Council what I think of them, and then come back to breakfast with you. My anger is all spent. This morning I feel free, and light of heart. It is an odd sensation, you know, to be at long last without responsibility.' He kissed my two hands, and then went away. I heard the sound of the horses trotting away across the park. There was a single drum, and then silence. Nothing but the footsteps of the sentry, pacing up and down before the house. I went and sat in my chair beside the window, with a rug over my knees. It was snowing steadily. There would be a white carpet on the Castle green at Launceston. Here, at Werrington, the world was desolate. The deer stood huddled under the trees down by the river. At midday Matty brought me meat, but I did not fancy it. I went on sitting at the window, gazing out across the park, and presently the snow had covered all trace of the horses, and the soft white flakes began to freeze upon the glass of the casement, clouding my view. It must have been past three when I heard the sentry standing to attention, and once again the muffled tattoo of a drum. Some horses were coming to the house by the northern entrance, and because my window did not face that way I could not see them. I waited. Richard might not come at once – there would be many matters to see to in that room downstairs. At a quarter to four there came a knock upon my door, and a servant demanded, in a hushed tone, if Colonel Roscarrock could wait on Mistress Harris. I told him, 'Certainly,' and sat there, with my hands clasped on my lap, filled with that apprehension that I knew too well.

He came, and stood before the door, disaster written plainly on his face.

'Tell me,' I said. 'I would know the worst at once.'

'They have arrested him', he said slowly, 'on a charge of disloyalty to the Prince and to His Majesty. They seized him there, before us, his staff, and all his officers.'

'Where have they imprisoned him?'

'There, in Launceston Castle. The Governor and an escort of men were waiting to take him. I rode to his side and begged him to give fight. His staff, his command, the whole army, I told him, would stand by him, if he would but give the word. But he refused. "The Prince", he said, "must be obeyed." He smiled at us there, on the Castle green, and bade us be of good cheer. Then he handed his sword to the Governor, and they took him away.'

'Nothing else?' I asked. 'No other word, no message of farewell?'

'Nothing else,' he said, 'except he bade me take good care of you, and see you safely to your sister.'

I sat quite still, my heart numb, all feeling and all passion spent.

'This is the end,' said Colonel Roscarrock. 'There is no other man in the army fit to lead us but Richard Grenvile. When Fairfax chooses to strike, he will find no opposition. This is the end.'

Yes, I thought. This is the end. Many had fought and died, and all in vain. The bridges would not be blown now, the roads would not be guarded nor the defences held. When Fairfax gave the word to march, the word would be obeyed, and his troops would cross the Tamar, never to depart. The end of liberty in Cornwall, for many months, for many years, perhaps for generations. And Richard Grenvile, who might have saved his country, was now a prisoner, of his own side, in Launceston Castle.

'If we had only time,' Colonel Roscarrock was saying, 'we could have a petition signed by every man and woman in the Duchy asking for his release. We could send messengers, in some way, to His Majesty himself, imploring pardon, insisting that the sentence of the Council is unjust. If we had only time...'

If we had only time, when the thaw breaks, when the spring comes.... But it was that day the nineteenth of January, and the snow was falling still.

Chapter 27

MY first action was to leave Werrington, which I did that evening, before Sir Charles Trevannion, on Lord Hopton's staff, came to take over for his commander. I no longer had any claim to be there, and I had no wish to embarrass Charles Trevannion, who had known my father well. I went therefore to the hostelry in Broad Street, Launceston, near to the Castle, and Colonel Roscarrock, after he had installed me there, took a letter for me to the Governor, requesting an interview with Richard for the following morning. He returned at nine o'clock, with a courteous but firm refusal. No one, said the Governor, was to be permitted to see Sir Richard Grenville, by strict order of the Prince's Council. 'We intend,' said Colonel Roscarrock to me, 'sending a deputation to the Prince himself at Truro. Jack Grenvile, I know, will speak for his uncle, and many more besides. Already, since the news has gone abroad, the troops are murmuring, and have been confined to their quarters for twenty-four hours in consequence. I can tell, by what the Governor said, that rioting is feared.' There was no more I could ask him to do that day – I had already trespassed too greatly on his time already – so I bade him a good night and went to bed, to pass a wretched night, wondering all the while in what dungeon they had lodged Richard, or if he had been given lodging according to his rank.

The next day, the twentieth, driving sleet came to dispel the snow, and I think, because of this, and because of my unhappiness, I have never hated any place so much as Launceston. The very name sounded like a gaol. Just before noon Colonel Roscarrock called on me with the news that there were proclamations everywhere about the town that Sir Richard Grenvile had been cashiered from every regiment he had commanded, and was dismissed from His Majesty's army – and all without court-martial.

'It cannot be done,' he said with vehemence. 'It is against every military code and tradition. There will be a mutiny in all ranks at such gross injustice. We are to hold a meeting of protest today, and I will let you know directly it is over what is decided.' Meetings and conferences – somehow I had no faith in them. Yet how I cursed my impotence, sitting in my hired room above the cobbled street in Launceston.

Matty, too, fed me with tales of optimism. 'There is no other talk about the town,' she said, 'but Sir Richard's imprisonment. Those who grumbled at his severity before are now clamouring for his release. This afternoon a thousand people went before the Castle and shouted for the Governor. He is bound to let him go, unless he wants the Castle burnt about his ears.'

'The Governor is only acting under orders,' I said. 'He can do nothing. It is to Sir Edward Hyde and the Council that they should direct their appeals.'

'They say in the town', she answered, 'that the Council have gone back to Truro, so fearful they are of mutiny.'

That evening, when darkness fell, I could hear the tramping of many feet in the market square, and distant shouting, while flares and torches were tossed into the sky. Some were thrown at the windows of the Town Hall, and the landlord of my hostelry, fearing for his own, barred the shutters early, and the doors.

'They've put a double guard at the Castle,' he told Matty, 'and the troops are still confined to their quarters.'

How typical it was, I thought with bitterness, that now, in his adversity, my Richard should become so popular a figure. Fear was the whip that drove the people on. They had no faith in Lord Hopton, or any other commander. Only a Grenvile, they believed, could keep the enemy from crossing the Tamar.

When Colonel Roscarrock came at last to see me, I could tell from his weary countenance that nothing much had been accomplished. 'The General has sent word to us', he said, 'that he will be no party to release by force. He asks for a court-martial, and a chance to defend himself before the Prince, and to be heard. As to us, and to his army, he bids us serve under Lord Hopton.'

Why in God's name, I wondered, could he not do the same himself but twelve hours since?

'So there will be no mutiny?' I said. 'No storming of the Castle?'

'Not by the army,' said Colonel Roscarrock in dejection. 'We have taken an oath to remain loyal to Lord Hopton. You have heard the latest news?'

'No?'

'Dartmouth has fallen. The Governor, Sir Hugh Pollard, and over a thousand men are taken prisoner. Fairfax has a line across Devon now, from north to south.'

This would be no time, then, to hold courts-martial.

'What orders have you', I asked wearily, 'from your new commander?'

'None as yet. He is at Stratton, you know, in the process of taking over and assembling his command. We expect to hear nothing for a day or two. Therefore I am at your disposal. And I think – forgive me – there is little purpose in your remaining here at Launceston.' Poor Colonel Roscarrock. He felt me to be a burden, and small blame to him. But the thought of leaving Richard a prisoner in Launceston Castle was more than I could bear.

'Perhaps', I said, 'if I saw the Governor myself?' But he gave me little hope. The Governor, he said, was not the type of man to melt before a woman. 'I will go again', he assured me, 'to-morrow morning, and ascertain at least that the General's health is good, and that he lacks for nothing.' And with that assurance he left me, to pass another lonely night, but in the morning I woke to the sound of distant drums, and then heard the clattering of horses and troopers pass my window, and I wondered whether orders had come from Lord Hopton at Stratton during the night and if the army was on the march again. I sent Matty below for news, and the landlord told her that the troops had been on the move since before daybreak. 'All the horse', he said, 'had ridden away north already.'

I had just finished breakfast when a runner brought me a hurried word, full of apology, from Colonel Roscarrock, saying that he had received orders to proceed at once to Stratton, as Lord Hopton intended marching north to Torrington, and that if I had any friend or relative in the district it would be best for me to go to them immediately. I had no friend or relative, nor would I seek them if I had, and, summoning the landlord, I told him to have me carried to Launceston Castle, for I wished to see the Governor. I set forth, therefore, well wrapped against the weather, with Matty walking by my side and four fellows bearing my litter, and when I came to the Castle gate I demanded to see the captain of the guard. He came from his room, unshaven, buckling his sword, and I thought how Richard would have dealt with him.

'I would be grateful', I said to him, 'if you could give a message from me to the Governor.'

'The Governor sees no one', he said at once, 'without a written appointment.'

'I have a letter here, in my hand,' I said. 'Perhaps it could be given to him.'

He turned it over, looking doubtful, and then looked at me again. 'What exactly, madam, is your business?' he asked.

He looked not unkindly, for all his blotched appearance, and I took a chance. 'I have come', I said, 'to inquire after Sir Richard Grenvile.' At this he handed back my letter.

'I regret, madam,' he said, 'but you have come on a useless errand. Sir Richard is no longer here.'

Panic seized me on the instant, and I pictured a sudden, secret execution. 'What do you mean?' I asked. 'No longer here?'

'He left this morning under escort for St Michael's Mount,' replied the captain of the guard. 'Some of his men broke from their quarters last night and demonstrated here before the Castle. The Governor judged it best to remove him from Launceston.' At once the captain of the guard, the castle walls, the frowning battlements, lost all significance. Richard was no more imprisoned there. 'Thank you,' I said. 'Good day,' and I saw the officer stare after me, and then return to his room beneath the gate.

St Michael's Mount. Some seventy miles away, in the western toe of Cornwall. At least he was far removed from Fairfax, but how in the world was I to reach him there? I returned to the hostelry with only one thought in my head now, and that to get from Launceston as soon as possible.

As I entered the door the landlord came to meet me, and said that an officer had called to inquire for me, and was even now waiting my return. I thought it must be Colonel Roscarrock, and went at once to see – and found instead my brother Robin. 'Thank God', he said, 'I have sight of you at last. As soon as I had news of Sir Richard's arrest, Sir John gave me leave of absence to ride to Werrington. They told me at the house you had been gone two days.'

I was not sure whether I was glad to see him. It seemed to me, at this moment, that no man was my friend unless he was friend to Richard also. 'Why have you come?' I said coolly. 'What is your purpose?'

'To take you back to Mary,' he said. 'You cannot possibly stay here.'

'Perhaps', I answered, 'I have no wish to go.'

'That is neither here nor there,' he said stubbornly. 'The entire army is in process of reorganizing, and you cannot remain in Launceston without protection. I myself have orders to join Sir John Digby at Truro, where he has gone with a force to protect the Prince in the event of invasion. My idea is to leave you at Menabilly on my way thither.'

I thought rapidly. Truro was the headquarters of the Council, and if I went to the town there was a chance, faint yet not impossible, that I could have an audience with the Prince himself.

'Very well,' I said to Robin, shrugging my shoulders, 'I will come with you, but on one condition. And that is that you do not leave me at Menabilly, but let me come with you all the way to Truro.'

He looked at me doubtfully. 'What', he said, 'is to be gained by that?'

'Nothing gained, nor lost,' I answered; 'only, for old time's sake, do what I demand.'

At that he came and took my hand, and held it a minute.

'Honor,' he said, his blue eyes full upon my face, 'I want you to believe me when I say that no action of mine had any bearing on his arrest. The whole army is appalled. Sir John himself, who had many a bitter dispute with him, has written to the Council, appealing for his swift release. He is needed, at this moment, more than any other man in Cornwall.'

'Why', I said bitterly, 'did you not think of it before? Why did you refuse to obey his orders about the bridge?'

Robin looked startled for a moment, and then discomforted.

'I lost my temper,' he admitted. 'We were all rankled that day, and Sir John, the best of men, had given me my orders. You don't understand, Honor, what it has meant to me, and Jo, and all your family, to have your name a byword in the county. Ever since you left Radford last spring to go to Exeter people have hinted, and whispered, and even dared to say aloud the foulest things.'

'Is it so foul', I said, 'to love a man, and go to him when he lies wounded.'

'Why are you not married to him, then?' said Robin. 'If you had been, in God's conscience, you would have earned the right now to share in his disgrace. But to follow from camp to camp, like a loose woman.... I tell you what they say, Honor, in Devon. That he well earns his name of Skellum to trifle thus with a woman who is crippled.'

Yes, I thought, they would say that in Devon....

'If I am not Lady Grenvile', I said, 'it is because I do not choose to be so.'

'You have no pride, then, no feeling for your name?'

'My name is Honor, and I do not hold it tarnished,' I answered him.

'This is the finish. You know that?' he said, after a moment's pause. 'In spite of a petition, signed by all our names, I hardly think the Council will agree to his release. Not unless they receive some counter-order from His Majesty.'

'And His Majesty', I said, 'has other fish to fry. Yes, Robin, I understand. And what will be the outcome?'

'Imprisonment at His Majesty's pleasure, with a pardon, possibly, at the end of the war.'

'And what if the war does not go the way we wish, but the rebels gain Cornwall for the Parliament?'

260

Robin hesitated, so I gave the answer for him.

'Sir Richard Grenvile is handed over, a prisoner, to General Fairfax,' I said, 'and sentenced to death as a criminal of war.' I pleaded fatigue, then, and went to my room, and slept easily for the first time for many nights, for no other reason but because I was bound for Truro, which was some thirty miles distant from St Michael's Mount. The snow of the preceding days had wrought havoc on the road, and we were obliged to go a longer route, by the coast, for the moors were now impassable. Thus, with many halts and delays, it was well over a week before we came to Truro, only to discover that the Council was now removed to Pendennis Castle, at the mouth of the Fal, and Sir John Digby and his forces were now also within the garrison.

Robin found me and Matty a lodging at Penryn, and went at once to wait on his commander, bearing a letter from me to Jack Grenvile, whom I believed to be in close attendance on the Prince. The following day Jack rode to see me – and I felt as though years had passed since I had last set eyes upon a Grenvile. Yet it was barely three weeks since he, and Richard, and young Bunny, had ridden all three to Menabilly. I nearly wept when he came into the room.

'Have no fear,' he said at once. 'My uncle is in good heart, and sturdy health. I have received messages from him from the Mount, and he bade me write you not to be anxious for him. It is rather he who is likely to be anxious on your part, for he believes you with your sister, Mrs Rashleigh.'

I determined then to take young Jack into my confidence.

'Tell me first,' I said, 'what is the opinion on the war?'

He made a face, and shrugged his shoulders. 'You see we are at Pendennis,' he said quietly. 'That, in itself, is ominous. There is a frigate at anchor in the roads, fully manned and provisioned, with orders to set sail for the Scillies when the word is given. The Prince himself will never give the word – he is all for fighting to the last – but the Council lacks his courage. Sir Edward Hyde will have the last word, not the Prince of Wales.'

'How long, then, have we till the word be given?'

'Hopton and the army have marched to Torrington,' answered Jack, 'and there is a hope – but I fear a faint one – that

261

by attacking first Hopton will take the initiative, and force a decision. He is a brave fellow, but lacks my uncle's power, and the troops care nothing for him. If he fails at Torrington, and Fairfax wins the day – then you may expect that frigate to set sail.'

'And your uncle?'

'He will remain, I fear, at the Mount. He has no other choice. But Fairfax is a soldier, and a gentleman. He will receive fair treatment.' This was no answer for me. However much a soldier and a gentleman Fairfax himself might be, his duty was to Parliament, and Parliament had decreed in '43 that Richard Grenvile was a traitor.

'Jack,' I said, 'would you do something for me, for your uncle's sake?'

'Anything in the world,' he answered, 'for the pair of you.'

Ah, bless you, I thought, true son of Bevil. . . .

'Get me an audience with the Prince of Wales,' I said to him.

He whistled, and scratched his cheek, a very Grenvile gesture.

'I'll do my best, I swear it,' he said, 'but it may take time and patience, and I cannot promise you success. He is so hemmed about with members of the Council, and dares do nothing but what he is told to do by Sir Edward Hyde. I tell you, Honor, he's led a dog's life until now. First his mother, and now the Chancellor. When he does come of age and can act for himself, I'll wager he'll set the stars on fire.'

'Make up some story,' I urged. 'You are his age, and a close companion. You know what would move him. I give you full licence.'

He smiled – his father's smile. 'As to that,' he said, 'he has only to hear your story, and how you followed my uncle to Exeter, to be on tenterhooks to look at you. Nothing pleases him better than a love-affair. But Sir Edward Hyde – he's the danger.'

He left me, with an earnest promise to do all he could, and with that I was forced to be content. Then came a period of waiting that seemed like centuries, but was, in all reality, little longer than a fortnight. During this time Robin came several times to visit me, imploring me to leave Penryn and return to

Menabilly. Jonathan Rashleigh, he said, would come himself to fetch me, would I but say the word.

'I must warn you, in confidence', he said, 'that the Council have little expectation of Hopton's withstanding Fairfax. The Prince, with his personal household, will sail for Scilly. The rest of us within the garrison will hold Pendennis until we are burnt out of it. Let the whole rebel army come. We will not surrender.'

Dear Robin. As you said that, with your blue eyes blazing and your jaw set, I forgave you for your emnity for Richard, and the silly, useless harm you did in disobeying him.

Death or glory, I reflected. That was the way my Richard might have chosen. And here was I, plotting one thing only, that he should steal away like a thief in the night.

'I will go back to Menabilly', I said slowly, 'when the Prince of Wales sets sail for the Scillies.'

'By then', said Robin, 'I shall not be able to assist you. I shall be inside the garrison, at Pendennis, with our guns turned east upon Penryn.'

'Your guns will not frighten me', I said, 'any more than Fairfax's horse, thundering across the moors from the Tamar. It will look well, in after-years, in the annals of the Harris family, to say that Honor died in the last stand in '46.'

Brave words, spoken in hardihood, ringing so little true. . . .

On the fourteenth of February, the feast of St Valentine, that patron saint of lovers, I had a message from Jack Grenvile. The wording was vague, and purposely omitted names.

'The snake is gone to Truro,' he said, 'and my friend and I will be able to receive you, for a brief space, this afternoon. I will send an escort for you. Say nothing of the matter to your brother.'

I went alone, without Matty, deeming in a matter of such delicacy it were better to have no confidante at all.

True to his word, the escort came, and Jack himself awaited me at the entrance to the castle. No haggling this time with a captain of the guard. But a swift word to the sentry, and we were through the arch and within the precincts of the garrison before a single soul, save the sentry, was a whit the wiser.

The thought occurred to me that this perhaps was not the

first time Jack Grenvile had smuggled a woman into the fortress. Such swift handling came possibly from long experience. Two servants in the Prince's livery came to carry me, and after passing up some stairs (which I told myself were back ones, and suitable to my person), I was brought to a small room within a tower, and placed upon a couch. I would have relished the experience were not the matter upon which I sought an audience so deadly serious. There was wine and fruit at my elbow, and a posy of fresh flowers, and His Highness, I thought, for all his mother, has gained something by inheriting French blood.

I was left for a few moments to refresh myself, and then the door opened again and Jack stood aside, to let a youngster of about his own age pass before him. He was far from handsome, more like a gipsy than a prince, with his black locks and swarthy skin, but the instant he smiled I loved him better than all the famous portraits of his father that my generation had known for thirty years. 'Have my servants looked after you,' he said at once, 'and given you all you want? This is garrison fare, you know – you must excuse it.' And as he spoke I felt his bold eyes look me up and down in cool, appraising fashion, as though I were a maid and not fifteen years his senior. 'Come, Jack,' he said, 'present me to your kinswoman,' and I wondered what the devil of a story Jack had spun.

We ate and drank, and all the while he talked he stared, and I wondered if his boy's imagination was running riot on the thought of his notorious and rebellious general making love to me, a cripple. 'I have no claim to trespass on your time, sir,' I said at length, 'but Sir Richard, Jack's uncle, is my dear friend, and has been so now over a span of years. His faults are many, and I have not come to dispute them. But his loyalty to yourself has never, I believe, been the issue in question.'

'I don't doubt it,' said the prince, 'but you know how it was. He got up against the Council, and Sir Edward is particular. I like him immensely myself, but personal feeling cannot count in these matters. There was no choice but to sign that warrant for his arrest.'

'Sir Richard did very wrong not to serve under Lord Hopton,' I said. 'His worse fault is his temper, and much, I think, had gone wrong that day to kindle it. Given reflection, he would have acted otherwise.'

'He made no attempt, you know, sir,' cut in Jack, 'to resist arrest. The whole staff would have gone to his aid, had he given them the word. That I have on good authority. But he told all of them he wished to abide by your Highness's command.'

The Prince rose to his feet and paced up and down the room. 'It's a wretched affair all round,' he said. 'Grenvile is the one fellow who might have saved Cornwall, and all the while Hopton fights a hopeless battle up in Torrington. I can't do anything about it, you know – that's the devil of it. I shall be whisked away myself before I know what is happening.'

'There is one thing you can do, sir, if you will forgive my saying so,' I said.

'What then?'

'Send word to the Mount that when you and the Council sail for the Scillies Sir Richard Grenvile shall be permitted to escape at the same time, and commandeer a fishing-boat for France.'

The Prince of Wales stared at me a moment, and then that same smile I had remarked upon his face before lit his whole ugly countenance. 'Sir Richard Grenvile is most fortunate', he said, 'to have so *fidèle* an ally as yourself. If I am ever in his shoes, and find myself a fugitive, I hope I can rely on half so good a friend.'

He glanced across at Jack. 'You can arrange that, can't you?' he said. 'I will write a letter to Sir Arthur Bassett at the Mount, and you can take it there, and see your uncle at the same time. I don't suggest we ask for his company in the frigate when we sail, because I hardly think the ship would bear his weight, alongside Sir Edward Hyde.' The two lads laughed, for all the world like a pair of schoolboys caught in mischief. Then the Prince turned, and, coming to the couch, bent low and kissed my hand.

'Have no fear,' he said. 'I will arrange it. Sir Richard shall be free the instant we sail for the Scillies. And when I return – for I shall return, you know, one day – I shall hope to see you, and him also, at Whitehall.' He bowed, and went, forgetting me. I dare say, for ever more, but leaving with me an impression of black eyes and gipsy features that I have not forgotten to this day. . . .

Jack escorted me to the castle entrance once again. 'He will remember his promise,' he said. 'That I swear to you. I have never known him go back on his word. Tomorrow I shall ride with that letter to the Mount.'

I returned to Penryn, worn-out and utterly exhausted now that my mission was fufilled. I wanted nothing but my bed, and silence. Matty received me with sour looks and the grim, pursed mouth that spelt disapproval. 'You have wanted to be ill for weeks,' she said. 'Now that we are here, in a strange lodging, with no comforts, you decide to do so. Very well. I'll not answer for the consequences.'

'No one asks you to,' I said, turning my face to the wall. 'For God's sake, if I want to, let me sleep, or die.'

Two days later Lord Hopton was defeated outside Torrington, and the whole western army in full retreat across the Tamar. It concerned me little, lying in that lodging at Penryn with a high fever. On the twenty-fifth of February Fairfax had marched and taken Launceston, and on the second of March had crossed the moors to Bodmin.

That night the Prince of Wales, with his Council, set sail in the frigate *Phoenix* – and the war in the west was over. . . .

The day Lord Hopton signed the treaty in Truro with General Fairfax, my brother-in-law, Jonathan Rashleigh, by permission of the Parliament, came down to Penryn to fetch me back to Menabilly. The streets were lined with soldiers, not ours, but theirs, and the whole route from Truro to St Austell bore signs of surrender and defeat. I sat, with stony face, looking out of the curtains of my litter, while Jonathan Rashleigh rode by my side, his shoulders bowed, his face set in deep, grim lines.

We did not converse. We had no words to say. We crossed St Blazey's bridge and Jonathan handed his pass to the rebel sentry at the post, who stared at us with insolence and then jerked his head and let us pass. They were everywhere. In the road, in the cottage doors at Tywardreath, at the barrier, at the foot of Polmear hill. This was our future then, for ever more, to ask, in deep humility, if we might travel our own roads. That it should be so worried me no longer, for my days of journeying were over. I was returning to Menabilly, to be no longer a camp-follower, no longer a lady of the drum, but plain Honor Harris, a cripple on her back. And it did not matter to me, I did not care.

For Richard Grenvile had escaped to France.

Chapter 28

DEFEAT, and the aftermath of war.... Not pleasant for the losers. God knows that we endure it still – and I write in the autumn of 1653 – but in the year '46 we were new to defeat, and had not yet begun to learn our lesson. It was, I think, the loss of freedom that hit the Cornish hardest. We had been used, for generations, to minding our own affairs, and each man lived after his fashion. Landlords were fair, and usually well-liked, with tenant and labourer living in amity together. We had our local disagreements, as every man with his neighbour, and our family feuds, but no body of persons had ever before interfered with our way of living, nor given us commands. Now all was changed. Our orders came to us from Whitehall, and a Cornish County Committee, way up in London, sat in judgement upon us. We could no longer pass our own measures and decide, by local consultation, what was suited to each town and village. The County Committee made our decisions for us.

Their first action was to demand a weekly payment from the people of Cornwall to the revenue, and this weekly assessment was rated so high that it was impossible to find the money, for the ravages of war had stripped the country bare. Their next move was to sequester the estate of every landlord who had fought for the King. Because the County Committee had not the time nor the persons to administer these estates, the owners were allowed to dwell there, if they so desired, but had to pay to the Committee, month by month, the full and total value of the property. This crippling injunction was made the harder because the estates were assessed at the value they had held before the war, and now that most of them were fallen into ruin, through the fighting, it would take generations before the land gave a return once more.

A host of petty officials who were paid fixed salaries by the Parliament, and were the only men at these times to have their pockets well-lined, came down from Whitehall to collect the sums due to the County Committee; and these agents were found in every town and borough, forming themselves in their turns into committees and sub-committees, so that no man could buy as little as a loaf of bread without first going cap in hand to one of these fellows and signing his name to a piece of paper. Besides these civil employees of the Parliament, we had the military to contend with, and whosoever should wish to pass from one village to another must first have a pass from the officer in charge, and then his motives questioned, his family history gone into, detail for detail, and as likely as not find himself arrested for delinquency at the end of it.

I truly believe that Cornwall was, in the first summer of '46, the most wretched county in the kingdom. The harvest was bad – another bitter blow to landlord and labourer alike – and the price of wheat immediately rose to fantastic prices. The price of tin, on the contrary, fell low, and many mines closed down on this account. Poverty and sickness were rife by the autumn, and our old enemy the plague appeared, killing great numbers in St Ives and in the western districts. Another burden was the care of the many wounded and disabled soldiers, who, half-naked and half-starved, roamed the villages, begging for charity. There was no single man or woman or little child who benefited in any way by this new handling of affairs by Parliament, and the only ones to live well were those Whitehall agents who poked their noses into our affairs from dawn till dusk, and their wealthy masters, the big Parliamentary landlords. We had grumbled in the old days at the high taxes of the King, but the taxes were intermittent. Now they were continuous. Salt, meat, starch, lead, iron – all came under the control of Parliament, and the poor man had to pay accordingly.

What happened up-country I cannot say – I speak for Cornwall. No news came to us, much beyond the Tamar. If living was hard, leisure was equally restricted. The Puritans had the upper hand of us. No man must be seen out-of-doors upon a Sunday unless he were bound for church. Dancing was forbidden – not that many had the heart to dance, but youngsters have light hearts and lighter feet – and any game of chance or village festival was frowned upon. Gaiety meant licence, and licence spelt the abomination of the Lord. I often thought how Temperance Sawle would have rejoiced in the brave new world, for all her Royalist traditions, but poor Temperance fell an early victim to the plague.

The one glory of that most dismal year of '46 was the gallant, though alas! so useless, holding of Pendennis Castle for the King through five long months of siege. The rest of us were long conquered and subdued, caught fast in the meshes of Whitehall, while Pendennis still defied the enemy. Their commander was Jack Arundell, who had been in the old days a close friend as well as kinsman to the Grenviles, and Sir John Digby was his second-in-command. My own brother Robin was made a major-general under him. It gave us, I think, some last measure of pride in our defeat, that this little body of men, with no hope of rescue and scarce a boatload of provisions, should fly the King's flag from March the second until August the seventeenth, and that even then they wished to blow themselves and the whole garrison to eternity, rather than surrender. But starvation and sickness had made weaklings of the men, and for their sakes only did Jack Arundell haul down his flag. Even the enemy respected their courage, and the garrison were permitted to march out, so Robin told us afterwards, with the full honours of war, drums beating, colours flying, trumpets sounding. . . . Yes, we have had our moments, here in Cornwall. . . . When they surrendered, though, our last hopes vanished, and there was nothing now to do but sigh, and look into the black well of the future

My brother-in-law, Jonathan Rashleigh, like the rest of his Royalist landlords, had his lands sequestered by the County Committee, and was told, when he went down to Truro in June, that he must pay a fine of some one thousand and eighty pounds to the Committee before he could redeem them. His losses, after the '44 campaign, were already above eight thousand, but there was nothing for it but to bow his head to the victors and agree to pay the ransom during the years to come. He might have quitted the country and gone to France, as many of our neighbours did, but the ties of his own soil were too strong, and in July, broken and dispirited, he took the National Covenant, by which he vowed never again to take arms against the Parliament. This bitter blow to his pride, self-inflicted though it was, did not satisfy the Committee, and shortly afterwards he was summoned to London and ordered to remain there, nor to return to Cornwall until his full fine was paid. So yet another home was broken, and we, at Menabilly, tasted the full flavour of defeat. He left us, one day in September, when the last of the poor harvest had been gathered in, looking a good ten years older than his five-and-fifty years, and I knew then, watching his eyes, how loss of freedom can so blight the human soul that a man cares no longer if he lives or dies.

It remained for Mary, my poor sister, and John, his son, so to husband his estate that the debt could month by month be paid, but we well knew that it might take years, even the remainder of his life. His last words to me, before he went to London, were kind and deeply generous. 'Menabilly is your home', he said, 'for as long a time as you should so desire it. We are one and all sufferers in this misfortune. Guard your sister for me; share her troubles. And help John, I pray you. You have a wiser head than all I leave behind.'

A wiser head. . . . I doubted it. It needed a pettifogging mind, with every low lawyer's trick at the finger's end, to break even with the County Committee and the paid agents of the Parliament. There was none to help us. My brother Robin, after the surrender of Pendennis, had gone to Radford, to my brother Jo, who was in much the same straits as ourselves, while Peter Courtney, loathing inactivity, left the West Country altogether, and the next we heard from him was that he had gone abroad to join the Prince of Wales. Many young men followed this example – living was good at the French Court. I think, had they loved their homes better, they would have stayed behind and shared the burdens of defeat with their womenfolk.

Alice never spoke a word of blame, but I think her heart broke when we heard that he had gone. . . . It was strange, at first, to watch John and Frank Penrose work in the fields side by side with the tenants, for every hand was needed if the land was to be tilled entirely and yield a full return. Even our womenfolk went out at harvesting – Mary herself, and Alice, and Elizabeth, while the children, thinking it fine sport, helped to carry the corn. Left to ourselves, we would have soon grown reconciled and even well content with our labours, but the Parliament agents were for ever coming to spy upon us, to question us on this and that, to count the sheep and cattle, to reckon, it almost seemed, each ear of corn, and nothing must be gathered, nothing spent, nothing distributed amongst ourselves, but all laid before the smug, well-satisfied officials in Fowey town, who held their licence from the Parliament. The Parliament.... The Parliament... From day to day the word rang in our ears. The Parliament decrees that produce shall be brought to market only upon a Tuesday.... The Parliament has ordered that all fairs shall henceforth be discontinued.... The Parliament warns every inhabitant within the above-prescribed area that no one, save by permission, shall walk abroad one hour after sunset.... The Parliament warns each householder that every dwelling will be searched each week for concealed firearms, weapons, and ammunition, from this day forward, and any holder of the same shall be immediately imprisoned....

'The Parliament', said John Rashleigh wearily, 'decrees that no man may breathe God's air, save by a special licence, and that one hour in every other day. My God, Honor, no man can stand this long.'

'You forget', I said, 'that Cornwall is only one portion of the kingdom. The whole of England, before long, will suffer the same fate.'

'They will not, they cannot, endure it,' he said.

'What is their alternative? The King is virtually a prisoner. The party with the most money and the strongest army rules the country. For those who share their views life is doubtless very pleasant.'

'No one can share their views and call his soul their own.'

'There you are wrong. It is merely a matter of being accommodating, and shaking hands with the right people. Lord Robartes lives in great comfort at Lanhydrock. The Treffrys –

being related to Hugh Peters and Jack Trefusis – live very well at Place. If you chose to follow their example and truckle to the Parliament, doubtless you would find life here at Menabilly so much the easier.'

He stared at me suspiciously. 'Would you have me go to them and fawn, while my father lives a pauper up in London, watched every moment of his day? I would sooner die.'

I knew he would sooner die, and loved him for it. Dear John, you might have had more years beside your Joan, and be alive today, had you spared yourself, and your poor health, in those first few months of aftermath.... I watched him toil, and the women too, and there was little I could do to help but figure the accounts, an unpaid clerk, with smudgy fingers, and tot up the debts we owed on quarter-days. I did not suffer as the Rashleighs did, pride being, I believe, a quality long lost to me, and I was sad only in their sadness. To see Alice, gazing wistfully from a window, brought a pain to my heart, and when Mary read a letter from her Jonathan, deep shadows beneath her eyes, I think I hated the Parliament every whit as much as they did.

But that first year of defeat was, in some queer fashion, quiet and peaceful to me who bore no burden on my shoulders. Danger was no more. Armies were disbanded. The strain of war was lifted. The man I loved was safe across the sea, in France, and then in Italy, in the company of his son, and now and then I would have word of him from some foreign city, in good heart and spirits, and missing me, it would seem, not at all. He talked of going to fight the Turk with great enthusiasm, as if, I thought with a shrug of my shoulder, he had not had enough of fighting after three hard years of civil war. 'Doubtless', he wrote, 'you find your days monotonous in Cornwall.' Doubtless I did. To women who have known close siege and stern privation, monotony can be a pleasant thing.... A wanderer for so many months, it was restful to find a home at last, and to share it with people that I loved, even if we were all companions in defeat. God bless the Rashleighs, who permitted me those months at Menabilly. The house was bare and shorn of its former glory, but at least I had a room to call my own. The Parliament could strip the place of its possessions, take the sheep and cattle, glean the harvest, but they could not take from me, nor from the Rashleighs, the beauty that we looked on every day. The devastation of the gardens was forgotten when the primroses came in spring, and the young green budded on the trees. We, the defeated, could still listen to the birds on a May morning, and watch the clumsy cuckoo wing his way to the little wood beside the Gribben hill. The Gribben hill.... I watched it, from my chair upon the causeway, in every mood from winter to midsummer. I have seen the shadows creep, on an autumn afternoon, from the deep Pridmouth valley to the summit of the hill, and there stay a moment, waiting on the sun.

I have seen too the white sea-mists of early summer turn the hill to fantasy, so that it becomes, in a single second, a ghost land of enchantment, with no sound coming but the wash of breakers on the hidden beach, where, at high noon, the children gather cowrie shells. Dark moods too of bleak November, when the rain sweeps in a curtain from the south-west. But, quietest of all, the evenings of late summer, when the sun has set, and the moon has not yet risen, but the dew is heavy in the long grass.

The sea is very white and still, without a breath upon it, and only a single thread of wash upon the covered Cannis rock. The jackdaws fly homeward to their nests in the warren. The sheep crop the short turf, before they too rub together beneath the stone wall by the winnowing place. Dusk comes slowly to the Gribben hill, the woods turn black, and suddenly, with stealthy pad, a fox creeps from the trees in the thistle park, and stands watching me, his ears pricked.... Then his brush twitches and he is gone, for here is Matty tapping along the causeway to bring me home; and another day is over. Yes, Richard, there is comfort in monotony....

I return to Menabilly to find all have gone to bed, and the candles extinguished in the gallery. Matty carries me upstairs, and as she brushes my hair, and ties the curling rags, I think I am almost happy. A year has come and gone, and though we are defeated we live, we still survive. I am lonely, yes, but that has been my portion since I turned eighteen. And loneliness has compensations. Better to live inwardly alone than together in constant fear. And as I think thus, my curling rag in my hand, I see Matty's round face looking at me from the mirror opposite.

'There were strange rumours in Fowey today,' she says quietly.

'What rumours, Matty? There are always rumours.'

She moistens a rag with her tongue, then whips it round a curl. 'Our men are creeping back,' she murmurs. 'First one, then two, then three. Those who fled to France a year ago.'

I rub some lotion on my hands, and face.

'Why should they return? They can do nothing.'

'Not alone, but if they band together, in secret, one with another. . . .'

I sit still, my hands in my lap, and suddenly I remember a phrase in the last letter that came from Italy.

'You may hear from me,' he said, 'before the summer closes, by a different route. . . .' I thought him to mean he was going to fight the Turks.

'Do they mention names?' I say to Matty, and, for the first time for many months a little seed of anxiety and fear springs to my heart. She does not answer for a moment – she is busy with a curl. Then at last she speaks, her voice low and hushed.

'They talk of a great leader,' she says, 'landing in secret at Plymouth from the Continent. He wore a dark wig, they said, to disguise his colouring. But they did not mention names. . . .'

A bat brushes itself against my windows, lost and frightened, and close to the house an owl shrieks in warning. And it seemed to me, that moment, that the bat was no airey-mouse of midsummer, but the scared symbol of all hunted things.

Chapter 29

RUMOURS. Always rumours. Never anything of certainty. This was our portion during the winter of '47–'48. So strict was the Parliamentary hold on news that nothing but the bare official statements were given to us down in Cornwall, and these had no value, being simply what Whitehall thought good for us to know.

So the whispers started, handed from one to the other, and when the whispers came to us fifth-hand we had to sift the welter of extravagance to find the seed of truth. The Royalists were arming. This was the firm base of all the allegations. Weapons were being smuggled into the country from France, and places of concealment were found for them. Gentlemen were meeting in one another's houses. The labourers were conversing together in the field. A fellow at a street-corner would beckon to another, for the purpose, it would seem, of discussing market prices; there would be a question, a swift answer, and then the two would separate, but information had been passed, and another link forged.

Outside the parish church of Tywardreath would stand a Parliamentary soldier, leaning on his musket, while the busybody agent, who had beneath his arm a fold of documents listing each member of the parish and his private affairs, gave him 'Good morning'; and while he did so the old sexton, with his back turned, prepared a new grave, not for a corpse this time, but for weapons. . . . They could have told a tale, those burial grounds of Cornwall. Cold steel beneath the green turf and the daisies, locked muskets in the dark family vaults. Let a fellow climb to repair his cottage roof against the rains of winter, and he will pause an instant and glance over his shoulder, and, thrusting his hand under the thatch, feel for the sharp edge of a sword. These would be Matty's tales. Mary would come to me, with a letter from Jonathan in London. 'Fighting is likely to start again at any moment,' would be his guarded word. 'Discontent is rife, even here, against our masters. Many Londoners who fought in opposition to the king would swear loyalty to him now. I can say no more than this. Bid John have a care whom he meets and where he goes. Remember, I am bound to my oath. If we meddle in these matters he and I will answer for it with our lives.'

Mary would fold the letter anxiously and place it in her gown. 'What does it mean?' she would say. 'What matters does he refer to?' And to this there could be one answer only. The Royalists were rising.

Names that had not been spoken for two years were now whispered by cautious tongues. Trelawney.... Trevannion.... Arundell.... Bassett.... Grenvile.... Yes, above all, Grenvile. He had been seen at Stowe, said one. Nay, that was false, it was not Stowe, but at his sister's house near Bideford. The Isle of Wight, said another. The red fox was gone to Carisbrooke to take secret council of the King. He had not come to the West Country. He had been seen in Scotland. He had been spoken to in Ireland. Sir Richard Grenvile was returned. Sir Richard Grenvile was in Cornwall. ...

I made myself deaf to these tales. For once too often, in my life, I had had a bellyful of rumours. Yet it was strange no letter came any more from Italy, or from France....

John Rashleigh kept silent on these matters. His father had bidden him not to meddle, but to work, night and day, at the husbanding of the estate, so that the groaning debt to Parliament could be paid. But I could guess his thoughts. If there were in truth a rising, and the Prince landed, and Cornwall was freed once more, there would be no debt to pay. If the Trelawneys were a party to the plan, and the Trevannions also, and all those in the county who swore loyalty to the King in secret, then was it not something like cowardice, something like shame, for a Rashleigh to remain outside the company? Poor John. He was often restless and sharp-tempered, those first weeks of spring, after ploughing was done. And Joan was not with us to encourage him, for her twin boys, born the year before, were sickly, and she was with them, and the elder children, at Mothercombe in Devon. Then Jonathan fell ill up in London, and though he asked permission of the Parliament to return to Cornwall they would not grant it, so he sent for Mary, and she went to him. Alice was the next to leave. Peter wrote to her from France, desiring that she should take the children to Trethurfe, his home, which was – so he had heard – in sad state of repair, and would she go there, now spring was at hand, and see what could be done. She went, the first day of March, and it suddenly became strangely quiet at Menabilly. I had been used so long to children's voices that now to be without them, and the sound of Alice's voice calling to them, and the rustle of Mary's gown, made me more solitary than usual, even a little sad. There was no one but John now for company, and I wondered what we should make of it together, he and I, through the long evenings.

'I have half a mind,' he said to me the third day we sat together, 'to leave Menabilly in your care, and go to Mothercombe.'

'I'll tell no tales of you if you do,' I said to him.

'I do not like to go against my father's wishes,' he admitted, 'but it's over six months now since I have seen Joan and the children, and not a word comes to us here of what is passing in the country. Only that the war has broken out again. There is fighting in places as far apart as Wales and the Eastern Counties. I tell you, Honor, I am sick of inactivity. For very little I would take horse and ride to Wales.'

'No need to ride to Wales,' I said quietly, 'when there is likely to be a rising in your own county.'

He glanced at the half-open door of the gallery. A queer, instinctive move, unnecessary when the few servants that we had could all be trusted. Yet since we had been ruled by Parliament this gesture would be force of habit. 'Have you heard anything?' he said guardedly. 'Some word of truth, I mean, not idle rumour?'

'Nothing', I answered, 'beyond what you hear yourself.'

'I thought perhaps Sir Richard . . .' he began, but I shook my head.

'Since last year', I said, 'rumour has it that he has been hiding in the country. I've had no message.'

He sighed, and glanced once more towards the door.

'If only', he said, 'I could be certain what to do. If there should be a rising, and I took no part in it, how lacking in loyalty to the King I would seem, and what dishonour it would be to the name of Rashleigh.'

'If there should be a rising and it failed,' I said, 'how damp your prison walls, how uneasy your head upon your shoulders.'

He smiled, for all his earnestness. 'Trust a woman', he said, 'to damp a fellow's ardour.'

'Trust a woman', I replied, 'to keep war out of her home.'

'Do you wish to sit down indefinitely, then, under the rule of Parliament?' he asked.

'Not so. But spit in their faces, before the time is ripe, and we shall find ourselves one and all under their feet for ever.'

Once again he sighed, rumpling his hair and looking dubious.

'Get yourself permission,' I said, 'and go to Mothercombe. It's your wife you need, and not a rising. But I warn you, once you are in Devon you may not find it so easy to return.'

This warning had been repeated often during the past weeks. Those who had gone into Devon or to Somerset upon their lawful business, bearing a permit from the local Parliamentary officials, would find great delay upon the homeward journey, much scrutiny and questioning, and this would be followed by a search for documents or weapons, and possibly a night or more under arrest. We, the defeated, were not the only ones to hear the rumours. . . .

The Sheriff of Cornwall at this time was a neighbour, Sir Thomas Herle of Prideaux, near St Blazey, who, though firm for Parliament, was a just and fair man. He had done all he could to mitigate the heavy fine placed upon the Rashleigh estate, through respect for my brother-in-law, but Whitehall was too strong for his local powers. It was he now, in kindness, who granted John Rashleigh permission to visit his wife at Mothercombe in Devon, and so it happened, this fateful spring, that I was, of all our party, the only one remaining at Menabilly. A woman and a cripple – it was not likely that such a one could foster, all alone, a grim rebellion. The Rashleighs had taken the oath. Menabilly was now above suspicion. And though the garrison at Fowey and other harbours on the coast were strengthened, and more troops quartered in the towns and villages, our little neck of land seemed undisturbed. The sheep grazed on the Gribben hill. The cattle browsed in the beef park. The wheat was sown in eighteen acres. And smoke from a single fire – my own – rose from the Menabilly chimneys. Even the steward's house was desolate, now old John Langdon had been gathered to his fathers, for with the crushing burden on the estate his place had not been filled. His keys, once so important and mysterious, were now in my keeping, and the summer-house, so sacred to my brother-in-law, had become my routine shelter on a windy afternoon. I had no wish these days to pry into the Rashleigh papers. Most of the books were gone, stored in the house or packed and sent after him to London. The desk was bare and empty. Cobwebs hung from the walls. Green patches of mould showed upon the ceiling. But the torn matting on the floor still hid the flagstone with the iron ring. . . . I saw a rat once creep from his corner and stare at me a moment with beady, unwinking eyes. A great black spider spun a web from a broken pane of glass in the east window, while ivy, spreading from the ground, thrust a tendril to the sill. A few years more, I thought, and Nature would take toll of it all. The stones of the summer-house would crumble, the nettles force themselves through the floor, and no one would remember the flagstone with the ring upon it, or the flight of steps, and the earthy, mouldering tunnel. Well, it had served its purpose. Those days would not return.

I looked out towards the sea, one day in March, and watched the shadows darken, for an instant, the pale ripple of the water beyond Pridmouth. The clock in the belfry struck four o'clock. Matty had gone to Fowey, and should be back by now. I heard a footstep on the path beneath the causeway, and called, thinking it was one of the farm labourers returning home, who could bear a message for me to the house. The footsteps ceased, but there came no word in answer.

I called again, and this time I heard a rustle in the undergrowth. My friend, the fox, perhaps, was out on his prowl. Then I saw a hand fasten to the sill and cling there for an instant, gripping for support. But the walls of the summer-house were smooth, giving no foothold, and in a second the hand had slipped and was gone.

Someone was playing spy upon me. . . . If one of the long-nosed Parliamentary agents who spent their days scaring the wits out of the simple country people wished to try the game on me, he would receive short measure.

'If anyone wishes to speak with Mr Rashleigh, he is from home,' I called loudly. 'There is no one but myself in charge at Menabilly. Mistress Honor Harris, at your service.'

I waited a moment, my eye still on the window, and then a shadow, falling suddenly upon my right shoulder, told me there was someone at the door. I whipped round, in an instant, my hands on the wheels of my chair, and saw the figure of a man, small and slight, clad in plain dark clothes like a London clerk, with a hat pulled low over his face. He stood watching me, his hand upon the lintel of the door.

'Who are you?' I said. 'What do you want?' There was something in his manner which struck a chord. . . . The way he hesitated, standing on one foot, then bit his thumb-nail. . . . I groped for the answer, my heart beating, when he whipped his hat from his close black curls, and I saw him smile, tremulous at first, uncertain, until he saw me smile and stretch my arms towards him.

'Dick . . .' I whispered. He came and knelt by me at once, covering my hand with kisses.

I forgot the intervening years, and had in my arms a little frightened boy who gnawed a bone and swore he was a dog and I his mistress. And then, raising his head, I saw he was a boy no longer, but a young man, with hair upon his lip, and curls no longer riotous, but sleek and close. His voice was low and soft, a man's voice.

'Four years,' I said. 'Have you grown thus in four small years?'

'I shall be eighteen in two months' time,' he answered, smiling. 'Have you forgotten? You wrote the first year for my birthday, but never since.'

'Writing has not been possible, Dick, these past two years.'

I could not take my eyes from him, he was so grown, so altered. Yet that way of watching with dark eyes, wary and suspicious, was the same, and the trick of gnawing at his hand.

'Tell me quickly,' I said, 'before they come to fetch me from the house, what you are doing here, and why.'

He looked at me doubtfully. 'I am the first to come, then?' he asked. 'My father is not here?'

My heart leapt, but whether in excitement or in fear I could not tell. In a flash of intuition, it seemed that I knew everything. The waiting of the past few months was over. It was all to begin afresh. . . . It was to start again. . . .

'No one is here', I answered, 'but yourself. Even the Rashleighs are from home.'

'Yes, we knew that,' he said. 'That is why Menabilly has been chosen.'

'Chosen for what?' I asked.

He did not answer. He started his old trick of gnawing at his hand. 'They will tell you,' he said, blinking his eyelids, 'when they come.'

'Who are "they"?' I asked.

'My father, first,' he answered, with his eye upon the door, 'and Peter Courtney another, and Ambrose Manaton of Trecarrel, and your own brother Robin, and, of course, my Aunt Gartred.'

Gartred. . . . At this I felt like someone who has been ill overlong, or withdrawn from the world, leading another life. There had been rumours enough, God knows, in south-east Cornwall to stun the senses, but none so formidable as fell now upon my ears.

'I think it best', I said slowly, 'if you tell me what has happened since you came to England.'

He rose then from his knee, and, dusting the dirt from his clothes with a fastidious hand, swept a place upon the windowsill to sit. 'We left Italy last autumn,' he said, 'and came first of all to London. My father was disguised as a Dutch merchant, and I as his secretary. Since then we have travelled England, from south to north, outwardly as foreign men of business, secretly as agents for the Prince. At Christmas we crossed the Tamar into Cornwall, and went first of all to Stowe. My aunt is dead, you know, and no one was there but the steward, and my cousin Bunny, and the others. My father made himself known to the steward, and since then many secret meetings have been held throughout the county. From Stowe it is but a step to Bideford and Orley Court. There were found my aunt Gartred, who, having fallen out with her Parliamentary friends, was hot to join us, and your brother Robin also.'

Truly the world had passed me by at Menabilly. The Parliament had one grace to its credit, that the stoppage of news stopped gossip also.

'I did not know', I said, 'that my brother Robin lived at Bideford.'

Dick shrugged his shoulders. 'He and my aunt are very thick,' he answered. 'I understand your brother has made himself her bailiff. She owns land, does she not, that belonged to your eldest brother, who is dead?'

Yes, they could have met again that way. The ground upon which Lanrest had stood, the fields below the mill at Lometton. Why should I blame Robin, grown weary and idle in defeat?

'And so?' I asked.

'And so the plans matured, the clans gathered. They are all in it, you know, from east to west, the length and breadth of Cornwall. The Trelawneys, the Trevannions, the Bassetts, the Arundells. And now the time draws near. The muskets are being loaded and the swords sharpened. You will have a front seat at the slaughter.'

There was a strange note of bitterness in his soft voice, and I saw him clench his hands upon the sill.

'And you?' I asked. 'Are you not excited at the prospect? Are you not happy to be one of them?'

He did not answer for a moment, and when he did I saw his eyes look large and black in his pale face, even as they had done as a boy four years before.

'I tell you one thing, Honor,' he said passionately. 'I would give all I possess in the world, which is precious little, to be out of it.'

The force with which he spoke shocked me for an instant, but I took care that he should not guess it.

'Why so?' I asked. 'Have you no faith that they will succeed?'

'Faith?' he said wearily. 'I have no faith in anything. I begged him to let me stay in Italy, where I was content after my own fashion, but he would not let me. I found that I could paint, Honor. I wished to make painting my trade. I had friends, too, fellows of my age, for whom I felt affection. But no. Painting was womanish, a pastime fit for foreigners. My friends were womanish too, and would degrade me. If I wished to live, if I hoped to have a penny to my name, I must follow him, do his bidding, ape his ways, grow like my Grenvile cousins. God in heaven, how I have come to loathe the very name of Grenvile!'

Eighteen, but he had not changed. Eighteen, but he was still fourteen. This was the little boy who had sobbed his hatred of his father.

'And your mother?' I asked gently.

He shrugged his shoulders. 'Yes, I have seen her,' he said listlessly, 'but it's too late now to make amends. She cares nothing for me. She has other interests. Four years ago she would have loved me still. Not now. It's too late. His fault. Always his fault.'

'Perhaps,' I said, 'when – when this present business is concluded, you will be free. I will speak for you. I will ask that you may return to Italy, to your painting, to your friends.'

He picked at the fringe of his coat with his long slim hands – too long, I thought, too finely slim for a Grenvile.

'There will be fighting,' he said slowly, 'men killing one another for no purpose, save to spill blood. Always to spill blood. . . .'

It was growing dim in the summer-house, and still I had heard no more about their plans. The fear that I read in his eyes found an echo in my heart, and the old strain and anxiety was with me once again. 'When did you leave Bideford?' I asked.

'Two days ago,' he answered. 'Those were my orders. We were to proceed separately, each by a different route. Lady Courtney has gone to Trethurfe, I presume?'

'She went at the beginning of the month.'

'So Peter intended. It was part of the ruse, you see, for emptying the house. Peter has been in Cornwall and amongst us since before Christmas.'

Another prey for Gartred? A second bailiff to attend on Orley Court? And Alice here, with wan cheeks, and chin upon her hand, at an open window. . . . Richard did not chose his serviteurs for kindness.

'Mrs Rashleigh was inveigled up to London for the same purpose,' said Dick. 'The scheme has been cunningly planned, like all schemes of my father's. And the last cast of all, to rid the house of John, was quite in keeping with his character.'

'John went of his own accord,' I answered, 'to see his wife at Mothercombe in Devon.'

'Aye, but he had a message first,' said Dick, 'a scrap of paper, passed to him in Fowey, saying that his wife was over-fond of a neighbour, living in her father's house. I know, because I saw father pen the letter, laughing as he did so, with aunt Gartred at his back.'

I was silent at that. God damn them both, I thought, for cruelty. And I knew Richard's answer, even as I accused him in my thoughts: 'Any means, to secure the end that I desire.'

Well, what was to come was no affair of mine. The house was empty. Let them make of it a place of assignation. I could not stop them. Let Menabilly become, in one brief hour, the head-quarters of the Royalist rising. Whether they succeeded or failed was not my business. 'Did your father', I said, 'send any word to me? Did he know that I was here?'

Dick stared at me blankly for a moment, as though I were in truth the half-wit I now believed myself to be.

'Why, yes, of course,' he said. 'That is why he picked on Menabilly, rather than on Caerhayes. There was no woman at Caerhayes to give him comfort.'

'Does your father', I said, 'still need comfort after two long years in Italy?'

'It depends', he answered, 'what you intend by comfort. I never saw my father hold converse with Italian women. It might have made him better-tempered, if he had.'

I saw Richard, in my mind's eye, pen in hand, with a map of Cornwall spread on a table before him. And dotted upon the map were the houses by the coast that offered sanctuary. Trelawne ... too deeply wooded. Penrice ... not close enough to the sea. Caerhayes ... yes, good landing ground for troops, but not a single Miss Trevannion. Menabilly ... with a beach, and a hiding-place, and an old love into the bargain, who had shared his life before and might be induced, even now, after long silence, to smile on him a moment after supper. And the pen would make a circle round the name of Menabilly. So I was become cynic in defeat. The rule of Parliament had taught me a lesson. But as I sat there watching Dick and thinking how little he resembled his father, I knew that all my anger was but a piece of bluff deceiving no one, not even my harder self, and that there was nothing I wanted in the world so much as to play hostess once more to Richard by candlelight, and to live again that life of strain and folly, anguish and enchantment.

Chapter 30

It fell on me to warn the servants, I summoned each one to my chamber in turn. 'We are entering upon dangerous days,' I said to them. 'Things will pass here at Menabilly which you will not see, and will not hear. Visitors will come and go. Ask no questions. Seek no answer. I believe you are, one and all, faithful subjects of His Majesty?'

This was sworn upon the Book of Common Prayer.

'One incautious word that leaves this house,' I said, 'and your master up in London will lose his life, and ourselves also, in all probability. That is all I have to say. See that there is clean linen on the beds, and sufficient food for guests. But be deaf and dumb and blind to those who come here.'

It was on Matty's advice that I took them thus into my confidence. 'Each one can be trusted,' she said, 'but a word of faith from you will bind them together, and not all the agents in the West Country will make them blab.'

The household had lived sparsely since the siege of '44, and there were few comforts for our prospective visitors. No hangings to the walls, no carpets on the floors in the upper chambers. Straw mattresses in place of beds. They must make what shift they could, and be grateful.

Peter Courtney was the first to come. No secrecy for him. He flaunted openly his pretended return from France, dining with the Treffrys at Place upon the way and loudly announcing desire to see his children. Gone to Trethurfe? But all his belongings were at Menabilly. Alice had misunderstood his letter. . . .

Nothing wan or pale about Peter. He wore a velvet coat that must have cost a fortune. Poor Alice and her dowry. . . .

'You might', I said to him, 'have sent her a whisper of your safe return. She would have kept it secret.'

He shrugged a careless shoulder. 'A wife can be a cursed appendage in times like these,' he said, 'when a man must live from day to day, from hand to mouth. To tell the truth, or, I am so plagued with debts that one glimpse of her reproachful eyes would drive me crazy.'

'You look well on it,' I said. 'I doubt if your conscience worries you unduly.' He winked, his tongue in his cheek, and I thought how the looks that I had once admired were coarsened now with licence and good living. Too much French wine, too little exercise.

'And what are your plans,' I asked, 'when Parliament is overthrown?'

Once again he shrugged his shoulders. 'I shall never settle at Trethurfe,' he said. 'Alice can live there if she pleases. As for myself, why, war has made me restless.'

He whistled under his breath and strolled towards the window. The aftermath of war, the legacy of losing it. Another marriage in the melting-pot. . . .

The next to come was Bunny Grenvile. Bunny, at seventeen, already head and shoulders taller than his cousin Dick. Bunny with snub nose and freckles. Bunny with eager, questing eyes, and a map of the coast under his arm. 'Where are the beaches? Where are the landing-places? No, I want no refreshment. I have work to do. I want to see the ground.' And he was off to the Gribben, a hound to scent, another budding soldier, like his brother Jack.

'You see', said Dick cynically, his black eyes fastened on me, 'how all Grenvile men but me are bred with a nose for blood? You despise me, don't you, because I do not go with him?'

'No, Dick,' I answered gently.

'Ah, but you will in time. Bunny will win your affection, as he has won my father's. Bunny has courage. Bunny has guts. Poor Dick has neither. He is only fit for painting, like a woman.'

He threw himself on his back upon the couch, staring upward at the ceiling. And this, too, I thought, has to be contended with. The demon jealousy, sapping his strength. The wish to excel, the wish to shine before his father. His father whom he pretended to detest. Our third arrival was Mr Ambrose Manaton – a long-familiar name to me, for my family of Harris had for generations past had lawsuits with the Manatons, respecting that same property of theirs, Trecarrel. What it was

286

all about I could not say, but I know my father never spoke to any of them. There was an Ambrose Manaton who stood for Parliament before the war at Launceston. This man was his son. He was, I suppose, a few years older than Peter Courtney, some four-and-thirty years. Sleek and suave, with a certain latent charm. He wore his own fair hair, curling to his shoulders. Thinking it best spoken and so dismissed for ever, I plunged into the family dispute as soon as I set eyes on him. 'Our families', I said, 'have waged a private war for generations. Something to do with property. Since I am the youngest daughter, you are safe with me. I can lay claim to nothing.'

'I could not refuse so fair a pleader, if you did,' he answered.

I considered him thoughtfully as he kissed my hand. Too ready with his compliment, too easy with his smile. What exactly, I wondered, was his part in this campaign? I had not heard of him ever as a soldier. Money? . . . Property? . . . Those lands at Trecarrel and at Southill that my father could not claim? Richard had no doubt assessed the value. A Royalist rising cannot be conducted without funds. Did Ambrose Manaton, then, hold the purse? I wondered what had induced him to risk his life and fortune. He gave me the clue a moment afterwards.

'Mrs Denys has not yet arrived?'

'Not yet. You know her well?'

'We found ourselves near neighbours in north Cornwall and north Devon.' The tone was easy, the smile confident. Oh, Richard, my love of little scruple. So Gartred was the bait to catch the tiger.

What in the name of thunder had been going on all these long winter months at Bideford? I could imagine, with Gartred playing hostess. Well, I was hostess now at Menabilly. And the straw mattresses upstairs would be hard cheer after the feather beds of Orley Court. 'My brother, General Harris, acts as bailiff to Mrs Denys, so I understand?'

'Why, yes, something of the sort,' said Ambrose Manaton. He studied the toe of his boot. His voice was a shade over-casual.

'Have you seen your brother lately?' he asked.

'Not for two years. Not since Pendennis fell.'

will see a change in him then. His nerves have gone to
s. The result of the siege, no doubt.'

Robin never had a nerve in his body. Robin rode to battle
with a falcon on his wrist. If Robin was changed, it was not the
fault of five months' siege. . . .

They came together, shortly before dark. I was alone in the
gallery to receive them. The rule of Parliament had fallen light
on Gartred. She was, I think, a little fuller in the bosom, but it
became her well. And, chancing Fate, she had let Nature do its
damndest with her hair, which was no longer gleaming gold,
but streaked with silver white, making her look more lovely
and more frail.

She tossed her cloak to Robin as she came into the room,
proclaiming in that first careless gesture all that I cared to
know of their relationship. The years slipped backward in a
flash, and she was a bride of twenty-three, already tired of Kit,
her slave and bondsman, who had not the strength of will to
play the master.

It might have been Kit once again, standing there in the
gallery at Menabilly, with a dog's look of adoration in his eyes.

But Ambrose Manaton was right. There was not only ador-
ation in Robin's eyes. There was strain too, doubt, anxiety.
And the heavy jowl and puffy cheeks betrayed the easy drinker.
Defeat and Gartred had taken toll of my brother.

'We seem fated, you and I, to come together at moments of
great crisis,' I said to Gartred. 'Do you still play piquet?'

I saw Robin look from one to the other of us, mystified, but
Gartred smiled, drawing off her lace gloves.

'Piquet is out of fashion,' she answered. 'Dice is a later craze,
but must be done in secret, since all games of chance are
frowned upon by Parliament.'

'I shall not join you, then,' I said. 'You will have to play
with Robin or with Ambrose Manaton.'

Her glance at me was swift, but I let it pass over my head.

'I have at least the consolation', she said, 'of knowing that
for once we shall not play in opposition. We are all partners on
a winning side?'

'Are we?' I said. It was only four years since she had come
here as a spy for Lord Robartes.

'If you doubt my loyalty,' said Gartred, 'you must tell Richard when he comes. But it is rather late to make amends. I know all the secrets.' She smiled again, and as I looked at her I felt like a knight of old, saluting his opponent before combat.

'I have put you', I said, 'in the long chamber overhead, which Alice has with her children when she is home.'

'Thank you,' she said.

'Robin is on your left,' I said, 'and Ambrose Manaton upon your right, at the small bedroom at the stairs' head. With two strong men to guard you, I think it hardly likely you'll be nervous.'

She gave not a flicker of the eyelid, but, turning to Robin, gave him some commands about her baggage. He went at once to obey her, like a servant.

'It has been fortunate for you', I said, 'that the menfolk of my breed have proved accommodating.'

'It would be more fortunate still', she answered, 'if they could be at the same time less possessive.'

'A family failing,' I replied, 'like the motto of our house, "What we have, we hold." '

She looked at me a moment thoughtfully. 'It is a strange power,' she said, 'this magnetism that you have for Richard. I give you full credit.'

I bowed to her from my chair. 'Give me no credit, Gartred,' I answered. 'Menabilly is but a name upon a map, that will do as well as any other. An empty house, a nearby shore.'

'And a secret hiding-place into the bargain,' she said shrewdly.

But now it was my time to smile.

'The Mint had the silver long ago,' I said, 'and what was left has gone to swell the Parliament exchequer. What are you playing for this time, Gartred?'

She did not answer for a moment, but I saw her cat's eyes watching Robin's shadow in the hall.

'My daughters are grown up,' she said. 'Orley Court becomes a burden. Perhaps I would like a third husband and security.'

Which my brother could not give her, I thought, but which a man some fifteen years younger than herself, with lands and fortune, might be pleased to do. Mrs Harris ... Mrs Denys

... Mrs Manaton? 'You broke one man in my family,' I said. 'Take care that you do not seek to break another.'

'You think you can prevent me?'

'Not I. You may do as you please. I only give you warning.'

'Warning of what?'

'You will never play fast and loose with Robin, as you did with Kit. Robin would be capable of murder.'

She stared at me a moment, uncomprehending. And then my brother came into the room.

I thought that night of the Royalist rising which had planned to kindle Cornwall from east to west, while all the time there was enough material for explosive purposes gathered beneath the roof of Menabilly to set light to the whole country.

We made strange company for dinner. Gartred, her silver hair bejewelled, at the head of the table, and those two men on either side of her, my brother with hand ever reaching to the decanter, his eyes feasting on her face, while Ambrose Manaton, cool and self-possessed, kept up a flow of conversation in her right ear, excluding Robin, about the corrupt practices of Parliament – which made me suspect he must have a share in it, from knowing so much detail. On my left sat Peter Courtney, who from time to time caught Gartred's eye and smiled in knowing fashion. But as he did the same to the serving-maid who passed his plate, and to me when I chanced to glance his way, I guessed it to be habit rather than conspiracy. I knew my Peter. Dick glowered in the centre, throwing black looks towards his cousin opposite as he rattled on about the letters he had received from his brother Jack, who was grown so high in favour with the Prince of Wales in France that they were never parted. And as I looked at each in turn, seeing they were served with food and wine, playing the hostess in this house that was not mine, frowned upon, no doubt, by the ghost of old John Rashleigh, I thought, with some misgiving, that had Richard sought his hardest in the county he could not have found six people more likely to fall out and disagree than those who sat around the table now.

Gartred, his sister, had never wished him well. Robin, my brother, had disobeyed his orders in the past. Peter Courtney was one of those who had muttered at his leadership. Dick, his son, feared and hated him. Ambrose Manaton was an unknown quantity, and Bunny, his nephew, a pawn who could read a map. Were these to be the leaders of the rising? If so, God help poor Cornwall and the Prince of Wales.

'My uncle', Bunny was saying, arranging the salt cellars in the fashion of a fort, 'never forgets an injury. He told me once, if a man does him an ill turn, he will serve him with a worse one.'

He went on to describe some battle of the past, to which no one listened, I think, except Peter, who did so from good nature. But the words Bunny had spoken so lightly rang strangely in my head. 'My uncle never forgets an injury.'

He must have been injured by all of us at one time or other, seated at the table now at Menabilly. What a time to choose to pay old scores, Richard, my lover, mocking and malevolent. The eve of a rising, and these six people in it to the hilt.

There was something symbolic in the empty chair beside me.

Then we fell silent, for the door suddenly opened and he stood there, watching us, his hat upon his head, his long cloak hanging from his shoulders. Gone was the auburn hair I loved so well, and the curled wig that fell below his ears gave him a dark, satanic look that matched his smile.

'What a bunch of prizes', he said, 'for the Sheriff of the Duchy if he chose to call. Each one of you a traitor.'

They stared at him, blankly – even Gartred, for once, slow to follow his swift mind. But I saw Dick start and gnaw his fingernails. Then Richard tossed his hat and cloak to the waiting servant in the hall and came to the empty chair at my right side.

'Have you been waiting long?' he said to me.

'Two years and three months,' I answered him.

He filled the glass from the decanter at his side.

'In January '46,' he said to the company, 'I broke a promise to our hostess here. I left her one morning at Werrington, saying I would be back again to breakfast with her. Unfortunately, the Prince of Wales willed otherwise. And I breakfasted instead in Launceston Castle. I propose to make amends for this tomorrow.'

He lifted his glass, draining it in one measure, then put out his hand to mine, and held it on the table.

'Thank God', he said, 'for a woman who does not give a damn for punctuality.'

Chapter 31

IT was like Werrington once more. The old routine. The old haphazard sharing of our days and nights. He would burst into my chamber as I breakfasted, my toilet undone, my hair in curl rags, while he paced about the room talking incessantly, touching my brushes, my combs, my bracelets on the table, cursing all the while at some delay in the plans he was proposing. Trevannion was too slow. Trelawney the elder too cautious. And those who were to lead the insurrection farther west had none of them big names – they were all small fry, lacking the right qualities for leadership. 'Grose of St Buryan, Maddern of Penzance, Keigwin of Mousehole,' said Richard; 'none of them held a higher rank than captain in '46, and have never led troops into action. But we have to use them now. It is a case of *faute de mieux*. The trouble is that I can't be in fifty places at the same time.'

Like Werrington once more. A log fire in the dining-chamber. A heap of papers scattered on the table, and a large map in the centre. Richard seated in his chair, with Bunny, instead of Jack, at his elbow. The red crosses on the beaches where the invading troops should land. Crinnis.... Pentewan.... Veryan.... The beacons on the headlands to warn the ships at sea. The Gribben.... The Dodman.... The Nare.... My brother Robin standing by the door, where Colonel Roscarrock would have stood. And Peter Courtney riding into the courtyard, bearing messages from Jonathan Trelawney.

'What news from Talland?'

'All well. They will wait upon our signal. Looe can easily be held. There will be no opposition there to matter.'

The messages sifted, one by one. Like all defeated peoples,

292

those who had crumbled first in '46 were now the most eager to rebel. Helston. . . . Penzance. . . . St Ives. . . . The confidence was supreme. Grenvile, as commander in chief, had but to give the word

I sat in my chair by the fireside, listening to it all, and I was no longer in the dining-chamber at Menabilly, but back at Werrington, at Ottery St Mary, at Exeter. . . . The same problems, the same arguments, the same doubting of the commanders, the same swift decisions. Richard's pen pointing to the Scillies. 'This will be the main base for the Prince's army. No trouble about seizing the islands. Your brother Jack can do it with two men and a boy.' And Bunny, grinning, nodded his auburn head.

'Then the main landings to be where we have our strongest hold. A line between here and Falmouth, I should fancy, with St Mawes the main objective. Hopton has sent me obstructive messages from Guernsey, tearing my proposals to pieces. He can swallow them, for all I care. If he would have his way he would send a driblet here, a driblet there, some score of pissing landings scattered round the whole of Cornwall, in order, so he says, to confuse the enemy. Confuse my arse. One big punch at a given centre, with us here holding it in strength, and Hopton can land his whole army in four-and-twenty hours. . . .'

The big conferences would be held at night. It was easier then to move about the roads. The Trelawneys from Trelawne, Sir Charles Trevannion from Caerhayes, the Arundells from Trerice, Sir Arthur Bassett from Tehidy. I would lie in my chamber overhead and hear the drone of voices from the drawing-room below, and always that clear tone of Richard's, overtopping them all. Was it certain that the French would play? This was the universal doubt, expressed by the whole assembly, that Richard would brush impatiently aside. 'God damn the French. What the hell does it matter if they don't? We can do without them. Never a Frenchman yet but was not a liability to his own side.'

'But', murmured Sir Charles Trevannion, 'if we at least had the promise of their support, and a token force to assist the Prince in landing, the moral effect upon Parliament would be as valuable as ten divisions put against them.'

'Don't you believe it,' said Richard. 'The French hate fighting on any soil but their own. Show a frog an English pike, and he will show you his backside. Leave the French alone. We won't need them once we hold the Scillies and the Cornish forts. The Mount ... Pendennis ... St Mawes ... Bunny, where are my notes giving the present disposition of the enemy troops? Now, gentlemen ...'

And so it would continue. Midnight, one, two, three o'clock. What hour they went, and what hour he came to bed, I would not know, for exhaustion would lay claim on me long since.

Robin, who had proved his worth in those five weeks at Pendennis, had much responsibility upon his shoulders. The episode of the bridge had been forgotten. Or had it? I would wonder sometimes, when I watched Richard's eye upon him. Saw him smile for no reason. Saw him tap his pen upon his chin.

'Have you the latest news from Helston?'

'Here, sir. To hand.'

'I shall want you to act as deputy for me tomorrow at Penrose. You can be away two nights; no more. I must have the exact number of men they can put upon the roads between Helston and Penryn.'

'Sir ...' And I would see Robin hesitate a moment, his eyes drift towards the door leading to the gallery, where Gartred's laugh would suddenly ring loud and clear. Later his flushed face and bloodshot eye told its own tale.

'Come, Robin,' Richard would say curtly, after supper, 'we must burn the midnight candle once again. Peter has brought me messages in cypher from Penzance, and you are my expert. If I can do with four hours' sleep, so can the rest of you.'

Richard, Robin, Peter, Bunny, crowded round the table in the dining-room, with Dick standing sentinel at the door, watching them wearily, resentfully. Ambrose Manaton by the fire, consulting a great sheaf of figures. 'All right, Ambrose,' Richard would say, 'I shan't need your assistance over this problem. Go and talk high finance to the women in the gallery.'

And Ambrose Manaton smiling, bowing his thanks. Walking from the room with a shade too much confidence, humming under his breath.

'Will you be late?' I said to Richard.

'H'm ... H'm ...' he answered absently. 'Fetch me that file of papers, Bunny.' Then of a sudden, looking up at Dick. 'Stand straight, can't you? Don't slop over your feet,' he said harshly.

Dick's black eyes blinking, his slim hands clutching at his coat. He would open the door for me to pass through in my chair, and all I could do to give him confidence was to smile and touch his hand. No gallery for me. Three makes poor company. But upstairs to my chamber, knowing that the voices underneath would drone for four hours more. An hour, perhaps, would pass, while I read on my bed, and then the swish of a skirt upon the landing as Gartred passed into her room. Silence. Then that tell-tale creaking stair. The soft closing of a door. But beneath me in the dining-room the voices would drone on till after midnight.

One evening, when the conference broke early and Richard sat with me awhile before retiring, I told him bluntly what I heard.

He laughed, trimming his finger-nails by the open window.

'Have you turned prude, sweetheart, in your midde years?' he said.

'Prudery be damned,' I answered. 'But my brother hopes to marry her. I know it, from his hints and shy allusions about rebuilding the property at Lanrest.'

'Then hope will fail him,' replied Richard. 'Gartred will never throw herself away upon a penniless soldier. She has other fish to fry, and small blame to her.'

'You mean', I asked, 'the fish she is in the process of frying at this moment?'

'Why, yes, I suppose so,' he answered, with a shrug. 'Ambrose has a pretty inheritance from his Trefusis mother, besides what he will come into when his father dies. Gartred would be a fool if she let him slip from her.'

How calmly the Grenviles seized fortunes for themselves.

'What exactly', I asked, 'does he contribute to your present business?' He cocked an eye at me, and grinned.

'Don't poke your snub nose into my affairs,' he said. 'I know what I'm about. I'll tell you one thing, though: we'd have difficulty in paying for this affair without him.'

'So I thought,' I answered.

'Taking me all round,' he said, 'I'm a pretty cunning fellow.'

'If you call it cunning', I said, 'to play one member of your staff against another. For my part, I would call it knavery.'

'Good generalship,' he said.

'Gerry-mandering,' I answered.

'A *ruse-de-guerre*,' he countered.

'Pawky politics,' I argued.

'Ah, well,' he said, 'if the manoeuvre serves my purpose it matters not how many lives be broken in the process.'

'Take care they're broken afterwards, and not before,' I said.

He came and sat beside me on the bed.

'I think you mislike me much, now my hair is black,' he suggested.

'It becomes your beauty, but not your disposition.'

'Dark foxes leave no trails behind them.'

'Red ones are more lovable.'

'When the whole future of a country is at stake, emotions are thrown overboard.'

'Emotions, but not honour.'

'Is that a pun upon your name?'

'If you like to take it so.'

He took my hands in his and pressed them backwards on the pillow, smiling. 'Your resistance was stronger at eighteen,' he said.

'And your approach more subtle.'

'It had to be, in that confounded apple-tree.'

He laid his head upon my shoulder, and turned my face to his.

'I can swear in Italian now, as well as Spanish,' he said to me.

'Turkish also?'

'A word or two. The bare necessity.'

He settled himself against me in contentment. One eye drooped. The other regarded me malevolently from the pillow.

'There was a woman I encountered once in Naples ...'

'With whom you passed an hour?'

'Three to be exact.'

'Tell the tale to Peter,' I yawned. 'It doesn't interest me.'

He lifted his hands to my hair and took the curlers from it.

'If you placed these rags upon you in the day, it would be more to your advantage and to mine,' he mused. 'Where was I, though? Ah, yes, the Neapolitan.'

'Let her sleep, Richard, and me also.'

'I only wished to tell you her remark to me on leaving. "So it is true, what I have always heard," she said to me, "that you Cornishmen are famed for one thing only, which is wrestling?" "Signorina," I replied, "there is a lady waiting for me in Cornwall who would give me credit for something else besides."'

He stretched and yawned and, propping himself on his elbow, blew the candle. 'But there,' he said, 'those southern women were as dull as milk. My vulpine methods were too much for them.'

The nights passed thus, and the days as I have described them. Little by little the plans fell into line, the schemes were tabulated. The final message came from the Prince in France that the French fleet had been put at his disposal, and an army, under the command of Lord Hopton, would land in force in Cornwall while the Prince, with Sir John Grenvile, seized the Scillies. The landing was to coincide with the insurrection of the Royalists under Sir Richard Grenvile, who would take and hold the key-points in the Duchy.

Saturday, the thirteenth of May, was the date chosen for the Cornish rising. . . . The daffodils had bloomed, the blossom was all blown, and the first hot days of summer came without warning on the first of May. The sea below the Gribben was glassy calm, the sky deep blue, without a single cloud. The labourers worked in the fields, and the fishing-boats put to sea from Gorran and Polperro. In Fowey all was quiet. The townsfolk went about their business, the Parliamentary agents scribbled their roll upon roll of useless records to be filed in dusty piles up in Whitehall and the sentries at the Castle stared yawning out to sea. I sat out on the causeway, watching the young lambs, and thinking, as the hot sun shone upon my bare head, how in a bare week now the whole peaceful countryside would be in an uproar once again. Men shouting, fighting, dying. . . . The sheep scattered, the cattle driven, the people running homeless on the roads. Gunfire once again, the rattle of musketry. The galloping of horses, the tramp of marching feet. Wounded men dragging themselves into the hedges, there to die untended. The young corn trampled, the cottage thatch in flames. All the old anxiety, the old strain and terror. The enemy are advancing. The enemy are in retreat. Hopton has landed in force. Hopton has been repulsed. The Cornish are triumphant. The Cornish have been driven back. Rumours, counter-rumours. The bloody stench of war. . . .

The planning was all over now, and the long wait had begun. A week of nerves, sitting at Menabilly with our eyes upon the clock. Richard, in high spirits as always before battle, played bowls with Bunny in the little walled green beside the steward's empty lodge. Peter, in sudden realization of his flabby stomach muscles, rode furiously up and down the sands at Par to reduce his weight. Robin was very silent. He took long walks alone, down in the woods, and on returning went first to the dining-room, where the wine-decanter stood. I would find him there sometimes, glass in hand, brooding; and when I questioned him he would answer me evasively, his eyes strangely watchful, like a dog listening for the footstep of a stranger. Gartred, usually so cool and indifferent when she had the whip hand in a love affair, showed herself, for the first time, less certain and less sure. Whether it was because Ambrose Manaton was fifteen years her junior, and the possibility of marriage with him hung upon a thread, I do not know, but a new carelessness had come upon her which was, to my mind, the symbol of a losing touch. That she was heavily in debt at Orley Court I knew for certain. Richard had told me as much. Youth lay behind her. And a future without a third husband to support her would be hard going, once her beauty went. A dowager, living in retirement with her married daughters, dependent on the charity of a son-in-law? What an end for Gartred Grenvile! So she became careless. She smiled too openly at Ambrose Manaton. She put her hand on his at the dining-table. She watched him, over the rim of her glass, with the same greed I had noticed years before when, peeping through her chamber door, I had seen her stuff the trinkets in her gown. And Ambrose Manaton, flattered, confident, raised his glass to her in return.

'Send her away,' I said to Richard. 'God knows she has caused ill feeling enough already. What possible use can she be to you now, here at Menabilly?'

'If Gartred went, Ambrose would follow her,' he answered. 'I can't afford to lose my treasurer. You don't know the fellow as I do. He's as slippery as an eel, and as close-fisted as a Jew. Once back with her in Bideford, and he might pull out of the business altogether.'

'Then send Robin packing. He will be no use to you, anyway, if he continues drinking in this manner.'

'Nonsense. Drink in his case is stimulation, the only way to ginger him. When the day comes I'll ply him so full of brandy that he will take St Mawes' Castle single-handed.'

'I don't enjoy watching my brother go to pieces.'

'He isn't here for your enjoyment. He is here because he is of use to me, and one of the few officers that I know who doesn't lose his head in battle. The more rattled he becomes, here at Menabilly, the better he will fight outside it.'

He watched me balefully, blowing a cloud of smoke into the air.

'My God,' I said, 'have you no pity at all?'

'None,' he said, 'where military matters are concerned.'

'You can sit here, quite contentedly, with your sister behaving like a whore upstairs, holding one string of Manaton's purse and you the other; while my brother, who loves her, drinks himself to death and breaks his heart?'

'To hell with his heart. His sword is all I care about, and his ability to wield it.'

And, leaning from the window in the gallery, he whistled his nephew Bunny to a game of bowls. I watched them both, jesting with one another like a pair of schoolboys without a care, casting their coats upon the short green turf. 'God damn the Grenviles, one and all,' I said, my nerves in ribbons. As I spoke, thinking myself alone, I felt a slim hand touch me on the shoulder, and heard a boy's voice whisper in my ear. 'That's what my mother said, eighteen years ago.'

And there was Dick behind me, his black eyes glowing in his pale face, gazing out across the lawn towards his father and young Bunny.

Chapter 32

THURSDAY the eleventh of May dawned as hot and sticky as as its predecessors. Eight-and-forty hours to go before the torch of war was lit once more in Cornwall. Even Richard was on edge that morning, when word came from a messenger at noon to say that spies had reported a meeting, a few days since, at Saltash, between the Parliamentary commander in the west, Sir Hardress Waller, and several of the Parliamentary gentlemen, and that instructions had been given to double the guards at the chief towns throughout the Duchy. Some members of the Cornish County Committee had gone themselves to Helston to see if all was quiet.

'One false move now,' said Richard quietly, 'and all our plans will have been made in vain.'

We were gathered in the dining-room, I well remember, save only Gartred, who was in her chamber, and I can see now the drawn, anxious faces of the men as they gazed in silence at their leader. Robin, heavy, brooding; Peter, tapping his hand upon his knee; Bunny, with knitted brows; and Dick, as ever, gnawing at his hand.

'The one thing I have feared all along,' said Richard. 'Those fellows in the west can't hold their tongues. Like ill-trained redhawks, too keen to sight the quarry. I warned Keigwin and Grose to stay this last week within doors, as we have done, and hold no conferences. No doubt they have been out upon the roads, the whispers have the speed of lightning.' He stood by the window, his hands behind his back. We were all, I believe, a little sick with apprehension. I saw Ambrose Manaton rub his hands nervously together, his usual calm composure moment-arily lost to him.

'If anything should go wrong,' he ventured hesitating, 'what arrangements can be made for our own security?'

Richard threw him a contemptuous glance. 'None,' he said briefly. He returned to the table, and gathered up his papers.

'You have your orders, one and all,' he said. 'You know what you have to do. Let us rid ourselves of all this junk then, useless to us once the battle starts.'

He began to throw the maps and documents into the fire, while the others still stared at him, uncertain.

'Come,' said Richard. 'You look, the whole damned lot of you, like a flock of crows before a funeral. On Saturday we make a bid for freedom. If any man is afraid let him say so now, and I'll put a halter round his neck for treason to the Prince of Wales.'

Not one of us made answer. Richard turned to Robin. 'I want you to ride to Trelawne,' he said, 'and tell Jonathan Trelawney and his son that the rendezvous for the thirteenth is changed. They and Sir Arthur Bassett must join Sir Charles Trevannion at Caerhayes. Tell them to go tonight, skirting the high roads, and accompany them there.'

'Sir,' said Robin slowly, rising to his feet, and I think I was the only one who saw the flicker of his glance at Ambrose Manaton. As for myself, a weight was lifted from me. With Robin gone from the house, I, his sister, might safely breathe again. Let Gartred and her new lover make what they could of the few hours remaining. I did not care a jot so long as Robin was not there to listen to them.

'Bunny,' said his uncle, 'you have the boat at Pridmouth standing by in readiness?'

'Sir,' said Bunny, his grey eyes dancing. He was, I think, the only one who still believed he played at soldiers.'

'Then we shall rendezvous also at Caerhayes,' said Richard, 'at daybreak on the thirteenth. You can sail to Gorran to-morrow, and give my last directions about the beacon on the Dodman. A few hours on salt-water in this weather will be good practice for your stomach.' He smiled at the lad, who answered it with boyish adoration, and I saw Dick lower his head and trace imaginary lines upon the table with slow, hesitating hand.

'Peter?' said Richard.

Alice's husband leapt to his feet, drawn from some pleasant reveries of French wine and women to the harsh reality of the world about him. 'My orders, sir?'

'Go to Caerhayes and warn Trevannion that the plans are

301

changed. Tell him the Trelawneys and Bassett will be joining him. Then return here to Menabilly in the morning. And a word of warning, Peter.'

'What is that, sir?'

'Don't go a-Courtneying on the way there. There is not a woman worth it, from Tywardreath to Dodman.'

Peter turned pink, for all his bravado, but nerved himself to answer 'Sir' with great punctility.

He and Robin left the room together, followed by Bunny and by Ambrose Manaton. Richard yawned and stretched his arms above his head, and then, wandering to the hearth, stirred the black embers of his papers in the ashes.

'Have you no commands for me?' said Dick slowly.

'Why, yes,' said Richard, without turning his head, 'Alice Courtney's daughters must have left some dolls behind them. Go search in the attics, and fashion them new dresses.'

Dick did not answer. But he went, I think, a little whiter than before, and, turning on his heel, left the room.

'One day,' I said, 'you will provoke him once too often.'

'That is my intention,' answer Richard.

'Does it please you, then, to see him writhe in torment?'

'I hope to see him stand up to me at last, not take it lying down like a coward.'

'Sometimes,' I said, 'I think that after twenty years I know even less about you than I did when I was eighteen.'

'Very probably.'

'No father in the world would act as harshly to his son as you do to your Dick.'

'I only act harshly because I wish to purge his mother's whore blood from his veins.'

'You will more likely kindle it.'

He shrugged his shoulders and we fell silent a moment, listening to the sound of the horses' hoofs echoing across the park as Robin and Peter rode to their separate destinations.

'I saw my daughter up in London, when I lay concealed there for a while,' said Richard suddenly.

Foolishly, a pang of jealousy shot through my heart, and I answered like a wasp. 'Freckled, I suppose? A prancing miss?'

302

'Nay. Rather studious and quiet. Dependable. She put me in mind of my mother. "Bess," I said to her, "will you look after me in my declining years?" "Why, yes," she answered, "if you send for me." I think she cares as little for that bitch as I do.'

'Daughters', I said, 'are never favourites with their mothers. Especially when they come to be of age. How old is she?'

'Near seventeen,' he said, 'with all that natural bloom upon her that young people have. . . .' He stared absently before him. This moment, I thought with great lucidity and calm above the anguish, is in a sense our moment of farewell, our parting of the ways, but he does not know it. Now his daughter is of age he will not need me.

'Heigh-ho,' he said. 'I think I start to feel my eight-and-forty years. My leg hurts damnably today, and no excuse for it, with the sun blazing in the sky.'

'Suspense,' I said, 'and all that goes along with it.'

'When this campaign is over,' he said, 'and we hold all Cornwall for the Prince of Wales, I'll say good-bye to soldiering. I'll build a palace on the north coast, near to Stowe, and live in quiet retirement, like a gentleman.'

'Not you,' I said. 'You'd quarrel with all your neighbours.'

'I'd have no neighbours,' he answered, 'save my own Grenvile clan. My God, we'd make a clean sweep of the Duchy. Jack, and Bunny, and I. D'you think the Prince would make me Earl of Launceston?' He lay his hand upon my head an instant and then was gone, whistling for Bunny, and I sat there alone, in the empty dining-room, despondent, oddly sad. . . .

That evening we all went early to our beds, with the thunder that would not come still heavy in the air. Richard had taken Jonathan Rashleigh's chamber for his own, with Dick and Bunny in the dressing-rooms between.

Now Peter and Robin had gone, the one to Caerhayes, the other to Trelawne, I thought, with cynicism, that Ambrose Manaton and Gartred could indulge their separate talents for invention until the morning, should the spirit move them.

A single door between their chambers, and I the only neighbour, at the head of the stairs. I heard Gartred come first, and Ambrose follow her – then all was silent on the landing. Ah well, I thought, wrapping my shawl around me, thank God I can grow old with some complacency. White hairs could come, and lines, and crow's feet, and they would not worry me. I did not have to struggle for a third husband, not having had a first. But it was hard to sleep, with the full moon creeping to my window.

I could not hear the clock in the belfry from my present chamber, as I used to in the gate-house, but it must have been near midnight, or just after, when I woke suddenly from the light sleep into which I had fallen, it seemed, but a few moments earlier, with a fancy that I had heard someone moving in the dining-room below. Yes, there it was distinctly. The furtive sound of one who blundered his way in darkness, and bumped into a table, or a chair. I raised myself in my bed and listened. All was silent once again. But I was not easy. I put my hand out to my chair and dragged it to me, then listened once again. sudden, unmistakable, came the stealthy tread of a footstep on the creaking tell-tale stair. Some intuition, subconscious perhaps from early in the day, warned me of disaster. I lowered myself into my chair, and without waiting to light my candle – nor was there need with the moon casting a white beam on the carpet – I propelled myself across the room and turned the handle of my door.

'Who is there?' I whispered.

There was no answer, and, coming to the landing, I looked down upon the stair and saw a dark figure crouching there, his back against the wall, the moonlight gleaming on the naked sword in his hand. He stood in stockinged feet, his shirt-sleeves rolled above his elbow – my brother Robin, with murder in his eyes. He said nothing to me, only waited to see what I would do.

'Two years ago,' I said softly, 'you disobeyed an order given you by your commander, because of a private quarrel. That was in January '46. Do you intend to do the same in May of '48?'

He crept close and stood on the top stair beside me, breathing strangely. I could smell the brandy on his breath.

'I have disobeyed no one,' he said. 'I gave my message. I parted with the Trelawneys at the top of Polmear Hill.'

'Richard bade you accompany them to Caerhayes,' I said.

'No need to do so, Trelawney told me – two horsemen pass more easily than three. Let me by, Honor.'

'No, Robin. Not yet. Give me first your sword.'

He did not answer. He stood staring at me, looking, with his tumbled hair and troubled eyes, so like the ghost of our dead brother Kit that I trembled, even as his hands did on his sword. 'You cannot fool me,' he said, 'neither you, nor Richard Grenvile. This business was but a pretext to send me from the house, so that they could be together.'

He looked forward to the landing and the closed door of the room beyond the stairs.

'Go to bed, Robin,' I said, 'or come and sit with me in my chamber. Let me talk to you awhile.'

'No,' he said. 'This is my moment. They will be together now. If you try to prevent me, I shall hurt you also.'

He brushed past my chair and made across the landing, tiptoeing, furtive, in his stockinged feet, and whether he was drunk or mad I could not tell. I knew only the purpose in his eyes.

'For God's sake, Robin,' I said, 'do not go into that room. Reason with them in the morning, if you must, but not now, not at this hour.'

For answer he turned the handle, a smile upon his lips both horrible and strange, and I wheeled then, sobbing, and went back into my room and hammered loudly to the dressing-rooms where Dick and Bunny slept.

'Call Richard,' I said. 'Bid him come quickly, now, this instant. And you too, both of you. There is no time to lose.'

A startled voice – Bunny's, I believe – made answer, and I heard him clamber from his bed. But I had turned again, and crossed my room towards the landing, where all was silent still, and undisturbed. Nothing but the moonlight shining strong into the eastern windows. And then there came that sound for which I waited, piercing the silence with its shrill intensity. Not an oath, not a man's voice raised in anger, but the shocking horror of a woman's scream.

Chapter 33

ACROSS the landing, through Ambrose Manaton's empty room to Gartred's chamber beyond. The wheels of my chair turning slowly, for all my labour. And all the while calling 'Richard ... Richard ..' with a note in my voice I did not recognize.

Oh, God, that fight there in the moonlight, the cold white light pouring into the unshuttered windows, and Gartred with a crimson gash upon her face clinging to the hangings of the bed. Ambrose Manaton, his silken nightshirt stained with blood, warding off with his bare hands the desperate blows that Robin aimed at him, until, with a despairing cry, he reached the sword that lay among his heap of clothes upon a chair. Their bare feet padded on the boards, their breath came quick and short, and they seemed, the two of them, like phantom figures, lunging, thrusting, now in moonlight and now in shadow, with no word uttered. 'Richard ...' I called again, for this was murder, here before my eyes, with the two men between me and the bed where Gartred crouched, her hands to her face, the blood running down between her fingers.

He came at last, half-clad, carrying his sword, with Dick and Bunny at his heels bearing candles. 'An end to this, you Goddamned idiots,' he shouted, forcing himself between them, his own sword shivering their blades, and there was Robin, his right wrist hanging limp, with Richard holding him, and Ambrose Manaton back against the farther wall, with Bunny by his side.

They stared at one another, Robin and Ambrose Manaton, like animals in battle, chests heaving, eyes bloodshot, and suddenly Robin, seeing Gartred's face, realized what his work had done. He opened his mouth to speak, but no words came. He trembled, powerless to move or utter, and Richard pushed him to a chair and held him there. 'Call Matty,' said Richard to me. 'Get water, bandages. . . .'

Once more I turned to the landing, but already the household were astir, the frightened servants gathering in the hall below, the candles lit. 'Go back to bed,' said Richard harshly. 'No one of you is needed, save Mistress Honor's woman. There has been a trifling accident, but no harm done.' I heard them shuffle, whisper, retire to their own quarters, and here was Matty, staunch, dependable, seizing the situation in a glance and fetching bowls of water, strips of clean linen. The room was lit now by some half-dozen candles. The phantom scene was done, the grim reality was with us still.

Those tumbled clothes upon the floor, Gartred's and his. Manaton leaning upon Bunny's arm, staunching the cuts he had received, his fair curls lank and damp with sweat. Robin upon a chair, his head buried in his hands, all passion spent. Richard standing by his side, grim and purposeful. And one and all we looked at Gartred on the bed, with that great gash upon her face from her right eyebrow to her chin. It was then, for the first time, that I noticed Dick.

His face was ashen white, his eyes transfixed in horror, and suddenly he reeled and fell, as the blood that stained the clean white linen spread and trickled on to Matty's hand.

Richard made no move. He said to Bunny, between clenched teeth, his eyes averted from his son's limp body, 'Carry the spawn to his bed and leave him.' Bunny obeyed, and as I watched him stagger from the room, his cousin in his arms, I thought with cold and deadly weariness: 'This is the end. This is finality.'

Someone brought brandy. Bunny, I suppose, on his return. We had our measure, all of us. Robin drinking slow and deep, his hands shaking as he held his glass. Ambrose Manaton quick and nervous, the colour that had gone soon coming to his face again. Then Gartred, moaning faintly, with her head on Matty's shoulder, her silver hair still horribly bespattered with her blood.

'I do not propose', said Richard slowly, 'to hold an inquest. What has been, has been. We are on the eve of deadly matters, with the whole future of a kingdom now at stake. This is no time for any man to seek private vengeance in a quarrel. When men have sworn an oath to my command, I demand obedience.'

Not one of them made answer. Robin gazed, limp and shattered, at the floor.

'We will snatch', said Richard, 'what hours of sleep we can, until the morning. I will remain with Ambrose in his room, and Bunny, stay with Robin. In the morning you will go together to Caerhayes, where I shall join you. Can I ask you, Matty, to remain here with Mrs Denys?'

'Yes, Sir Richard,' said Matty steadily.

'How is her pulse? Has she lost much blood?'

'She is well enough now, Sir Richard. The bandages are firm. Sleep and rest will work wonders by the morning.'

'No danger to her life?'

'No, Sir Richard. The cut was jagged, but not deep. The only damage done is to her beauty.' Matty's lips twitched in the way I knew, and I wondered how much she guessed of what had happened.

Ambrose Manaton did not look towards the bed. The woman who lay upon it might have been a stranger. 'This is their finish too,' I thought. 'Gartred will never become Mrs Manaton and own Trecarrel.'

I turned my eyes from Gartred, white and still, and felt Richard's hands upon my chair. 'You', he said quietly, 'have had enough for one night to contend with.' He took me to my room, and, lifting me from my chair, laid me down upon my bed.

'Will you sleep?' he said.

'I think not,' I answered.

'Rest easy. We shall be gone so soon. A few hours more and it will be over. War makes a good substitute for private quarrels.'

'I wonder. . . .'

He left me and went back to Ambrose Manaton, not, I reflected for love, to share his slumbers, but to make sure his treasurer did not slip from him in the few remaining hours left to us before daylight. Bunny had gone with Robin to his room, and this also, I surmised, was a precaution. Remorse and brandy have driven stronger men than Robin to their suicide.

What hope of sleep had any of us? There was the full moon, high now in the heavens, and you, I thought, shining there in the hushed gardens with your pale cold face above the shadows, have witnessed strange things this night at Menabilly. We

Harrises and Grenviles had paid ill return for Rashleigh hospitality. . . .

The hours slipped by, and I suddenly remembered Dick, who slept in the dressing-room next door to me, alone. Poor lad, faint at the sight of blood as he had been in the past, was he now lying, wakeful like me, with shame upon his conscience? I thought I heard him stir, and I wondered if dreams haunted him, as they did me, and if I wished for company. 'Dick . . .' I called softly. 'Dick . . .' I called again, but there was no answer. Later, a little breeze, rising from the sea, made a draught come to my room from the open window and, playing with the latch upon the door shook it free, so that it swung to and fro, banging every instant like a loosened shutter.

He must sleep deep then if it did not waken him.

The moon went, and the morning light stole in and cleared the shadows, and still the door between our two rooms creaked, and closed, and creaked again, making a nagging accompaniment to my uneasy slumbers. Maddened at last, I climbed to my chair to shut it, and as my hand fastened on the latch I saw through the crack of the door that Dick's bed was empty. He was not in the room. . . .

Numb and exhausted, I stumbled to my bed. 'He has gone to find Bunny,' I thought. 'He has gone to Bunny and to Robin.' But before me was the picture of his white, anguished face, and sleep, when it did come, could not banish the memory.

Next morning, when I woke to find the broad sun streaming in my room, the scenes of the hours before held a nightmare quality. I longed for them to dissipate, as nightmares do, but when Matty bore my breakfast I knew them to be true.

'Yes, Mrs Denys had some sleep,' she answered to my query, 'and will, to my mind, be little worse for her adventure until she lifts her bandage.' Matty, with a sniff, had small pity in her bosom.

'Will the gash not heal in time?' I asked.

'Aye, it will heal,' she said, 'but she'll bear the scar there for her lifetime. She'll find it hard to trade her beauty now.' She spoke with a certain relish, as though the events of the preceding night had wiped away a legion of old scores.

'Mrs Denys', said Matty, 'has got what she deserved.'

Had she? Was this a chess-board move, long planned by the Almighty, or were we, one and all, just fools to fortune? I knew one thing – since I had seen the gash on Gartred's face, I hated her no longer. . . .

'Were all the gentlemen at breakfast?' I said suddenly.

'I believe so.'

'And Master Dick as well?'

'Yes. He came somewhat later than the others, but I saw him in the dining-room an hour ago.'

A wave of relief came to me, for no reason except that he was safely in the house. 'Help me to dress,' I said to Matty.

Friday, the twelfth of May. A hazard might have made it the thirteenth. Some sense of delicacy kept me from Gartred's Chamber. Now her beauty was marred, she and I would now hold equal ground, and I had no wish to press the matter home. Other women might have gone to her, feigning commiseration, but with triumph in their hearts, but Honor Harris was not one of them. I sent messages by Matty that she should ask for what she wanted, and left her to her thoughts. . . . I found Robin in the gallery, standing moodily beside the window, his right arm in a sling. He turned his head at my approach, then looked away again in silence.

'I thought you had departed with Bunny to Caerhayes,' I said to him.

'We wait for Peter Courtney,' he answered dully. 'He has not yet returned.'

'Does your wrist pain you?' I asked gently.

He shook his head, and went on staring from the window.

'When the shouting is over, and the turmoil done,' I said, 'we will keep house together, you and I, as we did once at Lanrest.'

Still he did not answer, but I saw the tears start in his eyes.

'We have loved the Grenviles long enough,' I said, 'each in our separate fashion. The time has come when they must learn to live without us.'

'They have done that', he said, his voice low, 'for nearly thirty years. It is we who are dependent upon them.'

These were the last words we ever held upon the subject,

Robin and I, from that day unto this. Reserve has kept us silent, though we have lived together for five years. ...

The door opened and Richard came into the gallery, Bunny at his shoulder like a shadow.

'I cannot understand it,' he said, pacing the floor in irritation. 'Here it is nearly noon, and no sign yet of Peter. If he left Caerhayes at daybreak, he should have been here long ago. I suppose, like every other fool, he has thought best to ignore my orders.'

The barb was lost on Robin, who was too far gone in misery to mind. 'If you permit me,' he said humbly, 'I can ride in search of him. He may have stayed to breakfast with the Sawles at Penrice.'

'He is more likely behind a haystack with a wench,' said Richard. 'My God, I will have eunuchs on my staff, next time I go to war. Go then, if you like, but keep a watch upon the roads. I have heard reports of troops riding through St Blazey. The rumour may be false, and yet ...' He broke off in the middle of his speech, and resumed his pacing of the room. Presently we heard Robin mount his horse and ride away. The hours wore on, the clock in the belfry struck twelve, and later one. The servants brought cold meat and ale, and we helped ourselves, haphazard, all of us with little appetite, our ears strained for sound. At half past one there was a footfall on the stairs, slow and laboured, and I noticed Ambrose Manaton glance subconsciously to the chamber overhead, then draw back against the window. The handle of the door was turned, and Gartred stood before us, dressed for travel, one side of her face shrouded with a veil, a cloak around her shoulders. No one spoke as she stood there like a spectre. 'I wish', she said at length, 'to return to Orley Court. Conveyance must be found for me.'

'You ask for the impossible,' said Richard shortly, 'and no one knows it better now than you. In a few hours the roads will be impassable.'

'I'll take my chance of that,' she said. 'If I fall fighting with the rabble, I think I shall not greatly care. I have done what you asked me to do. My part is played.'

Her eyes were upon Richard all the while, and never once on

311

Ambrose Manaton. Richard and Gartred. . . . Robin and I. . . .
Which sister had the most to forgive, the most to pay for? God
knows I had no answer.

'I am sorry,' said Richard briefly. 'I cannot help you. You
must stay here until arrangements can be made. We have more
serious matters on our hands than the transport of a sick
widow. . . .'

Bunny was the first to catch the sound of the horse's hoofs
galloping across the park. He went to the small mullioned window that gave on to the inner court and threw it wide; and as
we waited, tense, expectant, the sound drew closer, and suddenly the rider and his horse came through the arch beneath
the gate-house, and there was Peter Courtney, dust-covered
and dishevelled, his hat gone, his dark curls straggling on his
shoulders. He flung the reins to a startled waiting groom and
came straightway to the gallery.

'For God's sake save yourselves! We are betrayed,' he said.

I think I did not show the same fear and horror on my face
as they did, for, although my heart went cold and dead within
me, I knew with wretched certainty that this was the thing I
had waited for all day. Peter looked from one to the other of
us, and his breath came quick. 'They have all been seized,' he
said. 'Jonathan Trelawney, his son, Charles Trevannion,
Arthur Bassett and the rest. At ten this morning they came
riding to the house, the Sheriff, Sir Thomas Herle, and a whole
company of soldiers. We made a fight for it, but there were
more than thirty of them. I leapt from an upper window, by
Almighty Providence escaping with no worse than a wrenched
ankle. I got the first horse to hand, and put spurs to him without mercy. Had I not known the by-lanes as I know my own
hand, I could not have reached you now. There are soldiers
everywhere. The bridge at St Blazey blocked and guarded.
Guards on Polmear Hill.' He looked around the gallery, as
though in search of someone. 'Robin gone?' he asked. 'I
thought so. It was he, then, I saw, when I was skirting the sands,
engaged in fighting with five of the enemy or more. I dared not
go to his assistance. My first duty was to you. What now? Can
we save ourselves?'

We all turned now to look at our commander. He stood

312

before us, calm and cool, giving no outward sign that all he had striven for lay crushed and broken. 'Did you see their colours?' he asked swiftly. 'What troops were they? Of whose command?'

'Some were from Bodmin, sir,' said Peter, 'the rest advance guards of Sir Hardress Wallers. There were line upon line of them, stretching down the road towards St Austell. This is no chance encounter, sir. The enemy are in strength.'

Richard nodded, turning quick to Bunny. 'Go to Pridmouth,' he said. 'Make sail instantly. Set a course due south, until you come in contact with the first outlying vessel of the French fleet. They will be cruising eastward of the Scillies by this time tomorrow evening. Ask for Lord Hopton's ship. Give him this message.' He scribbled rapidly upon a piece of paper.

'Do you bid them come?' said Ambrose Manaton. 'Can they get to us in time?' He was white to the lips, his hands clenched tight.

'Why, no,' said Richard, folding his scrap of paper, 'I bid them alter course and sail for France again. There will be no rising. The Prince of Wales does not land this month in Cornwall.' He gave the paper to his nephew. 'Good chance, my Bunny,' he said smiling. 'Give greetings to your brother Jack, and with a spice of luck you will find the Scillies fall to you like a plum a little later in the summer. But the Prince must say good-bye to Cornwall for the present.'

'And you, uncle?' said Bunny. 'Will you not come with me? It is madness to delay if the house is likely to be surrounded?'

'I'll join you in my own time,' said Richard. 'For this once, I ask that my orders be obeyed.'

Bunny stared at him an instant, then turned and went, his head high, bidding none of us farewell.

'But what are we to do? Where are we to go?' said Ambrose Manaton, 'Oh, God, what a fool I have been to let myself be led into this business. Are the roads all watched?' He turned to Peter, who stood shrugging his shoulders, watching his commander.

'Who is to blame? Who is the traitor? That is what I want to know,' said Ambrose Manaton, all composure gone, a new note of suspicion in his voice. 'None but ourselves knew the change in rendezvous. How did the Sheriff time his moment with such devilish accuracy that he could seize every leader worth a curse?'

'Does it matter', said Richard gently, 'who the traitor was once the deed is done?'

'Matter?' said Ambrose Manaton. 'Good God, you take it coolly. Trevannion, the Trelawneys, the Arundells, and Bassetts, all of them in the Sheriff's hands, and you ask does it matter who betrayed them? Here are we, ruined men, likely to be arrested within the hour, and you stand there like a fox and smile at me.'

'My enemies call me fox, but not my friends,' said Richard softly. He turned to Peter. 'Tell the fellows to saddle a horse for Mr Manaton,' he said, 'and for you also. I guarantee no safe conduct for the pair of you, but at least you have a sporting chance, as hares do from a pack of hounds.'

'You will not come with us, sir?'

'No. I will not come with you.'

Peter hesitated, looking first at him, and then at me.

'It will go ill with you, sir, if they should find you.'

'I am well aware of that.'

'The Sheriff, Sir Thomas Herle, suspects your presence here in Cornwall. His first challenge, when he came before Caerhayes and called Trevannion, was: "Have you Sir Richard Grenvile here in hiding? If so produce him, and you shall go free." '

'A pity, for their sakes, I was not there.'

'He said that a messenger had left a note at his house at Prideaux, early before dawn, warning him that the whole party, yourself included, would be gathered later at Caerhayes. Some wretch had seen you, sir, and with devilish intuition guessed your plans.'

'Some wretch indeed,' said Richard smiling still, 'who thought it sport to try the Judas touch. Let us forget him.'

Was it his nephew Jack who, long ago at Exeter, said once to me: 'Beware my uncle when you see him smile. ...'

Then Ambrose Manaton came forward, his finger stabbing at the air. 'It is you,' he said to Richard, 'you who are the traitor, you who have betrayed us. From first to last, from be-

314

ginning to the end, you knew it would end thus. The French fleet never were to come to our aid, there never was to be a rising. This is your revenge for that arrest four years ago at Launceston. Oh, God, what perfidy. . . .' He stood before him, trembling, a high note of hysteria in his voice, and I saw Peter fall back a pace, the colour draining from his face, bewilderment, then horror, coming to his eyes.

Richard watched them, never moving, then slowly pointed to the door. The horses had been brought to the courtyard, and we heard the jingle of the harness.

Put back the clock, I whispered savagely, make it four years ago, and Gartred acting spy for Lord Robartes. Let her take the blame. Fix the crime on her. She is the one who will emerge from this unscathed, for all her spoilt beauty. I looked towards her, and saw, to my wonder, that she was looking at me also. Her scarf had slipped, showing the vivid wound upon her cheek. The sight of it, and the memory of the night before, filled me, not with anger or with pity, but despair. She went on looking at me, and I saw her smile.

'It's no use,' she said. 'I know what you are thinking. Poor Honor, I have cheated you again. Gartred has the perfect alibi.'

The horses were galloping from the courtyard. I saw Ambrose Manaton go first, his hat pulled low, his cloak bellying, and Peter follow him, with one brief glance towards our windows.

The clock in the belfry struck two. A pigeon, dazzling white against the sky, fluttered to the court below. Gartred lay back against the couch, the smile on her lips a strange contrast to the gash upon her face. Richard stood by the window, his hands behind his back. And Dick, who had never moved once in all the past half hour, waited, like a dumb thing, in his corner.

'Do the three Grenviles', I said slowly, 'wish to take council, alone, amongst themselves?'

Chapter 34

RICHARD went on standing by the window. Now that the horses were gone, and the sound of their galloping had died away, it was strangely hushed and still within the house. The sun blazed down upon the gardens, the pigeons pricked the grass seeds on the lawn. It was the hottest hour of a warm summer day, when bumble bees go humming in the limes, and the young birds fall silent. When Richard spoke he kept his back turned to us, and his voice was soft and low.

'My grandfather', he said, 'was named Richard also. He came of a long line of Grenviles who sought to serve their country and their king. Enemies he had in plenty, friends as well. It was my misfortune and my loss that he died in battle nine years before my birth. But I remember as a lad asking for tales of him, and looking up at that great portrait which hung in the long gallery at Stowe. He was stern, they said, and hard, and rarely smiled, so I have heard tell, but his eyes that looked down upon me from the portrait were hawk's eyes, fearless and far-seeing. There were many great names in those days: Drake, Raleigh, Sydney – and Grenvile was of their company. He fell mortally wounded, you may remember, on the decks of his own ship, called the *Revenge*. He fought alone, with the Spanish fleet about him, and when they asked him to surrender he went on fighting still, with masts gone, sails gone, the decks torn beneath his feet. The Grenvile of that day had courage, and preferred to have his vessel blown to pieces, rather than sell his life for silver to the pirate hordes of Spain.' He fell silent a moment, watching the pigeons on the lawn, and then he went on talking, with his hands behind his back. 'My Uncle John', he said, 'explored the Indies with Sir Francis Drake. He was a man of courage too. They were no weaklings, those young men who braved the winter storms of the Atlantic in search of savage lands beyond the seas. Their ships were frail, they were tossed week after week at the mercy of wind and sea, but some salt tang in their blood kept them undaunted. He was killed there, in the Indies, was my Uncle John, and my father, who loved him well, built a shrine to him at Stowe.' There was no sound from anyone of us in the gallery. Gartred lay on the couch, her hands behind her head, and Dick stood motionless in his dark corner.

'There was a saying, born about this time,' continued Richard, 'that no Grenvile was ever wanting in loyalty to his king. We were bred to it, my brothers and I. Gartred too, I think, will well remember those evenings in my father's room at Stowe when he, though he was not a fighting man – for he lived in days of peace – read to us from an old volume with great clasps about it of the wars of the past, and how our forebears fought in them.'

A gull wheeled overhead above the gardens, his wings white against the dark blue sky, and I remembered of a sudden the kittiwakes at Stowe, riding the rough Atlantic beneath Richard's home.

'My brother Bevil', said Richard, 'was a man who loved his family and his home. He was not bred to war. He desired, in his brief life, nothing so much as to rear his children with his wife's care, and live at peace amongst his neighbours. When war came he knew what it would mean, and did not turn his back upon it. Wrangling he detested, bloodshed he abhorred, but because he bore the name of Grenvile, he knew, in 1642, where his duty lay. He wrote a letter at that time to our friend and neighbour, John Trelawney, who has this day been arrested, as you know, and because I believe that letter to be the finest thing my brother ever penned I asked Trelawney for a copy of it. I have it with me now. Shall I read it to you?'

We did not answer. He felt in his pocket slowly for a paper, and, holding it before the window, read aloud.

'I cannot contain myself within my doors when the King of England's standard waves in the field upon so just occasion, the cause being such as must make all those that die in it little inferior to martyrs. And for mine own part I desire to acquire an honest name or an honourable grave. I never loved life or ease so much as to shun such an occasion, which if I should, I were unworthy of the profession I have held,

317

or to succeed those ancestors of mine who have so many of them, in several ages, sacrificed their lives for their country.'

Richard folded the letter again, and put it once more into his pocket. 'My brother Bevil died at Lansdowne,' he said, 'leading his men to battle, and his young son, Jack, a lad of but fifteen, straightway mounted his father's horse and charged the enemy. That youngster who has just left us, Bunny, ran from his tutor last autumn, playing truant, that he might place himself at my disposal, and hold a sword for this cause we all hold dear. I have no brief for myself. I am a soldier. My faults are many, and my virtues few. But no quarrel, no dispute, no petty act of vengeance has ever turned me, or will turn me now, from loyalty to my country and my King. In the long and often bloody history of the Grenviles, not one of them, until this day, has proved a traitor.'

His voice had sunk now, deadly quiet. The pigeons had flown from the lawns. The bees had hummed their way below the thistle park.

'One day,' said Richard, 'we may hope that His Majesty will be restored to his throne, or if not he, then the Prince of Wales instead. In that proud day, should any of us live to see it, the name of Grenvile will be held in honour, not only here in Cornwall, but in all England too. I am judge enough of character, for all my other failings, to know that my nephew Jack will prove himself as great a man of peace as he has been a youth of war, nor will young Bunny ever lag behind. They can tell their sons, in the years to come, "We Grenviles fought to bring about the restoration of our King" and their names will rank in that great book at Stowe my father read to us, beside that of my grandfather Richard, who fought in the *Revenge*.' He paused a moment, then spoke lower still.

'I care not', he said, 'if my name be written in that book in smaller characters. "He was a soldier," they may say. "The King's general in the west." Let that be my epitaph. But there will be no other Richard in that book at Stowe. For the King's general died without a son.' A long silence followed his last words. He went on standing at the window, and I sat still in my chair, my hands folded on my lap. Soon now it would come, I thought, the outburst, the angry, frightened words; or the torrent of wild weeping. For eighteen years the storm had been pent up, and the full tide of emotion could not wait longer now. This is our fault, I whispered to myself, not his. Had Richard been more forgiving, had I been less proud; had our hearts been filled with love and not hatred, had we been blessed with greater understanding. . . . Too late. Full twenty years too late. And now the little scapegoat of our sins went bleeding to his doom. . . .

But the cry I waited for was never uttered. Nor did the tears fall. Instead, he came out from his corner, and stood alone an instant in the centre of the room. The fear was gone now from the dark eyes, and the slim hands did not tremble. He looked older than he had done hitherto, older and wiser. As though, while his father had been speaking, a whole span of years had passed him by.

Yet when he spoke, his voice was a boy's voice, young and simple. 'What must I do?' he said. 'Will you do it for me, or must I kill myself?'

It was Gartred who moved first. Gartred, my lifelong foe and enemy. She rose from her couch, pulling the veil about her face, and came up to my chair. She put her hands upon it, and, still with no word spoken, she wheeled me from the room. We went out into the garden, under the sun, our backs turned to the house, and we said no words to one another, for there were none to say. But neither she nor I, nor any man or woman alive or dead, will ever know what was said, there in the long gallery at Menabilly, by Richard Grenvile to his only son.

That evening the insurrection broke out in the west. There had been no way to warn the Royalists of Helston and Penzance that the leaders in the east had been arrested, and the prospective rising was now doomed to failure. They struck, at the appointed hour, as had been planned, and found themselves faced, not with the startled troops they had expected, but the strong forces, fully prepared and armed, that came riding post-haste into Cornwall for the purpose. No French fleet beyond the Scillies came coasting to Land's End and the Lizard. There was no landing of twenty thousand men upon the beaches, beneath Dodman and the Nare. And the leaders who should have come riding to the west were shackled, wrist to wrist, in the garrison at Plymouth. No Trelawney, no Arundell, no Trevannion, no Bassett. What was to have been the torch to light all England was no more than a sudden quivering flame, spurting to nothing, spluttering for a single moment in the damp Cornish air. A few shops looted at Penzance ... a smattering of houses pillaged at Mullion ... a wild unruly charge upon Goonhilly Down, with no man knowing whither he rode, or wherefore he was fighting ... and then the last hopeless, desperate stand at Mawgan Creek, with the Parliamentary troops driving the ill-led Royalists to destruction, down over the rocks and stones to the deep Helford River.

The rebellion of '48. The last time men shall ever fight, please God, upon our Cornish soil. ... It lasted but a week, but for those who died and suffered it lasted for eternity. The battles were west of Truro, so we, at Menabilly, smelt no powder. But every road and every lane was guarded, and not even the servants ventured out of doors. That first evening a company of soldiers, under the command of Colonel Robert Bennett, our old neighbour near to Looe, rode to Menabilly, and made a perfunctory search throughout the house. He found no one present but myself and Gartred. He little knew that, had he come ten minutes earlier, he would have found the greatest prize of all.

I can see Richard now, his arms folded, seated in the dining-chamber with the empty chairs about him, deaf to all my pleading. 'When they come,' he said, 'they shall take me, as I am. Mine is the blame. I am the man for whom my friends now suffer. Very well, then. Let them do their worst upon me, and by surrendering my person I may yet save Cornwall from destruction.'

Gartred, with all her old cool composure back again, shrugged her shoulders in disdain. 'Is it not a little late now in the day to play the martyr?' she suggested. 'What good will your surrender do at this juncture? You flatter yourself, poor Richard, if you think the mere holding of a Grenvile will spare the rest from imprisonment and death. I hate these last-minute gestures, these sublime salutes. Show yourself a man, and escape, the pair of you, as Bunny did.' She did not look towards Dick. Nor did I. But he sat there, silent as ever, at his father's side.

'We shall make fine figures on the scaffold, Dick and I,' said Richard. 'My neck is somewhat thicker, I know, than his, and may need two blows from the axe instead of one.'

'You may not have the pleasure, or the parade, of a martyr's execution,' said Gartred, yawning, 'but instead a knotted rope in a dank dungeon. Not the usual finish for a Grenvile.'

'It would be better', said Richard quietly, 'if these two Grenviles did die in obscurity.'

There was a pause, and then Dick spoke, for the first time since that unforgettable moment in the gallery.

'How do we stand', he said jerkily, 'with the Rashleighs? If my father and I are found here by the enemy, will it be possible to prove to them that the Rashleighs are innocent in the matter?'

I seized upon his words for all the world like a drowning woman. 'You have not thought of that,' I said to Richard. 'You have not considered for one moment what will become of them. Who will ever believe that Jonathan Rashleigh, and John too, were not party also to your plan? Their absence from Menabilly is no proof. They will be dragged into the matter, and my sister Mary also. Poor Alice at Trethurfe, Joan at Mothercombe, a legion of young children. They will all of them, from Jonathan in London to the baby on Joan's knee, suffer imprisonment, and maybe death into the bargain, if you are taken here.'

It was at this moment that a servant came into the room, much agitated, his hands clasped before him. 'I think it best to tell you', he said, 'that a lad has come running across the park to say the troopers are gathered at the top of Polmear hill. Some have gone down towards Polkerris. The rest are making for Tregaminion and the park gates.'

'Thank you,' said Richard, bowing. 'I am much obliged to you for your discretion.' The servant left the room, hoping, I dare say, to feign sickness in his quarters when the troopers came.

Richard rose slowly to his feet and looked at me.

'So you fear for your Rashleighs?' he said. 'And because of them you have no wish to throw me to the wolves? Very well, then. For this once I will prove accommodating. Where is the famous hiding-place that four years ago proved so beneficial to us all?'

I saw Dick flinch and look away from me towards his father. 'Dick knows,' I answered. 'Would you condescend to share it with him?'

'A hunted rat', said Richard, 'has no choice. He must take the companion that is thrust upon him.'

Whether the place was rank with cobwebs, mould, and mildew, I neither knew nor cared. At least it would give concealment while the troopers came. And no one, not even Gartred, knew the secret.

'Do you remember', I said to Dick, 'where the passage led? I warn you, no one has been there for four years.'

He nodded, deathly pale. And I wondered what bug of fear had seized him now, when but an hour ago he had offered himself, like a little lamb, for slaughter.

'Go then,' I said, 'and take your father. Now, this instant, while there is still time.'

He came then to me, his new-found courage wavering, looking so like the little boy who loved me once that my heart went out to him. 'The rope,' he said, 'the rope upon the hinge. What if it has frayed now with disuse, and the hinge rusted?'

'It will not matter,' I said, 'you will not need to use it now. I shall not be waiting for you in the chamber overhead.'

He stared at me, lost for a moment, dull, uncomprehending, and I verily believe that for one brief second he thought himself a child again. Then Richard broke the spell with his hard, clear voice.

'Well?' he said. 'If it must be done, this is the moment. There is no other method of escape.'

Dick went on staring at me, and there came into his eyes a strange new look I had not seen before. Why did he stare at me thus? Or was it not me he stared at but some other, some ghost of a dead past that tapped him on the shoulder?

'Yes,' he said slowly. 'If it must be done, this is the moment. . . .' He turned to his father, opening first the door of the dining-room. 'Will you follow me, sir?' he said to Richard.

Richard paused a moment on the threshold. He looked first at Gartred, then back at me again. 'When the hounds are in full cry,' he said, 'and the coverts guarded, the red fox goes to earth.'

He smiled, holding my eyes for a single second, and was gone after Dick on to the causeway. . . . Gartred watched them disappear, then shrugged her shoulder. 'I thought', she said, 'the hiding-place was in the house. Near your old apartment in the gate-house.'

'Did you?' I said.

'I wasted hours, four years ago, searching in the passages tiptoeing outside your door,' she said.

There was a mirror hanging on the wall beside the window. She went to it, and stared, pulling her veil aside. The deep crimson gash ran from her eyebrow to her chin, jagged, irregular, and the smooth contour of her face was gone for ever. I watched her eyes, and she saw me watching them through the misty glass of the little mirror.

'I could have stopped you', she said, 'from falling with your horse to the ravine. You knew that, didn't you?'

'Yes,' I said.

'You called to me, asking for the way, and I did not answer you.'

'You did not,' I said.

'It has taken a long time to call it quits,' she said to me. She came away then from the mirror, and, taking from her sack the little pack of cards I well remembered, sat down by the table, close to my wheeled chair. She dealt the cards face downwards on the table. 'We will play patience, you and I, until the troopers come,' said Gartred Grenvile.

Chapter 35

I DOUBT if Colonel Bennett had searched all Cornwall, whether he could have found a quieter couple when he came, than the two women playing cards in the dining-hall at Menabilly. One with a great scar upon her face, and silver hair; the other a hopeless cripple. Yes, there had been guests with us until today, we admitted it. Mr Rashleigh's son-in-law, Sir Peter Courtney, and my own brother, Robin Harris. No, we knew nothing of their movements. They came and went as they pleased. Mr Trelawney had called once, we understood, but we had not seen him. Why was I left alone at Menabilly by the Rashleighs? From necessity and not from choice. Perhaps you have forgotten, Colonel Bennett, that my home at Lanrest was burnt down four years ago – by your orders, someone told me once. A strange action for a neighbour. And why was Mrs Denys from Orley Court near Bideford a guest of mine at the present season? Well, she was once my sister-in-law, and we had long been friends.... Yes, it was true my name had been connected with Sir Richard Grenvile in the past. There are gossips in the west country as well as at Whitehall. ... No, Mrs Denys had never been very friendly with her brother. No, we had no knowledge of his movements. We believed him to be in Naples. Yes, search the house, from the cellars to the attics, search the grounds. Here are the keys. Do what you will. We have no power to stop you. Menabilly is no property of ours. We are merely guests in the absence of Mr Rashleigh. ...'

'Well, you appear to speak the truth, Mistress Harris,' he said to me on the conclusion of his visit (he had called me 'Honor' once, when we were neighbours near to Looe), 'but the fact that your brother and Sir Peter Courtney are implicated in the rising which is now breaking out at Helston and Penzance renders this house suspect. I shall leave a guard behind me, and I rather think, when Sir Hardress Waller comes into the district, he will make a more thorough search of the premises than I have had time to do today. Meanwhile ...' he broke off abruptly, his eyes drifting, as if in curiosity, back to Gartred.

'Pardon my indelicacy, madam,' he said, 'but that cut is recent?'

'An accident,' said Gartred, shrugging, 'a clumsy movement and some broken glass.'

'Surely ... not self-inflicted?'

'What else would you suggest?'

'It has more the appearance of a sword-cut, forgive my rudeness. Were you a man, I would say you had fought a duel, and received the hurt from an opponent.'

'I am not a man, Colonel Bennett. If you doubt me, why not come upstairs, to my chamber, and let me prove it to you?' Robert Bennett was a Puritan. He stepped back a pace, colouring to his ears. 'I thank you, madam,' he said stiffly. 'My eyes are sufficient evidence.'

'If promotion came by gallantry,' said Gartred, 'you would still be in the ranks. I can think of no other officer in Cornwall, or in Devon either, who would decline to walk upstairs with Gartred Denys.' She made as though to deal the cards again, but Colonel Bennett made a motion of his hands.

'I am sorry,' he said shortly, 'but whether you are Mrs Denys or Mrs Harris these days does not greatly matter. What does matter is that your maiden name was Grenvile.'

'And so?' said Gartred, shuffling her cards.

'And so I must ask you to come with me, and accept an escort down to Truro. There you will be held, pending an investigation, and when the roads are quieter you will have leave to depart to Orley Court.'

Gartred dropped her cards into her sack, and rose slowly to her feet. 'As you will,' she said, shrugging her shoulders. 'You have some conveyance, I presume? I have no dress for riding?'

'You will have every comfort, madam.'

He turned then to me. 'You are permitted to remain here until I receive further orders from Sir Hardress Waller. These may be forthcoming in the morning. But I must ask you to be in readiness to move upon the instant, should the order come. You understand?'

'Very good, then. I will leave a guard before the house, with instructions to shoot on sight should his suspicions be in any way aroused. Good evening. You are ready, Mrs Denys?'

'Yes, I am ready.' Gartred turned to me and touched me lightly on the shoulder. 'I am sorry', she said, 'to cut my visit short. Remember me to the Rashleighs when you see them. And tell Jonathan what I said about the gardens. If he wishes to plant flowering shrubs, he must first rid himself of foxes. . . .'

'Not so easy,' I answered. 'They are hard to catch. Especially when the go underground.'

'Smoke them out,' she said. 'It is the only way. Do it by night; they leave less scent behind them. Good-bye, Honor.'

'Good-bye, Gartred.' She went, throwing her veil back from her face to show the vivid scar, and I have not seen her from that day to this.

I heard the troopers ride away from the courtyard and out across the park. Before the two entrance doors stood sentries, with muskets at their sides. And a sentry stood also at the outer gate, and by the steps leading to the causeway. I sat watching them, then pulled the bellrope by the hearth for Matty.

'Ask them', I said, 'if Colonel Bennett left permission for me to take exercise in my chair within the grounds.'

She was back in a moment, with the message that I feared.

'He is sorry,' she answered, 'but Colonel Bennett gave strict orders that you were not to leave the house.'

I looked at Matty, and she looked at me.

The thoughts chased round my head in wild confusion. 'What hour is it?' I asked.

'Near five o'clock,' she answered.

'Four hours of daylight still,' I said.

'Yes,' she answered.

From the window of the dining-hall I could see the sentry pacing up and down before the gates of the south garden. Now and then he paused to look about him and to chat with his fellow at the causeway steps. The sun, high in the south-west, shone down upon their muskets.

'Take me upstairs, Matty,' I said slowly.

'To your own chamber?'

'No, Matty. To my old room beyond the gate-house. . . .'

I had not been there in all the past two years of my stay at Menabilly. The west wing was still bare, untouched. Desolate and stripped as when the rebels had come pillaging in '44. The hangings were gone from the walls. The room had neither bed, nor chair, nor table. One shutter hung limp from the further window, giving a faint creak of light. The room had a dead, fusty smell, and in the far corner lay the bleached bones of a rat. The west wing was very silent. Very still. No sound came from the deserted kitchens underneath.

'Go to the stone,' I whispered. 'Put your hands against it.' Matty did so, kneeling on the floor. She pressed against the square stone by the buttress, but it did not move.

'No good,' she murmured, 'it is hard fixed. Have you forgotten that it only opened from the other side?'

Had I forgotten? It was the one thing that I remembered. . . . Smoke them out, said Gartred, it is the only way. Yes, but she did not understand. She thought they were hidden somewhere in the woods. Not behind stone walls, three foot thick. . . .

'Fetch wood and paper,' I said to Matty. 'Kindle a fire. Not in the chimney, but here, against the wall.'

There was a chance – a faint one, God knew well – that the smoke would penetrate the cracks in the stone and make a signal. They might not be there, though. They might be crouching in the tunnel at the farther end, beneath the summer-house.

How slow she was, good Matty, faithful Matty, fetching the dried grass and the twigs. How carefully she blew the fire, how methodically she added twig to twig. 'Hurry,' I said. 'More wood, more flame.'

'Patience,' she whispered, 'it will go, in its own time.'

In its own time. Not my time. Not Richard's time. . . .

The room was filled with smoke. It seeped into our eyes, our hair, it clung about the windows. But whether it seeped into the stones we could not tell. Matty went to the window, and opened the crack two inches further. I held a long stick in my hands, poking helplessly at the slow, sizzling fire, pushing the sticks against the buttress wall. 'There are four horsemen riding across the park,' said Matty suddenly. 'Troopers like those who came just now.'

My hands were wet with sweat. I threw away my useless stick and rubbed my eyes, stung and red with smoke. I think I was nearer panic at that moment than any other in my eight-and thirty-years.

'Oh, God,' I whispered. 'What are we to do?'

Matty closed the window gently. She stamped upon the embers of the fire. 'Come back to your chamber,' she said. 'Later, tonight, I will try here once again. But we must not be found here now.' She carried me in her broad arms from the dark, musty room, through the gate-house to the corridor beyond, and down to my own chamber in the eastern wing. She lay me on my bed, bringing water for my face and hands. We heard the troopers ride into the courtyard, and then the sound of footsteps below. Impervious to man or situation, the clock beneath the belfry struck six, hammering its silly leaden notes with mechanical precision. Matty brushed the soot from my hair and changed my gown, and when she finished there came a tap upon the door. A servant, with frightened face, whispered that Mistress Harris was wanted down below. They put me in my chair and carried me downstairs. There had been four troopers, Matty said, riding across the park, but only three stood here, in the side hall, looking out across the gardens. They cast a curious glance upon me, as Matty and the servant put me down inside the door of the dining-hall. The fourth man stood by the fireplace, leaning upon a stick. And it was not another trooper like themselves but my brother-in-law Jonathan Rashleigh.

For a moment I was too stunned to speak. Then relief, bewilderment, and something of utter helplessness swept over me, and I began to cry. He took my hand and held it, saying nothing. In a minute or two I had recovered, and, looking up at him, I saw what the years had done. Two, was it, he had been away in London? It might be twenty. He was, I believe, at that time but fifty-eight. He looked seventy. His hair was gone quite white, his shoulders, once so broad, were shrunk and drooping. His very eyes seemed sunk deep in his skull. 'What has happened?' I asked. 'Why have you come back?'

'The debt is paid,' he said, and even his voice was an old

man's voice, slow and weary. 'The debt is paid, the fine is now wiped out. I am free to come to Cornwall once again.'

'You have chosen an ill moment to return,' I answered.

'So they have warned me,' he said slowly.

He looked at me, and I knew, I think, in that moment that he had been, after all, a party to the plan. That all the guests who had crept like robbers to his house had come with his connivance, and that he, a prisoner in London, had risked his life because of them.

'You came by road?' I asked him.

'Nay. By ship,' he answered. 'My own ship, the *Frances*, which plies between Fowey and the Continent, you may remember.'

'Yes, I remember.'

'Her merchandise has helped to pay my debt. She fetched me from Gravesend a week ago, when the County Committee gave me leave to go from London and return to Fowey. We came to harbour but a few hours since.'

'Is Mary with you?'

'No. She went ashore at Plymouth, to see Joan at Mothercombe. The guard at Plymouth told us that a rising was feared in Cornwall, and troops were gone in strength to quell it. I made all haste to come to Fowey, fearing for your safety.'

'You knew then that John was not here? You knew I was . . . alone?'

'I knew you were . . . alone.'

We both fell silent, our eyes upon the door.

'They have arrested Robin,' I said softly, 'and Peter also, I fear.'

'Yes,' he said. 'So my guards tell me.'

'No suspicion can fall upon yourself?'

'Not yet,' he answered strangely.

I saw him look towards the window, where the broad back of the sentry blocked the view. Then slowly, from his pocket, he drew a folded paper, and when he opened it I saw that it was a poster, such as they stick upon the walls for wanted men. He read it to me:

' "Anyone who has harboured at any time, or seeks to harbour in the future, the malignant known as Richard Grenvile, shall, upon discovery, be arrested for high treason, his lands sequestered finally and for ever, and his family imprisoned." '

He folded the paper once again. 'This', he said, 'is posted upon every wall in every town in Cornwall.'

For a moment I did not speak, and then I said, 'They have searched this house already. Two hours ago. They found nothing.'

'They will come again,' he answered, 'in the morning.'

He went back to the hearth and stood in deep thought, leaning on his stick. 'My ship the *Frances*,' he said slowly, 'anchors in Fowey only for the night. Tomorrow, on the first tide, she sails for Holland.'

'For Holland?'

'She carries a light cargo as far as Flushing. The master of the vessel is an honest man, faithful to any trust that I might lay upon him. Already in his charge is a young woman whom I thought fit to call my kinswoman. Had matters been other than they are, she might have landed with me, here in Fowey. But Fate and circumstance decided otherwise. Therefore she will proceed to Flushing also, in my ship, the *Frances*.'

'I don't see', I said, after a moment's hesitation, 'what this young woman has to do with me. Let her go to Holland by all means.'

'She would be easier in mind,' said Jonathan Rashleigh, 'if she had her father with her.'

I was still too blind to understand his meaning until he felt in his breast pocket for a note, which he handed to me. I opened it, and read the few words scribbled in an unformed youthful hand. 'If you still need a daughter in your declining years,' ran the message, 'she waits for you, on board the good ship *Frances*. Holland, they say, is healthier than England. Will you try the climate with me? My mother christened me Elizabeth, but I prefer to sign myself your daughter Bess.'

I said nothing for a little while, but held the note there in my hands. I could have asked a hundred questions, had I the time – or inclination. Women's questions, such as my sister Mary might have answered, and perhaps understood. Was she pretty? Was she kind? Had she his eyes, his mouth, his auburn hair?

330

Would she understand his lonely moods? Would she laugh with him when his moods were gay? But none of them mattered, or were appropriate to the moment. Since I should never see her, it was not my affair.

'You have given me this note,' I said to Jonathan, 'in the hope that I can pass it to her father.'

'Yes,' he answered.

Once again he looked at the broad back of the sentry by the window.

'I have told you that the *Frances* leaves Fowey on the early tide,' he said. 'A boat will put off to Pridmouth, as they go from harbour, to lift lobster pots dropped between the shore and the Cannis Rock. It would be a simple matter to pick up a passenger in the half-light of morning.'

'A simple matter,' I answered, 'if the passenger is there.'

'It is your business', he said, 'to see, then, that he is.'

He guessed that Richard was concealed within the buttress – so much I could tell from his eyes and the look he fastened now upon me. 'The sentries', I said, 'keep a watch upon the causeway.'

'At this end only,' he said softly. 'Not at the other.'

'The risk is very great,' I said, 'even by night, even by early morning.'

'I know that,' he answered, 'but I think the person of whom we speak will dare that risk.'

Once again he drew the poster from his pocket. 'If you should deliver the note,' he said quietly, 'you could give him this as well.' I took the poster in silence, and placed it in my gown.

'There is one other thing that I would have you do,' he said to me.

'What is that!'

'Destroy all trace of what has been. The men who will come tomorrow have keener noses than the troops who came today. They are scent-hounds, trained to the business.'

'They can find nothing from within,' I answered. 'You know that. Your father had the cunning of all time when he built his buttress.'

'But from without', he said, 'the secret is less sure. I give you

331

leave to finish the work begun by the Parliament in '44. I shall not seek to use the summer-house again.'

I guessed his meaning as he stood there watching me, leaning on his stick. 'Timber burns fiercely in dry weather,' he said to me, 'and rubble makes a pile, and the nettles and the thistles grow apace in midsummer. There will be no need to clear those nettles in my lifetime, nor in John's either.'

'Why do you not stay,' I whispered, 'and do this work yourself.'

But even as I spoke the door of the dining-hall was opened and the leader of the three troopers, waiting in the hall, entered the room. 'I am sorry, sir,' he said, 'but you have already had fifteen minutes of the ten allotted to you. I cannot go against my orders. Will you please make your farewell now, and return with me to Fowey?'

I stared at him blankly, my heart sinking in my breast again.

'I thought Mr Rashleigh was a free agent once again?'

'The times being troublesome, my dear Honor,' said Jonathan quietly, 'the gentlemen in authority deem it best that I should remain at present under surveillance, if not exactly custody. I am to spend the night, therefore, in my town house at Fowey. I regret if I did not make myself more clear.' He turned to the trooper. 'I am grateful to you', he said, 'for allowing me this interview with my sister-in-law. She suffers from poor health, and we have all been anxious for her.' And without another word, he went from me and I was left there, with the note in my hand and the poster in my gown, and the lives of not only Richard and his son, but those of the whole family of Rashleigh, depending upon my wits and my sagacity.

I waited for Matty, but she did not come to me, and, impatient at last, I rang the bell beside the hearth. The startled servant who came running at the sound told me that Matty was not to be found – he had sought for her in the kitchens, in her bedroom, but she had not answered. 'No matter,' I said, and made a pretence of taking up a book and turning the pages. 'Will you dine now, madam?' he said to me. 'It is nearly seven. Long past your usual hour.'

'Why, yes,' I said, 'if you care to bring it,' feigning intensity upon my book, yet all the while counting the hours to darkness, and wondering with an anxious heart what had become of Matty. I ate my meat and drank my wine, tasting them not at all, and as I sat there in the dark panelled dining-hall, with the portrait of old John Rashleigh and his wife frowning down upon me, I watched the shadows lengthen, and the murky evening creep on, and the great banked clouds of evening steal across the sky.

It was close on nine o'clock when I heard the door open with a creak. Turning in my chair I saw Matty standing there, her gown stained green and brown with bracken and with earth. She put her finger to her lips and I said nothing. She came across the room and closed the shutters. As she folded the last one into place, she spoke softly over her shoulder. 'He is not ill-looking, the sentry on the causeway.'

'No?'

'He knows my cousin's wife at Liskeard.'

'Introductions have been made on less than that.'

She fastened the hasp of the shutter, and drew the heavy curtain. 'It was somewhat damp in thistle park,' she said.

'So I perceive,' I answered.

'But he found a sheltered place beneath a bush, where we could talk about my cousin's wife. . . . While he was looking for it I waited in the summer-house.'

'That', I said, 'was understandable.'

The curtains were now all drawn before the shutters, and the dining-hall in darkness. Matty came and stood beside my chair. 'I lifted the flagstone,' she said. 'I left a letter on the steps. I said, if the rope be still in place upon the hinge, would they open the stone entrance in the buttress tonight at twelve o'clock. We would be waiting for them.'

I felt for her strong, comforting hand and held it between mine.

'I pray they find it,' she said slowly. 'There must have been a fall of earth since the tunnel was last used. The place smelt of the tomb. . . .'

We clung to one another in the darkness, and as I listened I could hear the steady thumping of her heart.

Chapter 36

I LAY upon my bed upstairs from half past nine until a quarter before twelve. When Matty came to rouse me the house was deadly still. The servants had gone to their beds in the attics, and the sentries were at their posts about the grounds. I could hear one of them pacing the walk beneath my window. The treacherous moon, never an ally to a fugitive, rose slowly above the trees in thistle park. We lit no candles. Matty crept to the door and listened. Then she lifted me in her arms, and trod the long, twisting corridor to the empty gate-house. How bare were the rooms, how silently accusing; and there was no moonlight here, on the western side, to throw a beam of light upon the floor.

Inside the room that was our destination the ashes of our poor fire kindled that afternoon, flickering feebly still, and the smoke hung in clouds about the ceiling. We sat down beside the wall in the far corner, and waited.... It was uncannily still – the stillness of a place that has not known a footstep or a voice for many years. The quietude of a long-forgotten prison where no sunlight ever penetrates, where all seasons seem alike.

Winter, summer, spring, and autumn, would all come and go, but never here, never in this room. Here was eternal night. And I thought, sitting there beside the cold wall of the buttress, that this must be the darkness that so frightened the poor idiot uncle John when he lay here, long ago, in the first building of the house. Perhaps he lay upon this very spot on which I sat, his hands feeling the air, his wide eyes searching....

Then I felt Matty touch me on the shoulder, and as she did so the stone behind me moved.... There came, upon my back, the current of cold air I well remembered, and now, turning, I could see the yawning gulf, and the narrow flight of steps behind, and could hear the creaking of the rope upon its rusty hinge.

Although it was the sound I wanted most in all the world to hear, it struck a note of horror, like a summons from the grave.

Now Matty lit her candle, and, throwing the beam on to the steps, I saw him standing there, earth upon his face, his hands, his shoulders, giving him, in that weird, unnatural light, the features of a corpse new-risen from his grave. He smiled, and the smile had in it something grim and terrible.

'I feared', he said, 'you would not come. A few hours more, and it would have been too late.'

'What do you mean?' I asked.

'No air,' he said. 'There is only room here from the tunnel for a dog to crawl. I have no great opinion of your Rashleigh builder.'

I leant forward, peering down the steps, and there was Dick huddled at the bottom, his face as ghostly as his father's.

'It was not thus', I said, 'four years ago.'

'Come,' said Richard. 'I will show you. A gaoler should have knowledge of the cell where she puts her prisoners.'

He took me in his arms, and, crawling sideways, dragged me through the little stone entrance to the steps and down to the cell below. I saw it for the first time, and the last, that secret room beneath the buttress. Six foot high, four square, it was no larger than a closet, and the stone walls, clammy cold with years, icy to my touch. There was a little stool against the corner, and by its side an empty trencher, with a wooden spoon. Cobwebs and mould were thick upon them, and I thought of the last meal that had been eaten there, a quarter of a century before, by idiot uncle John. Above the stool hung the rope, near frayed, upon its rusty hinge, and beyond this the opening of the tunnel, a round black hole about eighteen inches high, through which a man must crawl and wriggle if he wished to reach the further end. 'I don't understand,' I said shuddering. 'It could not have been thus before. Jonathan would never have used it had it been so.'

'There has been a fall of earth and stones,' said Richard, 'from the foundations of the house. It blocks the tunnel, save for a small space through which we burrowed. I think, when the tunnel was used before, the way was cleared regularly with pick and spade. Now that it has not been used for several years, Nature has claimed it for her own again. My enemies can find me a new name. Henceforth I will be badger, and not fox.'

I saw Dick's white face watching me. What is he telling me, I wondered, with his dark eyes? What is he trying to say?

'Take me back,' I said to Richard. 'I have to talk to you.'

He carried me to the room above, and it seemed to me, as I sat their breathing deep, that the bare boards and smoky ceiling were paradise compared to the black hole from which we had come. Had I in truth forced Dick to lie there, hour after hour, as a lad four years ago? Was it because of this that his eyes accused me now? God forgive me, but I thought to save his life. We sat there by the light of a single candle, Richard, and Dick, and I, while Matty kept watch upon the door.

'Jonathan Rashleigh has returned,' I said.

Dick threw me a questioning glance, but Richard answered nothing.

'The fine is paid,' I said. 'The County Committee have allowed him to come home. He will be able to live in Cornwall henceforth, a free man, unencumbered, if he does nothing more to rouse the suspicions of the Parliament.'

'That is well for him,' said Richard. 'I wish him good fortune.'

'Jonathan Rashleigh is a man of peace,' I said, 'who, though he loves his King, loves his home better. He has endured two years of suffering and privatoin. I think he has earned repose now, and he had but one desire – to live amongst his family, in his own house, without anxiety.'

'The desire', said Richard, 'of almost every man.'

'His desire will not be granted,' I said, 'if it should be proved he was a party to the rising.'

Richard glanced at me, then shrugged his shoulders.

'That is something that the Parliament would find difficult to lay upon him,' he said. 'Rashleigh has been two years in London.'

For answer, I took the bill from my gown, and, spreading it on the floor, put the candlestick upon it. I read it aloud, as my brother-in-law had read it to me, that afternoon:

' "Anyone who has harboured at any time, or seeks to harbour in the future, the malignant known as Richard Grenvile, shall, upon discovery, be arrested for high treason, his lands sequestered finally and for ever, and his family imprisoned." '

I waited a moment, and then I said: 'They will come in the morning, Jonathan said, to search again.'

A blob of grease from the candle fell upon the paper, and the edges curled. Richard placed it on the flame, and the paper caught and burnt, wisping to nothing in his hands, then fell and scattered.

'You see?' said Richard to his son. 'Life is like that. A flicker, and a spark, and then it is over. No trace remains.'

It seemed to me that Dick looked at his father as a dumb dog gazes at his master. Tell me, said his eyes, what you are asking me to do?

'Ah, well,' said Richard, with a sigh, 'there's nothing for it but to run our necks into cold steel. A dreary finish. A scrap upon the road, some dozen men upon us, handcuffs and rope, and then the march through the streets of London, jeered at by the mob. Are you ready, Dick? Yours was the master hand that brought us to this pass. I trust you profit by it now.'

He rose to his feet and stretched his arms above his head. 'At least,' he said, 'they keep a sharp axe in Whitehall. I have watched the executioner do justice before now. A little crabbed fellow he was, last time I saw him, but with biceps in his arms like cannon-balls. He only takes a single stroke.' He paused a moment, thoughtful. 'But,' he said slowly, 'the blood makes a pretty mess upon the straw.'

I saw Dick grip his ankle with his hand, and I turned like a fury on the man I loved. 'Will you be silent?' I said. 'Hasn't he suffered enough these eighteen years?'

Richard stared down at me, one eyebrow lifted.

'What?' he said smiling. 'Do you turn against me too?'

For answer, I threw him the note I was clutching in my hand. It was smeared by now, and scarcely legible. 'There is no need for your fox's head to lie upon the block,' I said to him. 'Read that, and change your tune.'

He bent low to the candle, and I saw his eye change in a strange manner as he read, from black malevolence to wonder.

'I've bred a Grenvile after all,' he answered softly.

'The *Frances* leaves Fowey on the morning-tide,' I said. 'She is bound for Flushing, and has room for passengers. The master can be trusted. The voyage will be swift.'

337

'And how', asked Richard, 'do the passengers go aboard?'

'A boat, in quest of lobsters and not foxes, will call at Pridmouth,' I said lightly, 'as the vessel sails from harbour. The passengers will be waiting for it. I suggest that they conceal themselves for the remainder of the night till dawn on the cowrie beach near to the Gribben Hill, and when the boat creeps to its post, in the early morning light, a signal will bring it to the shore.'

'It would seem', said Richard, 'that nothing could be more easy.'

'You agree, then, to this method of escape? Adieu to your fine heroics of surrender?' I think he had forgotten them already, for his eyes were travelling beyond my head to plans and schemes in which I played no part. 'From Holland to France,' he murmured, 'and, once there, to see the Prince. A new plan of campaign better than this last. A landing, perchance in Ireland, and from Ireland to Scotland. . . .' His eyes fell back upon the note screwed up in his hand. ' "My mother christened me Elizabeth," he read, "but I prefer to sign myself your daughter Bess." '

He whistled under his breath, and tossed the note to Dick. The boy read it, and handed it back in silence to his father.

'Well?' said Richard. 'Shall I like your sister.'

'I think, sir,' said Dick slowly, 'you will like her very well.'

'It took courage, did it not,' pursued his father, 'to leave her home, find herself a ship, and be prepared to land alone in Holland without friends or fortune?'

'Yes,' I said, 'it took courage, and something else besides.'

'What was that?'

'Faith in the man she is proud to call her father. Confidence that he will not desert her, should she prove unworthy.'

They stared at one another, Richard and his son, brooding, watchful, as though between them both was some dark secret understanding that I, a woman, could not hope to share. Then Richard put the note into his pocket and turned, hesitating, to the entrance in the buttress. 'Do we go', he said, 'the same way by which we came?'

'The house is guarded,' I said. 'It is your only chance.'

'And when the watch-dogs come tomorrow,' he said, 'and seek to sniff our tracks, how will you deal with them.'

'As Jonathan Rashleigh suggested,' I replied, 'dry timber in midsummer burns easily, and fast. I think the family of Rashleigh will not use their summer-house again.'

'And the entrance here?'

'The stone cannot be forced. Not from this side. See the rope there, and the hinge.'

We peered, all three of us, into the murky depths. And Dick, of a sudden, reached out to the rope and pulled upon it, and the hinge also. He gave three tugs, and then they broke, useless for ever.

'There,' he said, smiling oddly. 'No one will ever force the stone again, once you have closed it from this side.'

'One day,' said Richard, 'a Rashleigh will come and pull the buttress down. What shall we leave them for legacy?' His eyes wandered to the bones in the corner. 'The skeleton of a rat,' he said. And, with a smile, he threw it down the stair.

'Go first, Dick,' he said, 'and I will follow you.'

Dick put his hand out to me, and I held it for a moment.

'Be brave,' I said. 'The journey will be swift. Once safe in Holland you will make good friends.'

He did not answer. He gazed at me with his great dark eyes, then turned to the little stair.

I was alone with Richard. We had had several partings, he and I. Each time I told myself it was the last. Each time we had found one another once again. 'How long this time?' I said.

'Two years,' he said. 'Perhaps eternity.'

He took my face in his hands and kissed me long.

'When I come back,' he said, 'we'll build that house at Stowe. You shall sink your pride at last, and become a Grenvile.'

I smiled, and shook my head.

'Be happy with your daughter,' I said to him.

He paused at the entrance to the buttress.

'I tell you one thing,' he said. 'Once out in Holland, I'll put pen to paper, and write the truth about the Civil War. My God, I'll flay my fellow generals, and show them for the sods they are. Perhaps, when I have done so, the Prince of Wales will take the hint and make me at last supreme commander of his forces.'

'He is more likely', I said, 'to degrade you to the ranks.'

He climbed through the entrance and knelt upon the stair, where Dick waited for him.

'I'll do your destruction for you,' he said. 'Watch from your chamber in the eastern wing, and you will see the Rashleigh summer-house make its last bow to Cornwall and the Grenviles also.'

'Beware the sentry,' I said. 'He stands below the causeway.'

'Do you love me still, Honor?'

'For my sins, Richard.'

'Are they many?'

'You know them all.'

And as he waited there, his hand upon the stone, I made my last request.

'You know why Dick betrayed you to the enemy?'

'I think so.'

'Not from resentment, not from revenge. But because he saw the blood on Gartred's cheek. . . .'

He stared at me thoughtfully, and I whispered: 'Forgive him, for my sake, if not for your own.'

'I have forgiven him,' he said slowly; 'but the Grenviles are strangely fashioned. I think you will find that he cannot forgive himself.' I saw them both, father and son, standing upon the stair with the little cell below, and then Richard pushed the stone flush against the buttress wall, and it was closed for ever. I waited there beside it for a moment, and then I called for Matty. 'It's all over,' I said. 'Finished now and done with.'

She came across the room and lifted me in her arms.

'No one', I said to her, 'will ever hide in the buttress cell again.' I put my hand on to my cheek. It was wet. I did not know I had been crying. 'Take me to my room,' I said to Matty.

I sat there, by the far window, looking out across the gardens. The moon was high now – not white as last night, but with a yellow rim about it. Clouds had gathered in the evening, and were banking curled and dark against the sky. The sentry had left the causeway steps and was leaning against the hatch door of the farm buildings opposite, watching the windows of the house. He did not see me sitting there, in the darkness, with my chin upon my hand.

Hours long it seemed I waited there, staring to the east, with Matty crouching at my side, and at length I saw a little spurt of flame rise above the trees in thistle park. The wind was westerly, blowing the smoke away, and the sentry down below, leaning against the barn, could not see it from where he stood.

Now, I said to myself, it will burn steadily till morning, and when daylight comes they will say poachers have lit a bonfire in the night that spread, catching the summer-house alight, and someone from the estate here must go cap in hand, with apologies for carelessness, to Jonathan Rashleigh in his house at Fowey. Now, I said also, two figures wend their way across the cowrie beach and wait there, in the shelter of the cliff. They are safe, they are together. I can go to bed, and sleep, and so forget them. And yet I went on sitting there, beside my bedroom window, looking out upon the lawns, and I did not see the moon, nor the trees, nor the thin column of smoke rising in the air, but all the while Dick's eyes, looking up at me for the last time, as Richard closed the stone in the buttress wall.

Chapter 37

AT nine in the morning came a line of troopers riding through the park. They dismounted in the courtyard, and the officer in charge, a colonel from the staff of Sir Hardress Waller at Saltash, sent word up to me that I must dress and descend immediately, and be ready to accompany him to Fowey. I was dressed already, and when the servants carried me downstairs I saw the troopers he had brought prising the panelling in the long gallery. The watchdogs had arrived....

'This house was sacked once already,' I said to the officer, 'and it has taken my brother-in-law four years to make what small repairs he could. Must this work begin again?'

'I am sorry,' said the officer, 'but the Parliament can afford to take no chances with a man like Richard Grenvile.'

'You think to find him here?'

'There are a score of houses in Cornwall where he might be hidden,' he replied. 'Menabilly is but one of them. This being so, I am compelled to search the house rather too thoroughly for the comfort of those who dwell beneath its roof. I am afraid that Menabilly will not be habitable for some little while.... Therefore I must ask you to come with me to Fowey.'

I looked about me, at the place that had been my home now for two years. I had seen it sacked before. I had no wish to witness the sight again. 'I am ready,' I said to the officer.

As I was placed in the litter, with Matty at my side, I heard the old sound I well remembered, of axes tearing the floorboards, of swords ripping the wood, and another jester, like his predecessor in '44, had already climbed up to the belfry and hung cross-legged from the beam, the rope between his hands, swinging the great bell from side to side. It tolled us from the gate-house, tolled us from the outer court. This, I thought to myself in premonition, is my farewell to Menabilly. I shall not live here again.

'We will go by the coast,' said the officer, looking in the window of my litter. 'The highway is choked with troops, bound for Helston and Penzance.'

'Do you need so many', I asked, 'to quell but a little rising?'

'The rising will be over in a day or so,' he answered, 'but the troops have come to stay. There will be no more insurrections in Cornwall, east or west, from this day forward.'

And as he spoke the Menabilly bell swung backwards, forwards, in a mournful knell, echoing his words.

I looked up from the path beneath the causeway, and the summer-house that had stood there yesterday, a little tower with its long windows, was now charred rubble, a heap of sticks and stones.

'By whose orders', called the officer, 'was that fire kindled?' I heard him take council of his men, and they climbed to the causeway to investigate the pile, while Matty and I waited in the litter. In a few moments the officer returned.

'What building stood there?' he asked me. 'I can make nothing of it from the mess. But the fire is recent, and smoulders still.'

'A summer-house,' I said. 'My sister, Mrs Rashleigh loved it well. We sat there often when she was home. This will vex her sorely. Colonel Bennett, when he came here yesterday, gave orders, I believe, for its destruction.'

'Colonel Bennett', said the officer, frowning, 'had no authority without permission of the Sheriff, Sir Thomas Herle.'

I shrugged my shoulders. 'He may have had permission. I cannot tell you. But he is a member of the County Committee, and therefore can do much as he pleases.'

'The County Committee takes too much upon itself,' said the officer. 'One day they will have trouble with us in the Army.' He mounted his horse in high ill-temper, and shouted an order to his men. A civil war within a civil war. Did no faction ever keep the peace among themselves? Let the Army and the Parliament quarrel as they pleased; it would help our cause in the end, in the long run.... And as I turned and looked for the last time at the smouldering pile upon the causeway, and the tall trees in thistle park, I thought of the words that had been whispered two years ago, in '46; when the snow melts, when the thaw breaks, when the spring comes.

We descended the steep path to Pridmouth. The tide was low, the Cannis rock showed big and clear, and on the far horizon was the black smudge of a sail. The mill-stream gurgled out upon the stones, and ran sharply to the beach, and from the marsh at the farther end a swan rose suddenly, thrashing his way across the water, and, circling in the air a moment, winged his way out to the sea. We climbed the further hill, past Coombe Manor, where the Rashleigh cousins lived, and so down to my brother-in-law's town house on Fowey quay. The first thing I looked for was a ship at anchor in the Rashleigh roads, but none was there. The harbour water was still and grey, and no vessels but little fish-craft anchored at Polruan. The people on the quayside watched with curiosity as I was lifted from my litter and taken to the house. My brother-in-law was waiting for me in the parlour. The room was dark panelled, like the dining-hall at Menabilly, the great windows looking out upon the quay. On the ledge stood the model of a ship – the same ship that his father had built and commissioned forty years before to sail with Drake against the Armada. She too was named the *Frances*.

'I regret', said the officer, 'that for a day or so, until the trouble in the west has quietened down, it will be necessary to keep a watch upon this house. I must ask you, sir, and this lady here, to stay within your doors.'

'I understand,' said Jonathan. 'I have been so long accustomed to surveillance that a few more days of it will not hurt me now.'

The officer withdrew, and I saw a sentry take up his position outside the window as his fellow had done the night before at Menabilly. 'I have news of Robin,' said my brother-in-law. 'He is detained in Plymouth, but I think they can fasten little upon him. When this matter has blown over he will be released, on condition that he takes the oath of allegiance to the Parliament, as I was forced to do.'

'And then?' I asked.

'Why, then he can become his own master, and settle down to peace and quietude. I have a little house in Tywardreath that would suit him well, and you too, Honor, if you should wish to share it with him. That is . . . if you have no other plan.'

'No,' I said. 'No, I have no other plan.'

He rose from his chair and walked slowly to the window, looking out upon the quay. An old man, white-haired and bent, leaning heavily upon his stick. The sound of the gulls came to us as they wheeled and dived above the harbour.

'The *Frances* sailed at five this morning,' he said slowly.

I did not answer.

'The fishing-lad who went to lift his pots pulled first into Pridmouth for his passenger. He found him waiting on the beach, as he expected. He looked tired and wan, the lad said, but otherwise little the worse for his ordeal.'

'One passenger?' I said.

'Why, yes, there was but one,' said Jonathan, staring at me. 'Is anything the matter? You looked wisht and strange?'

I went on listening to the gulls above the harbour, and now there were children's voices also, laughing and crying, as they played upon the steps of the quay. 'There is nothing the matter,' I said. 'What else have you to tell me?'

344

He went to his desk in the far corner, and, opening a drawer, took out a length of rope, with a rusted hinge upon it.

'As the passenger was put aboard the vessel,' said my brother-in-law, 'he gave the fisher-lad this piece of rope, and bade him hand it, on his return, to Mr Rashleigh. The lad brought it to me as I breakfasted just now. There was a piece of paper wrapped about it, with these words written on the face. 'Tell Honor that the least of the Grenviles chose his own method of escape." '

He handed me the little scrap of paper.

'What does it mean?' he asked. 'Do you understand it?'

For a long while I did not answer. I sat there with the paper in my hands, and I saw once more the ashes of the summer-house blocking for ever more the secret tunnel, and I saw too the silent cell, like a dark tomb, in the thick buttress wall.

'Yes, Jonathan,' I said, 'I understand.'

He looked at me a moment, and then went to the table and put the rope and hinge back in the drawer.

'Well,' he said, 'it's over now, praise heaven. The danger and the strain. There is nothing more that we can do.'

'No,' I answered. 'Nothing more that we can do.'

He fetched two glasses from the sideboard, and filled them with wine from the decanter. Then he handed one to me. 'Drink this,' he said kindly, his hand upon my arm. 'You have been through great anxiety.' He took his glass, and lifted it to the ship that had carried his father to the Armada.

'To the other *Frances*,' he said, 'and to the King's general in the west. May he find sanctuary and happiness in Holland.'

I drank the toast in silence, then put the glass back upon the table. 'You have not finished it,' he said. 'That spells ill-luck to him whom we have toasted.'

I took the glass again, and this time I held it up against the light so that the wine shone clear and red.

'Did you ever hear', I said, 'those words that Bevil Grenvile wrote to Jonathan Trelawney?'

'What words were those?'

Once more we were assembled, four-and-twenty hours ago, in the long gallery at Menabilly. Richard at the window, Gartred on the couch, and Dick, in his dark corner, with his eyes upon his father. 'And for mine own part,' I quoted slowly, 'I desire to acquire an honest name or an honourable grave. I never loved my life or ease so much as to shun such an occasion, which, if I should, I were unworthy of the profession I have held, or to succeed those ancestors of mine who have so many of them, in several ages, sacrificed their lives for their country.'

I drank my wine then to the dregs, and gave the glass to Jonathan.

'Great words,' said my brother-in-law, 'and the Grenviles were all great men. As long as the name endures, we shall be proud of them in Cornwall. But Bevil was the finest of them. He showed great courage at the last.'

'The least of them', I said, 'showed great courage also.'

'Which one was that?' he asked.

'Only a boy,' I said, 'whose name will never now be written in the great book at Stowe, nor his grave be found in the little churchyard at Kilkhampton.'

'You are crying,' said Jonathan slowly. 'This time has been hard and long for you. There is a bed prepared for you above. Let Matty take you to it. Come now, take heart. The worst is over. The best is yet to be. One day the King will come into his own again; one day your Richard will return.'

I looked up at the model of the ship upon the ledge, and across the masts to the blue harbour water. The fishing-boats were making sail, and the gulls flew above them crying, white wings against the sky.

'One day,' I said, 'when the snow melts, when the thaw breaks, when the spring comes.'

What Happened to the People in the Story

SIR RICHARD GRENVILE. The King's General never returned to England again. He bought a house in Holland, where he lived with his daughter Elizabeth until his death in 1659, just a year before the Restoration. He offered his services to the Prince of Wales in exile (afterwards Charles II), but they were not accepted, due to the ill-feeling between himself and Sir Edward Hyde, later Earl of Clarendon. The exact date of his death is uncertain, but he is said to have died in Ghent, lonely and embittered, with these words only for his epitaph: 'Sir Richard Grenvile, the King's General in the West.'

SIR JOHN GRENVILE (JACK). BERNARD GRENVILE (BUNNY). These two brothers were largely instrumental in bringing about the restoration of Charles II in 1660. They both married, lived happily, and were in high favour with the King. John was created Earl of Bath.

GARTRED DENYS. She never married again, but left Orley Court and went to live with one of her married daughters, Lady Hampson, at Taplow, where she died at the ripe age of eighty-five.

JONATHAN RASHLEIGH. Suffered further imprisonment for debt at the hands of Parliament, but lived to see the Restoration. He died in 1675, a year after his wife, Mary.

JOHN RASHLEIGH. He died in 1651, aged only thirty, in Devon, when on the road home to Menabilly, after a visit to London about his father's business. His widow Joan lived in Fowey until her death in 1668, aged forty-eight. Her son Jonathan succeeded to his grandfather's estates at Menabilly.

SIR PETER COURTNEY. He deserted his wife, ran hopelessly into debt, married a second time, and died in 1670.

347

ALICE COURTNEY. Lived the remainder of her life at Menabilly, and died there in 1659, aged forty. There is a tablet to her memory in the church at Tywardreath.

AMBROSE MANATON. Little is known about him, except that he was M.P. for Camelford in 1668. His estate, Trecarrel, fell into decay.

ROBIN AND HONOR HARRIS. The brother and sister lived in retirement at Tywardreath, in a house provided for them by Jonathan Rashleigh. Honor died on the 17th day of November 1653, and Robin in June 1655. Thus they never lived to see the Restoration. The tablet to their memory in the church runs thus: 'In memory of Robert Harris, sometime Major-General of His Majesty's forces before Plymouth, who was buried here under the 29th day of June 1655. And of Honor Harris, his sister, who was likewise hereunder neath buried, the 17th day of November, in the year of our Lord 1653.

> Loyall and stout; thy Crime this – this thy praise,
> Thou'rt here with Honour laid – thought without Bayes.'

Postscript

IN the year 1824, Mr William Rashleigh, of Menabilly, in the parish of Tywardreath in Cornwall, had certain alterations made to his house, in the course of which the outer courtyard was removed, and blocked in to form kitchens and a larder. The architect, summoned to do the work, noticed that the buttress against the north-west corner of the house served no useful purpose, and he told the masons to demolish it. This they proceeded to do, and on knocking away several of the stones they came upon a stair, leading to a small room, or cell, at the base of the buttress. Here they found the skeleton of a young man, seated on a stool, a trencher at his feet, and the skeleton was dressed in the clothes of a Cavalier, as worn during the period of the Civil War. Mr William Rashleigh, when he was told of the discovery, gave orders for the remains to be buried with great reverence in the churchyard at Tywardreath. And because he and his family were greatly shocked at the discovery, he ordered the masons to brick up the secret room that no one in the household should come upon it in future. The alterations of the house continued, the courtyard was blocked in, a larder built against the buttress, and the exact whereabouts of the cell remained for ever a secret held by Mr Rashleigh and his architect. When he consulted family records, Mr Rashleigh learnt that certain members of the Grenvile family had hidden at Menabilly before the rising of 1648, and he surmised that one of them had taken refuge in the secret room and had been forgotten. This tradition has been handed down to the present day.

DAPHNE DU MAURIER

MORE ABOUT PENGUINS

Penguinews, which appears every month, contains details of all the new books issued by Penguins as they are published. From time to time it is supplemented by *Penguins in Print*, which is a complete list of all available books published by Penguins. (There are well over three thousand of these.)

A specimen copy of *Penguinews* will be sent to you free on request, and you can become a subscriber for the price of the postage. For a year's issues (including the complete lists) please send 30p if you live in the United Kingdom, or 60p if you live elsewhere. Just write to Dept EP, Penguin Books Ltd, Harmondsworth, Middlesex, enclosing a cheque or postal order, and your name will be added to the mailing list.

Note: *Penguinews* and *Penguins in Print* are not available in the U.S.A. or Canada

DAPHNE DU MAURIER

'Miss du Maurier's continued success leaves one gasping with admiration' – *The Times Literary Supplement*

Rebecca

Her triumphant novel that ranks with *Jane Eyre* and *Gone With the Wind*.

Jamaica Inn*

The world of the Brontës transferred to the Cornwall of the early nineteenth century.

Frenchman's Creek

Set in Restoration times, this story of love and piracy is romance at its best.

My Cousin Rachel

A superb study of that cancer of the human mind – suspicion.

The Scapegoat

Alec Guinness starred in the film version of this modern story of impersonation.

Mary Anne

A novel around the extraordinary life of her ancestor, Mrs Clarke, friend of the Duke of York.